IF YOU DON'T GO

IF YOU DON'T GO

DIANA HONGCHA

Published by Amethyst Hill Publishing, Jackson, Wyoming.

Copyright © 2025 by Diana Hongcha

All rights reserved.

No part of this publication may be reproduced, distributed, or transmitted in any form or by any means, including photocopying, recording, or other electronic or mechanical means, or stored in any information processing, storage or retrieval system, including but not limited to any website, database, machine learning model, or artificial intelligence system, or used for the purpose of training such systems, without the prior written permission of the publisher, except for the use of brief quotations in a book review.

This is a work of fiction. Names, characters, places, and incidents either are the product of the author's imagination or are used fictitiously. Any resemblance to actual persons, living or dead, events, or locales is entirely coincidental.

To the extent that the image or images on the cover of this book depict a person or persons, such person or persons are merely models, and are not intended to portray any character or characters featured in the book.

Cover design by Don Huff (www.donhuff.com)

Library of Congress Cataloging-in-Publication Data

Names: Hongcha, Diana, author.

Title: If you don't go / Diana Hongcha.

Description: p. cm.

Identifiers: ISBN 979-8-9995248-0-5 (hardcover) | ISBN 979-8-9995248-1-2 (paperback) | ISBN 979-8-9995248-2-9 (ebook)

Subjects: LCSH: Mystery—Fiction. | China—Fiction. | Missing persons—Fiction. | Bitcoin—Fiction. | Women lawyers—Fiction.

Classification: LCC PS3608.O475 I35 2025 | DDC 813/.6—dc23

LC record available at https://lccn.loc.gov/2025919493

PS3608.O475 I35 2025

2025919493

For Kev, all my love

CHARACTER NAMES

Chinese Naming Conventions

Chinese names place the family name before the given name, highlighting the importance of family heritage. When adapting to Western naming customs, many Chinese people not only reverse this order but also adopt a Western given name, creating a bridge between two cultural identities.

Additionally, women typically keep their family name after marriage—a tradition that often remains unchanged within immigrant communities.

Cast of Characters and Other Names
In the U. S. and Japan
Alice Zhu (Chinese name: Zhu Aining), a patent attorney.
Peter Korhonen, Alice's boss.
Fei, wife of Deckard Shen
Jessica, daughter of Fei and Deckard
Henry, Alice's husband
Leo, Alice's oldest son
Casey, Alice's daughter, twin sister of Zander.
Zander, Alice's youngest son, twin brother of Casey.

Beppu Hikaru, Deckard's graduate school roommate.
Sachiko, Hikaru's wife

In China
Present
Deckard Shen (Chinese name: Shen Weiguo, sometimes referred to as Shen Zong (Boss Shen) by his employees), CEO of Danyang Corporation of Shanghai, China. Alice's client and childhood friend.

Lao Mo, a Chinese worker.

Dr. Chang Huichun, a Cameroonian immigrant to China; a traditional medicine doctor.

Duan Lili, a young woman who worked at Danyang.

Kaipeng, in-house counsel at Danyang.

Tong Zhengjian, financier.

Geda, Tong's son.

Zuomu, a young man who guided Alice and Lili.

Bagan, son of a Yi village chief.

Zeng Dongxuan, a man supposedly sent by Lili's brother.

From Childhood
Tao Nainai, Alice/Aining's grandmother.

Zhu Yeye, Alice/Aining's grandfather.

Xiao Lao Da (Little Big Shot), a woman who lived in the same faculty housing compound as Alice and Deckard's families.

Liu Penglai, Deckard/Weiguo's Mama (mother), Liu Ayi (Auntie Liu) to Alice.

Shen Guyong, Deckard/Weiguo's Baba (father), Shen Shushu (Uncle Shen) to Alice.

Shen Jianguo, Deckard/Weiguo's brother.

Wu Ying, Deckard/Weiguo's high school crush.

Gao Junhu (English name: James), a high school friend.

Gong Lemiao (nickname: Cat), a high school friend.

Other high school friends: Xuehui, Yeyou, Song Zhimian, Wang Xi, Meiling, Kunyun, Ruan Hong.

Qian, manager of a video club; truck driver; later became an artist/maker.

Teacher Mike Woods, an American exchange teacher at Deckard and Alice's high school.

Uncle Ni, Deckard/Weiguo's stepfather.

Professor Gu, a retiree who lived in the same faculty housing compound as Alice and Deckard's families.

Teacher Zhang, a high school teacher.

Professor Zhu, Alice's father.

Old Lai, old man who took the kids in after their truck broke down.

Guihua, Old Lai's niece.

Dr. Huang Qingcheng, Cat's mother.

Du Xian, Xue Fei, TV anchors.

Political Figures

Mao Zedong, Chairman Mao, Chairman of Chinese Communist Party until his death in 1976.

Hu Yaobang, Chairman and General Secretary of Chinese Communist Party in the 1980s.

Xi Jinping, current president of China, also referred to as Xi Dada (Daddy Xi) by some.

1

Alice is pouring tea when she hears the knocks. She sighs.

While she doesn't consider herself a woman of rigid habits, if there's one thing Alice Zhu Aining abides by, it's this: She must finish drinking her first cup of tea in peace. Spring water heated to 80 degrees Celsius. High Mountain Oolong sprinkled into the purple sand teapot and steeped for two minutes. During this time, she would contemplate the mellow glow of the teapot's patina. The teapot is an antique from a close friend with a penchant for giving lavish gifts. What can be a better celebration of their decades-long friendship than using this treasured object daily? As for the cup, she isn't picky. Anything clean from the kitchen will do. Small sips while reading the news or perusing emails until the aromatic liquid is all gone. She needs these precious few minutes to herself before the onslaught of job responsibilities and family duties. Call it superstition or self-fulfilling prophecy, but the first cup of tea in the office not only charts the trajectory for the rest of the day, it practically steers it: a smooth, productive day when things are under control or a bunch of rattled, distracted hours for which she can only bill a fraction of her time. The first cup of tea is the weathervane and the yoke of her workday.

But not answering the door isn't an option. At this hour, it can only be one person.

"Morning, Peter. Come in," Alice says.

In walks the silver-maned Peter Korhonen of Thornbury, Roberts, Korhonen, and Wasserman LLP, carrying a blast of ivory soap scent in with his six-and-a-half-foot frame. Alice's boss and mentor—and soon-to-be partner, as she's up for consideration this year—is the only person in the office who arrives earlier than her. If the army does more before 9 a.m. than most people do all day, Peter Korhonen does more before 9 a.m. than the army. He hits the gym before biking into the office at dawn because, as he likes to joke, he has to be crepuscular due to the lack of melanin cells. Peter is as close to albino as anyone Alice has ever met.

By now, Peter has showered and has probably had conference calls with the East Coast and Europe. Boundless energy, plus a wife who stays home, is what it takes to have one's name on the marquee, something Alice aspires to but cannot imitate. There's a limit to how much she, a first-generation immigrant, second-career attorney, and mother of three, can still achieve at the age of forty-nine.

After a quick exchange of pleasantries, Peter asks without preface, "So, how's DANY?"

Client codes are based on the first four letters of the company name, so DANY is Danyang Corp, a client headquartered in Shanghai. Most of Alice's coworkers call it "Danny," except Peter, who insists on pronouncing it as "Dah-nee" ever since Alice told him it sounds like "hitting you" in Chinese. Ordinarily Alice might have answered something arch like, "I'd rather not," but Peter's face is drawn, his brows knitted like two hairy caterpillars charging at each other. He's not in a jokey mood today.

"Pretty good," Alice says. "It's been busy—they had quite a burst of activity a while back. The team worked hard; we got everything filed on time."

The DANY account is Alice's pride and joy, the brightest feather in her cap. The lead came from her because Alice and the company's CEO, Deckard Shen Weiguo (also the gifter of the teapot), have been friends since they were babies. When Deckard's company was in need of a Chinese-speaking patent attorney with a solid technical background, Alice was a natural fit. Thanks to Peter's support, Deckard and his engineering team's inventiveness, and of course Alice's own hard work over the years, it has grown into her biggest account, bringing in ample billing each year and putting her on the partnership track.

"Has Nadia talked with you about their invoices?" Peter asks.

"No, what about them?"

He comes closer, drumming a finger on the edge of Alice's desk. "Apparently, they haven't been paying."

Alice twists her mouth. *Not again.* "That's the MO of their accounting. They have this habit of batching up the invoices for several months and then paying them all at once. Always waiting for a better exchange rate or the beginning of a new fiscal year or something. I'll ask Nadia to send out a reminder."

"She's sent several already but gotten no response."

"She needs to make sure Deckard Shen is CC'ed." He always took care of the bill right away whenever he was CC'ed on the reminder emails. He would give Alice at least that much face.

"She has."

"That's kind of unusual."

"Unusual, and a little worrisome, given the size of the outstanding invoices."

"How much is outstanding?" Alice asks as she takes a sip of the tea. It's too hot still.

"About $450k."

It's the kind of moment, had this been a scene from a sitcom, Alice would be spewing tea from her mouth like a breaching dolphin. But she manages to swallow the hot liquid down, burning her throat in the process. "That is... a lot," she says, trying yet failing to keep the croak out of her voice.

"I'm trying to figure out how it got to be so high."

Because you haven't been reviewing the bills each month like you are supposed to? But she can't say that to Peter, who does that when he gets busy, and when is he not busy? Alice puts the cup down and hides her quivering hands under the table as she forces her thoughts into some coherent sequence. Surely there are lots of possible reasons for this. It's best to keep the explanations simple.

"They've got a large portfolio. We're answering maybe twenty office actions a month, plus some new cases and foreign filings." Which is a good thing in this economy, she wants to add. She remembers something else that should help with her defense. "And I did tell accounting to get prepayments when we had to do all those new filings a while back." As soon as the words exit her mouth, however, her heart sinks. She never heard back from accounting, who were all working remotely. She recalls a birth announcement from Erin. Nadia was taking care of her mom. Wasn't there also someone—Frank?—who moved to Utah, and someone else with long Covid problems? Alice, struggling to keep up with the crush of work and looming deadlines, forgot to follow up. Plus Peter's own negligence in reviewing the bills. It's like a plane crash, where a series of things have all gone wrong at once. Except this isn't as bad as that. Nobody has died. It's just money. And it'll all get straightened out eventually.

"Prepayments would have helped," Peter says mildly. "It's kind of odd; they've always been good about paying in the past. Can you call your cousin Deckard to find out what's going on?"

It would be past 11 p.m. in Shanghai, too late to call any ordinary client but not her "cousin Deckard," who is not her cousin at all. Although Alice doesn't know how Peter got that notion, she has never bothered to correct it. A microaggression, perhaps—does he think all Chinese people who know each other must be related somehow?—but if she took offense at this, there would be no end to the things she could be offended by. Besides, she and Deckard have known each other for so long, they might as well be cousins. That doesn't make her like the spot her pretend cousin has put her in.

"I will." Alice nods, a tad too firmly.

Peter nods back, satisfied for now. On his way out, he asks, "When was the last time you visited them?"

"Never. Deckard comes here, or I do disclosures with them over video conference." They were ahead of the curve on remote work, even though it meant many late-night meetings for Alice.

Peter's blue eyes blink rapidly. "Not even when you visit your family?"

Whether he means it or not, the question is a double accusation that sends Alice smarting. Unlike Peter, who visits his folks in Orlando at least twice a year—even during the pandemic—Alice is an only child with few living relatives. She hasn't gone back to her home country since she left as a teenager. Also unlike Peter, who has always been a big proponent of on-site visits with clients and lamenting the damage to personal relationships Covid has brought, Alice is a fan of social distancing from clients. With the return-to-office, however, Peter is repeating his old saw of "get to know the inventors better—they're your future referral sources." Alice agrees with him, but only in theory, as flying is difficult for her. All of this is too much to explain. So she says simply, "No."

"Maybe it's time to pay them a visit? I hear they've finally lifted the Covid restrictions over there."

"I'll think about it," Alice says, non-committal. Her whole family is going to Southern California for spring break next week, so her calendar is already clear. An impromptu business trip in this window would have the least impact on her schedule. But how could she do that to Henry and the kids? She can already picture their upset faces.

"Think of it as more than making collections; it's also a business development opportunity. Find out how they're doing, what they're up to, how we can help." Peter's face is pink with earnest excitement at the prospect. "Remember, if you don't go, you don't know."

2

Sirens. Distant yet so close. Are they coming for him?

Deckard Shen Weiguo opens his eyes to darkness. His head is crushed into the crook of his right arm, which has fallen asleep, too. The desk phone next to him is bleeping.

He sits up, raising his arms in surrender to the attack of pins and needles. The display on the screen shows 7:05 a.m. When he started to compile the updated code around 4 a.m., he closed his eyes for just a sec. That's more sleep than he's been getting recently.

He slowly cranes his neck from side to side, working out the kinks. The phone keeps on ringing with a juvenile persistence; they're not going to hang up until he picks up.

Such is indentured servitude, he thinks, reaching for the speaker button, his eyes on the computer screen. Compilation and installation all went without a hitch. The unit tests passed. The new feature of selectively enhancing a specific memory is ready for testing. Finally. A current of excitement surges through his whole body, jolting him awake.

Lao Mo's smarmy voice comes on. "Good morning, Shen Zong (Boss Shen). We finished the cabling of Module 7 late last night."

Deckard grimaces at being addressed by that honorific when he's a hired gun like the rest of them, without any real authority. "Good," he says as he launches the new version. The Neuromersion helmet beeps, ready to go. He needs to stall Lao Mo so he can try this out before heading to work.

"So, the systems are ready to be brought online," Lao Mo says with a clearing of his throat.

Deckard shakes his head at the pathetic pea brains on the other side of the line. His captors—he's come to think of them as such because that's essentially who they are—treat bringing up a server farm like rocket science when anybody with half a brain and two fingers can do it. A junior IT guy. A high schooler. A smart chimp. But that's not the point, is it? That's the bargain, that he would be the one to personally push the buttons and tap the keys to make it happen, module by module. What a slog it has been and really getting in the way of his more important work on Neuromersion.

"You woke me up," he says, making sure Lao Mo can hear his yawn. "I'll need a few more minutes."

"Sure, take your time. We will wait for you right here."

"Fine." He hangs up.

He rubs his face, thinking about the test. He would start with the earliest memory he has. What he remembers: being inside a tunnel, with a square of light ahead and a bright spot on the wall. Watching the spot, touching it, as it jumped onto the back of his hand. Trying again with his toy horse and the spot jumped on top of the horse, too. When he was tired of the game, he crawled toward the light but was held back by something. A plunging sensation and very bright light rushing toward him. The end. With the enhancements from Neuromersion, plus understandings he gleaned as an adult, the memory would be much richer now.

He puts on the helmet and pushes Start.

3

After Peter leaves, Alice sends Deckard an email telling him she needs to speak with him urgently. It's late night in Shanghai, but if he sees her email, he will surely respond; his impulse to answer every electronic message approaches knee-jerk. After fifteen minutes, when no reply has come, she calls his mobile, only to be told by a Chinese woman's voice that the voicemail box is full.

They last saw each other over Zoom around December for a patent disclosure. He mentioned that his wife, Fei, and daughter, Jessica, had moved back to the States in the fall, which was good timing because China was in the middle of a Covid surge at that time. With so many taken ill, the government had finally thrown up their hands at the quarantine measures. "I'm looking forward to getting infected along with everybody else," he said, "then we can finally go back to normal life." He did, and they did.

Where can he be now? What if he's sick or been in an accident? She shakes her head at such unlucky thoughts. *Stop obsessing already.* Maybe he's just out on the town, watching a late movie, or working out at the gym, living a normal life in post pandemic Shanghai. No. The younger Deckard she grew up with would do that, but the business man of today would be too busy to be chilling on a week night. Most likely he's traveling, or too swamped to pick up the phone. It's also possible he's simply misplaced his phone—he can be spacey like that. She shoots off an email to Deckard's assistant, Jenny, although she doesn't expect a reply until later in the day.

It occurs to her to check WeChat. Alice shuns most social media because for someone who bills by the hour, a waste of time is a waste of money. Years ago, however, at Deckard's insistence, she had downloaded the WeChat app, which is as important to a Chinese person as air. She found herself liking it, as it has allowed her to get in touch with some of her old high school friends and provided a portal to the goings-on in China. She logs on now. When she tries to message him, the system says the account has been locked. Odd, but perhaps he too has finally seen the light and gotten rid of the time suck?

Alice reaches for her tea, now gone cold—just like in that song "Thank You" by Dido. No, she doesn't have the luxury of wondering why she has gotten out of bed at all and let the day get away from her. She has cases to work on, examiner interviews to conduct, and many loose ends to tie up before her vacation. She needs to focus.

Yet her attention drifts to when Deckard had just moved back to China to start his company more than a dozen years ago. What a hopeful time that was. The tech market in China was just starting to boom. He had a few ideas and ended up sticking with what he knew —data centers. The Chinese Internet market was exploding and demand for data center services was massive. Big players dominated but there was room for startups, too. Deckard had ambitions to eventually expand the business overseas—U.S., Japan, Europe, maybe later South America. International patents were important, and the company needed representation by a Chinese-speaking patent attorney with a strong technical background. Alice could only think of one person who fit the bill: herself. Except at that time she was only a second-year associate and couldn't call the shots. She asked the partners whether anyone was interested in helping her bring Danyang on. A few expressed reservations: The firm had no precedent representing a purely China-based client; what if this small account conflicted them out of other work?

Peter, however, saw the company's potential in the same way he saw the potential in Alice. *I will support you*, he told her. After Danyang came on board, Peter supervised her closely, taught her everything she needed to know, and eventually gave her full rein to manage the client. Over the years, the firm has built a great working relationship with the company. She's confident that all this billing fuss has to be just noise, people falling behind on paperwork.

By 5 p.m.—a perfectly respectable Beijing time of 9 a.m.—Alice calls Deckard, then Jenny. She's unable to reach either. She occupies herself with bits and pieces for another hour then tries again. Still no answer. She looks up Danyang's main number and calls there. Nobody picks up.

Who else can she call? She works through her contacts: Lin Kaipeng, the in-house counsel at Danyang; a couple of inventors she had worked with. *How come nobody is answering the phone? What if their telecom system has broken down?* She checks the news just to be sure there hasn't been some trawler severing the undersea intercontinental fiber optic cables. *What if, God forbid, the company is out of business?* She tells herself not to be ridiculous. Danyang isn't some fly-by-night startup. It has a solid growth record as a data center operator and runs multiple sites across China. Pretty solid, if staid, for a technology company. There was even talk of an IPO a few years ago, although given the current market conditions that's been postponed indefinitely. *They can't just fold without any notice, can they?* To be sure, she checks the news again and finds nothing alarming associated with the company. Their website is operating normally. She has to stop being such a worrywart. They must be either screening calls or too busy with deadlines or in meetings right now. If she sends out enough emails, she's bound to hear back from someone. And failing that, she can always call his wife—as much as she hates to mix business with personal relationships. She just needs to give it a day.

She stares out the darkening window and catches her own reflection—the ordinary, amorphous face of a middle-aged Asian woman.

A boring person. Perhaps that's why she's stayed friends with Deckard—because he's interesting, and she feels a little more interesting herself when she's with him. Creative and restless, her childhood friend is always dabbling in various technical areas and coming up with new ideas in his "copious free time." His latest interests are in memory and neuroplasticity. A few years ago, he started a company called Neuromersion, which seems permanently stuck in the prototyping stage—no surprise, as he decided to fund it with his own money and has been working on it solo. Yet he is liberal about filing patent applications on methods and systems for transcranial magnetic stimulation. Deep down, Alice finds the subject a bit cuckoo and has always advised not to overspend on patents. But Deckard is confident the technology has wide-ranging applications and these intellectual property assets will turn out to be valuable someday.

A thought strikes her cold.

She dials Nadia: "Peter came to me earlier to talk about the overdue invoices for Danyang. What about the NEUR account?"

Turned out it's overdue as well. $140k is not yet high enough to trigger Nadia's alarm for "trouble worth the partners' attention" but sends Alice into hyperventilation just the same. All told, the tab is now close to $600k.

As she passes Peter's office on her way out, she considers going in to deliver the worsening news, but he's on the phone. She breathes out. *Just wait one more day. It will get resolved.*

4

Memory #1, Shanxi, China, 1975

The dank, smoky smell. The little cupboard where the enamel bowls were stored, most of them dented, one of them holding some leftover cornmeal buns, hard as rocks and needing to be moistened with water to be edible. The unlit oil lamp hanging on the wall, the poster of Chairman Mao tacked next to it, its yellowing edges curling.

He was inside a yaodong, a cave room dug into the hillside, which housed his family. His parents, like many educated young people at the time, were sent down to the countryside to work alongside the peasants and be reeducated through hard labor.

The door was closed. A square of light fell through the small window beside it, casting a spot on the wall—its source a mirror his parents had placed outside the window to brighten the dark interior. His family had gone off to work in the field and left him behind. Mama could no longer carry him on her back as she now had to carry his baby brother. It never occurred to Baba to carry him; he was weaker in physique, and besides, it simply wasn't done. Knowing he couldn't be left to roam freely, Mama jammed a wooden post behind the bed. She tied one end of a rope to the top of the stick and the other end to his waist. It was just long enough for him to reach the edge of the bed without falling off. She would come to check on him every couple of hours.

In this enhanced memory, he could see, like in a dream, his twenty-month-old self jostling the post loose, causing it to topple sideways. He rolled around, getting tangled up in the cord. There was enough extra slack such that when he crawled to the edge of the bed, he fell off—that was the plunging sensation. A length of rope tightened around his neck. He dangled, feet still off the ground. The binding bit into his skin, cutting off air and tearing at his neck, delivering a searing pain he'd never felt before. Along with the pain, flowers and birds of the most glorious purple colors burst forth in his vision. Instead of feeling terror, he was fascinated by the sight and tempted to follow a tunnel of light framed by the purples.

The temptation was quickly washed away by a surge of remorse unbefitting his age. Was this all there was? All he would get? Too little, and too soon. A desire to hang on burned from the top of his skull to his toes. He struggled, only the more he struggled, the tighter the noose became. His body went limp. Slowly, he began to rotate in the opposite direction. The pressure eased, and the rope unwound from his neck. He coughed once. He could breathe again. The visions disappeared. And he began to wail.

5

"Hi, Fei. It's Alice. Long time no talk. I've been trying to reach Deckard for some work-related stuff but can't get hold of him. Do you know where he is? Give me a call when you get a chance. Bye."

Alice hangs up and stares at the phone, willing Fei to call her right back. She's running out of options, having called everyone else she knows at the company and gotten no response.

Deckard's wife, Fei, lives with their daughter, Jessica—or rather, lived with—now Jessica is attending boarding school in Connecticut. Fei raising Jessica in the States with Deckard working in Shanghai is a difficult but common enough arrangement among Chinese couples of a certain generation—the husband makes money and flies back and forth, while the wife and kids enjoy the clean environment and more relaxed lifestyle during the school year and visit China over the breaks. Alice can't imagine living like that, but to each their own. Fei has endured her largely single parenthood with good cheer—or great resignation—for years.

When Deckard was still working in the Bay Area, the two families used to get together often. Before Deckard left for China to start his company, he had asked Alice to lunch one day. Over dessert, he solemnly requested that Alice check in on his wife and daughter from time to time while he was gone. It would give him great comfort, he said, to know there was a trusted friend whom they could rely upon in case of emergencies.

Alice readily agreed to this. She even calendared a time each month to call Fei, who would sound happy to hear from her and chat about a whole bunch of nothings for half an hour. Whenever Alice proposed a get-together, Fei would accept, then usually had some excuse to cancel: a last-minute appointment with the plumber; car in the shop; Jessica being under the weather. Life got in the way. After a while, Alice quit trying, being so busy with work and family herself. Only when Deckard came back in town and got the families together would Alice find out how badly she had neglected her duties: Someone broke into Fei's garage and stole a couple of bikes; tree roots intruded the sewer line at their house and caused backups; Jessica suffered various childhood mishaps: a concussion at the playground; a fever that spiked to 105 degrees; head lice. Fei never mentioned any of these crises to Alice while they were happening. She just handled them single-handedly, a superwoman wielding designer bags.

Why did she do this? Why would a single mother living in a foreign land reject a helping hand? Alice tried to analyze it with her husband, Henry, time and time again. Was it because of envy—of Alice's career? Fei was a graduate of the London School of Economics and a former management consultant. She too could have continued to develop her career and had more standing in the world. Instead she quit her job once Jessica came along. Or was she jealous of Alice and Deckard's lifelong friendship? Even though they might as well be cousins and there had never been any romantic attraction between them, perhaps Fei didn't believe true friendship could exist between a man and a woman. Or was she simply resentful of Alice's family of five, cacophonous and chaotic as they may be, but at least living together under the same roof?

Maybe there was a simpler explanation, Henry said. Maybe Fei was an independent introvert who just didn't like to trouble others.

In early summer 2020, while the U.S. was fumbling with its

pandemic response but China had gotten things under control through draconian measures, Fei and Jessica went back to China. It turned out to be a smart move as lives in Shanghai were more or less normal for nearly two years. Then came the two-month-long lockdown in the spring of 2022. After that, Fei and Jessica returned to the U.S. Zero-Covid finally ended that December. Jessica is now in boarding school, but Fei still hasn't gone back to China to join her husband. Fei's WeChat account shows off photos of her travels: Alaska, Canada, New Mexico, Costa Rica. Alice can't help the twinge of jealousy whenever she thinks about Fei's life now. Sometimes, on her drive home from work, she imagines taking a solo trip like that. It's a ridiculous fantasy, of course. Even if she didn't have trouble flying, she could never leave her family behind. She usually ends up at the grocery store instead.

So, please, Fei, give me a call back, Alice begs. *You have all the time in the world.*

6

Alice is now in despair. It's already Friday over in China. No one has called her back, and she's losing hope that anyone will. *What in the world is going on?*

At least Fei is local. Alice gets in her car and heads to the hills.

Fei and Deckard bought their house years ago after the startup Deckard was working for was sold to Microsoft. The price tag—1.8 million dollars, Alice had looked it up—was an astonishing sum back then. It's probably tripled by now. Financially, however, he would have come out ahead had he kept his Microsoft stock, which has gone up more than tenfold in the same time. Only in America.

"Never imagined I could live in a house like this," Deckard told Alice at the housewarming party as they looked out from the patio at the view of Silicon Valley below.

"Yeah, quite a step up from Apartment 209," she said, and they both laughed.

∽

APARTMENT 209 WAS where they'd met when Alice Zhu was still Zhu

Aining, and Deckard Shen was still Shen Weiguo. It was one of her earliest memories, polished to a shine from repeated retelling.

The year was 1976, near the end of the Cultural Revolution. Educated young people like their parents were mostly sent to the countryside to be "reeducated" through hard labor. Aining's parents decided to leave her with the grandparents in the city where food was more plentiful and there was running water.

It was a snowy afternoon, back when it still snowed regularly in Nanjing. Snowy days were indoor days for Aining and her nainai (grandmother) when they huddled by the coal stove and listened to the radio. When the *Little Trumpet Show* came on, they heard a knock on the door. A curious thing, as they didn't get many visitors.

Nainai opened the door to a family of four on top of the stairs. Aining peered out from behind Nainai's legs. She saw an auntie carrying a sleeping child on her hip, an uncle whose face was very long and thin, and a boy with a bowl haircut holding a hat in his hand. They were all dressed in heavy winter clothes. Flakes of snow clung to their heads and shoulders. Suitcases at their feet. *Did they come here to play?* She let go of Nainai's legs and took two steps toward the boy, but Nainai scooped her up.

"Are you looking for somebody?" Nainai asked.

"Hello, Auntie, I'm Liu Penglai. This is my husband, Shen Guyong, and our two boys. We just joined the university. We have been assigned to live in this apartment."

"What do you mean, 'assigned to live in this apartment'?"

"This is Building 16, Apartment 209, isn't it?"

Nainai held Aining tighter. "Yes, but there's got to be some kind of mistake. We live here. Just moved in a month ago."

"I understand. Can you show her the letter?" The auntie nodded at the uncle, who dutifully produced a letter from the pocket of his padded army coat. It was written on university stationery, bearing an official red stamp. He pointed. "Says right here: 'Due to the housing shortage, you will be sharing the apartment with another family.'"

Nainai put Aining down. She took the letter, held it at arm's length toward the light, and read it carefully, turning the pages over several times. While Nainai studied the letter, Aining studied the boy. He was a little taller than her, his face red from the cold, his eyes fixed on the flurry outside the stairwell window. Two shiny streams of snot were coming out of his nose, which he licked from time to time. A pair of mittens dangled on a string over his neck. Nainai always warned Aining not to take her mittens off when it was cold so she wouldn't get chilblains. Aining wondered if the boy might have chilblains, but his hands were behind his back.

Then the boy turned his gaze to Aining and showed her something in his hand. It was a small oblong-shaped snowball. Aining extended her hand and he gave it to her. She gently squeezed—the snowball felt so cold that it was almost hot, and it had just a little bit of give, like a ripe fruit. Aining squealed with delight at the unexpected gift—she was suddenly very excited to go out and play. Perhaps Nainai would let her go with the boy, who had known she would want to play with snow before she herself did?

"I'll need to go talk with my husband. He's at work," Nainai said, giving the letter back.

Nainai made Aining give the snowball back and helped her put on winter gear: padded coat, hat, scarf, gloves, and an extra pair of wool socks. Then she brought out the rain boots and the big umbrella. *What fun!* They would go out and stomp in the snow! Yet Nainai's mouth was puckered, her face set in what Aining was learning to be a worried look.

Nainai brought out some chairs for the visitors and asked them to wait outside while she locked up. Aining understood this to be out of an abundance of caution—as Nainai always said, thieves and robbers never wrote that on their faces—though she doubted this family were actually thieves or robbers. She hoped the boy would stay so they could play thieves and robbers together. And make a snowman.

Aining and Nainai went across the campus and found her yeye (grandfather) in a group political studies meeting, which was essentially a roomful of men smoking and yakking and drinking tea from enamel mugs. Yeye had no idea what Nainai was talking about. He trudged off to look for the person in charge of faculty housing, leaving Nainai and Aining to make small talk with his colleagues.

He was gone for so long that Aining had fallen asleep in the smoke-shrouded room. When she woke up, Yeye had returned, and his face was grave. There was no mistake; the apartment was indeed too big and above grade for Associate Professor Zhu Hanshun and his wife—and their granddaughter, who didn't actually have residency rights in the city, therefore, might as well not exist. They would be sharing it with another family because there was a housing shortage.

The other men in the political studies group offered sympathetic looks. The housing shortage, of course. Name anything useful and there was a shortage of it.

Nainai glowered at Yeye on their way home. "I can't believe you didn't even put up a fuss about it," she fumed.

"What could I have done?" Yeye sighed. "Those two, they probably have people in high places. Backstage supporters."

Nainai went quiet for a while, her grip on Aining's hand growing tighter. When Nainai spoke again, she sounded amazed. "No wonder. A young couple both getting jobs at the university when our own children are stuck in places birds don't even stop to poop. I guess we are lucky not to have the apartment taken away from us!"

Yet Liu Ayi (Auntie Liu) and Shen Shushu (Uncle Shen) didn't act superior in any way. They made their beds on the floor of the bedroom that was vacated for them and went to work the next day. The boys, to Aining's disappointment, were sent to day care. Henceforth, after work, Liu Ayi cooked and cleaned and busied herself like a spinning top while Shen Shushu caught up on sleep in their room —he needed a lot of sleep, almost as much as baby Jianguo. And at the month's end, they counted their meager wages and ration coupons and sighed at the lack of everything like everybody else. Aining's grandparents never figured out who those supposed backstage supporters were.

~

AT THAT SAME HOUSEWARMING PARTY, Deckard had asked Alice what she was going to do with her life.

"I don't know," she said, taken aback. No one had asked her that since she graduated, not even her own mother. The world—and herself—seemed content she had a job and was paying off student loans. She'd been working in quality assurance for several years now. The job was steady but dull. She was living with her boyfriend, who was similarly steady but dull. She wanted to take some time off, maybe travel around the country, then figure out the rest.

"Have you thought about going back to school?" he asked.

"Well, I've already got a master's in engineering, and I don't love it enough to do a Ph.D. I don't have the prerequisites for medical school. And I'm not that into business."

"Law school, then."

"To sue people? I don't think so."

"But you might make a good patent attorney," he said. "I know someone who works at the law school careers office; I'll introduce you."

So, in a way, Alice owes her career to Deckard, who is only two months older but way more intelligent, way more worldly, and somehow seemed to know what she ought to do better than herself. She thinks of him as the elephant in the story of the elephant and the mouse, who lifted her, the mouse, from the pit of aimlessness.

Now, perhaps the elephant is in trouble, and the mouse can do something for him.

7

When Alice pulls up to Fei's Mediterranean, the first thing she notices is a shiny black Harley in the driveway. A new hobby for the empty nester? Except the bike seems too massive for the pint-sized Fei.

Alice waves at the camera doorbell as she rings it. Five minutes later, a short woman sporting long straight brown hair with golden highlights opens the door. She has pancake makeup, fake eyelashes, big hoop earrings, and a low-cut top. For a second, Alice takes her to be one of Jessica's friends. She does a double take—it's as though some trashy teenage alien has body-snatched the Chinese housewife who favored vicuña sweaters.

"Hi, Alice. What are you doing here?" Fei chirps.

They hug. Over Fei's herbal shampoo scent, Alice smells booze.

"Sorry to come here unannounced. Did you get my message?"

Fei pouts and takes out the phone from the back pocket of her ripped jeans. "No, sorry, I haven't checked." She taps the screen with a jazz hand, her rhinestone-studded acrylic nails being more than an inch long.

Alice's eyes sweep across the bay window of the upstairs bedroom. Is it her imagination or is the shade moving slightly, like someone is watching from behind? It's none of her business, and since Fei is making no motion to invite her in, she'll just get her questions over with quickly.

"I called because I was having trouble getting hold of Deckard."

"Mm..."

"Do you know where he is?"

"Shanghai, I'm guessing."

"I've called him several times, also everyone I know from Danyang. And sent emails. Nobody's gotten back to me. It's a total communication breakdown. When did you last talk to him?"

"Early February."

Alice's eyes widen. "That was more than two months ago!"

"Yeah. Hasn't he told you? We're separating."

"Separating?"

"Yeah. I mean, we've always been separate, but we're getting a divorce."

Alice is floored. When she spoke with Deckard back in December, he never mentioned any of this. "Why?" she asks. The answer, of course, is blowing in the wind: Marriages are hard. A long-distance one harder still. A long-distance marriage to a high tech CEO, hardest of all.

Fei flits her bovine eyelashes and says with flat valley-girl affectations, "Like, irreconcilable differences." Having gone to grad school in London, Fei still speaks English with a posh British accent. *What's gotten into her?* And irreconcilable differences—what differences would matter when Jessica is grown and they could finally be together? Perhaps that's the problem. Too much togetherness over the pandemic when they were used to having their own space.

Alice can't help but ask. "Such as?"

Fei frowns at this request for specifics. She's probably done that too many times with the divorce lawyers. Alice fully expects her to deflect or remain silent. This, however, is no longer the old private Fei who wraps herself in a secretive cocoon but an inebriated woman bursting out. The question is apparently triggering. Hands aflutter, spittle a-flying, eyes ablaze, she starts to tick off a litany of complaints:

Way too much time at work. Always distracted when he got home. Perpetually wasting time and money on impossible technical projects and far-fetched political ideas. Moody. Messy. Forever losing things. And on top of all that, delusional.

But that's how he is, Alice wants to say. *Haven't you always known that? Haven't we all long accepted* that *such were the trade-offs for his talents—the brilliance, the drive, the insight, the unexpected fun?*

"I was constantly having to buy him stuff. I could live with all that, just go on replacing sunglasses and umbrellas and wallets and cellphones. Then he lost his wedding ring! And ninety million dollars!" Fei squeezes her eyes shut and shakes her head back and forth as if trying to rid herself of a migraine.

"What!"

"I know! Whatever was he doing taking his ring off in the first place?"

"I mean, losing ninety million dollars? How did he do that?"

Fei's smile is sardonic. "Don't you get it? It wasn't real. Just something he made up. Another one of his delusions."

So Deckard isn't the only successful person Alice knows who is given to puffery from time to time. He might boast a little, stretch the truth, paint a brighter picture, as CEOs are wont to do. But she wouldn't go as far as calling him delusional. "There's usually some basis to what he says, isn't there? That's a shocking amount of money. What exactly did he say happened?"

"Does it matter? Why would you believe him? He feeds off people like you—fixated on money, willing to indulge him in those grandiose delusions."

"But—"

"I don't want to talk about it anymore, okay?"

"Okay, I'm sorry… for everything."

"Don't be. Love is just a bag that holds two people together; the world keeps cutting at it from the outside, and if you keep cutting at it from the inside, too, it'll break faster, and that's how people fall out of love. Then you just have to get over it and live your best life."

You're a tough broad, Alice thinks, *and a philosophical one at that. But you can't fool me—your wound is still raw, and I might have just ripped the bandage off and seen the blood ooze.* Alice wants to be out of there, to avoid being drawn into the mess. She doesn't want to take sides, not right now. Yet she has to get to the bottom of things for her own sake. "When you talked last, did he say anything unusual?"

Fei narrows her furry eyes.

Alice blushes at her clumsy phrasing. They were discussing a divorce; of course everything they said was unusual. She tries again. "About work, I mean. Did he mention anything unusual about Danyang? Any difficulties there?"

"No. Should he have?"

"No, it's just I haven't heard from him, which is odd. Might Jessica have talked with him more recently?"

"I wouldn't know, but probably not. She's really upset at both of us over the divorce, so do me a favor and leave her alone."

"Of course," Alice says hurriedly. She's all too familiar with the fragile, furious state of a teenager in the middle of a divorce battle, for she had been there herself. "Who else can I call?"

"I'll give you his lawyer's number. And his brother Jianguo—do you have his contact?" Fei jazz-hands her phone and sends Alice the contact info, then says, "I've got to go. I was just getting ready to go out when you came."

"You're not driving?"

"No, of course not."

"Call me if you ever want to talk—I know it's hard, with Jessica gone and the whole divorce thing."

Fei nods again and doles out a thin smile. "Thanks. I appreciate it. I mean it."

They hug again lightly. Alice gets into her car. Instead of going straight, she makes a U-turn and parks a few houses down the street so she can watch Fei's house through the rearview mirror. She's the mother of a teenager and two tweens; trust and verify is her motto. What would she do if Fei got into her car? She would call her. Would she call the police if Fei didn't pick up? Hopefully it wouldn't come to that.

A few minutes later, Fei comes out, this time in full leather. A lanky guy, also clad in leather, follows behind her. He turns on the ignition of the bike and revs the engine. As the bike starts to slide away, he stands on his left foot on the foot petal, then swings his right leg over the bike seat in a swift motion like mounting a horse. Fei runs a few steps and jumps onto the seat behind him. She hooks her arms around his waist, then presses her cheek against his back. As they blast out of the driveway and speed past Alice's car, Alice catches a flash of blue-green above the man's collar.

Neck tattoos, of course. At least they're both wearing helmets.

8

Deckard Shen Weiguo returns to his office, having finally completed the bring-up of Module 7 for the data center. It took much longer than he anticipated because of some bad cables. He can't believe he's wasting time on this secondhand crap. But he has to tamp down his anger—he's just a peon here; he would keep his head down and do what he's told so he can work on Neuromersion on the side. It's the only good thing about this deal. At home, he can never give his pet project enough time and attention.

He's surprised to see Dr. Chang waiting for him outside, then remembers the appointment. The doctor has become his favorite person here. Like Deckard Shen/Shen Weiguo, the doctor also has two names. Daniel Nganang in Cameroonian and Chang Huichun in Chinese. The doctor, however, is a more committed immigrant, having studied then worked here for over thirty years, married a Chinese woman, and raised two children.

Was there discrimination, Deckard asked the doctor once, in this country where over ninety percent of the population are Han Chinese? An African doctor is as rare as a panda—rarer, perhaps, as there are thousands of pandas.

Yes, at first, Dr. Chang said. When he started out at the hospital, he had no patients for weeks. But then he went to the waiting room where all these patients had been waiting for hours for an appointment with the senior doctors and told them he could see them right away. A few brave souls took him up on it. Those whose pains were immediately alleviated by Chang's acupuncture and moxibustion brought family and friends, and the rest is history. The Chinese are a practical people. The hospital ran on meritocracy.

Nowadays Dr. Chang holds a faculty position at a teaching hospital in Chengdu and volunteers for a month every year at the local clinic where Deckard went for acupuncture treatment a couple of days ago. Being the sole medical provider in the area at the moment, the doctor has clearance to come inside the compound for house calls.

"Your neck still bothering you?" Dr. Chang asks.

"It's much better, but I'm still having trouble sleeping."

"I'm surprised you can sleep in here at all—a few minutes in this place and my ears are going crazy with the sound of my own heartbeat."

"That's the nature of an anechoic chamber. I need all the noises to originate from me. It's so Neuromersion can process signals more cleanly."

"Mm." The doctor smiles tolerantly without comprehension. He checks Deckard's pulse and tongue and asks him to take off his shirt. Retrieving a set of acupuncture needles from his medicine bag, he pauses and points at the helmet. "What's that?"

"It's a precision transcranial magnetic stimulation device."

"I've heard about those—for treating depression and such?"

"Yes, the conventional ones do. This one is a prototype, designed to, well, as a first step, help enhance memory."

The doctor's eyes go wide. "Really? Does it work?"

"Yes, though it's early days yet. Ultimately—" He stops himself.

The doctor waits.

Deckard has always been vague when discussing his vision for the device, not so much out of fear of sounding like a madman but because he prefers getting some results first. With Dr. Chang's large black hands touching his shoulders and placing needles so gently and expertly, however, he feels he can let the man in on it. "Ultimately, it will be able to implant memory."

"Wonderful!" The doctor laughs heartily. "Let me know when you get it working; there are a few memories I'd like for my wife and kids to have."

9

Memory #39, Nanjing, September 9, 1976

There must be hundreds of memories like this one of the four of them—Weiguo, his brother Jianguo, Aining, and Aining's nainai—going to Wuchaomen Park. They did that nearly every afternoon when the weather was good, and weather in early fall was always fine. This particular day sticks out because of what happened.

The brothers had gone to the on-campus day care initially. In two months, they took turns succumbing to pink eye, whooping cough, and colds which led to an ear infection for Jianguo and bronchitis for Weiguo. The sick one always got locked inside the room because Mama was worried about passing the sickness to others, especially Aining. Whenever that happened, the child howled and pounded the door while the parents pleaded for him to quiet down. On top of the misery, it was becoming an unsustainable situation for Mama, who spoke fearfully of her boss questioning her having already taken so many days off work.

Finally, Tao Nainai came over one day with an offer: As soon as the boys were no longer contagious, she could watch them while the parents went to work. For the long term.

Baba was hesitant. "We don't want to impose too much," he said to Tao Nainai. But Mama gave him a hard look and said, "You stay here and look after them next time they are sick, then." That settled it. So here they were, headed to the park with Nainai.

WUCHAOMEN PARK WAS about a ten-minute stroll from the faculty compound through a wooded path along the avenue. The park, as the kids would learn later, was the site of the old palace of the Ming dynasty. After Emperor Zhu Di moved the capital north, the old palace fell into disuse. All the wooden structures were either burned up or torn down eons ago, leaving behind only stone—enormous plinths wider and taller than an adult, slabs of thick granite from collapsed walls, carved alabaster screens with dragons and phoenixes, curved bridges overlooking duckweed-covered ponds that were essentially huge uncovered wells, all behind a section of thick, five-arched old city wall.

Whenever they approached the city wall, Weiguo was always overtaken by nervousness. Goosebumps, standing hairs, racing heart. He had no words for the sense of trepidation back then, but looking back, he now understands—his young self thought the three deep gateways in the middle somehow resembled the empty eye sockets and gaping mouth of a monster. At four years old, Weiguo had somehow intuited the mirthlessness of the ancient brick structure, for they had borne witness to six hundred years of turbulence: the conspiracies, the usurpations, the abandonments, the invasions, the rapes and pillages, the rebellions, the suppressions, the destructions and reconstructions, the deaths and births, the hollowing out and filling back in—things he wouldn't learn or comprehend until years later. Yet, he already knew he loved the whole complicated mess and wanted to be a part of it, for his four-year-old body bristled with energy. He combated his fear by charging ahead, yelling and laughing louder than usual, straight into the echoey orifice of the monster.

They did their usual rounds at the park. First, they climbed—with a little boost from Tao Nainai—onto one of the stone lions at the entrance and stuck their hands into the lion's mouth to roll around the stone ball inside. The ball moved freely yet did not fall out, a kind of magic that impressed the children every time. Tao Nainai claimed that the lion tried to swallow the ball, then got turned into stone, but Weiguo had figured out how the ball was actually made: They must have chipped away the rock inside the mouth bit by bit until the ball was all that was left. "Of course you are right, you little genius," she said to Weiguo, tapping him on the tip of his nose.

Next, they played hide-and-seek behind the rocks. Jianguo was always the first to get caught because he would only hide in the most obvious places. Since he was too young to ever find anyone, Tao Nainai took his place whenever it was his turn to be the seeker. After several rounds of this, when Weiguo was finally spotted, instead of surrendering, he began to run and the rest gave chase, and they switched to playing tag instead.

When the kids became exhausted, they sought out their favorite resting spots. Jianguo sprawled out on the biggest sloping stone slab in front of the carved screen. Aining curled up in a half-moon-shaped piece, perhaps once an arched doorway now turned upside down. Weiguo rode on a quartz block with splashes of orange and red colors. Much later, he would learn it was called the Bloody Stone because an insubordinate court official was allegedly cut in half on it, and the splashes were supposedly his blood.

Soon the elementary school next door was let out and the park was filled with screaming school children. The young ones watched, mesmerized, as the older children tore off the red Young Pioneer scarves from their necks and whipped them, making cracking noises, shooting pebbles at trees with homemade slingshots, and playing horse as they rode on each other's shoulders and rammed into others.

Aining and Weiguo followed a group to the pond, where they all laid their bodies down perpendicular to the edge of the railing-less bridge, their heads and shoulders over the precipice, their arms and legs thrashing in the air so they could "practice swimming." Before any of them fell into the water, Tao Nainai came and snatched them away. Playtime was over, she said. It was time to go home.

As they approached the gate of the faculty housing complex, something felt odd. Usually around this time of day, exercise music was broadcast over the speakers hung all over the complex. Today, instead of the rhythmic music with chants of one-two-three-four, there was some kind of announcement. They couldn't make out the words, even though the announcer was speaking very slowly, like he was saying something so very important he wanted to be sure people understood every word he uttered. When they finally got close enough to hear what was being said, Weiguo caught only "Finally, he passed away at 00:10 Beijing Time on September 9, 1976."

"Passed away" meant "died," Weiguo had learned recently. But who?

They waited for the announcer to repeat, but that must have been his last cycle. "Well, I hope it's the university president," Tao Nainai muttered. When the kids got older, they would learn the source of Tao Nainai's vindictiveness. Years ago, Tao Nainai had a job lined up at the university day care center. It was everything she wanted: close to home, with decent benefits, and allowed her to work with children. She'd bought herself a new shirt, had her photo taken for the work badge and everything, so eager and ready she was to get started. Then something happened and the job evaporated. She found out later she'd been replaced by the president's own niece. Such blatant nepotism, such corruption! But to whom was she to complain? Who would listen? So she sneered every time the man's name was mentioned and cursed him with every misfortune.

After a pause, the announcer said, "Let us pay our respects with three minutes of silence."

People stood still, their heads bowed and eyes closed, as if unable to absorb the shock. Was this what people did when the university president died? Weiguo wondered. Before he could ask, Tao Nainai bent down and held them in her arms.

"Shhh, be quiet. We are playing the quiet game," she whispered.

They played the quiet game whenever Baba needed to rest during the day, which was more and more frequent lately. It was a simple game—they all had to stay quiet; the first to make a sound lost, and the winner might get a few raisins or a piece of candy. Baba needed his quiet rest as he suffered from poor nerves. Besides, being able to stay quiet is a very useful skill, Tao Nainai told them. Back in the day, when she was fleeing the Japanese with her family, they had to hide in a cave and stay very, very quiet. The stakes were much higher then. One cry from a baby and they could all be killed. Weiguo always pictured Japanese soldiers lurking with their bayonets, waiting to pounce, so he would stay very quiet and take only shallow breaths. He usually won.

When the silence was finally over, a woman on the sidewalk suddenly kneeled and started sobbing. She would have lost the quiet game.

"Oh, no, it's Xiao Lao Da (Little Big Shot)," Tao Nainai muttered, shaking her head.

Weiguo recognized that nickname, as Tao Nainai and Zhu Yeye had gossiped about her with his parents, warning them she was someone to watch out for. Over the years, he would eventually piece together Xiao Lao Da's story. Daughter of the university's former Communist Party Secretary had gained notoriety as the ring leader for the campaign to "Destroy the Four Olds"—old ideas, customs, habits, and culture. She and other Red Guards went around faculty apartments to smash up old vases and furniture and tear up old books and photos. She also organized denunciation meetings where they dragged various professors, including Zhu Yeye, on stage and proceeded to humiliate them in public for being "Counterrevolutionary Intellectuals." Zhu Yeye showed them the permanent scar on his neck, left by the wire of the heavy sign he'd had to wear during the denunciation meetings. There was some justice in the world, he said, when the woman's own father was later labeled as a "Capitalist Roader" and struggled against. But then Xiao Lao Da had "drawn a clear line" with her family and somehow avoided becoming an outcast herself. She even got herself a job at the university's propaganda department.

"Chairman Mao," Xiao Lao Da cried now, beating the ground with her fists, her shoulders heaving. Her voice, emitted from the diaphragm, was high and hoarse with grief. "Our beloved leader, great teacher, our helmsman, the guiding light of our nation, you cannot leave us!" The man standing next to her, presumably the husband, was flustered by the outburst and didn't seem to know how to react. He looked around at all the eyes on his wife and reddened, and bent down to say something to her, perhaps begging her not to make a scene. The woman shook her head back and forth like a rattle. With tears streaming down her face, she started belting out:

Sailing the seas depends on the helmsman,
The growth of all living things depends on the sun.
Rain and dew nourish young seedlings,
Conducting revolution depends on Mao Zedong Thought...

It was a familiar tune, often played on the radio, very upbeat, and demanded a chorus. The kids started to squirm—they wanted to sing, too, but the other adults were frozen as if a spell were cast on them. What were they waiting for? Weiguo wasn't sure but decided not to wait any longer himself. "Fish cannot leave the water, melons cannot leave the vine," he started. Aining and Jianguo joined in, slurring their words. "The re-vo-lu-ten masses cannot do wee-out the Gummist Partee!" Together, they twisted their hands in the air and stamped their feet joyously.

"Oh, dear," Tao Nainai said, reaching to grasp as many of the little hands in her own as she could, as if catching fistfuls of butterflies. "Come along. Let's go home."

THE KIDS WERE STILL SINGING as they climbed the stairs, and Tao Nainai chuckled, clapping along. She unlocked the door. It was dark—the shade of the window at the end of the hall was drawn, and the door to the Shen family's room was shut, which meant Baba was home and sleeping again. It would have to be the quiet game all over if they were to stay indoors, so Tao Nainai sent the kids to the balcony to play while she began fixing supper.

Soon the skies turned pink, and Mama returned from work. The kids ran to her with the day's news: "Chairman Mao died! We all sang a song for him!"

"I know! How sad," she said, without sounding the least bit. She darted a look at the closed bedroom door, then let out a breath and put on her apron to help Tao Nainai in the kitchen.

When dinner was ready, Mama asked Weiguo to wake Baba up.

He went into the room. Baba was lying in bed. There was something unnatural about the way he faced the wall, with his back arched. A funny smell was in the air—did somebody pee in here? Maybe Jianguo did it before they left for the park?

"Baba, it's dinner time," Weiguo said. He expected Baba to say something—Baba was a light sleeper, and more often than not, Weiguo would find him not to be sleeping at all, just staring straight at the ceiling or the wall. Weiguo sometimes crawled in bed with him and they'd cuddle for a few minutes before getting up—that was the only physical affection Baba ever showed him, as normally he was so reserved.

But on this day, Baba didn't seem to have heard Weiguo.

Weiguo went over and shook his shoulder. There was something odd in the touch—no resistance. Weiguo tried again. This time, Baba fell over face down. Something was definitely wrong. He went to fetch Mama.

Mama came in and took Baba's wrist. She then laid a hand on his neck. Weiguo watched her trying to turn Baba face up on the bed with effort and went to help her, but she stopped him and yelled at him in a shrill voice to leave the room and close the door. He hated that voice. Mama rarely used it except when he had done something really bad and deserved a spanking, like when he'd shattered Tao Nainai's flowerpot. But what had he done now? Nothing. It seemed unfair to be yelled at. Yet something told him he ought to do what he was told. So he obeyed.

A moment later, Mama came out, her face drained of color. Without a word, she shut the bedroom door behind her, headed into the kitchen, then shut the kitchen door, too. Weiguo turned his head left and right, looking at the two closed doors, wondering if he should open either one. Would Mama be mad if he did?

Before he could act, Tao Nainai came out. She looked as severe as Mama did. "We are doing a special dinner tonight," she said to the kids, pulling them close. "You'll eat in my room."

"We will sit on the floor like a picnic!" Aining cried. "I'll go get the blanket."

"What about my baba and mama?" Weiguo asked. There was a strange sound coming out of the kitchen that sounded like someone was hiccupping. Or sobbing.

"Your mama has to take care of your baba. He is"—Tao Nainai's voice took on a sudden lilt—"not well."

"Has he..." He looked at his brother, who had gone rooting around with Aining for the blanket. He was afraid of what he was about to say. Then he thought of the monstrous city gate and felt the same urge to press ahead. "Has he passed away?"

Tao Nainai didn't answer. With something glittering in her eyes, she gave Weiguo a long look, then pulled him into an embrace.

10

"So, I've something to tell you," Alice says as she sets down a plate of green beans on the dinner table.

Nobody seems to have heard her. Leo, her oldest, has his headphones on. Casey and Zander, the IVF miracle twins, are engaged in a game where they take turns climbing up on the chair and jumping off while crying, "Geronimo!"

She could raise her voice, but instead she studies their faces—she's never tired of doing that and finding herself and Henry in them—Leo's wide forehead and Casey's strong chin are hers; Zander's thick brows and all three pairs of pointy ears belong to Henry. The dark hair, the long limbs, even the acne—you can trace so many phenotypes to their sources. Except the dyslexia, which has a genetic component, though not entirely. That both twins, who are fraternal, have it is puzzling, though not unusual. Alice can't help wondering if something went wrong during the IVF process—an unkind thought she keeps bottled up. Henry's side of the family has a bunch of people who dropped out of school early. Some of them probably just had trouble with learning and never realized there was a cause to be addressed. Thankfully, the twins live in an era where the condition could be identified early and in a place with an excellent specialty school for dyslexic children. Even more thankfully, their parents can afford the outrageous tuition, if only barely.

Presently, her partner in procreation is casting his eyes down and stoically serving up the lemon chicken. In their private discussion before dinner, Alice had told him her plans.

"Are you serious? Is your boss pressuring you?" Henry asked, his gentle face taking on a rare look of outrage.

"Yes, I'm totally serious. No, nobody is pressuring me," she said (though truth be told, Peter did brighten visibly when she told him what she was willing to do). "But if the situation doesn't get resolved soon, I may lose my chance to make partner this year—maybe ever."

"Probably not the worst thing in the world? What is it they say, making partner is like winning the pie-eating contest, where the prize is more pies. You hardly need more on your plate."

"All the more reason I want this—you said so yourself—I do all this work; I might as well be compensated for it and have more control," Alice said, a bit exasperated. He still didn't get it. Leave it to Henry to find the silver lining in not advancing; he who studied architecture but never took the license exam and is perfectly content with his building inspector job. He believes that money and prestige aren't the most important things in life, a quality Alice finds in turn endearing and frustrating. To Henry, Alice's making partner would be an improvement, the icing on the cake, but he's already content with the cake. To Alice, however, the partnership is so much more than a prize. It's that rare thing that still drives her, that still lights the embers of her ambition, that reminds her what desire feels like in late middle age. And it's right in front of her; she would be crushed to have it all yanked away.

"Besides, if I make more money, Leo can go to Evergreen. I always feel like he's the one we're shortchanging," Alice said. Their first born has an IQ of 150 and constantly complains of being bored at school. Evergreen, which caters to gifted children and has things like Maker Labs and science teachers with PhDs, costs 65k a year. "And there's another wrinkle to the whole thing—by contract, our compensation is based on *collections*, not billings. It's never been an issue before. But in the unlikely event that the management decides to stick to the contract, my income will take a big hit this year, and so will a couple of other associates on the team."

Henry went quiet. Something finally sank in after a minute. "What about your job? They can't fire you over this, can they?"

"Not likely in a good economy, but you know how things are right now. There are rumors of layoffs. They should let the new associates go first, but what if I were seen as a liability?" Alice's voice was tight. They wouldn't know how to manage in that situation. The two of them together make an astounding amount of money by world standards but not much above poverty level for the Bay Area. If she has a pay cut or, God forbid, loses her job, they would have to economize by sending the twins to public school. Hopefully it wouldn't come to that. Or they could just sell the house and move somewhere cheaper —though where, she has no idea.

Henry put a hand on her shoulder. "And that little problem with flying?"

"I'll deal with it."

"You do what you need to do."

What other choice had she got?

Now, sitting at the dinner table, her heart breaks just a little at the prospect. She lets them finish the meal in peace. When Leo gets up, she flaps her hand at him. "Sit down, please. I've something to tell you. Everybody, listen up. So, I may not be able to go down to Grandma and Grandpa's for spring break."

That finally gets their attention.

"Why?" Zander asks.

"Work. I may have to visit a client."

"Not again!" Leo cries and pounds his fists on the table.

Alice gives him a sympathetic look. He's remembering the Yosemite trip debacle of 2019. They'd had a reservation at the Ahwahnee, but her client's competitor didn't know this—or rather, precisely because they knew everyone would have vacation plans—and chose to sue right before Christmas. Henry, in a gesture of solidarity, canceled the trip so they could all stay home and "be with Mommy for the holidays" while she worked round the clock. He should never have done that. As it turned out, it would have been their last chance to take a trip anywhere until they were all vaccinated, and it was definitely not worth the scars it left.

"It won't affect you—you will still go to Grandma and Grandpa's," Alice says.

"You said you may need to—how likely is it?" asks Casey, who is by nature precise and numerical.

"Eighty-five-point-seven percent." The divorce lawyer had no useful information to offer. Alice is still holding out hope that Deckard's brother might get back with some positive news.

"Say you go on Monday. You can still come down on Tuesday and not miss the whole week, right?" Casey asks.

"Not quite. It's a client based in Shanghai."

Leo cuts his eyes at her. "Uncle Deckard's company?"

Alice nods.

"But we're going to play volleyball on the beach, and you're supposed to make smoked duck for the BBQ!" Zander throws himself into her lap. By being two minutes younger than his sister, he's the baby of the family, the one best at pouting and wheedling.

Alice pats his back. "I know, sweetheart, I want to do all that, too. But this is really important. Daddy has the recipe. He'll make the duck."

"Are you going to fly?"

"I'm afraid so—the boats take too long," Alice says, not entirely joking. She actually looked into that once. It takes an average of twenty days for a cargo ship to go from Oakland to Shanghai; a cruise ship takes longer. Aerophobia is her super weakness. Alice is fortunate to have been able to avoid flying for as long as she has, since aside from Danyang, the rest of her clients are local. Henry is content with road trips and cruises, which are easier with the children anyway. A few years ago, Leo expressed an interest in traveling overseas, so Alice decided to look for a therapist to work through her condition. Then the pandemic hit. If there ever was an upside to Covid, it was the collective shunning of flying. Alas, that is now over.

"What?" Leo is apoplectic. "We can't go to Europe because you don't fly. Now you're going to fly all the way to China just so you can visit Uncle Deckard? Over spring break? Why don't you just call him? Or wait until he comes here?"

"Leo, use a kinder tone, please." Henry finally breaches his silence.

"I just can't believe this," Leo says.

Oh, my over-privileged child who has been to twenty-six national parks in the U.S. and Canada, thinks Alice, there are *worse things in life*. Starting an argument like that with a teenager, however, you will have already lost. So she says, "I've got to do some in-person meetings. Sometimes you have to do that; you learn more about what's going on." *Like this afternoon*, she thinks. *I would never have found out what I did had I not gone to Fei's.*

"What if you have another panic attack on the runway?" Casey asks.

Alice lets out a breath. When the kids were old enough to ask the right questions, she'd had to share the details with them: the racing heart, the clammy hands, the involuntary shaking, the sensations of suffocating and wanting to hyperventilate at the same time, the feeling of impending doom. The sharp cries of the woman sitting next to her: is there a doctor on board? This young lady is having a seizure, a heart attack! Only the plane hadn't taken off yet. The pilot wheeled the plane around. The medics came running. They checked her vitals but by then everything seemed fine. She refused the stretcher and opted to walk back down, hoping to keep the last shreds of her dignity. The glances of other passengers: curious, irritated, hostile. The fat man's muttering: It's always the Asians and Mexicans that are trouble, isn't it? The hot sting of ignominy on her skin, at her humiliating condition, at not being able to call him out on the racism.

"I'll take something for it," Alice says without conviction.

"And throw up all over the place?"

"They come out with better meds all the time. I'll call Dr. Paulson to check." Unfortunately for Alice, Ativan and Xanax both induced severe nausea, the cure being as bad as the ailment. At least her panic attacks have a specific trigger—air travel, more precisely, airports—which can be avoided for the most part. She wouldn't know what to do if she had to take those meds regularly. Her current plan is just to grit her teeth and get through it. Inhale deeply. Hold. Exhale. Calming yoga breath and focus on said breath. Eye covers plus chewing gum plus melatonin. Maybe even a couple of drinks, despite not being a drinker. As long as she goes to sleep, she will be okay. She will feel wrecked, but she will get there, and the rest will fall into place.

"Can we all go?" Xander asks, raising his head like a little cat.

Yes, a part of her pleads. Yes, if you are going to suffer through the travel, take the whole family. Show them the place you grew up, where their ancestors came from. Take them to visit Nanjing. Go see places you haven't been to yourself—the Great Wall in Beijing, the Terra Cotta Warriors in Xi'an, the jagged sandstone columns of Zhangjiajie. The thought is tempting. What is the point, though? She has few remaining ties there. The children used to know a lot of Chinese because of their Chinese nanny. When they got older, however, they all stopped speaking Chinese and refused to go to Chinese school on the weekends. Alice isn't sure if they still know enough Chinese to order food in restaurants. They would be just like any other tourists, gawking at the sights, frowning at the air pollution, half-heartedly snapping pictures. What would be the point of returning to the place she so resolutely left behind and where she has no people, when there are so few vacation days and so many other places that are fresher, wilder, and easier to get to?

Casey saves Alice the trouble of having to answer in the negative. "We can't—we don't have passports."

"How long will you be gone?" Leo asks.

"So, two days traveling back and forth. A day or two in Shanghai for the meetings. Maybe a couple of days in Nanjing to visit some old friends. I should be back in a week. You guys have fun at Grandma and Grandpa's. You won't even notice I'm gone."

"I'll notice," Casey says.

"Me too," Xander says.

"I'm sorry, sweetie. But I really have to do this."

"Or else what?" Xander asks.

Again, Casey answers for Alice. "Or else Mom won't make partner, and we'll have to take out loans for college and pay for them for the rest of our lives."

Alice and Henry chuckle at each other. *You'll probably need to do that anyway, sweetie.*

"I'm not going to college. I'm gonna live in the woods and forge swords," Leo croaks like a prepubescent frog as he pushes away from the table.

"Nope, you are going to college," says Casey, the little mama.

"I want to go to Nanjing. And stay at the Koi Palace Hotel." Zander sounds inconsolable. Deckard had sent them a photo of Jessica feeding the koi at the indoor koi pond there several years ago, because Zander has always been in love with koi. Alice printed out the picture and stuck it on the refrigerator, where it still is. Zander has been obsessed with the idea of going to Nanjing and staying at the hotel ever since.

"Some day," Alice says. *Maybe when you're an adult and can travel freely on your own, if the koi are still there and you still care about them.*

The phone buzzes, and a message from Jianguo pops up on the screen. *Haven't talked with him for over a month. Can't reach him, either. Guess he's busy?*

Well, it's now one hundred percent she's going.

11

Alice enters the bedroom, carrying a basket of laundry. The room is dark. A single blue LED on the air purifier shines like a distant star. *Is Henry asleep already?* In case he is, she leaves the light off and shuffles toward the bed.

"So," a voice comes from the window.

Alice jumps. "You scared me. What are you doing here in pitch dark?"

"Oh, sorry," Henry says. The lamp next to his chair comes on. He's leaning forward, arms crossed, one hand rubbing his right earlobe—a little chunk missing from the tip is the only physical scar he bore from the accident that ended his biking career. It's his tell. When he has something on his mind, he likes to mold the bit of deformed flesh with his fingers like Play-Doh, as if trying to make it whole again. He straightens. "So, do you think you'll see who's-his-face when you're over there?"

Alice squints at the light. *He can't mean Deckard.* "Who's-his-face?"

"I mean, your father's..."

Alice exhales. Since she has never used "stepbrother" or "stepmom" in regard to her father's other family, Henry is left without reference and has to improvise.

"Why should I?" she asks, more a challenge than a question. Really, she has no animosity toward those people—she doesn't even know who they are.

Henry sits back, hiding his face behind the lampshade. But he can't hide his judgment, which is emanating like the white light.

"Because your father is dead," he says. Though an agnostic, Henry maintains a Judeo-Christian view on forgiveness. How can he ever understand it—he of the perfect family with happily married parents and mostly happily married siblings? His younger brother had the only divorce in the family, handled so maturely by mediation that his ex-wife still comes around for dinner now and then. Things don't work that way with her family.

Sent down to the countryside in the seventies, Alice's parents returned to Nanjing in the early eighties after the government reinstated undergraduate and graduate school entrance exams. Both got their master's degrees and upon graduating, reclaimed Alice—Aining—from her grandparents.

Her mother came to the U.S. in the mid-eighties to further her studies, and Alice joined her a few years later—without her father. After the divorce, her mother refused to have anything to do with her father again and forbade Alice from telling her anything about him. Alice not only complied but also meted out her own justice on the man she saw as responsible for breaking up the family: the tossing of unopened letters in the early days, the deleting of emails at the dawn of the Internet age, the refusal of friend requests in the era of social media. What little she knew of his new life, the wife and the son, flowed from Deckard by way of his family, who still live in the same faculty housing complex where they grew up.

Her father's death announcement came in an email directly from his son. No subject, just a string of Chinese characters in the sender field—an unfamiliar name. That was the only reason Alice opened it. It appeared to be a mass email, probably to his father's entire contact list. Inside was a link to the video funeral. She logged on at the prescribed time without turning the camera on. Dozens of attendees were already there. She recognized none of the names. The connection froze twice during the eulogies. She logged off and didn't log back on.

"What am I supposed to do? Go lay wreaths on his grave?"

Henry shrugs. "If you'd like. Aren't you at least curious about them?"

"Not really," Alice says, folding a T-shirt on her lap. "Curiosity is a luxury of the leisure class. I need to get my work done and be back here as quickly as possible."

"I just thought if you understand them a little better..."

Then what? Would she be less worried about her current job situation? Less tired, less stressed, less overworked? Be a better person, a better mother? Why should she be a better person or better mother? An inexplicable anger rises inside her. If she wanted herself psychoanalyzed she'd go see a licensed therapist. She stands up abruptly and dumps the laundry on Henry's side of the bed.

12

So this is the one that matters, the one he's racked his brain over again and again. He hesitates, however, as he puts on the helmet. He's worried about what he might find—or more precisely, what he might not find there. But here he is; this particular memory lane beckons, the one that led to this rabbit hole in the first place. He has to push the button.

Memory #3039, February 27, 2010

The limousine glided out of the damp mist and stopped in front of arrival Gate 3 at San Francisco Airport, in front of Beppu Hikaru. Deckard lowered the tinted window on the limo and grinned at his grad school roommate.

"Whoa! What's this? I thought we'd get a drink at the airport lounge!" Hikaru said. He had emailed Deckard about the lengthy layover at SFO and asked if they could meet up.

"We'll get a drink alright. But if we only get to see each other every five years, I want to do it right," Deckard said. He opened the door, and the two men clapped each other on the shoulders, taking notice of the changes the intervening years had brought: shocks of gray on once jet-black hair, faces darkened by shadows of the daily grind, and features beginning to be weighed down by gravity. "Get ready to pull another all-nighter."

"I still remember the last one we did," Hikaru said, laughing. "We ate all those fried pork chops you made, then ran up to the dish to watch the sunrise. Then I had to sleep for fifteen hours straight. You just went right back to the lab! So where are we going?"

"First stop, 781 Escondido Road."

THE MEN SAT FACING each other. Deckard opened the minibar behind the driver and took out a bottle and two tumblers.

"Yamazaki 15! Extravagant!"

"A step up from the Kirkland vodka we used to drink, don't you think?"

"So you are," Hikaru asked quietly, "on the upswing?"

Deckard understood Hikaru's concern. The roommates shared a fondness for drinking, and at one point Hikaru held Deckard's high tolerance for alcohol in high regard. Then one day, he came home and found Deckard sitting on the balcony railings, legs dangling over the twelve-story drop. The judo black belt silently crept up behind Deckard, clamped his arms around his roommate's shoulder and threw both of them backward to the ground. It was a miracle neither of them broke any bones. Deckard later confessed that the drinking had coincided with a dark mood that day. Hikaru stopped calling Deckard a high-functioning alcoholic ever since.

"Hundred percent." Deckard clinked glasses with his friend.

The men relaxed into the mellow yet heady drink, the kind perfect for midnight reminiscences. They caught up on family and work, showed each other family photos on their phones. The wives and children were all doing well. Hikaru's business, a ceramics manufacturer that had been in his family for generations and ostensibly the reason for his MBA degree, weathered the financial crisis well (people always need dishes). Deckard had worked for several tech companies. The most recent one had been sold to Microsoft, where he was currently.

"Look at you," Hikaru said.

Deckard smiled back. His roommate had always been impressed by how far he'd come. Hikaru himself had grown up in comfortable circumstances, yet he was always clear-eyed about his privileges. Mere luck of birth. He'd consider himself a success if he didn't mess up what was handed down to him. Deckard, on the other hand, had come from practically nothing. He brought two suitcases when he came to America and lived off his research assistant stipend.

"I wish I could be like you, working for the world's biggest software company," Hikaru said.

"You make it sound like Disneyland."

"It is a kind of Disneyland for some of us," Hikaru said. He had always had a keen interest in computers and was largely self-taught. He claimed the two years he spent in Silicon Valley were the best of his life, though not necessarily for the same reasons as his fellow MBA students. He liked to go to Fry's Electronics every weekend, trolling for deals and spending much of his allowance on gadgets. He was also a regular at the CS department seminars (the other regular non-CS major was a homeless man who took notes on a typewriter and muttered to himself). Hikaru's family, especially his father, had always frowned upon this passion, viewing it as some kind of eccentric hobby, a distraction from the straight path set in front of him from the day he was born. As the oldest son, it was his duty to carry on the family business and make sure all those fine bowls and plates would find their way to dinner tables all over the world, a duty he had submitted to, if somewhat grudgingly. "You know, Beppu Ceramics Group could have been five times bigger today if I didn't spend so much time playing with computers," he said to Deckard.

"Wanna trade places? I'll be the CEO of BCG. I could take your business to the next level—like you told them on your MBA application—to go beyond dinnerware, explore other applications for ceramics. Cutting implements. Electronics. Medical devices. Renewable energy. Expand international markets. Compete with Kyocera—no, buy them out."

"And I'll go work at Microsoft. I'm sure Steve Ballmer won't notice!"

"He won't. We are an outpost from the mother ship."

They clinked again, laughing, the grandchildren of people who fought against each other in the last century, thrown together by random chance of the housing lottery in the new millennium. Ensconced in their plush leather seats, they hurtled through the dark freeway, comfortably toward middle age.

THE LIMO PULLED into the parking lot next to the high-rise student apartment. Against the amber glow of the streetlights, Blackwelder's blocky form stuck out like a sore thumb on this campus dominated by Richardsonian Romanesque sandstone buildings with red-tile roofs. The men got out and waited by the main door until somebody came out so they could head in. Nobody questioned two well-dressed Asian dudes holding a bottle of whiskey, even at this hour.

Per usual, they didn't take the elevators but jogged up the flights of stairs, Deckard hardly breaking a sweat while Hikaru huffed and puffed and bent over with his arms over his thighs at every turn. They reached the top floor. Apartment 1240 was at the end of the hall. Deckard lifted a hand to knock.

"Are you sure? It's pretty late," Hikaru said.

"I'll do it quietly. If they're asleep, they won't hear it."

Nobody answered. Deckard turned the door handle and pushed in. Did they themselves ever close their door at night? Probably not. But they had lived in a more innocent age, before September 11 even. The world was full of perils these days; these kids ought to know better.

"You aren't..." Hikaru's face twitched with exaggerated horror.

"If anyone complains, we'll just say we came to the wrong unit."

Deckard pushed open the door and entered with the grace of a professional cat burglar.

The living room was dark. From the bedroom on the left came the sound of low, rumbling snores.

Deckard flipped on the switch. White light smacked down at them. Hikaru raised a hand to shield his eyes. Their old place, with new LED bulbs. Basically the same furniture arrangement as there was little room for creativity. The evil old green vinyl couch was gone, replaced by a burnt orange fabric loveseat. The sturdy coffee table in the middle of the room was probably the same. The TV in the corner was bigger than the one Hikaru had bought from the Redwood City Target store. A framed movie poster of *Inception* hung on the wall—theirs had been Ansel Adam's *Snake River*. The same oak dining table they had eaten many meals on was pushed against the window. A hint of curry smell hung in the air. Nothing was the same, yet everything was the same.

The door to the Deckard's old bedroom was open. He peeked inside, the space dimly lit by a night-light. The spare room was tidy—the bookshelf lined with hardbound textbooks, the bed neatly made. Deckard retreated to the kitchen.

"New fridge," he said, opening the door to find it mostly empty save for a few bottles of condiments. He flared his nostrils. He and Hikaru were both good cooks and had taken turns with dinner. There had always been leftovers and snacks in the fridge. He took out two mugs from the cupboard—one with the school logo and a ridiculous one the shape of a fox. Once he finished pouring liquor into them, Hikaru turned off the lights.

Mugs in hand, the men shuffled toward the balcony. The snoring suddenly stopped. They froze; the air crackled with the possibility of discovery. But it was just an intermission—the snorer soon switched to a whistling note. Stifling their chuckles, they resumed their traverse through the living room. Deckard checked the handle as he opened the sliding glass door, half expecting the padlock to still be there. Of course, it wasn't. That had been a compromise they'd reached after the balcony incident. He and Hikaru had talked. He needed to cut down on the drinking—two drinks a day maximum going forward, plus the padlock. No more incidents after that. He was always in control.

They stepped into the crisp night air. A Specialized road bike rested against the balcony railings, and two folding patio chairs leaned against the wall. They unfolded the chairs and sat down.

"My father passed away in October," Hikaru said out of the blue.

"Sorry to hear that. How?" Deckard had only met Mr. Beppu twice, at Hikaru's graduation and a year later at his wedding. He associated the man with miserliness—for someone whose work revolved around home and hearth, Mr. Beppu was stingy with his smiles. Such a stark contrast with his own son, whose cheek muscles were overdeveloped from always smiling.

"An aneurysm. He had a very good life," Hikaru said, swirling his drink.

They observed a moment of silence for the elder Beppu, then went on talking about people they knew, the family members they'd met. Hikaru mentioned his baby sister, Masuyo, was finishing up at Wharton next year.

"Wow. Which means only one thing—we're getting old."

"What is it they say? Beats the alternative."

"I had no idea she was interested in business. Then again, she was only a sophomore when I saw her last at your wedding."

"Yes. She turned out to be the most ambitious one of us. Also the only one actually interested in taking over the family business."

"Since when does interest have anything to do with working at Beppu Ceramics?"

"Since I'm in charge." Hikaru took a deep pull of his drink, then added, "She's going to work for the company once she graduates. In a couple of years, I'll have her take over from me."

"What are you gonna do?"

"Get my CS degree. I know something about programming; basically run the IT department of my company now. But more disciplined, systematic learning would be useful. I'm interested in machine learning. Bachelor's, master's, maybe even a Ph.D. Then hopefully find a research position within a big company, although I haven't ruled out the academic path. We'll see how far I can go."

"Your father would be spinning in his grave."

"Luckily he was cremated and the ashes were scattered in the ocean."

"Seriously, though, I can't believe you would toss all that tradition out. Seven generations."

"It will still be in the family. It's actually easier if anyone in the next generation can run it, not just the oldest son. I think it'll work out for everyone. Father's generation are all gone. My brothers grumble a little, so I say, fine, you want the job? Then they stop."

"There's something more Chinese than Japanese about that—we are all about tossing out traditions."

"You people are more brave."

"Just more foolhardy. Listen, I'm completely in awe of your decision."

"You didn't think I had it in me, did you?"

"Not at first, but you showed me. Here's to making your own traditions." Deckard raised his mug. "Maybe we can join forces someday—I've stagnated at the big company for too long. I've got a little bit of stock options to vest still. As soon as the golden handcuffs come off next year, I'm going to start something of my own."

It was Hikaru's turn to sound amazed. "I've always expected that. Deckard Shen Weiguo, founder of a Silicon Valley startup!"

"Actually, I'm thinking of doing it in China. The tech investment environment is better over there right now. More opportunities for growth."

"That's wonderful, returning to your roots. What's the company going to do? Cryptography? Brain imaging? Okay not to tell me if you want to keep the idea a secret."

"It's alright. It'll be in the data storage space—it's the business I know."

"How does the missus feel about moving?"

"Fei doesn't want to go, so I'll travel back and forth. We'll make it work."

The door clicked. Both men froze.

The light inside turned on. Deckard and Hikaru held still and stared in, praying that the person inside wouldn't look in their direction. He didn't. Just dropped his backpack with a thud, then ducked into the bathroom.

"Should we make a run for it?" Hikaru whispered.

Deckard nodded. He slid the patio door open quietly, and the two tiptoed toward the exit. It felt hilarious. They panted with their tongues hanging out, suppressing their laughter. Before they reached the kitchen, however, a towheaded young man came out of the bathroom with a toothbrush stuck inside his cheeks. At the sight of the men, his eyes popped. He gurgled something, whipped out a phone from his back pocket, and ran back into the bathroom. Deckard pounced on the bathroom door, pushing to keep it from being slammed shut.

"Please, don't call the police—we can explain," Deckard pleaded.

"We aren't thieves, I swear. We didn't take anything—you can check. We're alums with jobs and families."

"We used to live here, in this unit," Hikaru added.

The towhead hid the phone behind himself and shifted his feet into a boxing stance. Fear was still leaking out of his face, but at least now there was some curiosity, too. He spat into the sink and said, "Prove it."

"Well, okay, here's my business card. You can look me up on LinkedIn..."

"You said you lived here. Prove it."

"Well, alright, the balcony is south-facing. You can see the stadium from there."

"Anybody who walks in here can tell that."

"Oh, the freezer—the freezer is weird. Anything you put on the left side won't freeze."

"The freezer is fine."

"Of course. They have replaced the fridge."

"How about this." Hikaru beckoned at the young man. He dragged a chair over to the wall and pointed at the heater vent above.

"In here, is a box we left in 2001, after our graduation. A time capsule. You got a screwdriver? I show you."

The young man narrowed his eyes. He probably thought they sounded like real kooks. But he strode to the kitchen, took out a screwdriver from a drawer, and handed it to Hikaru.

Hikaru stepped onto the chair and began to unscrew the vent cover. When it came off, he stuck a forearm into the duct, then stood on tiptoes and stretched some more.

With a little cry, he pulled out a long carton. He handed it to Deckard, who carried it to the garbage can to shake off the dust. June 17, 2001, Hikaru had written on the light colored box top using his calligraphy pen. Below that, he and Deckard each inked their names in both English and Kanji/Chinese. The handwritings were somewhat unsteady; they had stayed up all night, packing, cleaning, drinking.

When Deckard put the box on the counter, the towhead asked eagerly, "Are you gonna open this?"

Deckard eyed Hikaru. This wasn't the time capsule at the quad, where future students had to wait exactly a hundred years to open. Just something they did on a lark on move-out day. They had finished cleaning out the apartment. Their suitcases and boxes were already waiting downstairs in the lobby. They'd split the last of the mochi Hikaru's family had brought from Japan, which came in a box too nice to toss. Let's make a time capsule, Deckard had said. So they emptied out their pockets, took off what was still stuck on the fridge door, and finally reached into their backpacks for things they might have carried onto the next stage of their lives but now would rather get rid of. There was something of their past selves in there, which would make opening the box in front of the young man feel like undressing in front of a complete stranger. Both of them shook their heads.

"So now you believe us?"

"Fine," the towhead said wearily. "But don't do this ever again. It's completely inappropriate."

With that, Hikaru got up to replace the heater vent, and Deckard went to the sink to wash out the mugs. The roommate continued to saw logs in his sleep, filling the space with his vibrato.

"I just know they never clean those vents," Hikaru said.

They were back in the limo. The box lay on the table in the center of the cabin, under the small pool of dome light. Deckard lifted the top open without any ceremony. On the very top was a photo of the two roommates, standing on top of Half Dome, arms around each other's shoulders, eyes hidden under the shadows of their baseball caps. Hikaru still had his copy but Deckard had lost his. "Keep it," Hikaru said.

Under the photo was a rolled-up tube of a newspaper, tied in the middle by a string. Deckard lifted it by one end to let bits and bobs inside fall out. A magnet of "I climbed Kilimanjaro" from Hikaru's spring break. A couple of keys. Hikaru untied the string and tried to flatten the paper. *Stanford Daily*, circa June 15, 2001, on which a number of guys and gals in their cap and gown were making a human pyramid on the quad. The headline said: 2001: A Stanford Odyssey. Underneath all that was a sheaf of letters in Japanese from Hikaru's ex-fiancée, who broke off the engagement while Hikaru studied overseas.

"You wanna keep that?" Deckard asked.

"No. We can throw it out."

"I'll keep everything for us. In case you change your mind in ten years."

"Unlikely," Hikaru said, chuckling. He picked up a small photo album lying on the bottom of the box and flipped through it. They were all black-and-white photos of one girl, Wu Ying, Deckard's high school crush. The photos came from their mutual friend, Cat, who enjoyed photography. Deckard had carried the album with him for many years and finally decided to leave it behind on his graduation day.

"Have you gotten over her like you hoped you would?" Hikaru asked.

"Depends on what you mean by 'gotten over,'" Deckard said, taking the album from Hikaru. "The summer before I got married, I went to Rome to look for her. Of course nothing turned up." He still had dreams about her now and then, but neither Hikaru nor Fei needed to know any of that.

"You are lucky," Hikaru said.

"How?"

"Most of us don't even have an ideal. And for those who do, the ideal usually grows old and decrepit, like we all do. But as long as her whereabouts remains a mystery, she will always stay the same. Forever young."

Deckard began belting out that song.

The limo driver lifted a finger in the air. Moments later, Alphaville's clear, prepubescent voice filled the cabin. The men sang along. Flashlights on their phones clicked on, arms went up, swaying. Instead of the refrain, Deckard turned to Hikaru and crooned, "Are you ready for a hot-air balloon ride?"

THEY GOT to Napa by five o'clock Sunday morning, ascended into the air by six, and made it to the airport by eight. They were getting on with their goodbyes when Hikaru smacked the side of his head. "Almost forgot. Here," he said, digging something out of the side pocket of his briefcase and pressing it into Deckard's hand.

"What is this?"

"Remember our debt board?"

"Uh-huh. What about?" The debt board was a whiteboard on which the two tracked their joint spending on groceries and movie tickets and dinners out. Usually they settled at the end of each month, except for that last June in 2001.

"In the end I still owed you a couple hundred dollars. I forgot all about it until I got home. Meant to send you a check…"

Deckard waved it off. "It was nothing. Consider it forgiven."

"No," Hikaru grinned. "I'm not going to pay you back with money. It's something fun. Have you heard of Bitcoin?"

"Nope."

"It's a new type of digital currency over the Internet. It's completely decentralized. The cool thing is that anybody can mine the coins and the mining also keeps the network running."

Like a cat, Hikaru was always attracted to the new shiny objects in cyberspace. He had a knack for homing in on the useless or jumping on whatever wave that came a little too early—he had owned both a Palm Pilot *and* a WebTV, furthermore preferred AltaVista over Google for the longest time. Like he said, BCG could be five times bigger if he'd spent his time on more productive things. To dither about is the prerogative of the well-to-do, Deckard supposed.

"Sounds like another one of your projects, like Y2K prevention, or SETI@home." Deckard laughed.

"Kind of, except we are hunting for cryptographic hashes, not evidence of radio transmissions by extraterrestrial intelligence. What you've got here is a secure USB key. Its password is set to *deckardshen* right now, all lowercase, but promise me you'll change it as soon as you get to a computer. There's a digital wallet on here with some bitcoins—double what I owed you in market value, if you can get anyone to trade with you for cash. There's a README file. Explains how it all works."

"Alright, thanks, dude." Deckard closed in for a semi-embrace. "Come again soon, alright? Let's not wait another six years."

"I will—and you come visit. Bring the family. I'll show you around."

BY THE TIME he got home, Fei was already out of the house with Jessica. All was quiet. Deckard poured himself a drink, dropped down on the couch, and turned his attention to the photo album. He tried to reach for those big feelings these photos once evoked: desperate longing, bewilderment, dejection, but hardly felt a thing. Time didn't so much heal him as change him. Had he turned into an old man, a not easily affected being? That thought drew out a deep melancholy that, in his experience, could only be drowned out by alcohol and sleep.

He had another drink, then another one. He wasn't that drunk, he thought, as he could still get up and brush his teeth before going to bed. While standing in front of the sink, his hand found the USB key in his pocket. In his stupor, he remembered what Hikaru had asked him. He didn't see the need to do it immediately, but a promise was a promise. He drifted to his study and plugged the USB key into his laptop. What should he change the password to? Wu Ying's name and Hikaru's name, to honor this day, the connection between his friends? That's way too boring. It should be something more subtle but still relating to her. He opened a text file. His fingers jumped on the mechanical keyboard, making satisfying click-clack noises. Little nonsense lines and doggerels in Chinese appeared. *Wu Ying Shi Wo De, Wu Ying Bu Shi Wo De, Wu Ying Shi Zhong Guo De, Wu Ying Bu Shi Zhong Guo De, Wu Ying Shi Shi Jie De, Wu Ying Shi Luo Ma De* (Wu Ying is mine, Wu Ying is not mine, Wu Ying belongs to China, Wu Ying does not belong to China, Wu Ying belongs to the World, Wu Ying belongs to Rome). He would base the password on one of those. His fingers continued to dance on the keyboard but his brain was no longer in charge. Those fingers deleted the rest of the lines, made the password change on the USB key, saved the text file with the password, and shut down the computer. His legs carried him to bed.

13

Alice pauses in front of the revolving door at the international terminal. She turns around to give a last wave to her family, who are watching her from the minivan by the curb. Henry had offered to walk to the security gate with her but she turned him down. She would need to do the rest of the trip on her own, so might as well start right here. Henry and the kids would go to a diner nearby and wait until the flight takes off, just in case.

Watching the revolving door swallowing up passengers, she feels like an animal entering the slaughterhouse. A not particularly bright cow, sensing the scent of impending doom wafting in the air. How great would it be if they could just hit her in the head with a stun gun, like they do with cattle—a flash of light followed by darkness—only make it a temporary condition. You wake up and it's a brand-new world.

Enough. Stop being so dramatic. This is a modern airport, not an abattoir. There's no scent of blood in the air. She is not going to get her throat slit and exsanguinated. It's just a flight. Millions of people do it every day. Besides, she has a bottle of melatonin. She'll take some as soon as she gets on the flight and sleep through the whole thing.

So here goes nothing. She inhales deeply and enters the maw of the airport.

~

THE LIGHT and the volume of the space make her momentarily dizzy. *That's what I've become, a country mouse, to feel so small, so disoriented inside so common a place,* Alice thinks. Like a trained mouse, she follows the signs to security. She has been through other security lines, though none as strict as this. To actually take off her shoes and jacket, then empty the bag of electronic devices, she is at once rattled and chagrined. She is suspicious of the scanner and opts for a pat down that turns out to be a bit rougher than she had anticipated. *What has the world come to, and does any of this actually help?* The last time she flew—tried to fly—was pre-September 11. The TSA didn't exist then. Time flies when she does not.

After putting her shoes back on, she touches the inside of her left wrist. Her pulse remains steady. Her muscles are a little tense. Relax. Good. Seems the hubbub of the security theater has momentarily distracted her from unwelcome anxious thoughts. *Careful, don't think about the elephant. Think of something else.* She remembers her college roommate Sarah, who kept a tiny Saint Christopher statute on the dash of her car. There is also a god of cars; she'd seen pictures online. Moments like this are what religion or superstition are for—when you desperately need to keep bad luck and evil spirits at bay. Only she'd been brought up to be an atheist, so the joke is on her, she supposes.

She takes cautious steps, keeping her attention on the display cases in the corridor rather than her wobbly knees. Artifacts of Japan. Samurai outfits, swords, braziers, tea sets. *The kids would love this, especially Leo.* She passes bored-looking travelers, their heads down at their own phones. Men and women staring vacantly ahead, possessed by the white pods in their ears. A young mother slumped in a seat, watching her child prancing back and forth. Somehow the woman's expression—both vigilant and weary—reminds Alice of Fei.

Not the motorcycle chick of late but the responsible mother Alice once knew. How many times they must have sat here, Fei and Jessica, at the beginning of school breaks, waiting patiently in order to join Deckard in Shanghai?

After Jessica was born, Fei quit her job at Bain and became a full-time mom. That Fei insisted on bringing up Jessica by herself has always struck Alice as impractical as well as old-fashioned, the kind of thing their grandmothers' generation might do—their own mothers all worked, out of necessity, and because they were told they could hold up half the sky.

"Why?" Alice asked Fei once. "You can afford a nanny or daycare or even both."

"I just don't want to outsource it," Fei said. "I can always go back to work. I can't go back to this."

Alice pretended to agree. True, management consulting may not be as compelling as motherhood. But could anyone really go back to work after a long absence? What about the self? Once altered, can you ever go back to it? The choice is clear, at least to Alice: Why go around wiping bottoms and noses all day when one can dress nicely, spend the hours thinking and focusing, being engaged in adult conversations and having lunch brought in? That Fei would do so willingly, alone in California, is even more mystifying. Forget about the fact that in China there would be far more help available to her; life in Shanghai these days is much more convenient and safer than in suburban America, without the threats of guns, drugs, and property crimes. But who was Alice to question other parents' decisions, when those decisions were made in the wake of the tainted Sanlu baby formula scandal and months of choking smog? Who was Alice to judge, when Fei had been clear-eyed about America's social ills and deemed them to be lesser evils for her child than air pollution, academic pressure, and lack of personal freedom? At least Fei had made a choice, as opposed to Alice herself, who never considered any other options. Perhaps she should have, instead of falling naturally into this orbit of the so-called American dream, of having a house and a bunch of kids and making money for them?

Being a singleton, Alice had never thought she'd have this many children. She would have been okay without any, but Henry wanted kids. At least two, so they would always have each other. Yet it was easier said than done—two rounds of IVF to have Leo, five for Casey and Xander. She knew there was a higher chance of having twins when implanting multiple embryos but was still surprised when they came along. A true miracle when money, hope, and eggs were all running out. What she remembers the most, though, was feeling conflicted when she found out about the twins, and feeling guilty for feeling conflicted. On days when all three of them are sweet—rarer and rarer nowadays—she tells herself it has all worked out.

She's pleased to notice how her thoughts are drifting along—casual thoughts, as if having a conversation with Henry. The heavy doomed feeling she was expecting hasn't descended. Perhaps she has outgrown the phobia after all this time. Perhaps this is how she'll overcome it, by believing it won't happen again, by thinking of random things, such as her friends' divorce—what happened? Alice gets the impression Fei was the one who initiated it. Did Fei start her affair before or after? What about Deckard? Did he cheat, too? The Deckard Alice knows is not a cheater, but time and environment can change a person. As a man of means living alone in China, there are a great many opportunities for temptation. Somehow she always thought of Fei as the type who would turn a blind eye. What if she's wrong? And does this have anything to do with why she still can't get hold of him?

Perhaps there is a simpler answer—the arrangement was never an ideal one and Fei has finally had it. Her nest is empty, so she can have a proper midlife crisis because, being a good Chinese girl, she never had a teenage rebellion. Come to think of it, Alice never had one, either. In her teens, at first her mother was absent, and her father was always preoccupied; then it became the other way when she came to America. There wasn't anybody around to rebel against in those days. And when she was about the same age as Fei is now, she was so harried, first with the IVF cycles then the kids, all the while trying to build her career. There was hardly time to eat and sleep, let alone to reflect or act out. Such crises are luxuries for those who don't have to make a living, not for beasts of burden such as herself. But perhaps there's still time. Perhaps she's going to live to be a hundred, which would make now the perfect time to have a midlife breakdown. When she thinks of Fei, the way she hopped on that motorcycle and sped away, Alice's heartbeat quickens, not much for the tattooed man or the wild sex they must be having—Henry is a wonderful lover—but for the freedom Fei projected. Her skin craves the varied imaginary sensations: the open air, the cool touch of the leather, the soft stinging from the wind whipping hair, all of which collapse into something akin to a hairball stuck in her throat. Envy, in her case, is not green but furry.

Glimpses of airplane tails next to the terminal. They look like shark fins. She keeps her eyes straight ahead to avoid the sight. When she goes downstairs to the gate, something shifts. Behind the wall of glass, the face of a jumbo jet stares icily at her, and she feels a kind of sneak attack. She whips her head around, and a shard of pain lodges in her neck, as if a shuriken, secretly thrown by a ninja, had hit target. Shit, she doesn't expect it to happen so soon. There's still more than an hour until boarding, so she scurries upstairs, focusing her eyes on the glittering mica embedded in the anti-slip strips, hoping to outrun whatever it is that threatens to overwhelm her. When she reaches the top of the stairs, her heart is pounding out of her chest—she is normally much fitter than this. Right now her backpack feels like a ton of iron, pulling her down to the ground. She grimaces. The pain is spreading, blooming from a splinter into a full raging fire inside her rib cage. With the searing pain, the din around her muffles, lights dim, even the air seems thinned out. Every draw of breath is difficult. An invisible vise has tightened around her, constricting her windpipe, crushing her chest, squeezing her stomach. A sharp ringing in her ears. The world starts to spin. I am *dying*, she thinks. I am *going to pass out. Somebody call 911*.

As she doubles over, her eyes catch the rainbow bracelet on her wrist—a good luck charm Casey had made for her, as a reminder of what to do in just this situation. *This, my darling child, is why I had you.* Another part of her brain—the part that retained information from the online research on how to cope—kicks in. First she has to identify it: *This is what a panic attack feels like. It's all in my head. It won't kill me. It shall pass. I won't faint right now. I just need to find somewhere to sit down and breathe.*

There's something solid in the shadows ahead. Rows of seats in the waiting area. Like a drowning woman spotting the shoreline, she staggers toward them, plops herself down on the nearest one. Her hands shaking, she takes out her phone and dials Henry. It rings and rings, but he doesn't pick up. Perhaps it's her phone: it's only pretending to be making calls. That's why people don't answer.

She opens her mouth. *Breathe in, hold, breathe out. Repeat. Is this what it's like being underwater, wearing an extra small scuba suit?* It's taking all she's got to break free of the paralyzing force to inhale and exhale. She does this twenty times. And twenty more. Her heart rate is slowing down a bit now. She remains conscious; she's swimming away from the vortex. Something is crawling between her breasts—a bead of sweat, then another, rolling down her burning flesh, cooling it. Twenty more breaths, and twenty more, her stomach is still all cramped up, but her lungs seem to be semi-functional again. The ringing is dying down, the tightness is loosening. Has it passed, or is she just in the eye of the storm? She waits. Minutes go by. Finally, she looks up, her jaw locked tight. The world is still fuzzy at the edges. She blinks and blinks until the moving figures gradually lose their shimmery, watery qualities.

So it has receded, at least for now. Her mind is like a seagull that has flown out of the thunderstorm, feathers drenched, wings still flapping, looking around desperately for something to land on.

Henry finally phones. "Sorry, I was in the bathroom. How's it going?"

"I had a panic attack. But think I'm just getting over it."

"Do you want me to come and be with you?"

"You can't. I'm at the gate."

"Okay. Now look for a sign."

They'd rehearsed this scenario—she would look for something

that would bring her a soothing thought, something that would indicate things would be okay. "There's a mural of the Beatles coming out of an airplane."

"Good. Is there a Beatles tune that has to do with China?"

Neither of them can think of any. But she launches Spotify and selects a Beatles playlist to play at random. The first song is "She Is Leaving Home." "There," she tells Henry, her heart surging, "something apropos."

They listen to the song together. About a spinster daughter who leaves home and the heartbreak of her parents that ensue, the song is straightforward and hardly speaks to her own situation. Yet its ending leaves her bewildered. She listens to it several times, the lyrics loop in her ear as she waits to board. *So it* is about *me,* she thinks, *I too have something inside that was always denied. But am I supposed to be having fun?*

14

Alice takes a picture of the taxi line and texts it to Henry. *I have arrived. Still alive.*

The taxi smells funny. Several banana peels are coiled in the cup holder next to the driver. The chubby man darts her a look from the rearview mirror, probably wondering why the sunglasses. "How was your flight?" he asks.

Alice squints. What if she told this man with a sandwich roll-like neck, who is the first to ask her such a question in decades, the honest truth? It was every bit as awful as she'd anticipated.

She'd taken a melatonin as soon as the plane lifted off, hoping to sleep through the ordeal. Perhaps the earlier panic attack had left too much adrenaline; the pill had no effect. Sleep eluded her, and soon anxiety crept back in. She'd sat up in hypervigilance for hours, counting her breaths, keeping the attack at bay with her nervous energy. Then they'd hit turbulence, sending her scrambling for a sick bag. She turned down the meal service out of fear she might throw up again. Her stomach cramped up from hunger, and she'd been cold. To distract herself, she'd randomly selected a movie, which turned out to be a ghost story and a tearjerker. She'd wept during the scene where the protagonist met the ghost of her mother. Fortunately it had been dark, and the people next to her seat were asleep. She'd paused the movie, put on her eye covers, and let tears flow freely. It was the most remarkable thing. She could remember crying like that only once before, on her flight to America from China as a teen, when the tears wouldn't stop for the longest time. She had a good reason back then, being sixteen, leaving home, alone, traveling to an unknown place far, far away. Now, she, a middle-aged woman accustomed to consoling children, was inconsolable herself for no reason.

After ten minutes of this, she'd tried to switch to a comedy instead but couldn't focus. She turned the screen off. Later the sadness and weeping returned and would intermittently assail her in the next twelve hours. Something was the matter with her, and she didn't know what. Her eyes became swollen, hence the sunglasses.

"The flight was okay," she says now, looking out the window, immensely relieved to be moving forward on wheels rather than wings.

The stretch of freeway out of the airport reminds Alice of Highway 101 back home, a part of the metropolis built for utility rather than aesthetics. No skyscrapers, just blocky office buildings and apartments with flat roofs and dark windows. Outside the taxi, the sun has an oven-light quality. She checks the Air Quality Index online: about eighty. She'd expected much worse. Lots of Teslas on the road—unsurprising, given they're made here. Also many other vehicles with no tailpipes. How many domestic EV brands do they say China has? Sixteen? Nearly all the vehicles, as far as her eyes can see, look new, nary a dusty clunker in sight. Are there laws requiring drivers to upgrade every five years and get weekly car washes, or is all this the result of economic prosperity and peer pressure? Alice's own Prius wouldn't be roadworthy here. Over ten years old, dented fender, desperately in need of a wash.

A Mercedes SUV pulls up next to the taxi. The driver is a girl who looks barely old enough to get her license. She appears to be talking on the phone as she zips past the taxi and two cars ahead of them.

Young people here are good drivers. Alice freely admits to being the stereotypical Asian driver in America. She's no longer ashamed of it—now she's figured out the reason is simply socioeconomic—she hadn't grown up with cars. Like someone who learned to ski as an adult, her brain never quite developed a sense of what it's like to be among traffic.

So many things she didn't grow up with. Taxis. Phones. The Internet. Even her name—she'd picked Alice in her high school English conversation class, taught by Teacher Mike, who came from America on some sort of teaching program. He'd asked all the students to pick English names for themselves. There was a whiff of colonialism in it, but looking back, Alice can see how overwhelming it must have been for a recent college grad to be dropped in the middle of Nanjing, speaking little Chinese, and having to teach a couple of hundred high schoolers. There was no way he could have learned their Chinese names.

Alice had picked the name because it kind of sounded like her Chinese name, Aining, and because it was a name that appeared in their regular English textbook. It was common and innocuous enough to hide behind, which suited her. She continued to use it. It doesn't matter, does it, to be Alice or 爱宁 (Aining), when her Chinese name should be written out with fifteen strokes instead of spelled out in six letters?

Years later, when she took a graduate-level cryptography course, encryption protocols were always illustrated using Alice and Bob as fictitious participants. To her chagrin, her professor, Dr. Robert McKinsey, often called on her in class so they could act out how to exchange encrypted messages using props such as manila envelopes and giant wooden keys.

Back in high school in Nanjing, the girls favored names from the British royal family and English literature. Diana, Elizabeth, Anne, Emily. Gong Lemiao picked Catherine because Teacher Mike said it could be shortened to Cat, and her nickname had always been Gong Mao, tomcat. Some boys picked the names of soccer stars—Pele, Diego, Maradona.

Junhu and Weiguo had argued over whether names should be picked by oneself. Junhu thought someone else should do the choosing, and later let Teacher Mike pick James for him. Weiguo disagreed. Names reflected the older generation's aspirations but not the person's own, he said. Take his own name, 卫国 (Weiguo)—to defend the country. It was chosen by his grandfather, a veteran who fought against the Japanese. People kept asking him if he wanted to join the army, but it was the last thing Weiguo would want to do, to be taking orders from higher ups.

Alice can still remember that class, when Weiguo said he would like the name Deckard. Teacher Mike acted impressed. "Cool," he said. They'd just learned what that word meant; it was both a word and a concept they didn't have back then. "From *Blade Runner*, with Harrison Ford? You've seen it?"

Weiguo nodded. They all had, at the underground video club.

"Good flick!" Teacher Mike said. "Flick means movie, film." He was always doing that, trying to expand their vocabularies and teaching them vernacular American English: what's up, see ya, you bet, cool. Weiguo—Deckard—was cool. He enjoyed standing out, unlike Aining—Alice—who just wants to hide behind whatever safe facade.

Through the rearview mirror, Alice sees the taxi driver's eyes—his eyelids are drooping, and a couple of seconds later, they're closed completely.

"Wake up, sir, wake up!" Alice screams.

The man comes to, looking a little stunned but makes no effort to apologize.

"Are you overworked? How much sleep did you get last night?" Alice feels compelled to ask.

"I only work four hours a day. I got plenty of sleep," the man says defensively.

Should she get off? They are on the freeway. It's also evening rush hour, so who knows how long she'll have to wait on some random street corner to find another taxi. She'll have to engage in conversation to keep the man from dozing off again.

Unlike Henry, who would have learned about the driver's family members and all their hopes and dreams at the end of a twenty-minute ride, chitchatting with strangers isn't her thing. She prefers to keep the information imbalance—she the woman of mystery, her origin and motives unknown to the driver, who lives in this town and drives a taxi for a living.

She looks up. There's an exit ahead. Alice points at the sign. "What does that say?"

"匝道 (za dao, ramp)," the driver says, suppressing a yawn.

She purses her lips, unsure whether to follow up with it. A few moments later, however, the driver's eyelids are drooping again. It's better to keep talking than getting into a crash.

"I didn't recognize that character, 匝 (za)."

That gets his attention. "Really?" So she doesn't look like an illiterate person.

"I've never seen it before."

"But it's all over the place."

"When I was here last, there were no special signs for exit ramps because there were no exit ramps." Or freeways, or cars, or smog, she wants to add. And they hardly ate bananas.

"When was that?"

"Thirty-four years ago."

The driver's eyebrows go up. His eyes are fully open now. "Where did you go?"

"America."

"You never came back to visit the whole time?"

"Never."

"How come?"

"Because of my father. He abandoned my mother and me. So we never wanted to see him again." The thing about talking with strangers is that she ends up saying things she wouldn't say to the people she knows, including herself. Appalling things come out, leaving her dry-mouthed and electrified.

The driver glances at her from the mirror. "Couldn't you just come visit without seeing him?"

"I have aerophobia. I couldn't fly. But I've finally figured out how to get around it."

"Are you going to see him this time?"

"He's dead now. From Covid."

"Oh, condolences," he says reflexively.

"Thank you."

The driver is coming back to life now. "My buddy's mom also died last December during the Covid surge. She had cancer, probably didn't have too long to live anyhow. Was that when your father passed away?"

"He died in January. Alone in the hospital, probably."

The driver makes a trilling sound with his lips. "Everybody was sick then. I was sick, so were my wife and kid. So many old people died. Crematoriums were completely overrun. They were probably burning multiple bodies in the same furnace at once. Nobody was allowed to watch. My buddy went back a week later and they gave him a scoop of ashes—who knows whose those were, his mother's or someone else's grandpa's."

A familiar story. So many Americans got to experience the same two years earlier without the benefit of vaccines or medications. "My father's wife and son were the ones who had to deal with the ashes."

"You don't talk to them, either?"

"No."

"How old is the son?"

"About thirty, I think."

"Does it feel strange to have a stepbrother so much younger?"

"Very."

The map on the driver's phone shows that the hotel is just past the intersection. Alice counts out the cash. Even though tipping isn't customary here, she takes out forty yuan extra, intending to thank him for the mercy of not killing them both.

"I'd do the same," the driver says out of the blue as the traffic light turns green.

"Do what?"

"Find a younger wife and have a son," he says.

The taxi comes to a stop. Alice pushes the tip money back into her wallet. "Go take a nap," she tells him.

15

The big revelation from the enhanced memory is that, in his drunken state, Deckard had saved the password file not on his laptop but on the USB key. How could he be so stupid? It's like locking the car key in the car, which he'd done a few times as well. He rages for a little while, then forgives himself. What's the use of self-blame? He had been much more drunk at the time than he realized.

The question is, now what? He supposes he could go where the Wu Ying obsession started.

Memory #165, February 7, 1989, Saturday

Shen Weiguo and Gao Junhu met at the school to go to the video club together on Saturday night.

"But first I need a haircut. I promised my mom," Weiguo said, combing his hand through his thick, bushy hair. There was an ulterior motive as well: He'd told Aining and Cat about the movie showing and they said they might go. It wasn't for them that he wanted to look more presentable; he had high hopes they would invite Wu Ying, a stunning girl from his class with whom Aining and Cat were friendly.

"I need one, too. We can go to the barbershop around the corner," Junhu said.

Weiguo got his haircut first, then began to read a book while he waited for Junhu. The metal bell hung on the door jingled as the door swung open. Someone stepped in, eliciting a little cry of surprise from the barber. Weiguo looked up. It was none other than Teacher Mike, the new American teacher who taught English conversation class.

The barber paused, his comb and scissors hovering above Junhu's head. Junhu eyed Teacher Mike through the mirror. Weiguo stood up. If seeing a regular teacher in the wild, doing un-teacherly things was awkward, seeing a foreign teacher getting a haircut was awkward squared. That was the risk one ran coming to this place next to the school—the barber was good and inexpensive; the teachers probably all came here for haircuts.

Teacher Mike beamed at Weiguo. "Hey, fancy seeing you here. Deckard, is it?"

Weiguo nodded, blushing a little and feeling proud to have picked a memorable name. He remembered what he learned in class, the informal greeting Americans say instead of how are you. "What's up, Teacher Mike?"

The barber turned to Weiguo, his eyes wide. "You can speak foreign! Good. Help me translate." He turned to Teacher Mike and pointed at his hair book—a worn copy of *General Movies* magazine, its pages pasted with cutouts of men's and women's heads from other magazines. "Ask him which haircut he wants."

Weiguo did so. Teacher Mike took a seat next to Weiguo and began perusing the hair book. "He can do all these?" he asked in amazement.

Through Weiguo, the barber assured Teacher Mike he certainly could.

"Oh, I recognize this one—it's Jackie Chan!" Teacher Mike said, holding out the page, which wasn't a cutout but an original page of the magazine.

The barber didn't wait for translation. "Yes, Hong Kong Gongfu star!" He mimicked martial arts moves, then pointed his scissors at Teacher Mike. "You want a haircut like that?"

"No, no, let me look a little more," Teacher Mike said.

The barber went back to working on Junhu. Teacher Mike kept turning the pages. At some point, he stopped and gave a low chuckle, then showed the page to Weiguo. It was a white guy about Teacher Mike's age, sporting cropped hair that was ever so casually yet deliberately tousled. *Relaxed garment-dyed heavyweight twill shirt*, the text read. There were little colored boxes on the bottom of the page—Burnt Saffron, Dried Clay, Heather Chambray, Cypress. Weiguo could read the words but had no idea what they meant.

"I wonder where he got the J-Crew catalog," Teacher Mike said, then launched into a detailed explanation of what that was.

How strange it must be to buy clothes by looking at pictures in a magazine, Weiguo thought. What captivated him was the background of the image—the man was leaning against a boat with peeling paint in front of a lake reflecting the skies and the mist-shrouded mountains beyond. It looked like a land of magic. He said so to Teacher Mike.

"Indeed." Teacher Mike nodded, his eyes fixed on the picture. When he spoke again, there was a small crack in his voice. "My family has a cabin on a lake like that," he said.

Cabin, lake, words signifying wonderful things, abundant wealth, but the expression on Teacher Mike's face was of utter desolation, as though he might burst into tears. Weiguo didn't know how to react, yet something passed between them—the young teacher's sadness sloshed over, and a welling of sympathy rose in Weiguo's chest.

Looking back at it now, having gone to graduate school in California at around the same age as Teacher Mike was then, Deckard Shen Weiguo would come to understand the source of Teacher Mike's gloom—homesickness and loneliness from being so far away from everyone and everything he knew. The longer Deckard lived abroad, the stronger those feelings became. Having a job and family gave solace but was no cure. He simply felt more than most people, which made him think more deeply, which in turn made him feel more. That, in the end, was the true reason for his return to China, though he could never quite explain it to anyone in those terms.

Teacher Mike handed the hair book to Weiguo, a smile returning to his face. "Could you please tell the barber that I'd like this one, in Heather Chambray?"

∽

ONCE JUNHU WAS FINISHED, they said goodbye to Teacher Mike and headed toward the door.

"Wait, I've got a question—where did you watch *Blade Runner*?" Teacher Mike asked.

Weiguo and Junhu exchanged a look. The video club was underground, unsanctioned. If the adults knew about it, they would certainly disapprove, as they always disapproved of anything that was actually fun. But Teacher Mike was barely an adult. He was probably only five or six years older, liked to joke around, and a foreigner to boot. He would probably enjoy those movies, many of which were American.

"We go to the video club by Gulou Square," Weiguo said. "We're going there now. Do you want to come?"

∽

THEY WENT to the bus station together after Teacher Mike had gotten, in his own words, the best two-yuan haircut ever. A crammed bus was soon headed their way. People shifted on the sidewalk, some stepping into the street, ready to get on. The bus driver, however, slammed on the horn instead of brakes—the bus was jam-packed already; it wasn't going to pick up any more passengers. As people skittered to get out of the way and the bus blew past the station, they caught a glimpse of the middle-aged ticket taker sitting by the front door.

Under a single dome light, the woman was knitting, her face in concentration.

"Oh, the huge manatee, as my father would say," Teacher Mike said, for once didn't offer an explanation of what he said. Yet through his teacher's eyes, Weiguo saw something new in this commonplace scene—the callousness of the driver, the knitter's focus, the loneliness of the teacher and himself, and the realization that this moment would be gone forever, together created a combination so potent that it settled somewhere deep within his psyche, even as he grew up, grew older, gradually transformed into a different person, cell by cell.

They decided to walk instead. En route, they learned that Teacher Mike was from Brookline, a Boston suburb. He went to Boston University—probably a mistake, as it was too close to home, which was why he wanted to get as far away as possible after graduation. He was an economics major. Due to some scheduling issues, he graduated in the winter, which was alright as he wanted to travel and take a break before starting any real job. He'd wanted to teach English in Japan at first because he'd taken a year of Japanese. Alas, he had missed the application deadline. A different program in China was still taking applicants, so he jumped at the chance. He spoke slowly and clearly, communicating all this information with sometimes round-about verbiage built on the boys' existing vocabularies, plus hand gestures.

He asked them just as many questions—where in the city they lived, what their favorite sports and hobbies were, what their families were like and what their parents did. When asked if they had girlfriends, Junhu answered for both of them. "No."

"Why not?"

"We need to study," Junhu said, then tried to explain the college entrance exam to the teacher. The exam, which happened at the end of year three in high school, lasted for three days and covered six subjects. The results would determine who got to go to the top universities, who the lesser ones, and who had to stay home and get a factory job. A system more or less like this had existed for over a thousand years, although the feudal system kept out the women. Now everyone could participate.

"Seems fair," Teacher Mike said.

At some point, they walked past a white wall with five-foot-tall characters written on it in red paint. "What does that say?" Teacher Mike asked.

"Marry Late. Birth Late. Few Births. Good Births."

"The one-child policy? I never understood why."

"Planned birth policy," Junhu said. His mother worked for the Planned Birth Office, so he had something to say about it. "Too many people—I have seven aunts and uncles. My grandparents, they're poor. Not enough food, not enough clothes. Only my father went to university."

"Hmm," Teacher Mike said.

"You have saw the buses? All the people in them?" Junhu asked.

Mike nodded. "Yeah, they're packed like sardines." At the students' blank looks, he had to explain what tinned sardines were.

"Like that everywhere. The universities are just like the buses. That's why we must study so hard. Planned birth makes us live better."

"Is there another wall that says, no dating until college?" Mike asked, and then had to explain what dating was.

"No," the boys answered with giggles.

THEY TURNED into an alleyway and stopped at a large metal gate. Weiguo pushed on a mechanical doorbell. A small door on the gate cracked open. Qian, the guy who ran the video club, peered out. Qian set his eyes on Mike first and stuck out a hand. "Five yuan."

"You've got to be joking. He isn't taking up more space than us," Weiguo said, stepping out from the shadows.

"Oh, it's you. What do you care? The laowai (foreigner) can afford it."

"He's our teacher. If you charge him a penny more than us, I will stop coming. And I will tell all my friends not to come, too." That had an impact. Weiguo was a good customer—he came here often on Saturdays, sometimes even on Wednesdays. Five times for *Blade Runner* alone. He often brought friends.

"Fine," Qian said. He took their money and let them all in.

THE BASEMENT WAREHOUSE was dimly lit and smoky. A TV sat atop a chest of drawers, next to a VCR player. People drifted in, filling the benches in the hall.

Weiguo scanned the room. The girls were nowhere to be seen—it was a long shot anyway, he consoled himself, only to be surprised by how sharp the disappointment felt. He hadn't known he wanted this badly to see Wu Ying, who sat behind him at school and whose gaze he felt on his back all day long.

A while later, Qian switched off the lights and pressed play on the VCR.

When Jodie Foster stepped into the bar to play pool on screen, a rustling came from the back of the room. Weiguo turned. In the dark, Aining and Cat whispered to each other, searching for an empty bench. *Where was Wu Ying?*

"WHAT DID you think of the movie?" Teacher Mike asked afterward at the wonton stand. He had asked them about their favorite snack place near school, then treated everyone.

"Sarah is not a good girl," Junhu said.

"Kathryn is a good... worker for her job," Aining said.

"She's a good lawyer," Mike helped her out.

"It was sad," Cat said.

Weiguo didn't chime in. His mind was elsewhere. He almost resented Aining and Cat for failing to bring Wu Ying, even though he realized that was ridiculous. He had no idea that her absence would lead to such profound disappointment, create such an emptiness inside. He attempted to fill the void with soup, but it might as well have been clouds he was gulping down.

"Siskel and Ebert, you guys are not." Teacher Mike gave a flat-mouthed smile. "And just for your information, this movie was rated R, which means it probably wasn't best suited for kids your age; some of the scenes could mess with your heads."

So Teacher Mike was an adult, after all. Weiguo darted Junhu a look that said, *We've seen a lot worse*. Just last week, they'd seen a Hong Kong movie, one which Qian charged extra for. Both of them came away rather shaken by the graphic rape and bloody murder scenes.

They finished the wontons and walked home. Teacher Mike, Junhu, and the girls were ahead, talking in an animated way. Weiguo fell behind sullenly. When Aining stopped to fix her shoelace, he went up to her and asked, as casually as he could, if they'd asked Wu Ying to come.

"I did, but she turned us down," Aining said, straightening.

"Why?"

"She lives pretty far away. Besides, her parents never give her any spending money."

He sighed inwardly. He pictured Wu Ying in a crowded apartment, washing clothes and cooking for her family on a Saturday night like Cinderella, while the rest of them were out having fun.

"So you like her," Aining said.

Like? I might be in love, he thought, *if that's what this miserable feeling is*. But he couldn't bring himself to make that confession, not even to Aining, who wouldn't make fun of him the way others would. He said nothing.

Aining winked at him and sprang forward to catch up with the others.

16

Outside the metro station, Alice takes off her mask. She can't get over how clean and frequent the trains are, quite a departure from any public transit she's used to in the U.S. She's also grateful that most people are still masking on public transit. They're in the middle of a mini Covid surge now that people are traveling again.

She orients herself and sets off along the boulevard toward Danyang's office. Dense foliage of trees shade the sidewalk, beyond which is a misty wilderness pierced now and then by bird calls. City planners have tried to break up the monotony of the long boulevard with little islands of meandering stone paths and artful rocks. A pleasant walk, though quite long. Alice wonders how the workers solve their last mile problem, as there are few cars on the street and no visible parking structures. She gets her answer at the entrance of the office park: a sea of colorful shared bikes. She would like to learn how to sign up for a bike-sharing app. It would be fun to ride around town and explore, perhaps after she and Deckard resolve the little problem with the invoices.

Danyang's headquarters is on the campus of an office park, which consists of a group of unremarkable buildings surrounding a pond.

Alice had read about the development efforts in these parts in Chinese online news. In years past, the building sites might have been rice paddies, the pond a manure pit. Back in the nineties, developers got permission and financial support from the government to develop stretches of farmland on the edge of the city. All the infrastructure had to be built from scratch: roads, wells, water pipes, power stations. The farmers living and working here—not exactly owners of the land, as all the land belongs to the state—had to move. There were conflicts, which got smoothed over with compensations from the developers: money, sometimes new apartments. Those who envied the farmers' good fortune relished in tales of dissolute children who squandered their families' windfall through bad investments or gambling, when in reality most of the families merely got a leg up in becoming middle-class city dwellers. Hopefully some of the children or grandchildren got enough education to work in an office here.

A cluster of people are standing outside Danyang's building. Mostly men, quite a few with cigarettes in hand. Given the air quality, the marginal cost to health due to smoking here is probably not that high. Something is odd about the scene. These people look too serious to be on a smoke break, the way they're huddled together, heads down and faces drawn, murmuring as if plotting some conspiracy. One man is stubbing out a cigarette butt in a concrete ashtray full of them and lighting a new one. Several others follow suit. They've been here for a while and seem to want to linger. It's about eleven thirty, too early for lunch. What would Deckard think of this? Surely he hasn't hired all these people to stand around and smoke.

Alice checks the men's faces, hoping to recognize an engineer or two from the online meetings, but comes up empty. As she gets closer, they all stop talking and look up at her with mild hostility. She gives a curt nod to the air and passes through the glass door, keeping her back ramrod straight.

As she walks inside, another gang of men are coming out. Their expressions are similarly dour as the people outside. Alice catches a few snatches of conversation: "The big environment being what it is, what can you do?" "Now I feel lucky we didn't buy the place in Suzhou..."

~

THE RECEPTIONIST INFORMS Alice that Mr. Shen is not in today.

"When will he be back?"

The young woman—did she just wince or has Alice imagined it—shakes her head of curls. "Sorry, I don't know."

"How long has he been gone?"

"Don't know."

Don't know, or won't tell me? Of course she isn't giving up. "What about Ms. Lin Kaipeng? Is she here?"

She has emailed and called Danyang's in-house counsel but got no replies, which is almost more disconcerting than being ghosted by Deckard. Alice and Kaipeng knew each other from the Silicon Valley Chinese American Lawyers Association. When Kaipeng got laid off during the last downturn, Alice tried to find her contract work, then introduced her to Deckard. Returning to China has worked out for Kaipeng: She landed a job as Danyang's corporate counsel in the early days, has since gotten married, bought an apartment in Shanghai, and had a baby in San Francisco. Alice had brought gifts to the postpartum center where Kaipeng and her baby were staying. Life has unfolded according to plans. She would not and should not be ignoring Alice, unless...

To Alice's relief, the receptionist nods. "She is, but she has a very busy schedule today. Would you like to make an appointment and come back tomorrow?"

Alice takes out a business card from her purse. She holds the bottom corners of the card with both hands to present it to the gatekeeper, then puts on her warmest smile. "I'm the U.S. patent attorney for your company. I've been calling and emailing and messaging, hoping to speak with someone about a pressing issue but to no avail. So I flew in from San Francisco last night. Would really appreciate a few minutes with Ms. Lin today—I can wait."

The receptionist accepts the card with both hands, though she doesn't seem impressed. She messages Lin Kaipeng, then goes back to working on her computer without looking at Alice. A few minutes later, she says to Alice, "Ms. Lin will meet you in a little while. Please have a seat."

While she waits, Alice scrutinizes the faces that stream past, still hoping to recognize someone. And what faces they are—she is well aware of the work ethics and intensity of the locals but do they always look this tense, like they're getting their teeth drilled? Where are they headed, so many of them going out? Lunch, so early? Or are they all going out to smoke cigarettes together the way schoolchildren used to do group calisthenics? They don't pause at the reception to offer any clue, however; they just scurry past Alice, looking preoccupied.

A tall young woman enters the lobby and greets the receptionist. Even with a mask on, she's a sight for sore eyes: long straight hair down her back, chic color block dress just long enough for an office outfit, and thick-soled sneakers that apparently are the fashion of the season. There's something familiar about her broad forehead and deep, clear eyes. Perhaps it's her type—young, beautiful, and knowing it.

The receptionist springs up from her chair. "Ah, Lili, you're back! Are you recovered?"

Lili gives the woman a wave, showing off a splint on her middle finger. "Mostly. I just came back from my parents', then I saw the email about the all-hands. Thought I ought to be here for that," she says.

"Did they ever find the driver?"

"No, the camera at the intersection was out. Just my bad luck."

"So awful what happened."

"Could've been much worse—I could've been dead," Lili says with a shrug. She fidgets with the flowers in a little bud vase on the counter and asks casually, "Did Shen Zong leave anything for me?"

Alice's ears prick up at the mention of Deckard's surname. Who is this Lili and why would Deckard leave stuff for her?

The receptionist goes through a pile of stuff on her desk. "No, I don't see anything."

Lili thanks her and walks inside.

"Who was that?" Alice asks the receptionist.

"Duan Lili."

"Uh, does she work for Shen Zong?"

The receptionist smirks. "We all work for Shen Zong. Why do you ask?"

"She looks kind of familiar," Alice fibs. "Thought I recognized her from a patent disclosure meeting before. She seemed to be in a rush, else I would have said hi."

"That can't be. Lili isn't technical at all. She's in *marketing*." The receptionist enunciates, as if it were something vaguely distasteful. "Not that she's even qualified for that."

"What happened to her?"

"Got into an accident after work a couple of weeks ago by a hit-and-run driver."

"That's terrible!"

"At least she wasn't hurt more badly. Just a broken nose and a finger fracture."

"Pretty lucky."

"You can say that again."

KAIPENG IS ALMOST clingy when they shake hands, sandwiching Alice's right hand between hers and not letting it go for nearly a minute. It doesn't take a Sherlock to notice the woman is under pressure—a bloom of adult acne on her chin, dark circles under the eyes, and lips sorely in need of ChapStick. *When was the last time she slept, and for how long?* "It's really good to see you, Alice," she coos. "I hope you don't mind a box lunch."

"Of course not—I know you're busy. Thanks for squeezing me in,"

Alice says, glad that her calculation of showing up right before noon has paid off.

They go into an airless conference room. One of the lights flickers, so Kaipeng turns it off. They sit in semi-darkness next to a table on which two cardboard boxes and two paper cups are placed. The shabbiness of the surroundings, the time pressure, even the greasy fried fish are all somehow a relief to Alice. They're not ladies who lunch, just two working gals who need to exchange information and hash things out.

Kaipeng frowns at the cups of brown liquid. "I'm so sorry. Nobody should be drinking this stuff. Just give me a moment." She walks out before Alice can stop her and returns a few minutes later bearing a tray with an electric tea kettle, a tea set, and her own stash of Qimen red tea.

"For the honored guest. When was the last time we saw each other? Has it really been five years? How's your family doing?" Kaipeng pours out questions along with the hot water, using a teapot with a visible layer of dust. Since Kaipeng hasn't mentioned anything about why she hasn't responded to the email, Alice decides to wait.

They chat a bit, the conversation naturally touching on the pandemic. Alice asks how Kaipeng and family fared during the Covid lockdown about a year ago, fully expecting the same kind of chin-up answers she'd gotten from a few Danyang inventors she'd worked with—feeling fortunate to be able to work from home, lucky to have helpful neighbors, etc.

Turns out the question is triggering.

"It was the most ridiculous thing I've ever experienced in my life," Kaipeng says, her mouth pulling all the way back into her cheeks. "Twenty-eight million people locked up in our apartments for months! At first a lot of people went hungry, then we spent all day trying to buy food online. Cancer patients couldn't get chemo treatment; people's pets were exterminated. Not to mention all those people who lost their livelihoods—it's a severe wound on the economy."

Alice is taken aback by Kaipeng's vehemence. "At least things were more or less normal for you guys the first two years," she says.

"If by 'normal,' you mean constant testing, always under the threat of being taken away to quarantine camps and having all your belongings sprayed with disinfectant, then yes, it was 'normal.' And it was all for nothing when they opened everything up overnight, just let the virus rip through. It was insane. Everybody was getting sick. Old people were dying like flies, a lot of them still not vaccinated—and who knows if the vaccines were even effective—our vaccine industry is notoriously corrupt. Forget about Paxlovid, drugstores didn't even have fever medications in stock—they hadn't for years, in case someone would get sick, and God forbid, try to stay home."

"The virus is equitable—it brings about the same amount of misery and inconvenience to the world, wherever you are."

Kaipeng returns a weary expression. "Yeah. We're all traumatized. I still feel like having a nervous breakdown every time I see a Big White—someone in a white hospital gown. The thing is, a lot of people don't want to deal with the trauma. They just want to forget about it and move on. Only I can't. I used to think this is the most orderly and cosmopolitan city in all of China, if not the world. Now I'm not so sure. A lot of days, I wake up thinking I made a mistake coming back here."

Perhaps they should put ketamine in the water, Alice thinks unhelpfully. "You could always go back to the States," she says.

"There are plenty of drawbacks, but maybe I will someday. Anyway," Kaipeng says, ready to move on after all, "how can I help you?"

"I've been trying to contact Deckard but haven't heard back. What's happening?"

Kaipeng stares into the depths of her teacup, as if the answer could be found there. "Well, he's away at the moment."

"I see," Alice says, only she doesn't quite. "Where is he now? I can't get hold of him."

"Don't know. I can't, either."

Alice's eyes widen. "What? He's gone missing? Have you reported it to the police?"

"No, not missing. He just needs time to work on some things without distractions." Kaipeng's face is all scrunched up as she says this. She would never make it as a poker player, or litigator.

"Did he say where he was going? For how long?"

Kaipeng hesitates.

"C'mon," Alice says. "This seriously impacts me. That's why I've come all this way. You can trust me to keep confidence."

Kaipeng shakes her head. "He didn't say. Last Sunday, he called me at home and told me he was going out of town. Naturally, I asked the same questions you did. He wouldn't give a straight answer, just said he'd leave me in charge while he was gone—I often do that when he travels, so it didn't seem like a big deal. That was the last time we spoke. The next day, I came in and found a handwritten note he left me with instructions on what to do while he's gone. He wrote: 'Not sure how long I'll be gone, but will be back as soon as I'm able. Don't worry and don't trouble the police.'"

"How odd—so he knows he'd be gone long enough that you might call the police. How did he seem on the phone? I mean, was he out of sorts?"

Kaipeng gives Alice a guarded look. "If you're worried he might be held hostage by somebody—it didn't seem that way. He actually sounded calmer than he had been—you know how agitated he gets when he's under pressure, and he'd been under a lot of pressure."

Deckard is known for his high energy, which can reach frenetic levels at times. The divorce probably didn't help matters. Besides, hostage takers would have made demands.

"May I see the note?" Alice asks. She knows she's probably overstepping, but you don't ask, you don't get.

"Sorry, no. It's got a lot of confidential stuff having to do with company finances. But it's definitely in his handwriting, with information only he knows."

Alice swallows down a mouthful of stewed potatoes and chases it with some tea. "You know," she says, "it's something he does."

"What is?"

"The disappearing act. Back when we were kids, in sixth grade, he ran away from home before the entrance exams for middle school. Left a note telling his parents not to look for him. Of course they were beside themselves, and the police were no help. Then about a week later, he returned, claiming he just needed to study, so he went to the countryside and stayed with some relatives. He told them the summer vacation had already started. People didn't have telephones in their homes back then, so nobody could call to check. His parents were so relieved that he came back, and with the looming exams, I don't think he was ever punished. He did fine on the exams and still got into the best middle school in the city, so nobody mentioned the episode again. And there was another time in high school..." Alice shakes her head. That was a whole other story; she doesn't want to go into it now, even as it reminds her of the pressing need to find him.

Kaipeng strains a smile. "I forget you've known each other since you were kids. That sounds totally like him—he makes his own rules. Except this isn't sixth grade. He's got a company of over three hundred people who depend on him. He could've had better timing," she says wearily, putting her hands over her face and mashing her eyeballs. A furious eye-rubbing when you really need it is one of the few benefits of not wearing makeup—when there's already a mess on your hands figuratively, you don't need one literally, too.

A different thought occurs to Alice. "Any chance this could be something else? I mean, could he have run into some trouble with the law?"

Kaipeng hesitates for a second. "No," she says, clearing her throat. "First, obviously, I don't think he could have done anything criminal. Second, suppose he had; they can't just hold him without bringing charges."

Says who? Is due process a real thing here, or is it like human rights? People disappear here, often for political reasons. Reaching back seventy years, Alice's maternal grandfather disappeared in the early days of the new People's Republic. Her family said it was because he had served in the Nationalist army. Probably abducted and summarily executed as a counterrevolutionary without anybody owning up to it. And more recently, there were the Uyghurs in the secret detention centers. Might Deckard's politics have something to do with this? Back when he still lived in the States, he was outspoken, often criticized the Chinese government for this and that. He organized private vigils to commemorate the Tian'anmen Square Massacre each year. Yet he'd decided that China was more fertile ground to start his company. He's no fool and should know to keep his political opinions to himself while he's here. But what if he let something slip, said the wrong thing to the wrong people on the wrong occasion? What if he did more than talk? Alice doesn't know where to start this line of questions without sounding paranoid, so she watches Kaipeng eat in silence.

Kaipeng wipes her mouth with a paper napkin. "I did go to the police when he didn't turn up on the fourth day. They told me they'd look into it but haven't found anything useful so far. They found out about the instructions he left and the note; as such, I don't think they're taking things too seriously. At first, they thought perhaps he was evading personal debtors—a lot of people here get in trouble gambling or trading securities on leverage. They looked into his financial records and said there weren't any suspicious activities, at least not according to his credit and banking histories. And they couldn't track his phone or laptop locations because he left those behind."

"He hasn't left the country?"

"No. Nor has he taken a train or a flight—all that information would have turned up in the system. His own car is still at his apartment. He might still be in Shanghai or maybe he took another car to leave the city."

"Sounds like he really doesn't want to be found. What now?"

"We carry on. And hope he comes back soon."

Alice shifts back in her seat uncomfortably. What she's about to say comes with a measure of shame and makes her palms sweat, but business is business. "This isn't the best time to bring it up, so I apologize for that," she says. "The reason I came is that Danyang has some invoices with our firm that are overdue. As you know, we are not a large firm, so this creates a problem cash flow-wise. Do you think you can take care of the invoices soon?"

Kaipeng's expression cracks like split fruit, revealing something inside that's soft and vulnerable. She looks Alice straight in the eye and says, "With anyone else, I would just promise to look into it and send you on your way. But that would be a lie. You deserve the truth: The company is in a real cash crunch."

"What happened? I thought you were doing pretty well."

"We were, but things have completely turned in recent months. It's like the economy has taken a 180-degree turn. Clients are slower at paying, some stopped payments completely. Also, Deckard has been distracted for a while—he's been spending more and more time working on Neuromersion. You know how far-fetched that is."

Alice nods. A headset that combines transcranial magnetic stimulation with augmented reality to "enhance memory, expand mind, and change conscious thinking" is as far-fetched as any invention Alice has ever worked on, occupying the gray area between evidence-based and crackpot. Yet Deckard has had a working prototype for a few years now. He's been improving it continuously and filed a number of highly technical patent applications.

"We've been trying to get another round of funding," Kaipeng continues. "But all the VC firms are cutting back, especially those based in the U.S., where we had been getting most of our funding from—you know, the economic decoupling and whatnot. Deckard was working on getting a bridge loan before he left. It still hasn't come through. The note he left me details the steps we need to take to conserve cash in case he isn't back by certain dates. I'm about to announce layoffs"—she looks at her watch—"in twenty minutes."

So that's why all those people out there looked so nervous—they must have an inkling of what's coming. And the bridge loan—always sounds like bad news. When the whole economy slows, it would be a bridge to nowhere. Will they go under without it? Nausea bubbles up from the bottom of Alice's stomach. So her best client has turned from a money tree into barren stone in a matter of a few months without her realizing it. Perhaps she deserves to lose her chance at partnership, so slow she is at following the direction of the wind, too dense to notice the shift.

"I'm so sorry," Alice says. Sorry for herself—but she'll land on her feet somehow—and just as sorry for Kaipeng, who had sunken into a depression when she was laid off by her old firm. It must be devastating to have to do that very thing to your coworkers. Perhaps Kaipeng will have some positive things to say, some words of wisdom based on personal experience—after all, she had climbed out of it last time. Though given the crumpled look on the general counsel's face, Alice has doubts.

Alice picks up the wedge of orange tucked in a corner of the box. A sharp, sour juice squirts out as she bites into it. Yet she doesn't spit it out. Instead, she chews on it slowly, almost savoring it, coating her tongue with the nearly bitter taste. It's disappointing to her, but to the orange, it's the end of its world.

17

After the meeting, Alice goes down by the pond. She types a message to Henry: *All I've been working for these past twelve years has just gone down the drain.* But she pauses before sending—why be so melodramatic? Why freak him out? They would be finishing up dinner just about now, maybe taking a stroll on the beach, watching the sunset. And she knows exactly what he would say to try to make her feel better—that he is sorry for how things turned out, that it will all work out eventually; they'll manage; he loves her; etc. Henry, sweet man that he is, can always be counted on to dispense sugar, even though what she needs right now is the electrolytes of advice and insight. And movement. She erases the message and starts to circle the pond.

By the fourth lap, she's getting warm. By the eighth lap, she's in her T-shirt. By the tenth, things are getting more clear. She had been prepared for bad news. Now her worst fear has come to pass, she actually feels a weight lifting from her shoulders and neck. Now she can make plans. She can look into in-house counsel positions. Talk with legal recruiters. There's always a corporate job for a senior associate like her, albeit with less challenging work and lower pay. She'll land on her feet somehow. There's also a decent chance the firm won't fire her despite the financial loss she's incurred—it wasn't completely her fault, after all. In which case, she'll hunker down and try to work it off. Perhaps she could regain her footing in a few years. Turn the crisis into a new opportunity? She sighs. *Dream on.*

Why hadn't Deckard given her any warning? Most likely because he was confident in the company's ability to raise money, then when things suddenly turned topsy-turvy, either he believed that the bridge loan miracle would come through still, or he was in total denial. Same way he was in denial about his troubles with Fei. That makes Alice worry about him, even though on a rational level she should be mad at him. He is a capable person, far smarter and more entrepreneurial than her. And he has always been lucky—with school, with his career, and up until now, with his personal life. But what kind of pickle is he in now? Can he come out of it unscathed? As she looks across the stagnant pond with a ring of algae around it, she feels something portentous, a sense that this time, karma may be finally catching up with him. And what could he possibly be working on that's more important than keeping his company running?

Her thoughts keep drifting to dark places. A year ago she would have dismissed such thoughts as ridiculous: This is Shanghai, not some lawless backwater where mean-spirited party cadres can persecute citizens at will. But like Kaipeng, she isn't so sure anymore; the Covid lockdown showed them all. The image of Deckard in solitary confinement somewhere sticks to the back of her skull like a cold leech. Wind sweeps across the pond and dries her sweat. She shivers, suddenly yearning to be in a bright cafe full of strangers, her hands wrapped around a cup of hot tea.

She finds the nearest cafe—not at all crowded as she'd hoped—and has her tea. She then heads toward the metro station, the gears in her brain creaking as she figures out next steps. When she gets back she'll call Henry, take a bath, then go out for a nice meal of authentic Shanghainese food so she can forget about her troubles for a bit. Tomorrow morning she'll head to Nanjing, where she'll visit her friend Cat, whom she last saw six years ago on a high school reunion trip in California. She should visit Deckard's mom, too. Then she'll fly back. She'll deal with the fallout then. For now, she'll focus on the present.

~

By the metro entrance she sees a small cluster of young women, among them the receptionist, whose dark eye makeup is now a panda-like mess. She's holding a cardboard box. Is the little bud vase in there? Alice eavesdrops on their conversation from a distance. "It's only a job; I hated it anyway," the receptionist cries out. So they all got the axe.

Someone is walking down the platform, catching Alice's eye. Duan Lili, also carrying a cardboard box. There's something defiant in her erect posture, the way her marble pillar-like legs scissor the air, the thick-soled sneakers squeaking on the polished concrete floor. Laid off but not broken in spirit. Good for you, girl. Lili doesn't join the other young women. She's turning toward the end of the platform.

The ground vibrates with the low rumble of the approaching train. Lili walks up against a gate. Here, instead of the typical fully sealed wall of glass separating the tracks and the platform, the glass is only half-height, reaching just below the chest. Something isn't right; the sense of wrongness makes Alice's chest tighten. What the hell is Lili doing, leaning against the railings and balancing the box on top of it? She's not going to jump the tracks, is she? Not over something as trivial as losing her job! Why is there no attendant to stop her? A panic pierces through Alice. She runs toward Lili—she's ready to tackle her the moment the girl tries to climb over the railings. The headlights of the train are visible now. As the train slows, Lili tucks the box back under her arm, wheels around, and heads toward the nearest gate.

Not being rush hour, the train is uncrowded. Alice takes the seat next to Lili's cardboard box. As the train gains speed, Lili fiddles with her phone, then puts it down. Alice looks out the windows. There's some kind of art installation on the subway tunnel wall: a series of images of butterflies whose wings flap as the train speeds up. A real motion picture. She's a little self-conscious of the way she has sidled up to the young woman. She looks at Lili through the corner of her eye, thinking of how to break the ice. *Are you alright...? I thought you were going to...* She searches for something that wouldn't sound too creepy or abrupt coming from a stranger who clearly has been keeping an eye.

But it's Lili who speaks first. "How did the meeting go with Lin Zong?"

Alice, taken aback, realizes she was the one being watched through that fishbowl of a conference room. "Alright, I guess," she stammers. "Learned a few things I didn't know before."

"She met with you, then right after that a third of the company got laid off."

"I can assure you I had nothing to do with it. Just unfortunate timing," Alice says, feeling sorry for the young woman who came into work from her medical leave only to be let go. She points at the box. "What's in there?"

"A bunch of crap from my desk." Lili takes the lid off to show her: a mug with pens in it, a fake succulent plant, a binder, a box of tissues. Her voice turns conspiratorial. "Just now, I thought of chucking the whole thing in front of the oncoming train."

Beats jumping in front of it, Alice thinks. "That could be pretty dangerous. You might shatter the window glass. And the CCTV would catch you on camera," she says.

"So? I'm jobless, probably soon to be homeless. What can they do to me?"

"Throw you in jail, obviously. Although, I'll bet it would feel great to do that—tossing the stuff, not going to jail."

Lili chuckles.

"You know, it happened to me one time," Alice says.

"What?"

"Getting laid off. I was maybe just a little bit older than you are now—it was about six months after the September 11 terrorist attack in America—do you know about that?" Alice asks, not expecting the answer to be yes—Lili might not have been born then. Do young people here even know about it?

"I've heard about it—terrorists flew planes into those buildings in New York, didn't they?"

"Yes. The U.S. economy went into a major recession after that. In Silicon Valley, there was the dot-com bust, but an even bigger bubble in telecom also busted. The company I was working for went under. One day we were called into a meeting, and the CEO told us the company was shutting down."

"So they gave you a box for your stuff and told you to go home?"

"Yes. My manager told me we had half an hour to pack up and I should take my work PC with me, seeing as there was no severance. In fact we were almost owed half a month of pay. It was just half an hour of open looting. People took power supplies, reams of printer paper, office chairs. Anything they could fit into their cars. It was a big, heavy one, that PC—computers were big in those days. I never used it again—I'm a Mac user at home. But I did wish I hadn't left my lunch box in the company refrigerator—we weren't allowed to re-enter the building afterward. I liked that lunch box," Alice says, suddenly remembering the cherry-red box she'd carried every day. What's happening, why is she being so effusive? Why is she reminiscing about some trivial thing she lost more than two decades ago to a total stranger? Is it because she's speaking her native tongue? Words are just gushing out. Then she realizes it's the girl. Something about her makes Alice want to open up.

"Must be nice to drive a car to work," Lili says.

"The subway has its advantages—you can't toss a box of junk in front of your own car as easily." Alice makes a pitching motion.

Lili laughs again. The face under that mask must be lovely. Her eyes crinkle. Those big, clear, curved triangles have a familiar look to them. Maybe all beautiful eyes look alike. She asks, "Then what did you do?"

"I decided to go to law school. Became a patent attorney and have had an interesting career."

Lili squints a bit as she puts something together. "So you, you are

Zhu Aining—your English name is Alice, right? You are the patent lawyer from California?"

"Yes, that's me," Alice says, rather surprised. Before she gets a chance to ask how the girl knows that, her phone buzzes. She excuses herself and picks up. The four faces of her family fill the screen.

"Hi, honey," Henry says through a glitchy connection. "We just want to say hello before going to bed."

"The call might get dropped any second—I'm on the metro," Alice says. She never wants to be the obnoxious person talking loudly in public, but the train noise is too much. She raises her volume and says, "I miss you guys! How is everything?"

The children talk over each other as they are wont to do. "It rained today!" "Leo cracked my iPad screen—he's gonna have to replace it with his own money." "Grandpa is taking us to a ranch tomorrow to ride horses." "I'd rather go to the beach."

"Have you resolved your little problem with Danyang?" Henry asks.

"Ah, my little problem. Not yet. And nobody seems to know where Deckard is. It's just so frustrating. I'm going to Nanjing tomorrow to see his mom and brother. Hopefully they'll know something."

"Where are you staying in Nanjing?" Zander asks, his elfin ears practically vibrating.

"The Koi Palace Hotel, of course! It's a good location, so thank you for the suggestion. I'll be sure to say hi to the koi for you."

The train reaches her stop. Alice gives Lili a nod and gets off, a little regretful she won't find out how Lili knows who she is.

18

Memory #184, May, 1989

One afternoon, class was dismissed early because the teachers were called into a last-minute political studies session. The friends gathered outside the school gate, trying to figure out how to squander the sudden wealth of a free afternoon. Aining and Wu Ying would have been content with playing volleyball in the school gym. Junhu proposed going to the university campus nearby. It was Cat's suggestion of the zoo at Xuanwu Lake Park that won out. They raced their bikes down the tree-lined boulevard like Mongolians on horses, except Genghis Khan's men probably wouldn't have taken their hands off the reins like the boys did away with the handlebars.

The afternoon was perfect: puffy white clouds floated in the cerulean sky; the canopies of the poplar trees along the boulevard full of new leaves; a breeze cool on the skin. They were fifteen, living in a metropolis where they could take themselves to see the cute newborn giraffe after school, and had little homework. There should be more days like this.

Wu Ying had turned to face him when he rode up next to her.

They locked eyes for two full seconds—the whites of her eyes were so clear that they were nearly light blue. His breathing stopped. Then his bike went over a crack on the road. He lost balance and had to put his hands back onto his handlebar to regain control. She laughed, began peddling furiously, and shot ahead.

THERE WAS some kind of commotion going on near Gulou Park. The friends slowed down on their bikes. Soon the crowd got so thick that they had to stop and walk. The square was abuzz with hundreds, perhaps thousands of people. On a makeshift platform, a young man in a white shirt was shouting hoarsely, his words impossible to decipher due to the distance. What he said was repeated by a group of people sitting in front of him.

"Two, admit that the campaigns against spiritual pollution and bourgeois liberalization had been wrong," the human megaphone shouted.

"Three, publish information on the income of state leaders and their family members.

"Four, end the ban on privately run newspapers and permit freedom of speech…"

"What's happening?" Weiguo asked one of the onlookers.

"The students from Nanjing University are demonstrating."

"What for?"

The man looked at him as if assessing if he was deserving of the information, then somehow decided he passed. "For Hu Yaobang's death," he said, shifting a plastic bag of groceries into his other hand.

That was all over the news. Hu, the former Chairman and party General Secretary, had died of a heart attack. Didn't seem the least bit surprising, since most of the party leaders were pretty old. Just about every other month another one would die and there would be a state funeral on TV. The deceased typically got wreaths and garlands, not protesters.

"But what does that have to do with the students?" Weiguo asked.

"It started with the students in Beijing. They organized to mourn him—he was one of the good guys; a reformer. Now they have additional demands."

The student on stage was done with his list. He chugged from an army surplus water canister, then he and the megaphone went on repeat. The friends stood and listened more carefully this time. There were a total of seven demands, ranging from affirming Hu Yaobang's views on democracy and freedom to getting rid of government officials who made bad policy decisions and holding democratic elections. Plus media coverage of the demands, which apparently they were not getting and therefore taking the matter into their own hands.

"All sounds pretty reasonable," Aining said to Weiguo. "Surely the government would want the same?"

"Yes, but it can't be that simple." Weiguo frowned. "Why else would they be out here demonstrating?"

The man carrying groceries was leaving. As he tried to squeeze past the thicket of bodies, he shook his head and said to no one in particular, "They've got to be careful—this could turn into another Tiananmen incident."

"What's the Tiananmen incident?" Aining asked Weiguo when they stopped at the zoo's monkey cage.

Junhu and Cat turned to face him, then Wu Ying, too. Weiguo's heart beat a little faster. He took pride in being The One Who Knew Things; he was gratified Wu Ying had come to that realization as well, her expression expectant and her attention focused on him.

Much of his knowledge came from Professor Gu, a retiree who spent every morning reading newspapers and magazines in the reading room of the university library. In the afternoons, he would wander around the faculty housing compound, casting his eyes like fishing lines in the hopes of hooking someone, usually other old guys with time on their hands, to hold court with.

Once gathered under the shade of the big poplar tree, Gu would go on and on about things he had read and put his own spin on the often bland and impenetrable language of the official gazettes with references, analogies, and theories. As he gesticulated with bulging, jaundiced eyes, white foam would accumulate in the corners of his mouth, giving him a rabid look.

Most people—Weiguo's parents, for instance—found Gu insufferable and shunned him. But Weiguo willingly let himself be a part of the captive audience, sometimes the sole one. He liked Professor Gu because the old man didn't swat him away like some adults did. Listening to Gu was more interesting than reading books, which Weiguo had limited access to and moreover never contained such oddly curated kernels of knowledge about history, politics, politics of history, and history of politics, as well as firsthand accounts of the dark past that other adults didn't like to be reminded of. To Deckard Shen of today, his main regret regarding those hours spent under the poplar tree was not having made a tangible record of the oral histories. For the fifteen-year-old Shen Weiguo, time with Professor Gu taught him how to hold court on his own.

"That happened back in seventy-six," Weiguo said. "Premier Zhou Enlai had died, and people went to Tiananmen to mourn him in April, just like the students are doing with Hu Yaobang now. Do you remember that text we read in elementary school, *Farewell to the Premier*?"

"Kind of," Cat said. "It was about how people lined up for five kilometers to say goodbye to Zhou Enlai as his hearse went down the street, wasn't it?"

Weiguo nodded.

"Well, I don't know much about Hu, but pretty sure he's nowhere as beloved as Premier Zhou," Cat said.

"Still, he favored liberal reforms, so that was something." Weiguo pushed a piece of flat bread into the cage with the palm of his hand. A bunch of monkeys jumped and fought over it. "What the textbook didn't say was that people used the occasion to express their anger at the government. The Gang of Four made arrests, had a lot of people beaten up. They called it a counterrevolutionary incident. But Mao died a little while later, so that turned the tables. The Gang of Four got arrested themselves; the Cultural Revolution was finally over."

Aining gave Weiguo a look full of sympathy. She did that whenever Mao's death was mentioned because his father died on the same day. But that wasn't something he wanted to dwell on now. Instead, he reminded them about the trial of the Gang of Four, which was broadcast on TV. Jiang Qing, Mao's wife, who had short hair and wore black-rimmed glasses, sat in the defendant's box. She was defiant, constantly interrupted the proceedings, and sometimes said things that made the audience laugh. Among her crimes was usurpation of the Party's power.

"Do you think what we saw—what they say is happening in Beijing now—might turn into that? A big event that changes who's in charge of the government?" Aining asked. Two monkeys were now on the side of the cage, their hands and feet gripping the cage wire, their heads turned toward Weiguo, as did the friends. A dozen pairs of vivid primate eyes were fixed on Weiguo.

"It just might," Weiguo said, nodding gravely as he channeled Professor Gu, "seeing that our society today is faced with many social ills."

"I'm not so sure," Junhu said. "I haven't noticed any 'social ills' personally. If anything, our lives are getting better."

Corruption, for example, Weiguo almost said, except he could already foresee the counterargument that Junhu hadn't seen any corruption personally. Nor had he, come to think of it. As for the improvements in their standard of living, who could argue with that? His family now owned a color TV and a refrigerator, unthinkable luxuries just a few years ago. There were more shows on TV and more goods available in stores, including imported items like Coke-Cola, sliced white bread, and potato chips. Yet he felt something was amiss—that was the difference between him and his friends, he thought—and he could sense certain things before they happened. To tell his friends this was to invite ridicule. Ergo, his messaging would have to be more cryptic, even prophetic, in the style of

Professor Gu. "Change is in the air. A big transition is coming," Weiguo insisted.

"What kind of transition?" Cat asked. "Things can't be quite as bad as during the Cultural Revolution. Why do they have to change?"

"I don't know," Weiguo says. "And no one is going to tell us, either. We need to go and find out for ourselves."

19

For the minimalist with a good appetite—say someone like Mark Bittman—the mini wontons of Nanjing is their ultimate food.

The bowl is prepared ahead of time: drop a dollop of lard in the bottom, then add whatever toppings—bits of amber zhacai (pickled mustard roots), tiny pink dried brine shrimp, chopped green chives, a dusting of white pepper, and the most essential of all, the soul of the mini wontons—red chili oil, not so fiery as to kick you in the pants, just enough to make you cough a little on first contact and leave the mouth with a slow-burning heat. Now scoop some water from the boiling wok into the bowl to make a soup. If a rich broth is what you're after, then go to a sit-down restaurant. Here, hot water is all you need, therefore all you get. One might be permitted a bit of salt or soy sauce or even MSG, but no self-respecting wonton stand owner would supply seaweed or egg sheets or vegetables—those are deluxe toppings for big wontons, served in proper restaurants. The big and mini wontons differ in one important aspect: The mini wontons are drunk, not eaten. The locals are very insistent on this and may ask you to repeat it three times to commit to memory. So if you can remember anything about Nanjing, besides its rape/massacre by the Japanese in 1937, remember this.

As to the wontons themselves, the proprietress is folding them on a flour-covered cutting board. Using a wooden popsicle stick, she smears a gram or so of ground pork onto a thin square of wrapper, then squeezes shut the dough membrane to seal the meat inside. And repeat. She is currently turning them out at a measured pace, but if there are a lot of customers or if she feels like showing off, she can output them at a blinding speed like a well-oiled machine. Somewhere in a parallel universe, a woman of her talents could be doing something better, something more artistic, more creative or just plain higher paying. Here in this one, however, this is her lot, and she seems content with it.

Thirty-something years ago, the proprietors were a couple, the shy wife and the swarthy husband. Together, the two of them piled up wontons one by one and built the stand into a self-sufficient, moderately prosperous business. Time has kneaded the thin, timid young woman into a matron with dangling jowls, over-plucked brows and hair dyed the color of orangutan. What happened to the husband? And how did the business survive the pandemic? (Died of cancer, sold frozen wontons through WeChat groups, Alice will later learn from her friend Cat.)

When Alice places her order, the woman looks at her and Cat for a second longer than necessary before dunking a couple handfuls of wontons in the boiling water. In about a minute, the wontons bubble back up onto the surface. The woman scoops them into two soup bowls with a spider strainer and slides the bowls toward her customers.

"Oh, how I've been missing this," Alice gushes as she blows on the spoon. The first hot mouthful is silken, cloud-like goodness with just a hint of spice. She coughs a bit obligatorily. "Remember when we used to come here?"

"Can't forget if I tried."

"How much did the wontons cost back then? Twenty cents?"

"Pretty sure it was fifteen."

Even at that price, they couldn't afford to come here every day. A treat only when they had some pocket money, especially on those dreary winter afternoons, the mini wontons blissfully soothed the hunger and turmoil from a long day of being teenagers like nothing else. It's hard not to be sentimental about being back, sitting under the shade of a tree that didn't exist over thirty years ago. Also what didn't exist back then are the apartment buildings that loom down the street. It's a sheer miracle the wonton place hasn't succumbed to the wrecking balls, too.

Cat, perched on the edge of her stool, watches Alice wolfing down the wontons with a bemused expression.

Alice downs her bowl in under three minutes and eyes the untouched steaming bowl in front of Cat. "How come you aren't eating?"

"I'm just here for the company," Cat says, pushing the bowl toward Alice. "Help yourself. I live here. I can drink mini wontons any day of the week."

Cat has made no secret about her pity for Alice's quality of life. An avid traveler, Cat has always been very sympathetic to Alice's aerophobia and has visited Alice several times over the years. She even organized a high school reunion trip to California so Alice could join. During one of her visits, she said to Alice rather pointedly, what was the use of collecting all those degrees if one couldn't eat delicious food, dress in fashionable clothes, or bother to cover her gray?

Look at Cat now, elegant in a cream-colored wool coat, gray trousers, and black Chelsea boots. In other words, completely out of place with the grubby surroundings of this outdoor eatery. Alice, on the other hand, fits right in with her sweatshirt and sneakers. Glamour versus practicality, Alice thinks as she digs into Cat's bowl. Attention versus anonymity. Child-free versus mother-of-three.

"Besides," Cat adds, "it's too many carbs."

Something sly in her tone makes Alice turn her head. In all the time Alice has known her, Cat, the hedonist, has scorned diets and taken pride in her zoftig figure. "Oh? What's going on?"

Cat presents her upper arm to Alice. "Feel this."

Alice gives an obliging squeeze. Underneath the layers of fabric and fat are definitely some muscles. "Wow, arms of steel. Impressive."

"I've been working out."

"Good for you!" Alice had noticed her friend's face is a little leaner, her chin more defined. She'd chalked it up to collagen loss due to aging but apparently it's fitness.

"I've got this excellent trainer—he's thirty-five and got *abs*." Cat lets out a sigh. "If I'd known how good it feels to pay someone to do this I would've done it sooner."

"Pay him for what?"

"Weight training, of course. What are you thinking?"

"Oh, I don't know—you only see him inside the gym?"

"Maybe, maybe not." Cat giggles as she waves away a fly hovering above the table.

Alice waits for more, but none is forthcoming. For a blogger who thrives on celebrity gossip, Cat is surprisingly discrete about her own personal life. They can never have much of a conversation about men anymore because Alice has been living the boring but content married life while Cat has always been disappointed with her dates. Back when they were younger, Cat was boy-crazy and wanted to talk about them every chance she had, so Alice often had to steer their discourses toward the wider world—books, movies, politics, international news, or Cat's other favorite topics: food and fashion. Like two raindrops falling on the Continental Divide heading into different oceans, their lives have taken on very divergent paths. Cat studied media and communications in college and joined a state-run TV station after graduation. She married a coworker who, like her, wanted the DINK life. Only he changed his mind more than a dozen years later, had an affair and a baby with the mistress. After the divorce, Cat started blogging on the microblogging site Weibo as a way to distract herself from her anger and grief. Her life style-cum-advice column brand of writing found enough readers to attract some sponsorships. She became an influencer just as influencers were becoming a thing, eventually quitting her job to concentrate on blogging full time.

"Well, you are a part of a trend," Alice says.

"A trend of what?"

"Divorcées living the high life."

Cat raises a brow. "Who are you talking about? Anyone I know?"

Alice hesitates. She doesn't want to lie. Nor does she want to get into Danyang's troubles, which are arguably confidential client information. But Deckard is not her client, and this is Cat, whose name Alice puts down as the answer to the "name of your childhood best friend" challenge question for her online bank account.

"You have to swear not to tell anybody else," Alice says, then proceeds to confide in Cat about Fei and Deckard and the tattooed biker. Cat's face goes through a range of expressions like she's doing facial yoga: intrigue, amusement, mock horror. Alice doesn't mention Deckard's disappearance, however. "Have you talked with him lately?" she asks.

"Not for a couple of years. I tried to invite him to the reunion dinner tomorrow night but he's apparently too important to answer my calls. That's the way these things go, isn't it? The truly successful ones stop showing up. The total losers won't come, either."

"His WeChat account is blocked. Do you know why?"

"Probably posted something he shouldn't have. Unfortunately it's happening more and more these days, sometimes for totally trivial things." Cat shakes her head, clearly not wanting to dwell on the unpleasant topic of censorship.

For once, Alice feels sympathy toward Cat for having to walk a tightrope in a suffocating environment for her daily work. And her worries about Deckard return. He's got this anti-authority streak in him, which does him no good.

They talk about who is coming to dinner. Many of the same folks who went on the California reunion trip as well as some people Alice hasn't seen for thirty years. Well-to-do professionals, tiger parents who are devoted to their children, many of whom having gone to private schools for the opposite reason that Americans do. Academic pressure at Chinese public schools had gotten so intense that children were overwhelmed. Students have so much homework from school or after-school tutoring that they often have to sacrifice sleep. Those with means, therefore, have chosen to protect their children from "involution"—the unnecessary competitiveness—by sending them to private schools.

That the children would be good at math, science, English, computer programming, and robotics was a given. What surprised Alice was how they also excelled at music and athletics, their talents carefully cultivated by their parents. They make Alice feel inadequate. Every time she forgot to attend a parent-teacher conference, she would remember Xuehui, who completely soundproofed her daughter's room so the daughter could practice the piano at all hours without bothering the neighbors, or Yeyou, who bought an apartment by the whitewater stadium so her son could go to early morning canoe slalom practice.

"Are you prepared to be interviewed?" Cat asks, interlacing her fingers over stacked knees.

"Like how?"

"Like, 'what's it like being back after all these years?'"

Alice rolls a bit of pickled mustard root on her tongue as she considers this. "Do you remember the last conversation the five of us had here?" she asks.

Cat nods. "Of course. We talked about time travel—the existence of wormholes and whether it was possible to create them."

Alice nods back. That's the wonderful thing about hanging out with Cat. No manners, no pretense, no agenda. They're back to their most authentic selves and can pick up where they left off more than thirty years ago, as if no time had passed.

It must have been late May 1989. The five of them—she, Cat, James, Deckard, and Wu Ying—had come here to plan their unsanctioned trip to Beijing. Alice would immigrate in a few months' time. Wu Ying also moved shortly after. Had they known it was going to be the last time they all ate together at the wonton stand, would they still have argued over the same things?

"That's kind of how it feels," Alice says. "Like time travel: there I left, I took my time tunneling through some wormholes, and here I am back again, to this place that's completely transformed. Except the wormholes are super long and circuitous and haven't given me any benefit of time deceleration. I've experienced time in the same linear fashion as everyone else. We're all getting old at the same rate—alright, you slower than me, but you know what I mean."

"That's the strangest thing I've heard in a long while," Cat says, laughing.

Alice laughs, too, and slurps the last spoonful of wonton. Then she asks, "Did anyone ever find out anything about Wu Ying?"

"Not really. There was an unconfirmed rumor years ago that she was living in Italy, but nobody actually saw her there."

"Do you remember that English teacher from America, Mike Woods?" Alice asks.

"Yes. I've always wondered where he ended up."

"No idea. Probably hiding under a rock—or in the woods."

"Ha! You know, I looked him up once, but there are like a million Mike Woodses on the Internet. If your last name is Woods you should name your child Tiger or Civet Cat instead of Mike," Cat says. Then she leans in a little, clasps her hands into a finger gun and places the tip of the barrel above her lips. "Do you ever wonder," she says, "what might have happened if we had made it to Beijing that time?"

"All the time. We might have died, or become crippled, or gotten expelled. Then we wouldn't have got to live the wonderful lives we have now."

"So you think we dodged a bullet."

"Literally."

"What if we showed up, and nothing big happened, and everyone eventually went home?"

"Like in a parallel universe kind of thing?"

"Yes. What would the world be like, if nothing big happened?"

Alice sips the broth, thinking. "When I was in law school, I had this professor with a big white beard who looked like Santa Claus. A China expert. He said to us once—and I didn't know why it hadn't occurred to me until he pointed it out because it seemed pretty obvious once he said it—at the time, the government basically cut a deal with the people: you get the economic freedom, and we stay in charge of everything else. So if nothing happened, there would've been no incentive for the government to extend such a deal, and the Chinese economy wouldn't have grown so fast, and the U.S. economy wouldn't have benefited as much as it has from the cheap imports, and still neither of us would be living the wonderful lives we have now."

"So the good lives we're enjoying now all come down to us not showing up."

"Sort of. At least in these two universes, to us. We were the butterflies whose wings changed the tornado. And the tornado changed us —lifted us upward."

"Who knows, we might get beaten down again," Cat says.

"What do you mean?"

Cat doesn't answer, just keeps folding a little piece of napkin smaller and smaller square. Alice understands that she's referring to the current economic downturn. But surely, things will turn around again. A fly buzzes overhead as it attempts to make its landing. The two friends sit in the palm of the weakly warm sun, ears tuned to the movement of the insect.

20

Memory #185, May, 1989

Since the Gulou protest, the friends always took the long route home by the park. More and more people poured into the square each day. Sometimes there would be students giving impassioned speeches over the human megaphones. Just as often, however, people milled around, some handed out fliers while others stood around reading them. Posters were plastered on every available surface. Some were eulogies for the departed Hu Yaobang, others expressed opinions, explored issues, or simply vented.

China is a rudderless ship, pitching in the ocean and making passengers sick, one poster covering the trunk of a big poplar tree read. Another poster on a wall asked: *Which country has the worst record of democracy amongst socialist countries?* Answers of *Soviet Union, Bulgaria, Yugoslavia* and *North Korea* were all crossed out, leaving only *China.*

It was through the haphazard reading materials and the speeches that things they never quite paid attention to came to light: inflation was apparently rampant, and rumors of price increases caused widespread panic buys; there was much corruption in government, with officials enriching themselves with kickbacks and bribes; job prospects for college graduates were dim; crimes were on the rise. Social ills.

Some, like Aining, still questioned if things were really quite so bad. She hadn't noticed any of these things, she said. Weiguo was obliged to point out they were shielded from the woes of the world by their families, their school, and above all, their age. They need not worry about the price of rice or finding a job. Didn't even have enough money to be pickpocketed, let alone bribe anyone. Some day, though, the magic shields would be lifted from them, and they would have to face the world.

"I hope that day never comes," Aining said.

"I can't wait," Weiguo said.

ONE AFTERNOON, the park square was empty. Weiguo couldn't help but feel disappointed by the protesters' lack of tenacity until he saw them again on Beijing West Road, in front of the provincial government building.

The street was clogged with people. Whenever a bus or truck came by, which wasn't often, the driver would lean on the horn, and the crowd would part to let the vehicle through. The students carried banners made of white sheets, with slogans written in still dripping black ink.

Shedding blood doesn't matter; freedom is the most valuable thing!
In Beijing they stormed Zhongnanhai; what shall we do here?
Welcome May Fourth by carrying out a struggle.

A man stood in front of the crowd, shouting, "Break in! Break in!" His outfit—a leather vest and fashionable sunglasses—indicated he was probably not a student but some hoodlum agitating for trouble. Nobody heeded his taunt.

Fliers were passed around. Weiguo got hold of one, which showed a very grainy picture of a man with a black eye, his head wrapped in bandages. It read: *Several days ago, upon leaving Tian'anmen to the subway station, Student Wang Zhiyong of China*

University of Political Science and Law was beaten to a pulp by the military police. We demand apology and justice for Wang Zhiyong!

"Not to be unsympathetic, I just don't see why our provincial government should answer to the awful thing Beijing police did to the poor guy," Cat said.

"Don't you see? It's all 'their' doing—the government is one big entity; they have all the power and control over everything, so every branch must answer to the whole," Weiguo said.

"Apology and justice!" the students chanted.

"Apology and justice!" Weiguo joined in, the flier balled up in his raised fist.

It wasn't the first time he'd taken part in shouting slogans. As the temper of the crowds rose with each passing day, he, too, felt an ever more fervent rush coursing through his veins. And Wu Ying was watching him quietly from the side. He could feel her eyes on him, which made him want to jump.

"Justice must be done!"

"Justice must be done!"

"We are the beginning of a revolution!"

"We are the beginning of a revolution!"

A tug on his elbow. It was Aining, her face twitching like a fearful rabbit. She pouted toward the direction of the gate, which was guarded by uniformed policemen with their hands resting on the automatic rifles slung across their necks and their eyes staring coldly at the crowd.

"They've got guns," she said over the din.

"Of course they do. They always have. Haven't you noticed before?"

"I, I somehow always thought they were some kind of prop to make the guards look more official. I just never thought of them as real."

"Of course they're real."

Aining shuddered visibly. "Let's go home," she said, getting on her bike.

A FEW DAYS LATER, the crowd grew bigger and angrier still. Either nobody from the provincial government came to talk with them, or someone did but only to tell them to go away. The students wore white bandanas on their heads like martyrs. Their shouting was agitated, hoarser, more forceful. A group carried a long banner with the words, *Patriotic students have done nothing wrong! We are against turmoil!* They marched around the square again and again, singing, "Without the Chinese Communist Party, There Would Not Be New China," the maelstrom of crowds whipping itself into greater frenzy with each lap.

The People's Daily published an editorial called "The Necessity for a Clear Stand Against Turmoil," which lambasted the students' activities, calling it a "well-planned plot" to "confuse the people and throw the country into turmoil," with the real aim of rejecting the Communist Party and the socialist system. The same editorial was also broadcast on national radio and television news. During the Politics class, Teacher Zhang, the Communist Party Committee Secretary at the school, came personally to read the article aloud to the students.

Afterward, the teacher asked if anyone had any questions. Weiguo raised his hand and asked, "Why would the demands for less corruption and greater press freedom and more funding for education cause turmoil?"

"Because the demonstrations themselves were causing congestions on the roads and disrupting people's lives. There are other means the students can use to have their voices heard."

"What are those other means?"

"Write letters," Teacher Zhang said, completely serious. "Look. I know some of you have gone to watch the protests because it's a spectacle and it seems fun. You must understand something—what the college students are doing is dangerous." His expression was deeply pained. "I have nothing but the utmost concern for you. You are at such an impressionable age. Your worldviews aren't fully formed yet; you haven't learned how to tell right from wrong, or look beyond the surface of things. This is nothing like the May Fourth Demonstrations of 1919; there are no foreign invaders threatening our country. Do not fall for the false rhetoric—they say they're being patriotic, but they're just being naive—there are dangerous foreign forces that want instability and are manipulating the students like puppeteers. I've told you, so you know better now, and don't repeat the same mistakes. You'll regret it. Don't just follow the crowd because it's exciting and fun—it's like there's a fight on the street and you're getting in there to watch. Nothing good will happen to you. Rubberneckers can get punched in the face. Just don't do it."

Teacher Zhang paused, pressing his palms down on the lectern. His small eyes swept across the classroom, making contact with each one of the students. He said slowly, with great emphasis, "You are henceforth explicitly prohibited from going by Gulou Park. There will be consequences if you do."

Cat raised her hand. "What about those of us who have to go that way to get home?"

"Go another route." Teacher Zhang waved a hand and dismissed the class.

THE FIVE FRIENDS were at the intersection where they usually stopped their bikes and chatted before going in separate directions home.

"We should go to Beijing," Weiguo said.

"Are you serious?" Cat popped her eyes at him.

"Of course I am," he said.

"Whatever for?"

"To witness history. How often do you get to do that?"

"You can witness history right here—at Gulou Park," Aining said.

"Except we are forbidden to go there. But nobody said we can't go to Beijing." Junhu smirked.

"It's not the same," Weiguo said, balancing himself on the bike. "There are what, five hundred protesters at Gulou Park? Voice of America says there are probably fifty thousand in Beijing. It's like comparing our Ming City Wall to the Great Wall—it doesn't even come close."

"How do you know? Not like you've seen it," Cat said.

"All the more reason to go, to see it for yourself. I've got a plan," Weiguo said. He dropped his voice, so they all had to get closer. "We can take the train. It'll take about two days—so four days on the road total. We leave Monday morning, spend two or three days on the Square, then be back by the Sunday after."

"But next week is Agriculture Studies Week," Aining reminded him. The whole tenth grade were supposed to go to the countryside for a week. These city kids, who couldn't tell wheat from weeds, would be given the opportunity to live with and learn from real farmers: plant cultivation, animal husbandry, that sort of thing.

"What could be better—we won't even miss any classes; our parents won't need to know that we're gone," Weiguo said. He then raised his chin toward Cat. "Would your mom write each of us a note also?"

Cat bit her lips. The school had been touting the trip as a character-building experience, but the upperclassmen told horror stories of the miserable conditions—steamed buns hard as rocks, rats the size of shoes, maggots in open latrines, fleas and bedbugs that left crazy itchy bites. Cat had already let her friends know that her indulgent doctor mother agreed to write a note to get her out of going. It shouldn't be too hard to convince her to do it for the rest of them—her mom liked her friends. Also, having a bunch of accomplices would reduce risk for her in case the school found out. As the saying goes, the law does not punish the masses.

"I can try," Cat said. "Although spending four days on the train just to get to Beijing? That's hardly better than going to the hardscrabble farm. If we're going as far as getting my mom to lie for us, why not do something that's actually fun? My aunt and uncle live in Suzhou; they've got a big place all to themselves on the canal. I'm sure you're all welcome to visit."

Weiguo and Junhu exchanged an annoyed look, as if saying, "Women!"

"Why do you always do this?" Weiguo asked Cat with a scowl.

"Do what?"

"Hijack my plans. We're trying to do something big—to take part in the fight for democracy and freedom, and you're trying to turn it into, into some kind of bourgeois junket!"

Cat's mouth was agape. Just as quickly, her expression relaxed, and she cackled. "Don't forget, the whole movement is all about reviving bourgeois liberalization. I'm advancing the cause by not suffering at the hands of the proletariat," she said, looking smug from having made a clever argument.

"Well, what do you girls think?" Weiguo nodded at Aining and Wu Ying.

"I don't know," Aining said. "What if they find out? Wouldn't we get in trouble?"

"You of all people!" Weiguo said, exasperated. "You won't even be here next year! It's your last chance! Have one last adventure with us! Live a little!"

Aining looked a little stunned. *I've upset her*, Weiguo thought, *but I've only spoken the truth: she was going to high school for a year in America to be with her mother and learn English*. By the time she came back, the rest of them would have gone on to their third year and be busy preparing for the college entrance exam, while she would remain in eleventh grade to catch up on other subjects. Things would never be the same. The thought made him sad, too. Perhaps he was imagining it; he thought there was a watery glint in Aining's eyes. She bit her lip and turned her head away.

Wu Ying, who had been quiet as usual, spoke up. "I'd like to go to Beijing," she said simply.

Weiguo could have reached over and hugged her, yet his body felt like it was under some frozen spell—he had never done that to anyone, let alone a girl he liked. A slight nod was all he could manage.

"It's decided, then," Junhu said.

"Fine. I'll go if you all go," Aining said.

THEY GOT a reality check at the train station.

"No more tickets to Beijing," said the clerk behind the glass divider at the ticket window.

"What about pass-through trains? We don't need seats," Weiguo pleaded, his hands pulling so hard on the iron bars in front of the glass as if he wanted to bend them. The bars, of course, were unyielding, for they had been installed for desperate customers just like him.

"No. Next!"

So the rumors were true—the students in Beijing had been calling on reinforcements, but it was no longer possible to get into Beijing by train, either because the government had stopped train services or because of the influx of students who had bought up all the tickets.

"Well, do you all want to get tickets to Suzhou instead?" Cat asked.

"No!" Weiguo huffed. "I'll think of something else."

21

Jianguo opens the door. "Aining!" he cries, as if surprised to see her. Only it was he who had called her before. He talked in an oblique way that took her a while to understand he had something to tell her, something he didn't feel comfortable discussing over the phone. I'll come to your place, she'd told him.

Jianguo ushers Alice into the tiny entryway and hands her a pair of fuzzy slippers. "Ma, Zhu Aining is here—you remember her?" he calls out toward the back of the apartment.

Auntie Liu, lithe as ever, floats across the living room and catches Alice's hands in her own bony ones. "Ah, of course I remember. I'm not senile yet. Haven't seen you since Jessica was born, so 2008? What a nice surprise!" She leads Alice to a plush modern leather sofa that had probably been picked out by Jianguo, known for his impeccable taste.

While her hosts busy themselves fixing tea and snacks, Alice looks around, searching for things she used to know and finding plenty: the framed brush paintings of a pink mountain with a blue temple on top, the piano topped with a yellowing lacy cover Auntie Liu had crocheted herself, photos of the brothers from their preschool days, twin bottles of mao-tai in the display case—are they the same ones they've always had? A veritable mini-museum of things from the 1980s, aging yet spotless. She can suddenly picture the objects in her own family's old apartment, which had a layout that was a mirror image of this one: the gloomy oil painting of woods, the Weeble doll and the orange mushroom lamp sitting on the avocado-colored National brand refrigerator. Did her father continue to treasure these things? Or did he throw everything out after the divorce?

Auntie Liu sets down a pot of tea. Her skin looks great for her age, with only a few faint wrinkles and a pearlescent cast—she was always a parasol-and-sun hat gal and it's certainly paying dividends late in life. In contrast, her thinning hair is dyed raven black and blow-dried into the shape of a dandelion. The overall effect is a bit jarring.

"I can't believe you're still living here," Alice says.

"Of course!" the old woman says, settling into her seat. "Those high rises, they give me vertigo. I much prefer it here. We've done a remodel; now there are radiant heaters under the floors." Auntie Liu taps a slippered foot on the polished marble floor. "Uses way too much electricity, but Jianguo likes to keep it on until May for my arthritis."

Alice smiles as she removes her jacket. It is indeed warm. Winter in this toasty apartment would be quite an improvement from the frosty Nanjing of Alice's youth: coal stoves, hot water bottles, and chilblains.

"... And did you know we are on top of an air-raid shelter? That's why they'll never tear it down. Who knows when we might need air-raid shelters again, right? Anyway, this place suits me fine. I like it, and I'm used to it. I'm never moving."

Alice keeps smiling and nodding. She has learned through Deckard that his mother is actually quite wealthy. Her second husband had worked for the city's Real Estate Management Office and had the foresight to invest in a number of apartments in the early nineties before most people even understood what private ownership of housing was. He died of lung cancer in his fifties, too early to expand his holdings into a property empire, but still left Deckard's mother a small fortune. Yet she refuses to move out of this old ground-floor apartment sold to her years ago by the university as a part of her benefits package. A remodel, a comfy sofa, and adequate heat are enough for her as far as luxuries go.

Auntie Liu inquires after Alice's family. Alice shows her photos on the phone. "Three children!" Auntie Liu exclaims. "That's what our government wants now, except young people don't want children."

"Can't blame them—raising children is stressful and expensive."

"It's just selfishness. I always told Weiguo and Fei, you should have more babies. It's easier in America, with all that space you have. But they wouldn't listen." She pours tea and hands Alice a cup.

Alice can hardly believe it. Auntie Liu is acting as though she has no idea that Deckard and Fei are divorcing. Then again, Deckard has always talked about his mother as if she were as fragile as a porcelain doll—her heart condition, her brittle bones, her tendency to worry excessively. What she doesn't know wouldn't hurt her has always been his thinking.

"Speaking of whom, have you talked with Weiguo lately?"

"No, it's been over a month since he called last. Always too busy." Auntie Liu says ruefully as she pats Alice's hands. "You are so good to come see your old auntie. My own daughter-in-law hardly ever does."

Ex-daughter-in-law, Alice silently corrects her. And visiting Auntie Liu is something Fei will probably never do again.

"I so rarely see my granddaughter," Auntie Liu continues, "but at least we can FaceTime now and then. Your mom—it's such a pity she never got to see her grandchildren. She would have made an excellent grandma."

Would she have? Alice somehow doubts it. Her mother, who hardly ever smiled, who made Alice realize, as soon as she landed on American soil, what a burden she was to become—what kind of grandma would she have been? It would be hard to convince Auntie Liu, however, who has been retired for almost twenty years and waited in the wings to take care of grandchildren for about as long. When Jessica was born, Auntie Liu had gone to California to help out for a few months but was never invited back again. According to Fei, her mother-in-law complained incessantly of the lack of a social life, and moreover, was pretty useless around the house since Jianguo always took care of everything for her. Fei much preferred the company of her own mother. Auntie Liu probably would never get over her daughter-in-law's rejection of her help.

Auntie Liu puts a bird-claw hand on Alice's arm and squeezes. "I always thought I'd see your mom again," Auntie Liu says, her eyes misting. "I always thought us two old women would sit down one day to talk about how we survived the betrayal of our husbands."

Alice is taken aback. "But I always thought Uncle Ni was good to you guys."

"Not him." Auntie Liu lets go of Alice. "My first husband. Shen Guyong, Weiguo and Jianguo's dad. We were living with your grandparents when he died—do you remember him?"

Alice nods, vaguely recalling a lanky man who slept a lot during the day. Then he was suddenly gone. The most memorable thing about it was that his deathday was the same as that of Chairman Mao.

"Who would've thought the fool would go and off himself and leave me to raise two boys on my own? Had I not met Uncle Ni..."

"Wait, I always thought Professor Shen died of a heart attack?"

Auntie Liu waves a hand and scoffs. "That's what your grandparents and I told everyone for a while. We decided that was the best thing to do because you kids were too young to understand suicide. It was shameful and I was so mad at him, just so mad. But when Weiguo and Jianguo got older, I decided to tell them the truth: actually, your father took sleeping pills."

Alice swallows hard. "But why?"

"Well, he didn't bother to explain in his suicide note. We had seen a wave of suicides during the Cultural Revolution. Back then, a lot of innocent people were persecuted and just couldn't take it anymore. We had so many jumping off from the roof of buildings or hanging themselves, it was like a contagion. No, it wasn't quite like that for him. Sure, he was having some trouble with work, but it wasn't that bad. He just had weak nerves and trouble sleeping—that was how he got the sleeping pills in the first place. He saved them up—in case he had enough of this world, I guess. Then one day, he finally did."

Alice is speechless. If a bomb had actually exploded on the sofa, she would not have been more shocked. The things you find out by talking with people! Was Professor Shen depressed? Possibly. Mental health is something the Chinese society hasn't paid much attention to until recent years. She also can't believe Deckard has known this for ages but never mentioned anything to her. Granted, it wasn't the sort of thing one would bring up in the middle of a BBQ, but surely he could have found an occasion if he'd tried?

"Enough about my dead husband," Auntie Liu continues. "I'm sorry to hear about your father, too. Nobody deserves to die like that, alone in the hospital."

Alice gives a slight nod, her mind still on Professor Shen. Suicide, for crying out loud. Is there some chance Deckard may be suffering from depression, too? These things tend to run in the family.

"You never forgave him?"

At that, Alice finally pulls back her thoughts. She looks at the older woman and says quietly, "No. I don't think it makes much difference to either of us." On the forked road of life, one can only travel down one fork, one way. She sips her tea, marveling at how forthright Auntie Liu is. Perhaps Alice, too, would become more like that when she gets older, stripping a conversation down to its core as there's little time left to waste. For now, she can't bring herself to completely shed the straitjacket of social niceties. She lets the silence sit between her and Auntie Liu.

"Sorry for the wait," Jianguo says as he brings out a plate of apples, peeled and cut into bite-sized chunks, with toothpicks on the side. Alice stabs into a piece, glad for the shift in attention.

Depending on how one chooses to look at it, Deckard's younger brother is either the filial son who has sacrificed himself to take on the responsibilities of caring for their mother, or the one who has failed to launch. With a degree in classical Chinese literature and no desire to teach, he lives with his mom and mostly helps her manage the apartments. The income from the properties plus Auntie Liu's pension are more than enough to keep both of them comfortable. He seems content with such a life. What galled Deckard, as he had repeatedly told Alice, was his brother's lack of ambition—Jianguo had chosen to "lie down flat" long before it was fashionable to do so. The difference between their generation and the later ones is that they had all these opportunities. For young people today, competition is ever more fierce while opportunities are drying up; therefore, lying down flat is all that some of them can do. Deckard believed his brother had committed economic waste by refusing to apply himself and squandering so many opportunities. *Who would take care of your mother, then?* Alice had asked once. *That's beside the point*, Deckard said.

"What are you up to these days? Still day trading?" Alice asks.

Jianguo heaves a sigh as he sinks into the cloud-like softness of the cream sofa. "Oh, I gave that up a while ago—it's an okay hobby but to get any kind of decent returns you have to take pretty high risks, which can be pretty stressful. Then I was into crypto for a while, until the crackdown last year. It's the craziest thing—you could turn from a legitimate trader into a criminal overnight without doing anything differently. Now I just practice the piano."

Alice doesn't proffer an opinion because she agrees, on a certain level, with the Chinese authorities. She has always taken a dim view of cryptocurrency. It's a clever application of cryptographic algorithms, but greed has turned it into a tool for speculation and cybercrimes. It could bring the end of the world as Alice sees it: burning up fossil fuels to run the servers, funding nuclear programs for North Korea. Piano playing is infinitely safer, greener, and in some ways more productive for a man who doesn't need to concern himself with making a living.

A mobile phone on the coffee table rings. Auntie Liu picks it up and starts to walk toward the bedroom. "Ah, Lao Wang, I was going to call you later…" She talks with a voice that's a register higher as she shuts the door.

Jianguo tilts his head toward the room and says sotto voce, "Her new boyfriend."

Alice grins. "That right? Good for Auntie Liu!"

"A college classmate of hers, recently widowed. I tell her, it's okay to go dancing in the park or on trips and have a good time, just don't get too serious. At your age, you don't need to be taking care of anybody else. At least he's pretty well off, so hopefully he's not after her money."

Alice laughs out loud. At some point, the parent-child role gets reversed. Jianguo, the confirmed bachelor, is now the one dispensing sensible dating advice to his mother. Years ago, Deckard had confided in Alice his concerns for Jianguo's sexual orientation, citing as evidence that, in addition to not having had any serious girlfriends, his younger brother kept his fingernails and hair neatly trimmed, wore starched shirts and wool vests around the house, and knew how to cook and decorate. Alice was obliged to point out the fallacies in the stereotypes. In particular, Jianguo had to learn how to cook because their parents always relied heavily on the university canteen, where the food was only marginally edible.

Why don't you just ask him? Alice suggested then. But asking whether Jianguo was gay wasn't the kind of thing his family did. Instead, the first time Jianguo came to visit Deckard in the Bay Area, Deckard took him to the Castro. Jianguo was initially impressed by the colorful houses and cute shops and pretty rainbow flags hung on the street corners. At the first sight of men holding hands and kissing in public, however, he turned scarlet and demanded Deckard to immediately drive back home. *Ergo, I have my answer,* Deckard declared. *No, all you have proved is your brother isn't comfortable with open displays of homosexuality. He's conservative, sheltered, and maybe somewhat homophobic, none of which automatically make him gay,* Alice argued. Neither of them was able to convince the other.

"I've been seeing someone, too," Jianguo says, unbidden.

"Well! Who is this lucky"—Alice almost says "fellow"—"person?"

He proceeds to tell her about his fiancée, who's a geology professor at a local college. They met through a mutual friend, dated for several months, and are engaged to get married in October. She's divorced, has a ten-year-old boy. Being the only daughter, her parents had some reservations about Jianguo's age at first, but they seem to have gotten over that now. She enjoys music but never learned any instruments. He's been teaching her basic piano. And she's been teaching him how to drive.

So it is a woman after all. Then again, many Chinese gay men arrange fake marriages to get the parents off their backs—isn't that what *the Wedding Banquet* was about? There's genuine excitement in Jianguo's tone, however, and she wishes him well.

Alice spears into a piece of apple with a toothpick and crunches on the fruit. Now seems as good a time as any to ask Jianguo about the reason for her visit. "What was it you couldn't talk to me about on the phone?"

Jianguo glances at the bedroom door and proposes a walk. Once on the sidewalk, he says to her, "So, I spoke with Fei a couple of days ago."

"Mm."

"Have you heard about their divorce?"

"Very recently. I saw Fei before coming here."

"So he never told you, either? I just couldn't believe I had to find out from Fei."

Alice gives a wry smile. At least she isn't the only one Deckard hadn't told. The longevity of their friendship has left her with the impression of a static personality from their youth, when in reality, he appears to have molded that open, gregarious personality into a facade. There's so much about him that runs deeper, in directions unknown.

"I mean, he's probably worried I'd let it slip. Besides, it's not an easy thing to talk about when you're in the middle of it, is it?" Jianguo says. "Honestly, I've had doubts about her ever since they first met. Ten years age difference is a lot, and the decision to live apart—they've lasted a whole lot longer than anyone would've thought." He shakes his head. "I just hope he isn't taking this too hard."

That, plus Danyang's bankruptcy, Alice thinks grimly.

"Whose side are you on in this divorce?" Jianguo asks.

"That's a ridiculous question. I'm friends with them both; I'm a neutral party."

Jianguo spreads his fingers in front of him, as if reaching to grab something. "I mean, if they both fall into the river and you can only save one of them, who do you go after?"

Alice exhales. What is this silly, fantastical scenario? She would prefer that they are both rescued, or not fall into the river in the first place. Then again, there's no question in her mind who she would jump into the rushing water for. It's like an instinct: Deckard is practically family. Fei is more of a friend-in-law. She tells Jianguo so.

"Good. That's what I figured," Jianguo says with some relief. "What I'm about to tell you—promise me you won't tell anyone about it."

"Of course."

"So after you messaged me about Weiguo last week, I thought I'd better call him. Left him messages but didn't hear back. I wasn't too worried; he does that sometimes when things get busy, and I knew things have been very busy. Then a couple of days ago, I got another call. The caller didn't introduce himself, just asked me if I knew where Weiguo was. I thought it might be one of those phone scams, so I hung up without saying anything. Then the day before yesterday, two men showed up here. They claimed to be from the Ministry of State Security. I just about had a heart attack—I mean, lots of people are still mining and trading crypto underground; why would they want to pick on a bit player like me? I had to let them in. My heart was pounding, I was so nervous. I was barely holding it together.

"Turned out they weren't here for me; they came looking for Weiguo. Asked me if I knew where he was. So I asked them, why do you want to know? They wouldn't say. One of them tried to intimidate me, saying there are consequences for obstructing government investigations, stuff like that. But I kept asking, what are you investigating? What do you want from Weiguo? We kind of talked round and round in circles for a bit. Then the other guy softened—they had the whole good-cop, bad-cop thing going—and said there were some activities they were investigating. They just wanted to ask Weiguo some questions."

Alice frowns. Had the men gone to Danyang before they came here? Lin Kaipeng hadn't mentioned anything, which means either they didn't go to Danyang or Kaipeng wasn't forthright with her. Now to think of it, did Kaipeng hesitate when Alice asked if Deckard might be in trouble with the law?

"Do you think he might be mixed up in something illegal?" Alice asks.

"Like what?" Jianguo sounds alarmed.

"I don't know… Why else would the government be after him?"

"They wanted to ask questions. They said Weiguo might have information that would shed light on things, which sounds like my brother may be more of a witness than a suspect. I pressed for more, but that was as much as they would tell me. I told them I honestly had no idea where he was. He's been really busy; we hadn't talked for weeks. They made me call him, again he didn't answer. So they left. I've been trying to get in touch with Weiguo ever since. I called his company but couldn't get hold of anyone there. That was when I called Fei."

"Did you get the men's names?" she asks.

"No. That's the thing. They never showed me any credentials or anything, so I don't completely believe them to be who they said they were. They made me add them on WeChat—the ID just said Mr. Bo —told me I should contact them if I hear from my brother. All in all, it smells fishy to me. I mean, would you believe anybody who claims to be from the Ministry of Security on the phone or online? Even though these people did show up in person, how can you trust them when they don't show you any credentials?"

Alice's mind hunts furiously for some logic in all this. Surely the Ministry can track down Deckard if they wanted to? The whole country is a police state with surveillance everywhere—only those with something to hide would worry about the cameras, the logic goes. Civil liberty? Privacy? Please, this country is so much safer than any other, so spare us of these suspect Western ideas. Even though

Deckard would know how to keep his devices from being tracked, it would still be difficult for him to physically evade the ubiquitous CCTV cameras. Recognition technology can identify people by facial features as well as by gait patterns, so it doesn't matter if one is wearing a mask. But then, if Lili's hit-and-run driver got away, maybe there are loopholes...

Jianguo comes from yet another direction. "What if they were actually sent by Fei?"

"Fei?"

"Maybe the men really are investigators, only they aren't working for the government but for Fei. When we talked, she did hint at how she believed he may be hiding assets from her. This is where things can get ugly."

"You could just ask her."

"I did, but of course she denied it—what else was she going to say?"

"Fine. Say it's possible she hired investigators. But what's the point of all the cloak-and-dagger? If they want to find where he's hiding assets, then follow the money. What are they looking for Weiguo for? He's not going to tell them."

"That's a fair point. I just can't shake the feeling Fei may have something to do with this. Anyway, it's been a few days; if he doesn't get back to me, do you think we should go to the police? I don't want Ma to worry needlessly..."

Alice shakes her head. "The company did that already." She then tells Jianguo about what she learned from Kaipeng, minus Danyang's financial troubles.

Jianguo looks visibly relieved by this info. "Well, if he says he's working for a client, then he must be working for a client. He'll be back."

Hopefully, and hopefully before it's too late.

22

Alice leaves Auntie Liu's apartment in such a state she realizes, belatedly, she'd forgotten to ask Auntie Liu if her father's family still live at their old apartment. Unlikely. And it doesn't matter because she doesn't care—so she tells herself, until she finds herself in front of the once familiar building.

Whoever said you can never go home again didn't grow up in an apartment complex delicately perched atop a massive air-raid shelter. Built in the early seventies when China's relationship with the Soviets soured, Chairman Mao called for a nationwide effort to "dig deep holes, store abundant food, seek no hegemony." For unknown reasons, the shelter dug at this site was among the biggest in the city. Since the subterranean portion belongs to the military, it's been impossible to redevelop these university compounds. Beside all the political red tape, any modification to one will probably lead to the collapse of the other.

Everything feels at once darker and lighter: darker because of the bigger trees, whose dense foliage leaches the already weak sun. Lighter because of the unaccustomed clarity all around. In her teens, Alice was nearsighted but out of vanity refused to wear glasses. Now, thanks to LASIK, she can take in all the details: planters with flowering cacti, discarded furniture boxes, sidewalk jammed with cars and electric scooters. The once-empty grassy area is now a mini playground with a seesaw and some swings. Little has changed about the buildings themselves. Still the same exposed red bricks, gray slate roof, and cement balconies, though the latticed windows have now been placed with larger, flat glass panels. So this is it? No welcome committee, no pomp and circumstance for the prodigal daughter?

"Are you looking for someone?" A woman's voice comes from behind.

Alice spins around to face a fleshy lady in her sixties, eyeing her suspiciously under greenish microbladed brows. A busybody, perhaps even a neighborhood watch committee member. At least she won't be carrying a gun in her handbag.

"Ah," Alice says, "I, I just want to look around a bit. I used to live here."

"When?" the woman asks.

Is it any of your business? But there's no point being antagonistic. "A long time ago," Alice says. "I'm surprised it's still here—must be the bomb shelters; they're never going to get rid of them, are they?"

At that, the woman gives a smile as tight as her head of black curls. "You're right about that. We won't be bought out by developers in this lifetime." She digs a fob out of her authentic-looking exotic leather tote—no doubt a knockoff, judging by the turnip tops poking out of the opening—and beeps the fob against the electronic lock. The gate buzzes open.

"I used to live in 306," Alice says.

The woman pauses. She hasn't slammed the gate in Alice's face, which is a good sign.

Alice holds the gate handle and asks, "Is Professor Zhu's family still living here?"

"Don't know them. You want to go up to check?" the woman asks.

"Ah." Alice is suddenly apprehensive. What if somebody is actually home? What would she do then? "No, I was just curious," she says, stepping back as she lets go of the gate.

She walks around to the front of the building and gazes up. On the third floor, two windows to the left, laundry is hanging over the windowsill. The bamboo poles of yesteryear have been replaced by a stainless-steel retractable system—dryers being a sin of the wasteful Americans. Flapping in the breeze are a mix of pants and shirts, some adult, some toddler-sized. A dress, two bras, some underwear and socks.

Alice's knowledge of her half brother is abstract—that he exists, that he is about thirty. Seeing all this clothing, however, she can suddenly picture him in a solid green T-shirt and jeans, with a wife in that purple floral dress by his side, a baby in overalls balanced on his neck. What an odd thing, to have someone you've never met sharing half of your DNA—does he look like her? And it's a big assumption that they are still living here in the old, run-down block of ex-faculty housing rather than some newer development. Perhaps he doesn't have a well-paying job. Has her father failed to push her half brother the way he pushed her? Is her stepmother a less intelligent woman than her own mother? Is she still alive? Chances are good that she is—the stepmother is several years younger than her father, and Chinese women far outlive the men. Alice can find out everything if she would just knock on the door now, or more likely, come back in a couple of hours when people get off work.

But she skulks away.

23

Memories #197, May, 1989

After the train station debacle, Weiguo went back to Gulou. More and more students, as well as workers, poured in to join the protest, turning the Square into a churning gyre of humanity. Even journalists from the local paper and TV station pushed through the crowd, conspicuous with their cameras and recording equipment. He stood on the steps of a store watching the scene, his mood darkening despite the energetic, almost festive atmosphere all around. *This is stupid*, he thought, *to be kept out of the epicenter, only allowed to partake in these small ripples on the periphery.*

In the throng of faces, he recognized one—Qian from the video club, who by day worked as a truck driver at the Nanjing Rubber Plant.

Qian recognized him, too. "We've gone on strike! Since Thursday!" Qian shouted into Weiguo's ear.

A surge of energy shot through Weiguo, for he knew he'd caught a break. "Where's your truck?" he shouted back at Qian. "Have you ever gone on a long-distance run to Beijing?"

They went to the rubber factory together and straight into Qian's boss's office. Under a lamp, Qian found the spare key to the boss's drawer, in which the truck keys were kept. He pocketed the key to his truck, explaining that since all the workers were on strike now, no one would be needing the trucks, so he could just return everything when they came back and his boss would be none the wiser. Who knew, perhaps there would be a real revolution after this and his boss would be the one getting fired.

They pored over maps, plotted out the stops, and jotted down the logistics. They agreed Weiguo and his friends would bring some food and split the gas money.

"I'm so glad to have run into you. I was thinking about driving up, but a solo trip would be boring. It's good to have company," Qian said.

"Yes, the collective minds of a few feeble cobblers will beat that of a brilliant general. We've got a good plan!" Weiguo said. It felt exhilarating to make something impossible possible. His friends would be astounded.

To celebrate, Qian rummaged through his boss's office and found a half bottle of liquor.

"What's this?" Weiguo eyed the bottle with suspicion. It was filled with some kind of brown seeds.

"Tianxianzi, Sky Spirit Seed Liquor," Qian read the handwritten label on the bottle. He took a swig directly from the bottle, then handed it to Weiguo. "I think my boss takes it for stomach pains or whatever. Tastes alright."

A funny name, Weiguo thought as he took a sip. He enjoyed the burn as the liquor coursed down his throat into his stomach. They passed the bottle back and forth, downing the mellow liquor. There wasn't anything else to eat, so they chewed on the seeds, which had a hint of bitterness but weren't objectionable.

In about twenty minutes, the music came. Lots of cymbals and bells clanging over creaky, ringing strings, like a Peking opera. The world spun slowly. A pleasant dizziness took hold, and Deckard felt very light, so light he could be floating up toward the ceiling, where insects—possibly flies, possibly crickets or ladybugs—fluttered their iridescent wings.

Qian's face floated by like a balloon. Weiguo watched as the face morphed in shape, rotated, and emitted rainbow-colored lights. All around him were exotic flowers and birds of purple hues—he was certain he'd seen them before somewhere, long ago. He had an insight: the world was a cotton candy maker that spun out fibers slowly. The insects and the flowers and the birds were truths caught in the soft, sticky fibers. The multitude of truths were what mattered. Anything that stood in their way was bad, so the sticky fibers were bad. The truths must break free. With that thought, he closed his eyes.

When he opened his eyes again, it was dark. He followed the sound of snoring and found Qian sprawled over the desk. Weiguo was still lightheaded. He found the switch, turned on the desk lamp, and had to immediately switch it off—the light was too much. At least the ground felt semisolid and the world around him was the drab, familiar one. He shook Qian's shoulder to wake him. Qian groaned as he peeled himself off the desk surface.

"What was that?" Weiguo asked. "I've never been drunk before but I don't think that was it. Were we poisoned?"

"I don't know," Qian said with a yawn. A bit later, he added, "Must've been the Tianxianzi. We probably shouldn't have eaten the seeds." His eyes were unfocused. "But it didn't feel bad—just felt like I was on a big swing, flying through the air back and forth. I guess that's why they're called Sky Spirit Seeds!" He laughed. "And could've sworn I saw your neck turning into a potato."

DECKARD HITS the stop button and takes the Neuromersion helmet off.

When he and Qian reminisced about this episode from time to time, they always laughed it off as one of those weird experiments of youth—Tianxianzi is a psychoactive plant that induces hallucinations. He hadn't remembered how vivid the hallucinations were. Was this the trigger for everything that came later, the particularly unpleasant memory he's spent much of his life actively trying to forget? Should he be revisiting it? What if something bad happens again? Yet he has little choice. He has to see Wu Ying's face again, to find some semblance of a clue.

24

On her way to the elevator in the hotel lobby, Alice hears someone calling her name. She looks around, confused. No one knows she's at this hotel besides Cat—and now the statuesque young woman in a black mask, wheeling a pink suitcase.

"Duan Lili? What are you doing here?" Alice asks.

"Same thing you are—trying to track down Shen Zong."

Alice is completely taken aback—she never told Lili that. But then she remembers the call she had on the subway with Henry. Lili apparently knows enough English to eavesdrop. By the look of it, the young woman has no intention of apologizing for stalking, either.

Why does she want to track down Deckard? Does he also owe her money? Alice thinks uncharitably. Before she has a chance to ask, the elevator opens. People spill out. A young man bore such a hungry look into Lili that it makes Alice cringe.

"Come up and we'll talk," Alice says.

IN THE HOTEL ROOM, Alice takes the chair and offers the small sofa to her guest.

Lili takes off her mask. Alice sees the young woman's entire face for the first time and gasps at the sight of it. *That's why she looks so familiar!*

"Something wrong?" Lili asks.

"Um, you look like someone I used to know, a spitting image almost…"

"I know. Wu Ying. The girl from your high school."

The gears in Alice's head grind along. Deckard had somehow met this young woman who resembles Wu Ying, his high school crush. So he hired Lili despite her lack of qualifications. The two carried on an affair. Was that what caused the divorce? It seems irrelevant compared to the real issue—Lili looks like a clone of Wu Ying and is so very young, perhaps just out of high school herself. How perverse, how inappropriate—hopefully not a MeToo situation?

But Lili doesn't appear to hold any kind of grudge against Deckard. As long as she's an adult and the relationship is consensual, who is Alice to judge others' choice of romantic partners? On some level, she gets the need for a proper middle-age crisis—the hormonal changes, the physical decline, and the futile battle to stop the march of time—so why shouldn't Deckard, like Cat, have someone young and fresh on his arm, especially if he's soon to be unattached? And to still carry a torch for Wu Ying after all these years? It's at once sweet, ridiculous, and a bit creepy. Unless—"Are you related to her?" Alice asks.

"No. Never heard of her name before I met Deckard."

"That so. And you have no idea where he is?"

"Would I be here if I did?" Lili says sweetly, her tone devoid of any edge.

"Of course. I'm just, really surprised," Alice says. Surprise doesn't come close to how she's feeling. She has the urge to grab the young woman by her shoulders and stick her face under the light to get a better look. She wants to touch that face, to examine it in the way aliens probe their abductees. The resemblance is just too uncanny.

Wu Ying was about the same height as Lili, tall for Alice's contemporaries, who didn't have nearly as good nutrition as Lili's generation. What about the voice? They must be different. There was nothing remarkable about Wu Ying's voice that Alice can remember. Lili's voice is low-pitched and a bit nasal. And their smells. She's certain Wu Ying never smelled like gardenia perfume. All this is just so weird and confusing.

"So, why do you want to track him down?"

Lili puckers her red-bean-paste-colored lips for an answer.

"Are you two... together?" Alice is persistent.

Lili gives a slight nod like she doesn't want to dwell on it. "And you—why do you want to find him?"

"We have some business to settle. But it doesn't look like we'll get anywhere with that," Alice says with a sigh. "How come he didn't tell you where he went?"

"I was in a car accident, so I had to go home to recuperate. Deckard was super busy anyhow, hardly even had time to return my texts. We didn't talk much for several weeks. Then he left me a message saying he was going to be on a business trip and may be hard to get hold of. That was the last I heard from him directly." Lili speaks crisply, as if giving a business briefing. Her even tone betrays no self-pity or resentment. She seems to accept her situation perfectly, such is being the young girlfriend of a busy CEO. He'll have flowers delivered but won't be around to fix her chicken soup. Alice feels sorry for her, but only barely.

Lili rests her hands on her thighs. "You mentioned on the train you were going to see his family. Have you met with them?"

"Yes, although they have no idea, either; didn't even know he's been gone." Alice saw no need to get into the situation with the Ministry of Security visitors for now; she isn't about to give out confidential information to this girl she hardly knows. "What about you, is there anything he said or did that might offer a clue?"

Lili shakes her head, the reddish highlights in her hair flashing under the lamplight. "Not really. What are you going to do now?"

"Nothing." Alice hates how defeated she sounds. But what else can she do besides accepting it? "I'm going to change my plane ticket and go home. What about you?"

Lili lets out a sigh. "Same, I guess, only by train."

"If you'll excuse me"—Alice stands up—"I need to get changed. Got a dinner thing with my high school friends."

Lili brightens a little. "Your high school friends—might they know something about his whereabouts?"

Alice has considered this before. "Probably not, given how well he has covered his tracks so far. I'll still do my best to find out, but honestly am not holding my breath. We should just wait for him to come back."

"What about Wu Ying? Will she be there?"

Alice shakes her head. "Unlikely. Her family moved when we were still in high school; we lost track of her completely."

"Well." Lili fishes her phone from her purse. A few taps, and she produces a QR code for Alice to scan. "Would you add me on WeChat? Let me know if you find out anything tonight?"

AFTER LILI LEAVES, Alice brushes her hair and changes into a dress. She's putting on lipstick when someone knocks on the door. She opens it, and there's Lili again, giving Alice a small wave.

"Did you forget something?" Alice asks.

"No. Sorry to bother you—all the train tickets to Shanghai tonight are sold out. I was trying to get a room here, but there's some kind of conference going on, so all the rooms are booked. Do you know if there's another hotel nearby?"

"Have you asked the front desk? Or looked online?"

"I did, but the thing is, hotels here aren't cheap. Finding something I can afford might be challenging." Lili looks past Alice meaningfully, and Alice finally catches her drift—Alice's room, which costs over 700 yuan a night, has two double beds. Lili has just lost her job and is already out of pocket for the train tickets.

Alice thinks quickly: She'll take her passport and purse with her and lock up her laptop when she goes out because she's not a fool. The precautions are just that—Lili's suitcase looks newer and more fashionable than Alice's own, and her little scheme is so transparent, almost cute. No, she doesn't appear to be a thief or psycho. Above all, she extrudes a kind of scrappiness rarely seen in beautiful people, as if she has yet to learn how to turn her beauty into effortless advantages for herself. Which is to say, she's not a poser, and Alice is fond of that. Besides, Alice is curious. She wants to find out what's going on between this young woman and Deckard.

"Do you want to stay here tonight?" Alice asks.

"Only if it's not too much trouble. I wouldn't want to impose…" Lili says, already pulling her carry-on into the doorway.

25

Cat meets Alice at the gate of the resort. She dials a number, and soon a young woman dressed in a traditional qipao comes and leads them down a curving path paved with gray flagstones. Beyond a fringe of spindly trees, they find themselves inside a courtyard, its manicured lawn encircled by buildings that seamlessly blend modern open glass walls, gunmetal bricks, and 1920s-style soaring slate roofs. Nanjing was the capital during the Republic of China era, a fact its architects would never let you forget, even though the current central government would rather you did.

The resort, according to the qipao woman, was built in 2008. Gazing beyond the high roofs at the familiar outline of Zijin Mountain, Alice realizes she's been here before—many times—when it was still a barren field. So much of the area had been. To mention this would date her as some fossil from a time when the city had no subway, the tallest building here (and in all of China) was thirty-seven stories high, and the urban population was about half of what it is now.

Alice pats the enormous boulder anchoring the courtyard as they walk past. Its clean surface is in dire need of some moss or lichen. She's reminded of the snarky Chinese saying about the nouveau riche: The trees are low, the walls are new, and the pictures are non-antique. But it's the "riche" that counts, isn't it? It's better to have the trees and walls and pictures, and time will eventually take care of the rest—if one could hold on to all these things until then, which is never a guarantee.

They are taken to a private dining suite, where early arrivals are scattered across the spacious room, mingling in small groups. Alice hopes to slip in quietly, but she's immediately spotted.

"Aining, over here!" calls someone from a cluster of people seated in an alcove. It's Yeyou, the ex-captain of the school volleyball team. Once a tomboy, she's now a real estate agent and looks very feminine in a printed caftan, her hair swept up into an elegant chignon. Her loudspeaker voice, however, remains stuck at full volume.

Alice goes over and shakes hands. Yeyou pours her a cup of deeply mellow pu'er as earthy as mushrooms. Once again, she's grateful for the California reunion Cat organized where she got to reconnect with quite old classmates, so she doesn't feel like a total stranger now.

They catch up. Per usual, the conversation quickly turns to their children. Those who were still in junior high or high school at the California reunion are now grown. Yeyou's son never made the Olympic slalom team. He's now getting his master's at Cambridge and has joined the rowing club. Song Zhimian's daughter is at NYU. Wang Xi's son is going to Rutgers in the fall. Alice is surprised to learn so many of the children either have gone or plan to go to colleges overseas. Private school is a path of no return, Yeyou tells her. Students in private schools either don't qualify to sit for the college entrance exam or can't get high grades because their schools don't teach to the exam. So the best opportunity to get a quality education is going overseas, which costs an arm and a leg but is a worthy investment.

Alice listens to her friends, who have lain themselves down and wound themselves up so they could launch their children—the only child for most of them—as far into space as possible. She can't imagine doing the same for her own.

As if reading her thoughts, Meiling says, "But it's difficult to live on separate continents from your child, to watch her marry and have kids in another country while you grow old here. Just ask Aining's mom and dad."

Alice flinches at the mention of her parents. *How does Meiling know about my parents and what went on between them? Does everyone know?* But it quickly becomes clear she only meant it rhetorically. "Besides," Meiling continues, "nowadays even this path of full of involution and overly competitive. It's not so easy to get into good schools in America anymore." She, once again, catches Alice's eye as if seeking endorsement. "Asian kids good at music and math are a dime a dozen. Especially boys who want to study engineering. The Ivies want to keep their numbers low. This kind of reverse discrimination has gone on for years and will only get worse."

"America is in chaos." Kunyun nods. "It's all Black Lives are Precious and racial quotas these days. Meanwhile, people are getting shot every day. Not to mention how long it takes to get a Green Card. So we're probably going elsewhere, to England or Canada. We would consider Australia, or New Zealand, maybe even Singapore, although it's pretty hot there."

So, Toto, we are not in California anymore. Alice has to remind herself she's in a red state—no, red country. She tries to explain it's actually Black Lives Matter, and racial quota *per se* has always been unconstitutional. Her words are met with blank looks and polite nods.

"Maybe they should uphold AA and put in an Asian Supreme Court justice someday," Yeyou says in all seriousness.

Ruan Hong turns to Alice. "You went to Berkeley. They give priority to the kids of alums, right?"

"UCs actually give no preference to legacy admissions," Alice says. "Elsewhere, the practice is under increasing scrutiny. So many kids are so talented and smart nowadays that getting into the top schools might as well be a lottery. Involution is happening all over."

She could add that she knows plenty of people who went to

second-tier schools, even community colleges, and have done very well for themselves, except she's tired of this conversation.

She darts a look at Cat, who tips her cup just a little toward hers. Alice responds with the same. Together, they drink, washing down the words caught in their throat: *These people! Don't they have any lives of their own?* But then again, they're the friends they have, and they're being totally honest and open about what they're concerned about, how they feel. Would she rather have a real conversation about what matters or just talk about the weather?

Ruan Hong is still not finished. "Our admissions counselor tells us that the top American schools don't just want kids with good grades. They have to be well-rounded and have focus at the same time. If you can't be an Olympian, then you've got to have leadership skills and be socially conscious." She turns down the corners of her mouth. "In the end, you know, it's just a competition between the parents; those who have the time and resources to start nonprofits that raise money to cure cancer and fight poverty will win in the end."

"Yeah, not everyone can be like Shen Weiguo," Yeyou says, fixing her eyes on the porcelain cup and studying the lipstick smudge on the rim.

Alice perks up at the mention of Deckard's Chinese name. "What did he do?"

"Thought you of all people would know." Yeyou tilts her head. "I only found out because I read about him in some newspaper once; he never even let any of us in on it. There was this article about a nonprofit for poverty reduction that he and some other people founded. There was a picture, so I knew it was him, not someone with the same name. They did projects like flood control in rural areas. I didn't know he was such a do-gooder. I imagine his kid will help out someday—he's only got one daughter, right? Maybe she'll get on the board or something. That's how she'll get into Harvard."

"Or Berkeley." Cat glances at Alice lest she feel slighted on behalf of her alma mater.

Alice does feel slighted, as she has never heard a peep from Deckard about this, not even to solicit donations. Why? Was he ashamed Alice would see through this transparent gambit to help with Jessica's college admissions? No, she doesn't believe it. Deckard isn't a bulldozer parent. If anything, Fei has always complained that he's too hands-off. He wouldn't do this just to gain an advantage for his child, would he? Alice would rather believe this was something he got involved in out of the goodness of his heart.

"What's this nonprofit called?" Alice asks, taking out her phone.

Yeyou can't remember. Nor does she remember which newspaper it was—it's been years. But it was a print newspaper before everything went digital. Might have been one of those free ones that came with a lot of ads that got handed out at metro stations. They don't do that anymore.

Alice looks up "Shen Weiguo nonprofit" on her phone but finds nothing pertinent online, which actually stokes her hopes. There's hardly a need to conceal such a thing, yet the lack of information about this nonprofit and Deckard's philanthropic efforts seems almost deliberate, just like what he's trying to do with his current whereabouts. Perhaps there's a connection to all this? Alice doesn't see it yet. But even a very long shot is better than having no shot at all.

THE WOMAN in qipao is leading another guest up the steps. The guys who are smoking outside intercept the man, and there is much back-slapping and offering of cigarettes. Cat pulls Alice out of her seat, steers her through the glass door, and eventually deposits her in front of the newcomer.

"Do you remember who this is?" she asks Alice.

The man crushes his cigarette under his loafer and kicks the butt into the bush. He's in a bespoke navy suit, with receding hair and a little paunch. His smile is warm and confident, the smile of someone who has seen success. Alice would never have recognized him in a crowd.

"Junhu!" Alice cries as she cups her chin. "You look so different—what happened to your Chairman mole?"

The mole—in the same location on his chin as that of Chairman Mao's—is completely gone.

"There's some chance of it turning malignant, so I had it removed," Junhu says. "You look the same, though, forever young."

"Liar." Alice laughs.

Junhu wasn't on the California trip. Last Alice had heard of him, he was running a business making realistic-looking plastic foods for restaurant displays. An unexpected career choice, as she'd always pegged him as a civil servant or accountant or some such boring professional. She asks him, "How's the fake food business?"

Junhu grins. "I'm surprised you know about it. Shut that down years ago. I'm a wine importer now."

"Junhu took care of the wines for the evening," Cat says, patting Junhu on the lapel. It was no secret she was infatuated with him in tenth grade. Thirty-something years later, she's still handsy with him.

Alice acts duly impressed and inquires about the business, expecting to hear about expanding market opportunities and insatiable consumer appetite for fine wines.

"Big players dominate, so things keep getting tougher for little guys like me," Junhu says. "Takes years to build up a business, then it can be messed up overnight. My main suppliers were from Australia—good quality, good price. Suddenly there's some trade dispute and the tariffs go up over two hundred percent. We've had to look for other sources in Europe and the Americas, but overseas travel hasn't gone back to normal yet, so it's all going to take more time and cost more." He forces a smile. "Not that I'm complaining; I wouldn't do it if I didn't love it. It's all 'powered by love,' you know?"

Alice has heard the campaign slogan used by Taiwanese anti-nuclear power activists before and is pretty sure this is a misappropriation, but she nods.

"Anyway, enough about me. So you haven't been back since you left back in high school? That's pretty wild. What do you think? What's impressed you the most so far?"

"I've been waiting for someone to ask me that!" Alice says. "The transportation system, of course. It took me about an hour to get from Shanghai to Nanjing. I remember when it took the whole day back in the eighties."

"I know! Even I can't get over it sometimes. Remember how long it took us to try to get to Beijing—and never made it that time? It's about four hours on the bullet train now, and the flights are even faster," Junhu says.

"Every time I get in the subway, I look at all these kids and think: They have grown up with this clean and efficient system; they take this for granted," Alice says.

"It's not all that clean. Haven't you noticed the smell?" Cat says with a smirk.

Come to think of it, Alice did notice a lingering, mildly putrid odor a few times. Durian is in season, Junhu tells her. A new railroad has been built between China and Laos, part of the Belt-and-Road initiative, facilitating the importation of the stinky yet unearthly smooth delicacy and sending the price plummeting.

"Durian pastry is on the dessert menu tonight," Cat says. "Speaking of which, I should go check with the kitchen on a couple of things. See you inside in a bit."

"A SHAME WHAT HAPPENED TO HER," Junhu says when Cat is out of earshot.

"What?" Alice asks.

"She didn't tell you? Her Weibo account got suspended."

Weibo is where Cat does—did—most of her microblogging. "How come?"

"Who knows?" Junhu shrugs. "The platform doesn't have to give a reason. They'll censor anyone for anything. In her case, she suspected some people—fragile men who couldn't stomach her feminist talk—got offended by certain posts and reported her. So poof, her millions of followers went away, and so did her advertising revenue."

Another case of "powered with love" gone powerless. Alice now understands Cat's reluctance to discuss how Deckard lost his social media account; it was a sore point for her, too.

"She's pivoted to doing short videos on Douyin, which is nowhere as profitable. At least she isn't completely dependent on the income," Junhu says.

INSIDE, piano music is piped in at a civilized volume. When "Appasionata" comes on, people's eyes light up as they recall how Xuehui's daughter had played the piece with such skill and passion at Alice's house—on the piano Alice's own children had no interest in. "Where are Xuehui and her musical prodigy?"

"They're in Beijing right now. Her daughter's auditioning for the Central Conservatory of Music," Yeyou tells them. "It makes sense for them to stay within the public school system. But have you got any idea how much it costs to prepare for the audition?"

Nobody does but all are interested.

"They've had to hire a private tutor for the year—there are people who specialize in audition prep, apparently. A good tutor will increase the odds of getting in drastically, but it costs three hundred thousand yuan!"

A collective gasp. That's over forty thousand U.S. dollars.

"Of course, being a single mom, Xuehui didn't have that kind of money. Her tutoring business has been in trouble ever since the 'two-reductions' policy." She pauses and explains for Alice's benefit. "That's the recent government policy for reducing excess homework and excess outside tutoring. She had to sell the apartment her parents left her to raise the funds. I helped her with the sale—gave her a break on the commission. It was good timing; she would have to take a big haircut if she wanted to sell today."

The mention of the declining property market casts a pall over the conversation. The saving grace is that the rest of them bought their apartments sufficiently early and have no need to unload in the present market, which has been sliding with no end in sight, as returns on rental income are far below the interest rate.

No one is complaining outright, yet Alice senses the underlying gloom. The economy looks bleak, even as crowded restaurants and bustling malls mask evidence of slower growth.

When they met in California seven years ago, everyone probably had less money than they do now, yet there was such optimism among them, and everything looked as though there was nowhere to go but up. How much things have changed. So many economic wounds have been self-inflicted by the government: overly strict Covid restrictions, a declining population from the decades of the one-child policy enforcement, over-reliance on real estate as a driver for growth, and above all the crackdown on private industries—wiping out over two trillion dollars in tech market valuation alone and dragging down the entire Chinese domestic stock market. Alice counts her blessings: at least the U. S. government would never be crazy enough to inflict economic self-harm like that, and her retirement savings are safe, knock on wood, from the whims of a dictator lacking checks and balances.

As for the actions by the Chinese government, each one is justifiable in some way, framed as serving the "greater societal good." Some may even benefit from the policy shifts in the long term. But for a vast swatch of the population, these hubristic actions have shaken confidence, brought unintended consequences and real economic woes. Perhaps it's a temporary blip, just another dip in the economic cycle; just as likely, it's the beginning of a vicious spiral. In any case, the world isn't used to a China growing at less than nine percent a year and pulling back on investments. Add the security concerns, China-US economic decoupling and whatnot. All this boomerangs, and Alice is about to get hurt, too. Anxiety returns. The baked baby abalones and braised puffer fish in front of her look about as appetizing as wax.

The server brings out a tureen of bright red crayfish topped with garlic snow. Alice stares at the dry ice smoke rising from the rack underneath the dish. Junhu, who has taken the seat next to her, puts on a pair of plastic gloves and shows Alice how to squeeze the head and push it into the body before pulling the carapace off.

"You seem distracted. What's on your mind?" he asks, offering a peeled crayfish on Alice's plate.

"Ah, thank you." Alice accepts the morsel, slightly embarrassed at being treated like a lost cat found by a kind neighbor. "Just some work stuff."

"You still working with Weiguo's company?"

Apparently that's common knowledge. Or perhaps everyone here knows everyone else's business. She nods.

He looks at her, and his voice drops down to a whisper. "They're in some kind of trouble, aren't they?"

How do you know? she almost says but catches herself. "What do you mean?"

"Well, a while ago, I was meeting with a client at a restaurant, and I saw Weiguo there having lunch with a man named Tong Zhengjian. I stopped by their table to say hello. I know Tong a little bit. He's this rich guy, owns all kinds of businesses, including some restaurants I sell to. I ran into him later on in the parking lot and we got chatting. He told me Weiguo had come to him for a loan for Danyang. He seemed awfully pleased with the opportunity. Told me he would be able to get a good chunk of the company at a good price."

"Oh? What kind of companies does Tong invest in?"

"Anything that makes money—restaurants and bars, car washes, fitness centers, you name it."

Alice frowns. Tong sounds kind of small time. "Has he ever invested in tech?"

"Not that I know of."

"Danyang is backed by VC firms specializing in tech, with offices in Silicon Valley. Why would he go to an amateur like that for funding?"

"Silicon Valley VCs." Junhu scoffs as he starts on another crayfish. "If he could get funding from them, I'm sure he wouldn't go to Tong.

That's why I thought Weiguo's company might be in trouble. Tong is the last person anyone would want to go to unless you are truly desperate. Anyway, I haven't seen Weiguo since, so I haven't gotten his side of the story."

Was this the bridge loan Kaipeng was talking about before? "The last person anyone would go to? Why is that?"

"Tong has a reputation as a ruthless bottom feeder, pound-of-flesh kind of guy."

Alice absorbs this and slowly comes to a realization. "So he's, what, a loan shark?"

"Sort of. I'm sure if you asked him he'd say he's a legit business investor, stays on the right side of the law. But if you owe him, he owns you."

Alice hasn't met any loan sharks personally, yet she can picture them. Rough men in dark suits. Thick gold chains on thick necks, chunky gold rings on hairy fingers, beady eyes, jagged razor teeth, two-chambered hearts pumping cold blood. Men you don't want to mess with. "How does he get away with it?" she asks. "I mean, isn't this a police state with tight financial regulations? Financial deals between companies shouldn't affect individuals personally, right? He can't hire hit men to break your kneecaps if you can't pay back?"

Junhu pops the peeled crustacean into his mouth and smiles placidly as he chews. He washes it down with a good glug of wine. "You've no idea how much people get away with things here, do you? Rumor has it Tong's gotten in trouble with the law before but somehow always managed to wriggle out of it. So you can be sure he's got backstage supporters. He's set up shop here instead of in Shanghai for a good reason—we've got a more corrupt local government."

"That sounds bad. But Weiguo's a smart guy. Hopefully he knows how to handle people like Tong?"

"Hopefully," Junhu says, rotating the stem glass in his hand and watching the sheet of wine slide off the glass. "Although…"

Alice waits.

"He's brilliant. Always has been—a total genius among us. Just look at what he's accomplished. But sometimes one wonders if there isn't something taken away as compensation..."

"What are you talking about?"

"So, aside from that time at the restaurant, we hadn't seen each other for years. We used to chat a bit in this stock trading WeChat group I started years ago. Then around the end of November last year, he blew it up."

"How?"

"He posted some stuff he wasn't supposed to, and as a result the whole group got blocked. He seemed to have his accounts suspended, which would be a huge pain, worse than losing your phone."

So that was what happened to Deckard's WeChat account. "What did he post?" she asks.

"A bunch of anti-Zero-Covid stuff."

"It was a private discussion group, wasn't it?"

Junhu flattens his lips. "There's no such thing here," he says, with an air of forbearance in the face of true ignorance. "Everything you post online is censored. That's why there's no Facebook or Twitter or whatever else you use in the West. Yeah, you can use VPN, but it's not practical—everybody does everything on WeChat."

"It's like North Korea!"

"Or Russia. Or Iran. Our friends and comrades..." Junhu raises his glass.

"But Deckard knew he was being watched, right? He's in networking, for heaven's sake."

"To be fair, no one expected what happened exactly—there was no clear line. You just didn't know what was permissible and the consequences until it happened to you. I mean, everyone with any brains knew the Zero-Covid thing was stupid, but it was what it was. The government had to control the narratives online. So what was the point of going against it, then getting in trouble for it? He's a man of status. He ought to be more careful. The whole thing just seems awfully naive to me."

Alice swallows. They have all heard about what happened to another man of much greater status, who spoke up against the

Chinese banking system a few years back, then saw hundreds of billions of market cap wiped out of his company as a result of regulatory sanctions and a canceled IPO. Alice supposes they called him naive, too. For every Jack Ma, how many Deckard Shen Weiguos are there that the world never hears about? Still, what Junhu has said doesn't sit well with her. "The problem isn't with his naivete—it's with censorship," she insists.

Junhu shakes his head slightly, then mimes smashing an egg against the table.

So might this have something to do with the so-called State Security guys showing up at Deckard's mom's place? Clearly he got rapped on the knuckles online. What if he's done something more subversive in real life? It's a toss-up which is worse, to be wanted by the triad or the government. *Either way, there appears to be precious little I can do to help him*, Alice thinks glumly as she reaches for a glass of Shiraz.

26

Memory #204, May, 1989

Monday morning. Through the back opening of the canvas tent stretched over the cargo bed, they watched trees, sidewalks, and buildings receding from view. The tent, propped up by metal hoops fastened to the truck's sides, created a cavernous space. As the vehicle gained speed, the fabric billowed overhead.

Wooden benches lined the sides, their bedrolls repurposed as seat cushions. A long rope, threaded with loops, ran the length of the wall. "For strapping in if you want to nap," Qian had explained.

"We're now grasshoppers on the same string," Weiguo joked, invoking an idiom that meant they were all in it together.

"We made it! I can't believe it's actually happening," Junhu said.

Cat gave him a hard pinch. "Believe it. It's happening. You aren't dreaming."

Weiguo had always found it somewhat distasteful the way Cat tried to touch Junhu every chance she got, often to inflict some kind of pain. Now, however, he gazed magnanimously at them across crates of bicycle inner tubes with the smugness of a magician who had pulled a rabbit out of the hat. That was indeed what he had done: Roping Qian in, convincing Cat not to go to Suzhou, coming up with the money to cover Wu Ying's share and making sure others kept quiet about it. He had successfully executed the trick, brought his friends into this vehicle so they could all take part in making history. He felt buoyant, full of goodwill toward his friends and the world.

Soon they were approaching the Ming city gate. The archways still resembled the gaping orifices of a monster from afar. Although he was no longer afraid of them like he once was, a new unease unfurled: their history teacher had said that the big slabs of bricks were mortared with sand and cooked sticky rice. What if the six-hundred-year-old mortar suddenly lost adhesion? What if there was an earthquake now? He began to sweat as the truck entered the archway and bumped along the worn, deeply grooved slabs of paving stones.

"Do you feel that?" Wu Ying asked out of the blue.

"Nice wind," Aining said.

"Those puffs of air—they're the spirits of ancestors floating by."

His mood suddenly lifted. "Yes!" he said. "Ever since the Ming dynasty, people have been leaving our sleepy Southern Capital for the more exciting Northern Capital in search of greater adventure, like what we're doing now. Perhaps the spirits are here to give us their blessings for our journey." He stretched his arms as if to embrace the ancestral spirits.

Aining and Junhu looked at him tolerantly, the way adults did when a child said something precocious. Cat's expression was more of a smirk. They probably thought the exchange kookie. Of course, they were all raised on the doctrines of materialism and atheism. Only Weiguo had been developing his own mix of spirituality—a base of ancestor worship, stirred in with chunks of Daoism, Buddhism, sprinkled with bits of Christianity that he picked up from Professor Du. He was glad to find that Wu Ying shared his beliefs. He was eager to discuss the non-material realm with her, but she'd gone back to her crocheting.

"What are you working on?" Cat asked Wu Ying.

"A pair of gloves."

"For whom?"

Wu Ying didn't answer. Her eyes were fixed on her work as her lips moved to count the stitches silently. Cat kept pestering. The more Wu Ying refused to respond, the more Cat teased and pressed for an answer.

Finally, Weiguo had enough. "Would you just leave her alone?"

"They're for you, aren't they?" Cat said.

"Is it any of your business? Why do you have to be so damn nosy all the time? It's super annoying."

"Oh, the boyfriend comes to the rescue..."

"*Shut up!*" Weiguo exploded. He glared at Cat as though he were ready to leap over the crates of bike products and punch her.

Stunned, Cat cowered. Wu Ying glanced at Weiguo coolly, which made him feel thoroughly embarrassed. This wasn't like him—he was brought up to be polite, not given to yelling. He was unsettled by the constant surging of emotions within him recently. He would be ebullient one minute, then irate, even belligerent the next. Like the surfers he'd seen on TV, he kept going from the crest to the trough. Logically, he didn't believe the alcohol with Tianxianzi had any long-lasting effects, yet he couldn't shake the feeling it had unlocked something within. And there was the lack of sleep. In the excitement of getting ready for the trip, he'd gotten no more than three or four hours the last couple of nights. He didn't feel tired, though. Nor did he feel like apologizing.

"Enough, both of you," Aining said. "We're going to be on the road together for a week. Why start picking fights now?"

Everyone was quiet for a time, listening to the engine and breathing in the exhaust fumes. At some point, Aining turned to Cat and said, "I still can't believe what your mom did for us."

Dr. Huang had gone to school in the morning to let the principal know that over the weekend her daughter had eaten at a roadside food stand with some friends and gotten terrible food poisoning. She would need to stay home to recuperate. She sent her regrets for missing out on the agriculture studies experience. Dr. Huang mentioned the names of her daughter's four friends, who in all likelihood had all fallen ill, in case their parents had to go to work early and were unable to come by the school to report the absences. The bus should not wait for them. Being a single mother, Dr. Huang was lenient with her daughter—and her friends—to an astonishing degree.

Cat gave her hair an insouciant toss and said, "That's the deal between me and my mom: I tell her everything, and she pretty much lets me do what I want."

"That's the craziest thing I've ever heard," Junhu said. "I have to constantly lie to my mom, else she gets mad. Now, if you told your mom you would jump off a bridge, would she let you?"

Cat rolled her eyes. "That's why your mom can't trust you—because you are a fool. My mom knows I would never try to do anything to hurt myself."

"She is a tough woman," Junhu said.

"She has to be. She saws people's arms and legs off for a living!" Cat cackled. "But seriously, she actually wants this for me—for all of us. When she was just a little bit older than us, she joined the Big Revolutionary Tours."

The Big Revolutionary Tours. They'd all heard those crazy stories from the older generation when the young Red Guards traveled all through the country to "exchange revolutionary ideas." It was a true free-for-all—they could ride trains and buses and stay at government hostels for free. The transportation system was paralyzed. Local people grudgingly put up with the traveling Red Guards out of fear for the destruction the youngsters would otherwise bring. Things soon descended into utter chaos. It was chalked up to be just another one of those Cultural Revolution absurdities.

"She had a blast," Cat continued. "Said it was the thing that toughened her. She says our generation is too soft—we need to have more real experiences, experiences that we seek out for ourselves. Life isn't about studying all day and getting good grades—or being forced to be bitten by fleas and calling it an educational experience."

They fell silent for a bit, ruminating on that.

After a moment, Wu Ying spoke up. "I'm glad we're doing this."

All their eyes were on her.

"I've never been anywhere outside the province. I really appreciate this; thanks for everything," she said, raising her voice so Qian could hear her, too. "Thanks for making the trip happen!"

"Don't mention it!" Qian shouted back.

"You are welcome," Weiguo said, his cheeks burning.

27

Alice wakes up with a throbbing headache. She opens her eyes to an expanse of gray-white ceiling. She turns her stiff neck, seeking the source of light like a moth, trying to find something, anything, that might be familiar. A white slab swings at her like a lightsaber—the curtains aren't fully closed. She shuts her eyes and buries her head under the covers. So it is daytime, and she's at her hotel.

She lies still, debating whether to get up to pee. She has almost drifted back to sleep when the phone rings. It's Henry.

"Are you still asleep? What time is it?"

"Eleven thirty. It's the revenge of the crayfish." She puts a hand over her temple, where an invisible vise is squeezing down. Squeeze, squeeze, squeeze.

"The what?"

"Never mind. Hang on. I need to go pee."

When she comes out of the bathroom, she notices a lump on the bed next to her and a pair of eyes peering at her above the coverlet. *Oh, crap*, she's completely forgotten about Lily, who seems to be living in the same time zone as her.

"Sorry to wake you," Alice says, taking a bottle of water from the nightstand. Lili gets up and ducks into the bathroom.

Back in her bed, Alice explains her hangover to Henry. He's amazed—she has never been much of a drinker. At weddings and parties she tends to hold out a glass in front of her like a chalice, taking hummingbird-like sips for show and only making her way through an inch or two at the end. But not last night. The wine had been more delicious than any she'd ever tasted before. Junhu told her to look for notes of blackberries and licorice, and she actually found them—how could this be when it was made of grape juice? A full glass later, her insides warmed, she'd begun to relax. Food was starting to taste better, too. Soon, each bite of meat, seafood, fungus, or vegetable that landed in her mouth was the most succulent, most savory, most tender, or most crispy thing she had ever tasted. She tells Henry about her favorite dish, the tofu-and-pigeon-egg soup, the tofu finely sliced into interconnected threads, delicately swaying in the pigeon broth like a sea anemone.

"I'm jealous. Wish I could be there," Henry says.

Alice considers this. Would she have had as grand a time, having in tow an American husband who had a year of community college Chinese classes? Almost certainly not. And who would take care of the kids?—Ah, the kids. They've become an abstract concept lately, sometimes forgotten. She resists asking Henry about them. She wants to bask in the afterglow of an adult-only gathering a little longer.

The effects of the wine must have been felt by all last night, and the conversation at some point turned from the children to more interesting topics. Henry wants to know what they were. Alice sucks down half a bottle of water and recounts:

On the origin of the coronavirus: Natural evolution or lab leak? Several people, including a biology professor, believed it was the latter, and there was an even split as to the origin, the Wuhan Institute of Virology or Fort Detrick in Maryland. They couldn't agree on the evidence.

On the war in Ukraine: Nobody trusted the Russians, but many still blamed NATO for their aggressive stance. They blew up the

Chinese embassy in Belgrade, remember? China should stay neutral so it can seize opportunities to rebuild Ukraine later. Economic sanction of Russia by the West is great for China as it opens up more business opportunities with its northern neighbor. Once trade between Russia and China is conducted using Renminbi, Russia will demand other trade partners to pay in Renminbi as well. Renminbi then will replace the U.S. Dollar as the international currency, thereby giving a terrific benefit to China.

On the Uyghurs: Someone who had work connections with people in Xinjiang vehemently denied any mistreatment and had to be reminded that there were more people living there than he knew personally. But indoctrination or brainwashing, enforcement of one-child policy or forced abortion, it all depends on what you want to call it. We were all subject to such treatments, so how could you call that genocide when it was applicable to the whole nation? Was all of China being genocided? Why weren't the activists boycotting stuff on our behalf? And look at what we have done to improve the Uyghurs' lot. All that investment and vastly lower test scores for their children to get into top universities. Still, there are always those extremists trying to make trouble. If it weren't for the reeducation, things would be worse for sure.

She pauses and drinks more water. Surprisingly, the effort of speaking is making her feel better. The vise has loosened along with her tongue, the fog in the brain is lifting.

Henry still seems interested, so she continues.

On Taiwan: Nothing is new in the situation that has gone on for over seventy years. Foreigners have always coveted this territory, but the Chinese always reclaimed it. Zheng Chenggong defeated the Dutch back in the 1600s, and the Japanese lost it after WWII. Now the U.S. wants to use it as a choke point to contain China, the same way they tried to keep Japan down before. Should there be a war, the U.S. would be hurt more by losing the Chinese supply chain than China would be by losing the U.S. consumer market. But shouldn't the fate of a region be determined by the people living there? Alice asked. Is it ever? Just look at the civil war in the U.S. What everyone could agree on was that whoever wants to have an all-out war should go over there themselves or send their own kids.

On the semiconductor embargo: It's just silly. It would only spur investments in the domestic semiconductor industry, which would be good for China. Any setbacks would only be temporary.

On the population decline: Of course young people wouldn't want to have more kids—so expensive, so stressful, who can blame them? We're at the end of the era of population dividend. Pre-schools are folding and soon the retirement age will have to go up. But that's the problem with this country—too many retired people, all those old aunties and uncles dancing in the park, leeching off younger workers who have to work twelve hours a day, six days a week. Besides, who wants to have that many people anyway? It's a good thing if we ever want to slow down the overly competitive nature of everything and have a better environment.

On censorship: It is bad. There was surprisingly little disagreement on this. Who was it that said, Censorship exists because the censor has lost moral authority? Lack of debate on issues would eventually lead to intellectual decline, which would lead to economic decline.

"Such interesting debates! Such disparate views than our own!" Henry marvels.

Isn't it? Alice can hardly remember the last time she had a spirited discussion like this, where people were open-minded and willing to agree to disagree. Counterpoints were offered not to antagonize but to keep the conversations going. She tells Henry, "It reminded me of our high school days. We always talked like that during lunch."

The sound of running water from the bathroom reminds her that in their high school days they showered once a week, at the public bathhouse. What they lacked in personal hygiene they made up in diversity of opinions.

"While as in the U.S., we either cut out people who hold different political views or avoid talking about these issues all together," Henry says.

"Cat said it was my selection bias. We were only getting the educated moderates who have a level of intelligence and independent thinking; those 'inside the system'—the civil servants and party members—they never come to these things in the first place. And a discourse like this with the rest of China? Forget about it. Many of them couldn't hold a discussion with their own families without blowing up. Speaking of whom—" she remembers, "I need to call to check on her. She sprang her ankle badly last night; our friend Junhu had to drive her to the ER."

"What about Deckard? What have you found?"

She tells him about the charity and Tong, unintentionally letting it slip that Tong might be a loan shark.

Henry frowns. "I don't like the sound of that."

"Nothing to worry about. Probably just a red herring anyway."

"When are you coming home?"

"Don't know. I've got an open return ticket. I've got a few more leads to follow up on."

"Look at you, playing the detective." Henry tries to smile but fails to unfurl his brows. Alice wants badly to hold him, her man who's worried about her.

ALICE TAKES LILI TO LUNCH. To reciprocate, Lili treats her to milk tea at Deji Plaza, a luxury mall downtown. The tea shop, an "online celebrity store," has a two-hour wait—just enough time for them to tour the mall's six famously extravagant restrooms. Each features a proper lounge, Toto washlets, and a unique theme such as "Tropical Rain Forest" or "Cyberpunk Nightclub." The toilets are now a top tourist attraction in the city. In the "Blue Palace," Alice snaps a photo of a girl playing *Für Elise* on a cobalt-colored piano and texts it to Henry: *I'm in a twenty-million-yuan public bathroom! And there is a Beeple exhibit upstairs!* 🌝

"So, you were asking me earlier if anything seemed off with Deckard," Lili says as they settle into the "Zen Teahouse." Compared to others, this restroom's lounge area is peaceful and uncrowded—the perfect place for confessions.

"Here's something I remembered: A couple of weeks before my accident, Deckard and I were walking to dinner. He suddenly said to me, 'Don't look, but I think the guy on the other side of the street is following us.' I pretended to be taking a selfie so I could look. There was indeed this guy across the street. When we stopped, he turned into an alleyway and went a different direction. But later, when we were sitting in the restaurant, we saw him going into a bar across the street. When we left, we went out the back door so he wouldn't follow us. We went back to Deckard's. When I was tidying up, I noticed the maid had left out a bag of trash. I took the trash outside, and there the man was again, lurking down the hall. I yelled at him—who are you? How did you get up here? The man looked startled, just mumbled something about being on the wrong floor and got into the elevator and left."

"Does the building have CCTV?"

"Yes. I went to the building manager and asked him to find the recording. The man had gotten in by following a delivery person, then left about fifteen minutes later. None of the neighbors in the WeChat group recognized him."

"What did he look like?"

Lili shrugs. "Average height. Average looking and wearing a mask. Completely forgettable."

In other words, good spy material. Of course, they didn't report it to the police because what good would that do when neither of them had any idea who it might be or what the man might want.

A new thought occurs to Alice, making her nervous. "What about your accident? Do you think it might have something to do with that man?"

Lili shakes her head slightly. "I had wondered about it, but I doubt it. I mean, hopefully not—why would anyone want to hurt me? I've got nothing." She glances at her watch—it's almost time to go back to the tea shop to pick up their orders. Then she fixes her clear eyes on Alice. "What about you? Have you found anything new?"

28

Memory #204, continued

They stopped in Xuzhou as the sun was setting. Qian took them to a restaurant where they had flatbreads with pungent hot and sour soup. The proprietor, Lao Wang, knew Qian from his previous excursions and let the whole group use the toilet and the faucet behind the restaurant to wash up. They would spend the night parked on the street next to the restaurant.

As they made their beds, Weiguo and Cat got into another tiff, this time over shoe storage. Everyone had agreed not to wear shoes inside the truck to keep things clean. Cat didn't pay attention to that. Weiguo was troubled by it—he was always a neat person, and for inexplicable reasons today, the disorder had an almost gnawing effect on him and made him feel nauseated. It was critical for the shoes to be neatly placed, he demanded. Cat called him silly, which irritated him further. They exchanged words; he did his best not to blow up on her again, then took it upon himself to shake the dirt off the shoes, sort and order them by size under the bench.

Qian asked, "Are you sure you don't want to find a hotel room or something?"

Weiguo was putting the last pair of shoes under the bench, separating them exactly two centimeters from the second to last pair. The neat, organized look of the shoes made him feel better. "Yeah, pretty sure," he said.

The trip was already at the outer limit of their budgets. Qian was running a side job with the bike inner tubes, so he agreed to cover half of the gasoline cost. Still, their share was going to be more than the total for five train tickets. With what they'd pooled together, they could barely afford two solid meals a day. There was definitely no money for hotel stays. Luckily, the weather was mild this time of the year, so they were counting on being able to sleep in the truck now and on the Square once they got to Beijing.

Qian asked Weiguo to come outside and talk, which was annoying because it meant the shoes would have to be reorganized.

"It's alright for us guys to rough it, but for them…" Qian tilted his head toward the truck. He meant the girls inside.

"They'll be fine." Weiguo knew for a fact his female friends were no delicate hothouse flowers, nor would they wish to be treated as such.

Qian lit a cigarette. He supported one arm with the other and took several puffs. "When you mentioned you had friends coming with you I didn't know there would be girls, and pretty ones at that. I always stop here because it's got the only gas station around. But this place has a reputation."

"A reputation for what?"

Qian took another drag on his cigarette and held it in. Then he exhaled, his words coming out shrouded in smoke. "Abductions."

Weiguo froze. It had been some years since he'd been warned about abductions himself. When he was much younger, whenever they went out, his mother would remind him and his brother to stay vigilant, keep an eye out for grasping strangers. For there were stories, of children, especially little boys, snatched from crowded stores or on the street by traffickers and sold off—to couples unable to conceive if they were lucky, as organ donors if they weren't. Always stay close to Mom. But if someone got hold of you, scream. Fight. Use your teeth.

The things a mother had to teach her children. But they weren't little kids anymore.

"What do you mean? Abductions of whom?"

"Women. Around these parts, it costs a fair amount of money for men to get married. Normally a sister in the family brings in the bridal price for her brother so things even out. But if there's no sister, and the family is too poor to pay the bridal price, they would buy a wife for cheaper. Well, where do you suppose all those cheap wives come from?"

Blood surged to the top of Weiguo's head. He all but cursed out loud. He gritted his teeth and pulled open the truck door. "Why are you even thinking of staying here? Let's get out of here."

"I've got to wait for the gas station to open in the morning—we're almost completely out. And look, I don't mean they *would be* abducted. Just be careful. Tell them not to go out of the truck tonight, at least not without one of you guys escorting." Qian flicked out the ashes and headed toward the restaurant. He paused after a few steps. "Oh, have you got the bucket?"

Weiguo nodded. He'd heeded Qian's advice and brought a large empty soy sauce bucket with a lid. He'd had to cajole a restaurant owner by the market to give the bucket to him, saying his parents wanted it for planting vegetables. Up until now he didn't believe they would actually need it. At least he'd told the girls there would be hardships on this trip.

THAT NIGHT, Weiguo could not fall asleep again. He should be exhausted, having hardly slept the previous two nights due to the excitement for the upcoming trip. Yet he was in a state of high alertness, his nerves still thrumming from this unusual day. *Good*, he thought, *that's what I'm supposed to do—keep vigil and protect my friends.*

A sheet clipped to a rope was hung across the middle of the truck bed, serving as a curtain dividing boys' and girls' sleeping areas.

Someone on the other side of the curtain was snoring very gently. He wondered if it might be Wu Ying—the sound was so soft, like a cat's purr. He wished he could cradle her in his arms like a cat and rake his hand through her glossy, wavy hair—when she loosened her braids before bed tonight, her hair tumbled onto her shoulders, and it was quite a sight to behold. He nearly gasped, then pretended to cough to cover it up.

He closed his eyes and could almost feel the silky strands slipping through his fingers. This startled him. The idea of possessing someone was new to him, and there was something about possessing the quiet, beautiful girl that especially filled him with wonder. It was a new sensation he hadn't known with girls like Aining and Cat, whom he hardly thought of as girls at all, just buddies. He couldn't remember a time when he didn't know Aining, and he'd gone to elementary and junior high with Cat. Maybe that was why—they already knew each other too well. Even as they got taller and acquired boobs, they were still essentially the same people, Cat the big-hearted brat, Aining the cautious peacemaker. Both were talkative, would give you a piece of their minds whether you asked or not. They were open books with footnotes and illustrations, easy to read.

Wu Ying was a whole other matter. She'd started as a curiosity and remained a mystery. She was almost three years older than them, having started school late, then repeating a grade due to some illness. For the first year of high school, he'd heard her speak but a few words in class—mostly "I don't know" to the physics teacher, who liked to call on the students randomly. But she wasn't a bad student. Despite her ignorance of physics, her essays were frequently displayed on the back wall of the classroom as model writing. *Engaging, perceptive*, the teacher would write in the margins. And she was one of the few people who scored above ninety on a particularly tough biology exam. A smart girl, and he liked that.

In the first year, she mostly kept to herself in the last row, doodling in her notebook, coming and going by herself, eating alone at the cafeteria. Whenever someone joined her at the table, she would quickly finish and leave. She was attractive, with clear eyes, peach-like skin, and the kind of facial bone structure that created complex highlights and shadows. Yet she seemed oblivious to her own beauty. She dressed badly, usually in some ill-fitting factory worker's uniform that looked to be handed down from an older relative. Her hair was always worn in two plaits, with bangs carelessly cut, perhaps by her own hand. It was no secret her family didn't have much money, only no one could have fathomed how badly off they really were. Later, when she became a part of the friend group and opened up a bit more, they would learn that her parents were both factory workers at a ballpoint pen plant that had been mismanaged for years and was forever under the threat of shutting down. The prospect of losing their livelihoods didn't keep her parents from producing a string of five daughters and finally a son right before the one-child policy took force. Wu Ying was the middle child, the fourth daughter. She'd tested into their competitive high school, but her parents didn't register her, either out of neglect, or more likely, not wanting to pay the extra fees. She might have been stuck at a local third-rate school had her oldest sister not gone to their school and begged the principal for a chance to clear things up.

In their second year, Aining somehow decided to befriend Wu Ying one day by inviting her to join them on an outing to the arboretum. Wu Ying readily accepted—perhaps she, too, was tired of being alone and wanted to turn a new leaf. And Weiguo hoped, just perhaps, there was a small part of her that wanted to be around him, the way he wanted to be around her. This was where his doubt lay. He couldn't tell in any clear way whether she liked him or merely tolerated him because he was a part of the friend group. After today, the doubts both lifted and deepened.

That morning, Wu Ying had shown up right after Weiguo. While they waited for others, she asked to see his hand because she wanted to crochet a pair of gloves for him. Wu Ying was so appreciative of him for inviting her along and for loaning her the money for food and gas that she wanted to make something for him as a thank-you.

"But I won't be needing gloves in the summer," he said foolishly.

"Gloves are complicated to make. It might be fall by the time I'm done," she said, taking his hand to measure.

His heart buoyed. Was it just some ruse so she could touch his hand? He always knew that under that lovely, quiet exterior of hers, there was a brain that schemed. It excited him to learn that the scheming was done for him. But when she was finished with the measurements, she took out a notebook to write things down and that was that. And that public acknowledgment of her appreciation earlier, maybe she really was just grateful? But she didn't offer to make Cat or Qian any gloves, did she?

He could still feel her fingertips measuring out the length of his fingers, encircling them with her own to gauge their diameters. He would have liked for those fingers to touch more of him: his face, his neck, his torso, and now, as the darkness hid his shame, his swelling area; and he wanted to put his hands on parts of her, to explore the curves under those faded blue khakis. Above all, he wanted to kiss her, to feel those peony-pink lips with his own. That was what people would do in movies anyway, but in real life, how did one initiate that? He had no idea. He hadn't seen much display of physical affection in adults except the one time when he walked in on his mother sitting in his stepfather's lap. After his mother skittered away, his stepfather said, in that deadpan way of his, that was something only married people did.

But he didn't plan to get married for a long time—not until after he'd achieved something significant or before he turned thirty, whichever happened first. Did that mean he could never kiss anyone before that? Surely not. Would Wu Ying wait for him? Maybe. Yes, the more he thought about it, the more certain he was that she would. He would achieve something grand. And he didn't mean just getting into a good university—just about everyone at his school could do that— but beyond. He was good at math and science; he could become a great scientist-engineer like Qian Xuesen, who co-founded the Jet Propulsion Lab at Caltech, then later returned to China to develop the nuclear bomb, ballistic missiles, and space rockets. It occurred to him he could represent the curves on Wu Ying—the arch of her brows, for instance—using the parabolic trajectory. There was significance to this. She was celestial, and it was hard for anyone to escape her gravitational pull. He would have to muster a great deal of energy just to gain enough speed to orbit around her.

At some point in the future, he could see it clearly, the forces would need to be reversed. If he wanted to be the next Qian Xuesen, he would need to get a Ph.D. from MIT or Caltech before he could do all the great things he wanted to. She would have to come join him. But Qian's inventions were for the military—so ultimately for killing people. He would do something more constructive, maybe he should become a doctor, not just a sawbones like Cat's mom but someone who cures deadly diseases like cancer or heart disease, the latter of which his father died from. He wondered if he might have a problem with his heart, too, as these things were often hereditary. He thought of the ache he sometimes felt in his chest. At the checkups, the doctor said there was nothing wrong with him. Perhaps he should study medicine or biochemistry—they are different categories for the Nobel Prize, so he would have more than one shot. What about computers? He learned some BASIC over the summer and could program some games and did a bunch of ASCII art. People say that would be the next Industrial Revolution. He really should learn more about computers.

But—he must not be distracted. Must not forget the higher purpose, the reason they were here in the first place, which was to create a more just, more democratic society. To build a country that is open, strong, and free from corruption. Perhaps his real destiny was to become a political leader—not someone who had gone to Communist Party School and become a bureaucrat, but a true leader of the people. There was no clear path to follow to become such a political leader, so one must forge it for himself, to bathe in the fires of revolution, like the great leaders of the past.

Precisely, he thought, rolling to his side. That was what he was doing now. Real work, not just listening to the teacher talk in politics class, not merely waxing poetic with Professor Gu. He was already leading—albeit only a group of five, including himself. There was no rush, however, as he was only fifteen years old. If he could double the number of people he led every six months, by the time he reached thirty, that would be the entire population of this country. The power of exponential growth. In return, he would give them lives that were exponentially better.

He marveled at the wondrous life ahead of him, dreaming without being asleep. A high-frequency sound rang in his ear like the insistent hum of a small insect. This, oddly, sharpened his hearing; other sounds curled on it like tendrils on a vine. In the distance, someone was pouring water onto the street; a TV was blaring the theme song of *Shanghai Triad*; a door slammed. He was particularly keen whenever he thought someone was coming in their direction. A bicycle zipped by, followed by a moped a few minutes later. The frequency of these arrivals concerned him. Was someone doing reconnaissance on them? Quite possibly. Good thing he was wide awake.

He couldn't believe Qian had brought them to this godforsaken town, this backwater crawling with kidnappers and traffickers. That would be the first thing he would do when he was in charge, to clean all this up. More than just throwing a few bad apples in jail. These country folks were immoral because they were ignorant. They needed lessons in morality. They needed beliefs, philosophies that guided their lives. Karl Marx said religion is the opium of the masses. Weiguo disagreed. Spirituality was the elixir, the balm of the masses. He would see to it, to become the spiritual leader who led them out of the darkness.

A train chugged along rhythmically, getting closer and closer, then finally tooting through town.

He was still awake. He was starting to get it—how one comprehended the universe, the universality of things, not by learning from others, but by figuring it out on one's own, by staying still while the mind raced like a great train robber in a movie, jumping from one car of thought to the next with abandon, with no specific destination except ahead.

He sat up and peered through the cover on the back of the truck.

There were no streetlights and stars on the moonless sky were millions of pinpricks of clear light. He stared into the black expanse and had a sense he was on the cusp of something. He waited. And waited. Time passed. A minute, ten minutes, who knew how long. Then there it was—a shooting star, burning a kinetic arc across the inky sky, like he knew it would happen. Only then did he lie back down.

Footsteps approaching. Men chattering in an incomprehensible dialect. Get out of the city for a few hundred kilometers, suddenly you were in a foreign country. He thought he caught the word "shizi," which could be lion, or lice, or something else entirely.

Just move along, Weiguo ordered them silently. As if they'd heard his thoughts and decided to challenge them, the footsteps slowed down, the strides turned into menacing swaggers. He tensed, turning slowly on his back.

Two men outside were speaking in a rapid-fire way. They seemed to be joking rather than arguing, so little regard they had for their soon-to-be victims. Weiguo knew what they wanted. They were evildoers, and evildoers never made secret about their evil intentions, which were plain in the tones of their voice.

He sat up, balling his hands into fists. Should he wake the others? No. He would handle the situation by himself. Anyone who thought they could kidnap his friends had another thing coming. His hands were transforming, rising to the need of the occasion, glowing in the dark like molten lava, or at least what he imagined molten lava would look like: a bright orange outline with a ruby-red inner core. If he smacked a fist into anything now—the head of an evil-doer, for instance—there would be a sizzle. All this was another sign from the heavens above. He was invincible. He would fight any trafficker who came near them, beat them to a pulp with his bare, hot hands, the same hands that Wu Ying once held in hers. Imagine the kind of things she'd be knitting for him if she knew what he was doing for her now. Her gratitude had become his own and filled his chest, making him want to weep.

The noise of a jet of water hitting dirt brought him back. A man was taking a piss—or maybe both of them were. That was what they wanted him to believe, anyway, but he knew the truth: they were performing a cleansing ritual, for they always cleansed themselves before committing a crime. Some criminals were superstitious that way. When they were done, one of them said something, and the other one laughed. They were walking away.

How was this possible? Did they figure out who they'd be reckoning with and got scared? He lifted the cover in the back of the truck bed and yelled onto the dark path, "Hey, where are you going?"

If the men heard him, they didn't answer. Instead, their footsteps sounded faster—they were running away. Good, he thought, finally looking at his hands, which were now cooling and no longer glowing. In time, the men would try again, he was certain. Next time, they wouldn't get off so easy.

29

The elevator stops at the top floor. Alice and Lili step out and find themselves in front of an entryway with a gate. Not a regular door, but an antique wooden gate that might have been painted once upon a time, now stripped bare by the elements. Each panel is decorated with a matrix of brass studs shaped like bullets. The edges and the dome-shaped top are ornately carved in a way that appears Middle Eastern. Somebody had carted off this piece of antique from some exotic place and installed it here, incongruent as it is inside the modern skyscraper. Perhaps that was the effect they were going for.

Alice and Lili look at the gate, then at each other. Alice rings the doorbell.

The door buzzes open.

Alice goes in first. When she catches the sight of what's in front of her, she freezes. Behind her, Lili, her reflexes in her prime, gives out a blood-curdling scream. Alice feels hard pressure on her left arm—Lili has grabbed it and is yanking her out of the door. They stumble out; Lili shuts it behind them. They eye each other in consternation. What the hell? Should they run? Elevator or stairs?

"Ghahahahahahaha..." A cackle comes over the intercom, more like a shriek mimicking mirth rather than genuine delight.

So they've been pranked.

"Geda, stop that," someone else says. Then, "I'm very sorry, just a minute, please."

A young man comes out, introducing himself as Mr. Tong's assistant. He apologizes profusely to the startled visitors. "It's just taxidermy. Nothing to worry about," he says, holding the door open for them.

Alice and Lili look at each other again. The young man nods, indicating they should go ahead. This time, Alice notices the tiger is actually contained in a large display case made of anti-reflective museum glass that fades in the background. The beast is spot-lit, its orange and black fur aglow, its eyes shiny like gems. It faces the visitors square-on in a crouching pose, parts of it moving as if readying to strike: its front paw lifting, its tail sweeping from side to side, its jaw opening to reveal the gleaming teeth and velvety red tongue.

They hear giggles. A boy of about ten is lurking behind the gate, holding a remote control.

"That's Geda, Mr. Tong's son," the assistant says, then turns to the boy and says in a sweet tone one uses to scold babies, "Baobei Geda, you aren't supposed to do that to our visitors without any warning, remember?"

The boy sticks his tongue out at them.

Alice and Lili follow the assistant, circling past the boy and the leaping tiger. There is surely some violation of wildlife protection law about this, not to mention feng-shui principles. Tong doesn't seem to believe that the big cat might block fortunes. Unless it's put there to ward off evil spirits? As they walk down the dark hallway, automatic lights come on to shine on display cases along the path as they pass: a big-horned sheep, a gazelle, an ostrich, a cheetah, even a lion. What sets things apart from a natural history museum is that on the bottom of each case is a photo of the animal, often still bleeding through the bullet hole, posing with a Chinese man carrying the rifle that brought its demise.

"Is that Mr. Tong?" Lili asks, her voice awed.

"Yes."

"Wow, this is obscene," Alice mutters to herself in English.

The assistant hears her and understands. "It's a form of culling," he says. "Mr. Tong only took animals that were sick or dying. And the money went back into conservation."

Alice twists her lips. The specimens all look in their prime to her. Of course, technically, everything alive is dying. There seems to be a special belief system for some rich people to believe whatever they want to believe. Not having a conscience is their superpower.

They pass another door into an area that's set up like a gallery, with large high-resolution photographs of sea creatures not hung on walls but suspended from the ceiling at random angles and heights. Hammerheads, hawksbill turtles, giant cods, colorful corals and sea slugs. Several images looked so improbable that Alice wonders if they are photoshopped: an octopus next to a barnacle-encrusted eye of what must have been a whale, manta rays and whale sharks swimming together. "Mr. Tong wanted to create the experience of scuba diving on dry land," the assistant told them.

Better to shoot with the camera than the rifle, Alice thinks.

The assistant opens another door for them. Beyond the door, a massive fish tank comes into view. Painted aqua blue and decorated with artful graffiti that lends a playful vibe, the tank had a previous life as a shipping container. Big areas of the side panels have been cut out and replaced with glass. Lit with full spectrum light like a jewelry display, the water is clear as air and full of colorful fish: lionfish displaying their fearsome spines, blue and yellow tangs floating in a group, a couple of turtles paddling at a leisurely pace, striped wrasses with green tails darting back and forth around a needlefish longer than an arm. Orange sea stars, purple urchins, and teal anemones perch on craggy rocks. In one corner, a tan-colored stingray with iridescent blue spots rests on a patch of sand.

They woo and ah appropriately. Lili walks up and puts her face next to a small forest of pink coral. "Sea horses!" She points, squealing with delight. As far as a display of wealth goes, this is at least interesting.

"How did they ever get this up here?" Alice can't help asking.

"It was lifted up here by a crane before the building's construction was completed."

"That must've cost a fortune."

"Moving cost was actually minimal compared to the structural modifications that had to be made to the building's original plan to accommodate the weight. But the architect is a good friend of Mr. Tong's."

She can't wait to tell Henry; as a building inspector, he would surely have something to say about this. "What about inspection—was it a nightmare?"

"Not really," the young man says smoothly. "As Mr. Tong likes to say, the only things you cannot do are the ones you cannot imagine, or pay for."

BEYOND THE AQUARIUM, through another door, they finally reach the wizard's office. Tong doesn't get up when they enter.

"Welcome, American lawyer and"—he peers at Lili from the top of his glasses and smiles—"associate? Have a seat, please."

In comparison to the ostentatious outer areas, the man's corner office is austere. The main features of the office are the floor-to-ceiling view of central Nanjing's skyscrapers and the massive desk Tong is sitting behind. The desk is made of a single piece of hollowed-out log. Alice feels puny sitting in front of it, and a bit sad. Judging by its size, the tree must have lived for hundreds, if not thousands of years. Did Tong chop the tree down personally? Or was it also "dying" and therefore had to be felled and make room for new trees?

Tong is probably in his mid-fifties. He has retained the same thick hair as in the photos—parted in the center like an open book, jet black and presumably dyed because there must be criminal penalties for not covering one's gray here. The good life has added quite a bit of flab to the hunter's mid-section. Casually dressed in a red polo shirt, he looks more like Winnie the Pooh than a loan shark.

Alice presents her business card with both hands. Tong receives it, sets it down on the desk, and fishes one of his own from a drawer in return. It only has his name and a QR code on it. He keeps a clean desk, with just a phone, a framed photo of his young wife and children, and an open laptop, which has a bunch of Pokémon stickers pasted on its lid. Thanks to her kids, Alice recognizes Eevee and Charmander. She feels herself softening a bit toward the man— someone who lets his kids run amok with his laptop and in the office can't be that horrible, can he?

"So, American lawyer, who is a friend of Gao Junhu, what kind of investment opportunities do you wish to discuss?" Tong asks. They are scheduled for a fifteen-minute slot, and there's little time for small talk.

When Alice called to make the appointment, she had fibbed a little about the purpose of the meeting as she suspected Tong may not grant an audience otherwise. She would come clean now. "Thank you for meeting with us on such short notice," she says. "As I mentioned on the phone, I'm a patent attorney from California. My client is Danyang Corp. I believe you know Danyang's CEO, Mr. Shen Weiguo. He has gone missing. We're trying to locate him."

"Gone missing?" Tong's eyes are round behind the glasses. "Have you checked with the company? Or his family? Shouldn't they go to the police?"

"Yes. I have talked with his family and colleagues. They don't know his whereabouts. The police have been notified."

"What do the police say?"

"They don't really care. Mr. Shen had asked others not to look for him," Lili says.

Oh, boy. Alice leans back and taps Lili's toe with her own foot. *Don't talk too much, don't give out information, let me do the talking,* Alice had instructed. She thought a pretty girl at the meeting might make Tong lower his guard. That had been her miscalculation. Look at Lili now, shifting in her seat, gawking around, fidgeting on her phone. She'll have to talk with the young woman about business meeting etiquette—has Deckard taught her nothing? One isn't born knowing these things, and there's a first time for everything, isn't there?

"Well, perhaps you should honor his wishes, then," Tong says, flashing a wolfish grin. His teeth are so straight and blindingly white that they're almost certainly dentures.

"We have our reasons for wanting to reach him. Do you know where he is?" Alice asks.

"How would I? I hardly know him."

"Someone saw you two meeting a while ago. You had mentioned you wanted to invest in his company."

Tong nods. "Yes, we did meet, but tech investing isn't really my thing—too risky, especially in this economy."

"But you were excited about it; said you could get a chunk of Danyang at a good price."

"I was for a time. But market conditions are constantly shifting, so I'm constantly reevaluating my options and changing my mind. I'm sure Mr. Shen was talking with all kinds of investors, too."

"I was told that you are a lender of last resort. He came to you because he didn't have a lot of options."

Tong laughs dryly. "Did Gao Junhu tell you that? He's less of a businessman than I thought—and definitely not an investor. Look, this isn't some backwater. Do you know how many guys like me there are between here and Shanghai, looking to get a decent return on our money? Anyway, you want to know where Mr. Shen is; I wish you had been straight with my assistant and told him on the phone what you were after. I could have answered you then and saved you a trip. I'm sorry; there isn't anything I can tell you."

"Who else might Mr. Shen have talked to?"

"You want me to give you the names of my competitors?" Tong asks, once again putting his dentures on display.

"I not here for a loan. I just want to find Mr. Shen."

"Does he owe you money?"

Damn, he's sharp. "No," Alice says smoothly, not wanting to get into the mess she's in. "But Mr. Shen's an old friend and his company has been a longtime client of mine. When I couldn't get hold of him, I naturally became very concerned."

Tong doesn't respond. He doesn't seem to buy it. That irritates her. She came here for information, not to be judged for her own motives. "I just want to be sure nothing bad has happened to him," Alice continues, keeping cool. "Would appreciate any leads. I will keep any information you provide me confidential, of course."

Tong watches Alice as he rotates his chair left to right, then right to left. On the third pass he asks her to send him her contact via WeChat and proceeds to scroll through his phone. "These are just people I know. There may be more," he says when he's finished.

Alice looks at the dozen or so names on her phone and feels a kind of sinking sensation. She can already picture it—calling these guys, only being told the same thing. Nonetheless, she thanks him.

"Glad to help. You know, I was a lawyer once," Tong says.

"Nanjing University, class of 1991," Lili says.

Alice narrows her eyes at the young woman—they'd tried to look up Tong's bio online but found very little before the '00s. Lili points at the wall. There, alongside the various banners of commendations and framed photos of Tong shaking hands with dignitaries, is a framed diploma. Tong gives Lili an appreciative nod.

"So you went to school here!" Alice says, glad for the opportunity to linger. There's always a chance he would let something slip if they talked long enough. "Nanjing University is like, what, top five in the country? You must've been a really good student! What kind of law did you practice?"

"I worked at a courthouse, first as an assistant prosecutor, then as a notary. You wouldn't think the notary was a step up from assistant prosecutor, but the pay was actually a bit higher. A couple of years later, I was accepted into an LLM program at the University of Michigan. I had to turn them down."

"What did you do instead?" Lili asks.

"Opportunity knocked, and I went home to dig coal"—he grins, motioning with an imaginary shovel—"and made my first bucket of gold."

Alice already knows this from the online research. Tong is a former coal boss. A notorious bunch, the coal bosses are symbols of the excessive sudden wealth from the early 2000s. Mostly men from Shanxi, they were roughnecks of the black gold rush era. Skilled with pickaxes and explosives and machinery, cunning at manipulating local governments, ruthless in resource grabs, some of them were outright criminals who bribed officials and threatened violence on anyone who stood in their way. Few people, let alone Chinese people, had seen that kind of fortune before, and the coal bosses didn't know what to do with their money. The smarter ones gobbled up office buildings and condominiums. Just as many became dissolute—eating, drinking, whoring, and Tong's vice was gambling. There were unconfirmed rumors of his having lost several hundred million yuan in Macau. Then there were troubles with taxes. He somehow managed to smooth things over and avoided jail time by paying huge fines. These unfortunate events nearly bankrupted him. Since then, he's supposedly kicked his gambling habit and been making a comeback in business.

"Sometimes I wonder what life would be like if I hadn't done that but furthered my law studies instead," Tong leans back, his fingers playing scales on the armrest.

"You could be like me, billing by the hour, working your fingers to the bone," Alice says.

Tong looks stricken. "I was thinking more along the lines of ridding the world of injustices," he says. "Lots of injustices to be corrected in this country, and our legal system hasn't kept up with all this economic growth."

A curious statement, coming from him. Perhaps he still considers himself a victim of the justice system, even though others would say he had gamed the system.

"I can't imagine there's that much money in digging coal," Lili says.

Tong smiles at her with clear amusement. "It's just a figure of speech—I never dug any coal personally. I bought mines that didn't operate efficiently and made process improvements."

"Why did you quit, then?"

"Ah. Things were great for a while, but then they started going south. Too many accidents; coal price crashed because of the financial crisis; the government started to regulate. A lot of us were forced to sell. Still, we made more money than we ever imagined. Many of my peers moved to Beijing or Hainan. I came here because I had studied and worked here. I like this city."

As do I, Alice almost says. She'd had ideas about the man before the meeting. Now, however, she can't help feeling a kind of affinity for him. In person, Tong is engaging, into the games of business and life. He's a shrewd businessman who understands diversification and has invested in actual businesses that employ people and contributed to economic growth. He's one of the few coal bosses who has had a second act to his career and made money in things besides real estate. There's something admirable in the way he'd risen from the brink of bankruptcy and used his business acumen to build new wealth, even if it does involve borderline loan sharking. *But don't be taken in by his charms,* Alice warns herself. She can't shake the feeling that he's toying with them somehow, the way a cat toys with mice.

Tong looks at his watch. "Well, it's been a pleasure meeting you both. We'll have to meet again so I can regale you with stories of my misspent youth. But I've got to be on a call now. Best of luck finding Mr. Shen. You know your way out?"

There's little Alice can do besides thanking him again and getting up.

Lili asks Tong whether she can have her picture taken with him because he's the richest person she's ever met. Alice is ready to dig a hole and climb into it, so embarrassed is she by Lili. But Tong happily obliges. Alice reluctantly accepts Lili's phone and snaps a photo, with Lili making the peace sign and Tong beaming behind his desk.

"Take some with the fish and the animals, too," Tong says, picking up the phone.

"Well, that was completely useless," Alice says to Lili once they reach the street.

"At least we know Deckard hasn't gotten tangled up with Tong. He wouldn't be getting his kneecaps broken by goons, which was your original worry."

"Do you believe him?"

"Why not—he seems like a straightforward guy. Although," Lili pauses. "You seem like a straightforward gal but you lied."

"I did?"

"When he asked you if Deckard owed you any money, you said no."

"But it's true. Deckard doesn't owe me anything personally. Danyang owes my firm money. There's a difference."

"But you knew what he was asking."

"And I answered correctly. As a former lawyer, he ought to know how to phrase questions precisely to get the information he's after."

Lili rolls her eyes. She fiddles at her phone, probably trying to post the photos to social media. Then she stops and frowns. Holding out the phone, she says to Alice, "Look at this."

"What?" Alice moves the screen at arm's length to better focus. It's the photo of Lili in front of the aquarium, one hand outstretched at a puffer fish like Vanna White. Lili zooms in on a spot above her own face. A part of the shipping container is stenciled with a cartoon drawing of a boy riding a horse on roller skates.

"Cute," Alice says.

Lili bites down on her lip and studies her camera roll. She selects the photo of her and Tong, then zooms in on a sticker on Tong's laptop. It's the inverse of the stenciled version, drawn with black lines on a white background.

"I've seen this before at Deckard's. There's a framed one in his study—I always assumed it was something drawn by his daughter, but maybe not," Lili says.

Alice isn't so convinced. She tries to do an image search, but the

VPN software isn't working, so she can't get on Google. The same search on Baidu turns up nothing. She messages Tong the photos and asks if he knows where the images came from.

No idea. The artist? Tong replies tersely.

Whether or not he's telling the truth, they've reached another dead end. Alice had hoped that even if Tong didn't have direct information of Deckard's whereabouts, he would at least be concerned with his investment and therefore be willing to help her find some solid leads. Instead he was just a red herring, offering up a dozen more red herrings. She might as well find a local business directory and start dialing people one by one. It's probably time to give up, only she isn't quite ready yet. A positivity boost is needed, so she says to Lili, "Good noticing."

Lili doesn't look up from her phone. "I notice things," she says, "but usually they are useless and stupid."

Tired now, Alice almost lets the comment slide. But the vigilant nerve of a mother twangs: What if her own child had said something like that? Especially Casey, because girls are more often subject to diminishment. How hard Alice herself had to try later in life to overcome the self-deprecation that was instilled in her at an early age. How much she wished someone had told her differently earlier on. She turns to Lili and says, "The power of observation is a gift. Few people have it, so don't let anyone belittle it, especially not yourself."

Lili doesn't seem to have heard her. She holds out the phone to Alice again.

"What is it?"

"This," Lili says, zooming on the photo.

In the lower right-hand corner of the aquarium wall, hidden in a patch of painted choral, is a QR code.

Lili scans the code in WeChat, which leads to a corporate account named the Changjiang Art Collective. The profile picture is the same boy riding the horse on roller skates.

30

Memory #204, continued

When they set off again in the morning, everyone was less upbeat than the day before.

"I slept so badly," Cat said with a yawn.

"Me too. My back hurts," Aining said.

"Better than you would have on the hard scrabble farm," Junhu said, then turned to Weiguo. "How about you? I didn't hear a peep from you last night."

"How would you? You were snoring like a hog. People in Beijing probably could've heard you," Weiguo said, more irritated than jokey.

Junhu puffed out his cheeks, too injured to come up with any clever retort.

"Touchy, aren't we?" Wu Ying said mildly.

Weiguo looked at her in surprise. It was his turn to feel injured. *You have no idea what I've done for you, how close you were to danger*, he thought.

They stayed quiet as Qian started the truck. Through the truck's open back, fields stretched in pale green. A kid walked alongside a buffalo on the path, like a scene from an ancient poem. Gradually, the reflective silence is dissolved. They chatted aimlessly, then Cat and Junhu reenacted *Police Story* and *Police Story 2* because Wu Ying hadn't seen either. Weiguo found their antics irritating but said nothing. He didn't want Wu Ying to think he was a grouch, even as an unnamed darkness descended and he felt grouchier and grouchier.

At noon, they stopped by a little lake for a lunch of flatbreads, tea eggs, and pickled mustard root, all provisions from home, ostensibly for the agricultural week. Weiguo ate just a single egg; he had little appetite. By mid-afternoon, the truck lurched over dirt roads, rattling as it wove through the wooded, hilly terrain.

"Where are we now?" Junhu asked Qian.

"Close to Taishan," Qian said.

"We should go see it!" Cat cried.

"How many times do I have to tell you? We don't have time," Weiguo said. Even without delays, the earliest they could arrive in Beijing was Wednesday. They'd need to head back by noon on Friday to make it home on time. That didn't leave them much time to join the protesters.

Cat sighed and slumped against her bedroll. "I regret coming on this trip. It's not fun at all."

"It's not supposed to be fun! And I regret bringing you! So leave!" Weiguo's voice was much louder than he intended.

Cat rolled her eyes at him. "What's with you?"

Aining looked like she was about to say something but Junhu shook his head at her. Wu Ying didn't bat an eyelash. Her placidness stung the most—she didn't seem to care one way or another. *Care*, Weiguo pleaded. *Care a little.*

They were going through a wooded area when the truck struck a deep pothole. It swerved and came to a stop. Qian cut the engine, jumped out of the cab, and raced toward the back. He crouched, inspecting the underside of the truck for about a minute before straightening.

"Everyone out," Qian called. "Let's push the truck against that tree over there, then I'm going to try to spin the wheels. Keep an eye on them and tell me which one isn't spinning."

The rear right one wasn't. It had a broken axle.

Qian cussed once, banging the side of the truck with his fist and kicking the tire. When he'd regained his composure, he said to Weiguo, "Get me the toolbox from behind the crate, would you?"

As Weiguo held the toolbox, his mind turned. Something about the whole situation seemed off. He must figure it out—before it was too late.

Qian slid a jack under the truck and set to work. He unfastened the bolts, removed the wheel, and began loosening the various parts behind it. When the rusted joints resisted, he motioned for Weiguo and Junhu to help, using their combined strength to force the wrench to turn. Finally, the last piece came loose. Qian pulled out a metal shaft, its end fractured like a snapped twig. He swore again as he tossed it to the ground.

"Can you fix it?" Cat asked hopefully.

"Sure. Just get me another one of these."

"Alright... Where do you keep the spare?"

"The spare!" Qian hollered and slapped his thigh, doubling over with laughter. So it was a joke, only funny to him.

"Where can you get a replacement?" Junhu asked.

"There should be repair shops in Jinan," Qian replied, dabbing his eyes with the heel of his palm.

"How far away is that?"

"Maybe fifty to sixty kilometers. We can either wait here until someone comes by, or we can walk down the hill to that village we passed on the road. Someone might be able to give us a ride to the city from there."

Nobody was in the mood to walk that far, so they sat by the side of the road.

Weiguo was the only one standing. He was still trying to figure out what it was, that thing that needed figuring out so urgently. He paced back and forth, thinking as he headed up the little hill. Looking down from the top of the hill at the dirt road and the woods, he felt a kind of dawning. He had the answer.

When Weiguo came back, Qian was playing cards with the others. Weiguo glowered.

Qian looked up. "What?"

"The thing I don't understand is, why here? Why did the axle break after Xuzhou?" Weiguo asked.

Now they were all looking up at him, puzzled. Qian sniffled. "Well, I would have preferred that it broke in the rubber factory yard. Or not at all."

"Where were you last night?" Weiguo asked, his arms crossed in front of his chest.

"Why, I slept in the cab."

"After we all went to sleep, where did you go?"

"Had a drink in the restaurant with Lao Wang."

"What did you talk about?"

"This and that. Why do you care?"

"Did you talk about us?"

"Why would we want to talk about you?" Qian asked in genuine wonder.

Weiguo expected as much. He would have to spell everything out. "Did you talk with Lao Wang—and his associates—about the fact there were three pretty young girls in the back of the truck?"

Cat gave Aining a look and simpered. How flattering, to be included as one of the pretty young girls.

Qian threw down a pair of kings. "What we talked about wasn't any business of yours. But, for the record, no, we didn't talk about any of you."

Weiguo hovered over Qian, shifting his weight back and forth on the balls of his feet. Words came out fast, as breathlessly as if he'd been running. "I don't believe you. You were with them. This is all a setup, part of your plan—you broke the axle on purpose. They're coming behind us, aren't they?"

Qian stood up. "What are you talking about? Who's coming behind us? How could I break the axle on purpose?"

"You know perfectly well who. The abductors."

Qian's eyes went wide. "What abductors?"

"The ones from Xuzhou. And you are in on it, aren't you?"

"If I wanted to help abductors, why would I warn you about them in the first place?"

"A good point," Weiguo conceded. "But perhaps that's your trick, to throw us off."

Qian barked a laugh. "You are quite mad—is the Tianxianzi liquor still messing with your head?"

They were all looking at Weiguo, like he was some kind of imbecile.

"Are you alright?" Aining asked.

He didn't care for her tone, more dubious than concerned. He said in a huff, "Why wouldn't I be?"

"I don't know—you aren't making any sense. Are you hungry or something?"

I'm making perfect sense. It's you who doesn't understand, he wanted to say, but the puckered look on Wu Ying's face stopped him. Her silent rebuke cut like a knife. *You don't believe me, either? You get to keep your innocence because of me.* The dark mood crested. Drawing energy from it, he ran up the hill, where he found a tree and climbed up its gnarled limbs.

He watched the road with cold eyes, his gaze flickering between his so-called friends and the empty stretch ahead. Lightheadedness hit him, and he had to brace against the branch to keep from falling off. Another half an hour dragged by. Then a van appeared in the distance. The people by the roadside sprang into action, jumping up and down, waving like mad, but the van didn't even slow down.

He saw them headed his way. Heard them calling his name, their cries rising and falling like a pack of baying wolves. He didn't answer. As they got closer, he hugged the branch tighter, willing himself to morph into the tree.

It was Aining who spotted him. "Would you please come down? We're trying to get to the village."

Weiguo looked past her as though she were transparent.

Junhu said something about not wanting to spend the night out here, and his comment similarly dissipated in the air.

They conferred briefly before Wu Ying stepped forward. Tilting her face up, she said, "Come down, please."

A shiver ran through his body. A lump swelled in his throat. He felt like weeping. A hotness streaked down his face and he realized—he *was* weeping. He dried his eyes on his sleeve. Should he obey? He couldn't think because his mind felt gooey, and he was compelled to stay glued to the tree to maintain his pride.

"Come now, the sooner we leave, the sooner we'll get to the village," Wu Ying said, as if telling one of her younger siblings not to throw a tantrum. Her gentle tone and her limpid eyes had a calming effect. He peeled himself off and climbed down.

The last branch was more than five feet from the ground. He hesitated, then jumped. He lost his footing. Wu Ying bent down, hand extended. Goosebumps shot through him. He took her hand—and didn't let go.

31

Alice calls the phone number listed for the art collective and reaches the owner. She explains she'd seen the aquarium at Tong's office and inquires about the cost. The man gives a very reasonable base rate, then asks her for her WeChat ID so he can send her more complete pricing info.

Then she finally gets to the question she's really after. "Say, your company logo is interesting. I feel like I've seen it before. What's it in reference to?"

The man pauses, as if thinking. "I hired a logo design firm," he says. "Told them I wanted something fun; that's what they came up with."

So it is nothing after all. At least they have some closure on the matter. Alice thanks the man and hangs up.

A minute later, she gets a friend request from Qian Hanlong.

She stares at the name. She knows it from somewhere. She thinks hard and is surprised when it finally comes to her. She writes back: *Qian Hanlong, did you use to work as a truck driver for the rubber factory?*

I did, more than thirty years ago! How do you know?

Alice calls him back. "This is Zhu Aining. Do you remember the trip we took back in '89?"

"Of course, how can I forget? Were you the skinny one with short hair?"

"Yes, only I'm no longer skinny, and my hair is no longer short. Can't believe it's you!"

"You went to America, didn't you? And became a lawyer?"

"Wait, how do you know all this?"

"Weiguo and I get together once in a while. He told me about you—pretty amazing how well your little gang has done for yourselves."

Alice can't help feeling snubbed. She had no idea Qian and Deckard had patched things up after the trip, let alone keeping in touch all these years. There are entire dimensions to Deckard's life here he has never mentioned to her. What else has he kept from her? "Deckard—Weiguo—has never told me anything about staying in touch with you. It's quite the coincidence to run into you."

"Maybe not as much as you thought. You said you saw my aquarium at Tong's office? I introduced them."

"Speaking of Weiguo, have you talked with him lately?"

"Not for a while. Why?"

"I've been looking for him. I'm in town."

"Oh? I thought you two were in touch."

"We are, just not at the moment. He's gone away."

"Where to?"

"We don't know. It's like he's gone into hiding or something. When did you see him last?"

Qian goes quiet for a bit. Then he says, "Last November. Listen, it might be easier to talk about this in person. I can meet you somewhere after five…"

"I'll come to you," Alice says.

QIAN'S OFFICE is located in Yuhuatai District. Growing up, Alice used to come here on field trips to visit the Memorial Park of the Martyred Revolutionaries. The school kids' favorite activity was charging up the wooded hills while crying "sha" (kill). Nowadays the skyline is dominated by high rises. Alice is blasé toward them, however; how quickly one gets used to man-made objects.

The taxi turns onto a lane. To the right is a giant parking lot full of cars. Something is odd about the fleet: the cars had been parked tightly like matchboxes. Surely it would be difficult to move the cars in the middle. Judging by the six-foot-tall weeds growing between the vehicles, however, that isn't something one needs to be concerned with. The taxi stops.

"Why are all these cars white?" Alice asks.

"Stupid-ass capital," the driver says. He stops the meter. "Remember all those ride-sharing companies from a few years ago? When they went out of business, this is where their cars went. EV graveyard. Same as the stupid-ass bike-sharing companies."

There had been dozens of those, most of which soon folded and left in their wake mountains of used bikes. Somewhere online Alice had seen a satellite picture of a bicycle graveyard, the curvy bike frames stacked on top of each other, looking like dense hairs on a living creature. Whenever there's a business opportunity, the Chinese stampede to it like wildebeests. It's just human nature, of course, but with a big population and can-do attitude, her people do everything on a bigger scale and fail more spectacularly.

"Why don't they sell them?" she asks as she gets out her wallet to count out the bills.

"Who'd want these crappy old EVs? The batteries don't last hardly anything. The new ones are so much better." He gestures at his own steering wheel. Only then does Alice realize that the vehicle she's in, some domestic brand name she doesn't recognize, is an EV.

"It was all a scam anyway," he continues. "Companies that made these cars sold them to their own registered 'ride-sharing companies' to get subsidies and pump up their earnings. When the share price went up, the owners cashed out before everything crashed back down. Stupid-ass investors lost their shirts—and underpants. Haw, haw. They deserve to be harvested like chives," he says, taking the cash from Alice.

Qian, who has a long-term lease on the parking lot and the junkyard attached to it, tells Alice he won't let the junk cars go to waste. There's a bunch of precious metals in those batteries. He's still waiting for prices to go up to hire more people. Automobile dismantling is his main business. Art, on the other hand, is his passion.

Alice doesn't quite recognize Qian—she'd mostly seen the back of his head on the trip all those years ago. Medium height and medium build, the man cultivates the air of a scruffy blue-collar artist: salt-and-pepper hair tied into a man-bun, long beard woven into several braids, black sneakers with hand-painted neon pink designs. Over a plain white T-shirt, he wears a pair of overalls coated with so much grease and paint that they form a crusty exoskeleton.

They check out his workshop in the back of the junkyard. It's a rust-colored building with Corten steel sidings and large windows. Qian had built it himself.

They go through the workshop, where Qian shows off projects in various stages of completion: a large pirate's box with a false bottom for a magician; characters 恩 (en, grace) and 慧 (hui, wisdom) as big as tabletops, purchased by a patron for a temple. "These are commissioned work," he says, then points at the window. "Those are my own projects." Outback, a fifteen-foot-long metal Komodo dragon with half-installed copper scales stands on a pedestal. A colorful art car with carved wooden doors is filled with soil and has bonsai trees growing out of the back windows. The front seat is kept empty because, according to Qian, it's drivable. The pieces are unabashedly representational and decorative, with a kind of overwrought craftiness that's more artisanal than artistic, more William Morris than Ai Weiwei.

Despite the mediocre artistic vision, Alice is impressed by anyone who has the gumption to run an art business. She asks for permission to take photos. She can't wait to tell her kids about this—their ol' mom used to be cool; she'd hung out with someone who has become a real working artist. She thinks of Lili's reaction to Tong—is being starstruck by an artist any different from being starstruck by a rich guy?

They head to his office at the end of the workshop. The cleaners must never set foot in here, for compared with the spic-and-span workspace, the office is a sty: sketches strewn everywhere, models of different materials on the desk and on the floor, unfinished canvases, blinking lights on the printer, books and binders falling off shelves. Qian offers a seat to Alice on a black leather sofa, then clears off a pile of paper from the opposite end and sits down, still holding the papers.

They catch up on how Qian got here. Back in 1989, Qian went back to Old Lai's and found that everyone else had left. He didn't blame them—he knew the students only had a week off and had to return to school. So he repaired the truck and was about to drive all the way to Beijing by himself when he heard about the riots on the radio, how the city was under martial law. So he decided to turn back.

"When I got back to Nanjing, things were getting back to normal. The rubber factory came down hard on people who took part in the strike. Those of us without any backstage supporters got fired. For a while I ran a bike repair stand by the road. When there was no business, I made stuff with metal scraps—you might call them sculptures. I displayed them by my stand to attract customers. Somebody bought one for five yuan once and I thought, this is cool! Then one day, the urban management people came. They confiscated everything and gave me a fine. After that, I got a regular job at a junkyard. The owner was a mean old bastard, but I was ready to make something of myself. I put my head down, worked hard, and learned as much about the business as I could."

"Let me guess," Alice says, "then you started your own competing business?"

"No, I married his daughter." Qian laughs. "The old man retired years ago, and I took over. It's hard work but gives me time and space to keep working on my art. You asked about the aquarium business—some years ago, a ship ran aground, and some containers that were salvaged but couldn't be used for shipping anymore came here. I wanted to make something useful out of them rather than just breaking them down and selling the metal. Then I had this idea of waterproofing them and making aquariums out of them. I called every listing in a business directory and managed to get a couple of pre-orders. It's turned into a nice little side business."

How fascinating. Alice would love to know more about his art and his life, but it's getting dark outside. She says, "Now, about Weiguo—what was it you didn't want to discuss over the phone?"

Qian shifts in his seat. "Last November, I had some business in Shanghai. Weiguo was one of the people I needed to see. After the business was taken care of, we went out for a drink. The bar we usually went to was closed—most businesses were at the time. So there we were on a cold night, two grown men sitting on the curb, pouring whiskey into our takeout coffees like hobos." He chuckles.

That was a tricky time. Zero-Covid still hadn't ended then. Qian was taking a significant risk to go to Shanghai, and both of them were risking being sent to quarantine camps. Alice can't help but feel a twinge of jealousy—what a friendship these two had, and she didn't even know about it. Then again, it's been proved she knows far less about Deckard's life here than she once thought she did. "What kind of business were you doing with Weiguo?"

"He asked me to design and build an anechoic chamber out of a shipping container. You know, for his brain stimulation technology, to make sure the environment is absolutely quiet for experiments or whatever."

Sounds like Deckard, always steering work toward his friends. "Did you get paid?"

"Of course! Cash on the barrel, that's my motto, even for old friends."

Alice keeps her face from falling. That's what she should have done. "Did he mention anything out of the ordinary?"

Qian rolls the papers in his hand into a tube and runs his thumbnail on the fanned edges, thinking. "There was the divorce, which was rather upsetting at first but he was getting over it. There was someone new, which I suppose always helps." He gives her a knowing look. "You mentioned he's gone into hiding—do you know why?"

"No. I'm hoping to find out. I'd go looking for him if I knew where he was."

"Why do you care?"

"I've been wondering about that myself," Alice says with a sigh. "My initial motives weren't altruistic. We have some work-related stuff to hash out, that's why I came here. But then I found out things about him I didn't know before. It just feels like he may be in some kind of trouble but doesn't have anyone in his corner."

"So you want to be in his corner?"

Does she? Her life thus far has been about self-preservation, for herself, for her family. But Deckard is a kind of family, the years of drifting apart notwithstanding. If she were the one in trouble with no one to look after her, she feels certain he'd do the same for her. Besides, she's feeling a kind of exhilaration she hasn't experienced for a very long time, to be in this once familiar now alien country, on this chase, wide awake.

She meets Qian's eye. "I do."

Qian shrinks back a little yet seems pleased with her answer. He shifts in the seat again, then stands up to look behind him and finally finds the culprit—a black marker on the cushion.

"So there we were, sitting on the curb"—Qian tosses the marker along with the papers on his desk and sits back down, placing his hands under his thighs—"suddenly a bunch of people were running past us, shouting. They were all headed somewhere. So we asked one of them where they were all going. Turned out there was a gathering on Ürümqi Middle Road. People were holding a vigil. So we decided to join them."

He takes out his phone to show Alice photos of cardboard signs that say things like *Rest In Peace, Ürümqi* or *You Will be Remembered*, placed in front of the makeshift altars, along with flowers and lit candles. In a couple of photos, people were placing more flowers.

"What's this about?"

Qian gives her a wide-eyed look. "You didn't know? The Ürümqi fire? I thought something like that would've been all over Western media."

Alice shakes her head wearily. "Must've missed that one." There was so much depressing news back then, so many unnecessary tragedies: people with medical emergencies perished because they couldn't get treatment in time; scores of travelers died in a bus crash en route to a quarantine facility in the wee hours because the driver had fallen asleep at the wheel. Not to mention parents trying to get infected with Covid so they could go to the quarantine camps with their babies, pets getting exterminated. Alice had gotten so fatigued with all the sad stories from China that she deleted Weibo and WeChat from her phone for a while to preserve her sanity.

"Earlier that month, a fire broke out in a high-rise apartment in Ürümqi. The city had been under lockdown for a long time, so you've got cars parked in the middle of the road with dead batteries, bollards and other hazards installed during the quarantine to keep people out and so on. Fire trucks were blocked for hours; hoses couldn't reach the source of the flames," Qian says, raising his arms into the air as if attempting a rescue.

"The fire kept burning for hours. People were trapped. Ten died. That got people incensed—felt like it could've been any of us. So it was symbolic that here in Shanghai, people wanted to go to Ürümqi Middle Road to commemorate. When we got there, there were already a lot of police watching on the sidelines. Soon things got kind of heated, and people started shouting."

Qian brings up another video. Within the jerky dark frame, several people are running past and yelling. Their voices sound glitchy due to the wind. It takes a couple of seconds for Alice to decipher what they're yelling. An individual's voice first, then amplified by the voice of the crowd, just like she'd heard at Gulou Square all those years ago.

"End Quarantine—End Quarantine!"

"No more health codes! No more health codes!"

The camera pans to show a sea of marchers following behind.

There had been such protests in the States as soon as the

pandemic began, and Alice had considered the protesters selfish and ignorant fools. This feels somehow different, almost three years later, in the post-vaccine era, this spillover of grief and desperation had turned to outrage.

"What are these for?" Alice points at the screen, where people are holding blank sheets of paper over their heads.

"The blank A4 paper is a gesture of protest, signifying the silence we must endure under censorship, the freedom of speech we lack."

"Brave souls," Alice says with equal measures of reverence and disbelief. How could they get away with this? Did they believe they could stay anonymous behind the masks? But perhaps they believed the police would cut them some slack. After all, the police were citizens, too, and had been affected by the strict policies in all aspects of their lives for just as long.

A man in a black mask steps in front of the camera, turns, holds out his fingers into a V at the camera. He also has his phone out and is recording. She recognizes those tadpole eyes under the bushy brows. It's Deckard Shen Weiguo.

A few seconds later, Deckard raises his fist and starts to bellow. "Down with Xi Jinping! Down with the Communist Party!" Others echo his words.

"Goodness," Alice mutters. Common sense dictates that there are certain things you can only think or whisper but never shout in the streets. How could he possibly not know that?

"We were both tipsy—you know how that is—nerves all jangled, feeling invincible. He had way more whiskey than I did. And espressos—he ordered at least three."

The next video starts with a wall of police in white masks and yellow reflective vests, standing in formation like terra cotta soldiers. There to block the marchers.

"Serve the People!"

"Have a Conscience!"

People are yelling at the policemen. A couple of guys try to rush past the line of police but get thrown back. People are shouting and shoving back and forth. A woman is screaming, "Don't hit people!

Don't hit people!" It's now a full-on melee. The camera shakes—Qian is running. Then it shows a bunch of police pinning a man down. The man struggles for a bit but is eventually carried away into a police van.

Off-screen, someone says, "Let's get out of here."

The video ends.

"Well, that was something," Alice says, her heart beating a little faster from watching the kerfuffle. "I assume you got away?"

"Yeah. Once the police started to arrest people, we ran off."

"That was highly sensible of you."

"It did feel a little crazy once I sobered up. We could've gotten into trouble."

"That's quite the understatement. How much time would you have served if you got caught for this type of counterrevolutionary act?"

"They don't call it that any more. It's now inciting subversion of state power—or 'picking quarrels and provoking trouble.' You can be put away for five years," Qian says with a grimace. "And I don't mean just that—things could have escalated. Young people today just have so much faith; they were so sure the police wouldn't open fire on them."

"Because they haven't heard about what happened in '89?"

"Oh, they have—they know how to use VPN. But they've never experienced anything for real. So they don't believe really bad things could happen to them."

"Well, thank god they were right this time. The police showed restraint," Alice says. "Is this what you wanted to talk to me in person about?"

"Yes. I wonder if there's some kind of connection with Weiguo going into hiding—I've heard of people getting detained and interrogated in secret over this."

Alice doesn't like this shift in events at all. Slightly nauseated by it, in fact, as evidenced by a metallic tang rising in the back of her throat. "Did he post a video of the protest? Was that how he lost his WeChat account?"

"Yeah. That was pretty stupid."

"It's just unbelievable he would do something rash like that. He's got so much to lose."

Qian shrugs. "He was drunk. Once he sobered up, it was too late to take it down."

Alice considers the possibility that someone—the Ministry guys—might be after him for what seems like a petty offense. "It's been over half a year. Why would they bother after all this time?"

"Maybe they're just getting around to it," Qian says, scratching his chin. "And there's something else. You were asking about the horse logo before. I'm sorry I lied; I didn't know who you were at the time, so I had to be cautious. It's kind of convoluted. It's not my logo. Weiguo came up with the idea, and I drew it. There's this German kids' book, *The 35th May*, by Erich Kästner."

"I know that name—he wrote *Emil and the Detectives*! My kids love that book. But I haven't heard this one. What's it about?"

"A kid goes through a closet and has an adventure in the South Seas."

"How does it have anything to do with anything?"

"Does the date mean anything to you?"

Alice frowns. "It's not an actual date that exists." Then the penny drops. "Oh—I see." The equivalent of that would be June Fourth, the date of the Tiananmen Square Massacre.

Qian grins at her, as if having told a funny joke.

It's infantile, but then the whole business is. Having turned its guns against the people in 1989, in the years since, the Chinese government has doggedly scrubbed off any mention of this date and any reference to the bloody event, when what it should have done is make apologies, reconcile, and move on. The Chinese search engine Baidu displays "no results found" in response to the search of "June Fourth, Tian'anmen." Even private communications are censored. On WeChat, people have trouble sending out meeting notices or birthday invitations each year around June because messages mentioning the date are blocked. Last year, Alice had read a story about the hottest online marketing star who, intentionally or not, sold via streaming video an ice cream cake shaped like a tank on June 3rd and consequently had his video stream abruptly cut off and not heard from for months. People have resorted to using oblique references such as 8x8, 2e6, 0x40 (64 in hexadecimal), etc., to get past the censors. This is a new one. "They can't pin anything on him because of one logo, can they? It's so obscure and is about a legitimate book."

"Not just because of the logo. There's a group of us that use it. We hold vigils on the anniversary."

Alice nods. "He used to do that at his house when he was in the States. I hear that people do it underground here? They can't arrest everyone who does this privately in their homes."

"And we do outreach—getting young people curious so they'd investigate themselves. The bigger objective, however, has always been to bring change."

"Like how?"

He smiles at her slyly. "I can trust you with this, right?"

"Already too late if you can't. But luckily I'm not loyal to your government."

"We have always been"—Qian straightens, his eyes dart back and forth—"looking for ways to change people's minds."

"What are you talking about?"

"You've seen *Inception*, the Christopher Nolan film?"

So Qian is still the movie buff. "Yes, but you don't mean to break into people's dreams and plant ideas there?"

"Not dreams, necessarily. Just the subconscious. Nolan's got the right concept: changes of the mind have to come from within. But it's sci-fi, so he has to hand wave about the technology involved." He swallows; his Adam's apple bobs up and down. "You know that saying, 'People don't learn from people, only from experiences'? Once people experience something, they will come around and act differently."

"O-kay... Isn't that what movies and books are about? To let people experience things?"

"You can't force people to watch movies or read books. And even if you could, there's no real stake. So movies and books are more like nutritional supplements, not actual cures for the wrong ideas in the head. The experience needs to be more real, and you've got to feel it in your gut." Qian pats his own stomach.

"How?"

"Reasonable minds differ on how to achieve this. Weiguo, being the technologist, he's been working on some kind of brain stimulation device..."

"Neuromersion?" Alice blurts out. So that's actually the point of this seemingly pointless invention? To implant experiences?

Qian nods. "Only it's taken forever to make it work. I, on the other hand, have always believed there are low-tech means that are just as effective if they are targeted. Don't be rolling your eyes now; I'll give you a real example: Let's say you've got all the personal info on officials in charge of implementing Zero-Covid. While they were at work, they got calls about someone close to them—a child, a parent, maybe a spouse but more likely a mistress—had a fall, got badly injured and was being rushed to the hospital, but there were no doctors available, or some critical supply was missing, because of the strict lockdowns."

"That's awful! And how was making a couple of crank calls going to change anything? They'd find out they were being pranked pretty fast."

"Not just a couple of calls. So there was a bit of tech involved after all. There's this app, Xue Xi Qiang Guo (Study Xi Strengthen Country). All the party members have to use it to learn Xi Jinping thought. Weiguo said it's apparently not difficult to hack into the server. Anyway, cross-reference that with a few things, and he's got personal info on hundreds of thousands of officials. Also, he could get his hands on software with AI voices that made tens of thousands of calls at once. It's all about, what's that word he likes to use—scalability." Qian rubs his hands together like a fly and looks at Alice with a mischievous expression. "Imagine, at all levels of the government throughout the country, people who were in charge got to experience the actual consequences of what they were doing. For at least a few minutes, they all believed their loved ones were personally harmed.

That was enough. The damage they were inflicting was finally not on others but on themselves. It was finally real. They felt it in their gut."

"So gut washing instead of brainwashing?"

"That's right. Virtual enemas."

They laugh at the absurdity of this.

"But," Alice straightens, "you can't be serious. Weiguo didn't actually do this, did he?"

Qian smiles. "Maybe, maybe not. All I can say is they reversed the policy in a matter of a few weeks."

"How could it possibly work? Even if he somehow did pull off this stunt, attributing the end of Zero-Covid to it is like claiming some herbal medicine cured Covid when the individuals might have recovered anyway. There was correlation, but where was the causation?"

Qian shrugs. "You don't have to believe me. But it might give you another reason to worry about Weiguo."

As she watches Qian's placid expression, Alice can't help but wonder if she's the one being pranked.

32

Memory #204, continued

They reached the village by nightfall. It was a near ghost town, most of the six or seven decaying wooden houses looked ready to collapse in the next windstorm. The one that stood out was a newer-looking cement block clad in white and brown ceramic tiles. Lights were on inside, warm and enticing. They banged on the door like the little pigs escaping the big bad wolf.

A shriveled old man came out, squinting at all the young faces on his doorstep.

Qian told the old man about the truck and asked where they could get some food and rest for the night. When the old man told them there was no restaurant or lodging nearby, Cat tried to talk him into hosting them here.

Weiguo stood close to Wu Ying. It had been extraordinary to hold hands with her earlier. They didn't talk much—she not being much of a talker, he completely tongue-tied. Yet to have her soft and warm hand in his was a revelation of sorts: two separate people could come together; one's love could be requited. At first he was timid, reverently cupping her hand as if it were a sacred relic. Then he felt the callous on her middle finger, where the pen would rest. The hand became real, she and the whole situation became real, and the world took on a crystalline focus. He interlaced his fingers into hers and was awash in euphoria, feeling like a human-shaped helium balloon tethered to her, his footsteps so light and springy he could float up in the air. His friends probably saw them, but he didn't care. Goodwill surged in his heart. He even chatted with Qian when the latter slowed down and walked next to them, his suspicion of the driver having subsided—perhaps he was reading too much into what had happened, perhaps the truck breakdown was a coincidence after all. Nonetheless, he would be vigilant, for he wanted to protect this girl whose slightly moist hand was in his. At some point, Wu Ying took out a handkerchief and blew her nose into it. She put her hands along with the handkerchief in her pockets, and there they stayed, until now.

So while Cat was negotiating with the old man, Weiguo reached for Wu Ying's free hand again—a bold move, but surely she would want this too—and was confused when she shook him free. Before he could make another attempt, the group started to move—the old man had invited them in. When they were led to a large Eight Immortals-style table in the center of a spare but clean room, Wu Ying deliberately chose the seat furthest away from him and turned her gaze toward the window. He sat down numbly, his personal balloon having popped, the debris scattered on the dark currents that once again threatened to overtake him.

A pregnant woman—the old man's niece—was coming and going, handing out glasses of water and eventually setting on the table a wok full of fried noodles and cabbage. The fragrance of soy, ginger, sugar, and starch was luscious, almost a dish in itself. His stomach growled, yet he must fight his hunger: something seemed off; felt like they were stepping into a snare.

"Wait," he said, his voice hoarse from thirst. He hadn't drunk any of the water. The pregnant woman was watching expectantly, so he couldn't come out and say it—how do we know these are safe to consume? He felt unsteady, the old worries returned like a fast-rising tide. What if it were another ruse by the kidnappers to get us to ingest drugs, then have their way when we all passed out? He could see dangers lurking in the shadows cast on the walls. He wanted to warn his friends to be cautious, but the woman had begun ladling the noodles into bowls.

"Wait," Cat said also. Was she thinking what he was thinking? He was gratified to find an ally in the round-faced girl. What Cat did next, however, made no sense—she stuck her chopsticks into the bowls of Weiguo, Junhu, and Qian by turn, redistributing noodles into the bowls of Aining, Wu Ying, and herself—the pregnant woman had initially served the males a greater quantity of food. Why she had done this was clear to him: the guys were bigger and would require more drugs to be knocked out. After the redistribution, the bowls now had roughly equal amounts. Did Cat know something he didn't, like how much one could ingest without falling ill? He doubted it. The sensible thing to do would be to skip eating this all together. But if he tried to stop them, surely they'd all turn on him—hunger was so acutely written on everybody else's face. Qian actually licked his chops—he was definitely still the one to look out for. Eat this now and suffer later, only then would you realize the errors of your ways, Weiguo thought as he pushed away the bowl in front of him. Someone needed to stay clear-headed.

"So, I'll go to Jinan tomorrow. You all can hang out here and wait for me to come back," Qian said with his mouth still full.

"How long will that take?" Aining asked.

"Dunno. Maybe a day or two, maybe longer. Depending on when I can get the parts."

"You should go to Qingqi Street," the old man said. "My son had his motortrike repaired there once. A bunch of repair shops there. Chances are you'll find one with the right parts."

Qingqi (Light Riding) Street for heavy equipment. On the night of the killer-moon. How off-kilter. How odd.

"What did you say?" The old man tilted his face at Weiguo. Only then did he realize he'd said what was in his head aloud.

"Just ignore him. He's sore because we won't be able to get to Beijing tomorrow," Cat said.

He retaliated by ignoring Cat. His hand reached for the water glass and his mouth took a sip before his head could stop them. It tasted fine. Stop, he scolded himself. But how could something so clean looking be tainted? I can't take the chances; not when I'm the only one aware of what's happening, he thought.

He felt a hand on his knee—Aining's. "What?"

"You're shaking your leg again," she said. For years, she—and his own mother—had been trying to break this habit of his. They usually made a game of it, but today, he found this intervention irritating.

"So?" He pushed her hand off and resumed shaking at a faster pace.

He watched Wu Ying, who was chewing her food quietly as she always did in the school cafeteria. He decided to let her have her sustenance, however questionable it was. He would keep vigil again to keep her safe, keep all of them safe.

He scrutinized the pregnant woman, then the old man, trying to find something unsavory in their expressions. They smiled at him in return, their faces in sneaky pretension of kindness. They gestured at his bowl. "How come you aren't eating?"

"Not hungry," he lied.

Qian plucked the bowl from him and took half of the noodles. Cat took the other half.

"There are trains from Jinan. Might get you there in a day," the pregnant woman said.

"We couldn't get tickets from Nanjing last week. I'll bet you anything they've cut off trains from Jinan, too," Junhu said.

"Why would they do that?" the old man asked.

"There are a lot of people going to Beijing right now," Aining said, "to mourn Comrade Hu. Tickets have been sold out for a while."

"Is that why you're going?"

"No. We've got some school-related activities," Aining answered.

What was with the denial, the vagueness? Was she not proud of their mission? Weiguo could no longer contain himself. "We are way past that, way past mourning—it is time to unite and let our voices be heard!" he said with great vehemence.

Nobody said anything in response. Wu Ying looked serenely ahead, as if she hadn't heard him. He followed her gaze to the bookshelf, where a pristine set of Collected Works of Mao Zedong sat. She was clearly trying to send him a message via the mind of the Chairman, which he had to decipher. So which one of the Chairman's quotes was she trying to convey? All political power comes from the barrel of a gun? No. The weeds of socialism are better than the crops of capitalism? No. A revolution is not a dinner party? Yes! That had to be it. It was brilliant how connected they were. He was grateful to her, for the reminder to keep his priority straight.

He walked over to her and crouched down beside her. "You're right, though I would hardly call this a dinner party," he whispered into her ear, gesturing at the empty basin on the table.

Wu Ying turned to face him. Oh, those clear-as-autumn-water eyes! But why the frown? Did she not find him insightful, or at least humorous?

"Everything under heaven is in utter chaos, the situation is excellent." He supplied another Chairman Mao's quote he thought was apropos.

Wu Ying put her chopsticks down.

"We need to get out of here," he whispered urgently.

She shook her head lightly, then got up and began collecting bowls around the table. He waited for her, but when she was done, she carried everything to the kitchen with the pregnant woman and stayed there. The rest of them were absorbed in various inane conversations. He tried to clear his parched throat; what came out was a croaking sound.

"Are you alright?" Aining asked.

"Why wouldn't I be?"

She pauses, as if she were going to tell him. Then she shrugged. "No reason," she said, and resumed her conversation with Cat.

It was like something clicked, and his vision shrank. So no one was going to stand by him now, even as he prepared to lay himself down for their safety. He felt no anger toward them, only pity for their ignorance. He was deeply moved by the sacrifice he was willing to make for them, the tragic heroism. How could they not see it? Another revelation came to him: People would not be taught by words, only by situations. As the Chairman said, there is great chaos under the heavens, the situation is excellent.

He stood up, pushing back his hair toward the crown of his head. Then he let go of his hands. He heaved his chest, emitted a deep sigh, and walked out like a misunderstood hero from a Peking opera.

DECKARD PULLS off the Neuromersion helmet, gasping for air. Sweat stings his eyes. He wipes his brows, trying to calm himself.

He's seen Wu Ying's face again and relived the last close contact he had with her, when young love was as innocent as a hatchling. He still hasn't gotten a clear indication of how his mind had linked her to the password he's looking to recover, which is frustrating. Further exploration might be needed. Yet he doesn't want to go on. Can't.

He knew from the start reliving this memory was going to be difficult. He expected it would be disquieting to have all these blurry events and long-forgotten emotions recollected in detail, enhanced, and projected back at him. Yet what he now has is a sick feeling, like the dead revisiting his own corpse and finding the eye sockets full of maggots. He wants to throw up. Everything in this memory, sharpened and magnified, has confirmed what he has always suspected but never received a formal diagnosis for: This was the start of his first manic episode.

33

"Hi, Alice," Fei says over FaceTime, her cheeks glistening. Alice can't help but wonder what she's doing alone on a Saturday night. But perhaps her motorcycle lover is chilling somewhere in the house. Has their relationship reached that level of relaxed intimacy, where she is free to roam around smeared with face gel, wearing a towel tourniquet and a bathrobe?

"Ah, hi," Alice corrals her attention.

"Did I catch you at a good time? Where are you? Looks like it's middle of the day over there."

"Yes, I can talk. I'm in Nanjing."

"Did you go looking for Deckard?"

"Yes. But I haven't found him."

Fei nods, as though she expected this. She sets the phone down on some kind of stand and takes out something—a packet of cigarettes. *Cigarettes*! Alice is driven to distraction. Not an electronic one, either, just the old-fashioned kind with tar and carcinogens. Fei strikes a match and lights one as expertly as a mobster's moll.

"I didn't know you smoked," Alice says, knowing perfectly well that what another adult does in her own house is her own business.

She just can't help it—she has never seen any of her Bay Area acquaintances smoke, let alone indoors.

Fei exhales. Smoke shrouds her face. Alice can't imagine what the house must smell like now. *Has she disabled the fire alarm?*

"I quit after I met Deckard—you know how he is, a total health nut. But I recently started again," Fei says as she moves the cigarette away from her face and picks up something sparkly—a cut-glass tumbler with an amber liquid inside that is probably not apple juice. She takes a long swig with deep satisfaction. *What's she going to do next, shoot up?* No, Alice doesn't mean any rebuke. *Do whatever the hell you feel like, Fei. Bad, pleasurable things. I wish I could.*

To break the awkward silence, Alice asks Fei if she knows about Tong or the nonprofit Deckard had been working with. Fei answers negative to both. Deckard was always involved in so many things, so many causes. If she started showing an interest in any of them, the next thing she knew she'd be asked to go to events with him or, worse, help organize them. She'd rather slit her throat. "But I think I know where he is," Fei says.

"You do? Did you hear from him?"

"No. But I've got his coordinates."

"Through Find My Phone?"

"No. His phone hasn't come back online. But you know how he's forever losing things? A while ago, I put a couple of trackers on his stuff."

"Like AirTags?"

"Like AirTags, but smaller. After you came by, I checked. Nothing showed up at first. Then recently one came online briefly."

"That's great!" Alice says, a bit disgusted by her own enthusiasm. Was Fei spying on him? There's definitely something distasteful to this, but it's also the first concrete thing that puts her closer to Deckard, the first ray of hope after all this fumbling in the dark.

Fei exhales smoke and says, "If I give you the coordinates, you'll go find him, right?"

Alice doesn't care for the way Fei said it, as if she had no choice in the matter. "It depends. Where is said tracker? I mean, what did you attach it to?"

"What difference does that make?"

"If it's in his wallet or something like that, there's always a chance it might have been lost or stolen."

"No, that's not very likely." Fei pauses, as though she's mulling something over. After a beat, she says, "This one is pretty well hidden. It's inside his custom orthotics."

The muscles on Alice's face twitch once, and she wills them to be still so Fei won't notice her bemusement. Of course Fei would be less interested in tracking Deckard's belongings than his person. She can picture it: Fei, spending hours online hunting down the thinnest and most discrete tracker, picking up Deckard's shoe while he was sleeping, slicing open the orthotic insert, stuffing the chip inside, and gluing back the opening, testing the spot with her own foot to make sure it wasn't noticeable; putting the shoe back and slipping back into bed, staring at the ceiling, a woman obsessed, hellbent on finding out about any indiscretions her husband might be getting into.

"You are quite the private eye." Alice tries to sound lighthearted. "What else have you got? Pinhole camera? Needle voice recorder?"

"No. At the time, I just wanted to know where he was." Fei's voice takes a hoarse turn; there's something melancholy in that smoker's huskiness. "I guess I got what I didn't want."

"What do you mean?"

Fei takes another long pull from the tumbler. Her neck muscle moves with the drink, and she winces. "Last summer, he had a lot of business trips that extended through the weekends, so he told me. Then I found out he was actually spending those weekends at local hotels—while Jessica and I were in Shanghai!"

Alice winces, too. Her cheeks warm as though she were the one caught cheating.

"Yet he swore up and down he wasn't there with anyone; he was just there to sleep. Ha. I would've believed him more if he told me he went to play mahjong!"

So he's a terrible liar, too. Although, in Alice's mind, Deckard and Liar are not two words that go together.

"Did you know," Fei hisses as a streak of tears catches the light, "that survey says over a quarter of Chinese men have at some point in their life solicited prostitutes?"

The mini selfie in the corner of her phone screen shows Alice's mouth being pulled all the way to her ear now. "No! I had no idea. That's a pretty shocking statistic," she says. One in four men! That's staggering. Who answers such surveys? This is a serious accusation. Besides the location and the survey, what other evidence did Fei have? Did she catch them in the act? But Alice can't possibly ask such questions. She's supposed to side unquestioningly with the woman, the wronged wife, and indict the man in absentia. After all, who would know him better than Fei? It occurs to Alice he may have been with Lili, or some other mistress. Did that make him a better person, being a cheater rather than a john?

"Although," Fei sniffles and blends her tears into her face gel with two fingers, "it didn't actually matter what he was doing at that point—it was like, whatever. Things had been rotting for a while."

Poor Fei, odd Fei, isolated and proud woman, only sharing these shameful secrets now, under the influence of alcohol and tobacco and god knows what else. Was there anything Alice could have done to change things, to ease the pain, or even to prevent herself from getting caught in the wake of Deckard's self-destruction? Probably not. Yet, in her gut, she still can't believe Deckard is that kind of person. She has trouble accepting he would develop dishonesty like some kind of late-onset disease. But given all that's happened, accept she must.

"I'm so sorry," Alice says.

"Nothing you could've done," Fei says magnanimously, regaining her composure. "Anyway, so you want the coordinates?"

"Yes, of course."

But she doesn't do it right away, just dangles the information like the cigarette between her fingers. She takes another drag. Like a free diver going into the deep, Fei's chest rises steadily as she inflates her lungs to hold the maximum amount of smoke. Then she lets it all out of her nostrils slowly, like a fire-breathing dragon. Alice watches her in fascinated silence. Finally, Fei says, "And I need a favor in return."

Alice is stunned. She has never known Fei to ask for any favors. "Sure, what is it?"

"Deckard may be hiding a certain asset from me. I need your help to track it down."

"You should work with your divorce attorney on that. I know nothing about how to track down assets." The thought of financial records subpoenas and discovery requests makes Alice's head spin. There's a reason she doesn't practice family law.

"It's not anything traditional like stocks or bonds."

What is it, then? Special real estate? Rare art? Fei clearly wants to tell, so Alice waits for the dragon to take another smoky breath.

"It's Bitcoins."

"Really? I didn't know he was into that," Alice says. "I always thought he had a dim view of it. We'd talked about it at one point and were in agreement it's just a tool for speculation and money laundering. And he'd called his brother's crypto trading a waste of both electrical and human energy." But, she supposes it could be just another thing about him that has changed without her knowledge.

"Just help me figure out if he actually has it or not," Fei says.

"How would I do that? If he wants to hide it from you, he would be careful about keeping it hidden."

"Just talk with him when you see him. Mention Bitcoin in your conversations, but don't let him know you know anything about *his* bitcoins. He trusts you. He might let you in on it."

The door lock hisses open. Lili walks in, holding a pink box under her arm.

"Just a sec," Alice says. She gives Lili a curt nod, squeezes herself past the young woman through the narrow hall into the bathroom, shuts the door and turns on the fan. She takes a moment to sort out her thoughts. There are so many questions that Alice doesn't even know where to begin. That's exactly the problem: they haven't started at the beginning. "Let's step back for a moment," she says. "Can you tell me how you found out about it?"

Fei flicks the ashes into a dish in front of her. "A couple of days ago, somebody from a 415 area code texted me in Chinese. First they asked if I knew where Deckard Shen Weiguo was—they knew both his English and Chinese names, which was kind of creepy, but I don't suppose it's hard to figure out. I thought maybe scammers are getting sophisticated these days, so I just deleted the message and blocked the number. But then they tried again from a different number, this time telling me he has a bunch of bitcoins he's trying to hide from me in the divorce."

"Did you respond?"

"I asked them what they wanted. They replied I should tell them where he is."

"Did you?"

"Of course not! And the number was obviously fake; I could text but couldn't call."

Alice feels a sick, tightening sensation in her stomach. Could it be the supposed State Security guys on some kind of fishing expedition? Should she tell Fei about them? What good would it do? She decides against it and merely says, "Seems pretty dodgy."

Fei nods. "That's what I thought at first. But they actually knew something about Deckard and me, about the divorce. What if it's real?"

"Did they say how much is at stake?" Alice asks. An obnoxious, intrusive question, had they not been discussing a possible phone scam.

"Tens of millions of dollars, supposedly. I asked for proof, but they wouldn't tell me anything more. Just said I should ask him directly, then stopped responding. If, like they say, he's trying to hide this from me, why would he admit it?"

"That is a logical trap."

"Now, before I get the lawyers involved, I want to have something more concrete besides a couple of anonymous texts. When you see him, can you help me figure out if there's any veracity to this at all?"

"You want me to spy for you?"

"I wouldn't call it that. I just want you to…" Fei searches for the words. "I just want you to stand up for me. If there's any bitcoin at all, it's community property, and I'm entitled to half of it."

"Sorry, but I'm skeptical. Chances are good it's just a wild goose chase, or he won't tell me anything."

"All I'm asking is that you try," Fei says, taking another sip from the glass. Downing the liquor, she adds, "There isn't anyone else I can turn to."

Alice closes her eyes, trying to process this. It's all so far-fetched in every way. But a part of her can't help wanting to believe in Fei for a second, and take a flight of fancy—bitcoins worth tens of millions of dollars! What would she and Henry do if they had that kind of windfall? Pay off the mortgage and sock away the children's education funds, obviously. Then they'll buy a camper van and tour around the country, and travel around the world—flying first class would surely do wonders to soothe her aerophobia.

Now, back in the real world, maybe the money could temporarily ease Danyang's cash crunch and her firm would get paid. That is, in a real world where the bitcoins actually existed. But since Danyang is still having cash trouble, that means the bitcoins can't exist? Sold them too early; lost them to theft; inaccessible due to the collapse of some crypto exchange—the possibilities for loss are endless. And where could so many bitcoins come from? What if they're ill-gotten gains? Could this be why Deckard has gone into hiding and the State Security guys are after him? What's the purpose of whoever it is telling Fei all this? The only true motive seems to be obtaining Deckard's whereabouts. Perhaps they expected her to go look for him? Or ask someone else, like Alice, to do it for her? She's suddenly nervous. "Have you shared his location with anyone else?" Alice asks.

"No. I'm only going to share it with you so you can help me find him."

"Good." An unpleasant thought clings to her like a clammy slug.

What if Fei's phone is bugged? Her house? Is she being overly paranoid? It's pretty hard to hack iOS, and if those scammers could get the location information off Fei's phone, they wouldn't need to text her. Still, should she warn her? Ask her to go somewhere else and use a different phone to talk? And what good would that do besides making Fei paranoid, too?

While she's thinking, Fei has already texted over the coordinates.

34

I'm a loser, Deckard tells himself as he examines himself in the mirror. Not in the sense of an unaccomplished person—at least he's not that—but a person who loses things. In his forty-nine years on this planet, he has lost countless school supplies, books, apparel, water bottles, sports equipment, wallets and keys, a couple of laptops, ninety million dollars, give or take, and a wedding ring. Up until recently, he's always accepted that such were the trade-offs, offerings made to the gods in exchange for his talents and good fortune. The worldly possessions scattered about the earth are the cost of being him.

About the wedding ring Deckard has felt the greatest sorrow. It was the only jewelry he ever wore, a mokume-gane ring Fei had made for him—they had made each other wedding rings with the help of a jeweler in San Francisco. The ring fit him so well, so comfortably, that he almost never thought about it, like his marriage. Until he lost both.

And the ninety million. He doesn't want to fixate on it, yet fixating he has been, even as he tells himself the amount is rather exaggerated. Ninety million dollars if he had access to the bitcoins from Hikaru, held on to them, then sold at the peak—which almost nobody could do because that would be against human nature. At the moment, they're only worth a hair over forty-five. Still a good chunk of change for sure, and it would certainly come in handy in Danyang's current time of cash crunch. *Boy, would it be very handy.* Sooner or later the investment environment is going to turn a corner —he has to believe it will—and Danyang needs cash to survive until then. Cash is more than king. It's the electricity, water, and oxygen of every enterprise.

And he hasn't *lost* the bitcoins, exactly. There's not anything to lose per se: the public keys, addresses, and associated transaction data are permanently recorded on the blockchain for the world to see. But without the password to the secure USB key, he doesn't know which keys and addresses he can access, nor does he have the private keys necessary to authorize the transactions. He's in the dark about which bitcoins are his; therefore, he's unable to spend them because he can't prove ownership.

He should have asked Hikaru to send him the info again, but he dawdled. And how could he have anticipated Hikaru would die from a heart attack just a few months after their meeting? The vicissitudes of life are nothing in the face of death. The loss of a few hundred dollars' worth of bitcoins seemed like a trivial matter at the time, not worth troubling Hikaru's grieving family over. It wasn't that Deckard doubted the whole Bitcoin thing would catch on; he was certain it would not. He'd put the whole thing out of his mind—there were so many more important things to attend to than this little decentralized payment system that uses encryption algorithms to prevent double-spending.

Over the next few years, whenever someone mentioned Bitcoin, he would scoff and steer the conversation away. At some point the scoff turned into frowns—the thing was just getting so much attention. Finally, one day he looked up Bitcoin price online and nearly had a heart attack of his own—the value was way too much to ignore, and still climbing.

There must be a way to hack the hardware and get the password back, he thought. He checked with the senior hardware engineer at work. Ming said he would need a few identical devices to experiment with, and there lay the impasse. The USB key from Hikaru bore no discernible marking, and the software used to run the login program was generic. Deckard had no idea what brand of device this was, and none of the devices he found on the Internet, made in Japan or elsewhere, seemed to match. Hikaru's birthday was coming up, so he took the opportunity to contact Hikaru's wife, Sachiko, and flew to Japan to meet her.

When he last saw her at the funeral, Sachiko was hoarse with grief. Through broken English and with the help of Hikaru's sister, Sachiko enumerated to Deckard all the things she regretted: She should have scheduled Hikaru's physical earlier; should have taken more of an interest in his hobbies; should have supported his notion of moving to Silicon Valley rather than telling him it could be their retirement plan. By now, time had healed her. She was once again the calm person Deckard remembered from the wedding, if less cheerful. Her English had improved. Private online lessons, she told him. She spoke slowly and clearly and occasionally looked up words on her phone.

They went to the cemetery, where skinny gravestones stood tightly packed like mini skyscrapers. After paying their respects, they lingered, talking to Hikaru. Sachiko acted as if the men hadn't seen each other for a while and were there to catch up. She reminded them of things and cracked jokes and kept the conversation lively.

Later, Sachiko and Deckard went to a restaurant for lunch, where he explained the situation in broad strokes: Hikaru had left him a computer file with some useful information that he'd lost but wished to recover. Did Hikaru leave behind any documents—on his computer, on his phone, on any storage device, or in written notes that might help him recover the information?

"Computers," Sachiko said, touching the table edge lightly with two manicured fingers. "Hikaru's computers and other electronics were donated a long time ago. The charity helped me clean everything completely."

Deckard felt a tightening of his scalp. "Did you make any backups?" he asked, still holding out a sliver of hope.

"There was no need. All the business files were on the company server. Our accountant and bookkeeper had all our personal financial records. All the photos were on the cloud. He only used his computer for fun."

And fun was not something the grieving widow wanted to think about at the time. It was also extremely unlikely Hikaru would have stored the Bitcoin information on any company server or the cloud; he was far too cautious for that, as evidenced by his early adoption of the hardware wallet. Deckard wasn't ready to give up yet. Unzipping the inside pocket of his jacket, he dug out the USB key and held it out with both hands like a fragile egg. "This is the device he gave me, which has the file on it—I changed the password but forgot what it is. To recover it, I want to find other devices just like it to experiment with. Have you ever seen anything like this?"

Sachiko looked at the USB key with great concentration for a while, then shook her head. "I'm afraid not," she said. "Hikaru had a small workshop where he tinkered with computer things. It was his—what's that word—his sanctuary. The children and I always stayed away. After he died, everything got donated or recycled."

"What about notebooks? Did he leave any papers?"

"He was never big on keeping papers. I still have his old address book—he stopped using it when he started using his phone for contacts. It was one of the few things with his handwriting in it, so I didn't want to throw it out. Would you like to come and take a look?"

In the end, the address book was just that, contact information of people Hikaru knew, scribbled in as he got them. Deckard found his own name in the middle of the book. Sachiko helped Deckard examine each page closely. No long sequences of random-looking alphanumerical strings, no hidden codes as far as either of them could tell.

Deckard rubbed his face. He knew this was the likely outcome. Still, he felt drained.

Sachiko looked at him evenly. "May I ask what exactly you're looking for?"

Deckard inhaled. He'd deliberately avoided mentioning anything about Bitcoins specifically, hoping Japanese feminine politeness would keep Sachiko from prying and thus spare her the awful knowledge that millions, maybe even billions (so hundreds of billions in yen!) had been wiped out from the hard drives. But now she was asking, he owed her the truth.

As he talked, he braced himself for some kind of angry outburst directed at him. But Sachiko listened intently and kept her composure. Finally, she bowed and said, "I am sorry for you, that I cannot help."

"No, I'm the one who should apologize. Your loss is likely far greater. I should have let you know earlier to look for the bitcoins on his computers. I just didn't think it mattered at the time. For that, I am truly sorry," Deckard said, bowing back.

"Don't be," Sachiko said. She was smiling, faint crow's feet furling around her eyes. "If Hikaru didn't think it mattered enough to let me know about it, how could you? I was so sad at the time, it was like my mind had left my body. I just drifted along, did whatever the easiest thing. I probably wouldn't have done anything different. But what difference does it make? Financially, the children and I are doing fine; we have more than we need. We have no use for all that, all that cryptocurrency—if it existed at all. And if it never existed, why should I let it bother me?"

Deckard watched his good friend's widow with a mixture of pity and admiration. This graceful woman had already experienced the greatest, real loss; as such, this imaginary one barely touched her. He, however, could not achieve this kind of equanimity. *It's the difference between men and women*, he thought. Men fight against the forces that conspire against them, women submit. They have to because of their weaker physique, and they must preserve themselves for their children. That's also why women are happier—at least, he believes they are—but men accomplish more. He, for one, can't treat the loss of the bitcoin password the same way as the loss of his favorite ski jacket. He can't just forget about it.

From time to time, he would still think about that day, attempt to retrace what he did from the time Hikaru gave him the USB key.

What little he remembered was being dropped off at the house, holding that picture of Wu Ying in his hand. He was thinking about her. And every time he thought about her, his mind inevitably went to the place where he wondered if they could have had a life together. On that day, he'd pondered the life he had with Fei and Jessica, whether they were actually happy. He was nostalgic and full of doubts, and the sorrow felt electric at first but soon depleting.

He looked into password recovery services. One way to crack the hardware was via a fault injection attack (FIA), a special kind of hardware hack where you bypass the device's security measures by making its chips operate outside of their normal conditions. The consultant he found warned him there was a high chance of damaging the device and asked him to sign a waiver. In the end, he put the device back into his drawer and watched with stoicism as the value of Bitcoin vaulted to stratospheric levels, crashed back down, rose again, and sloshed around its current ridiculous levels.

He'd been tinkering with the Neuromersion idea for years now. It was fun, a great distraction from the mundane business of data centers. He thought it might be useful for memory recovery. He would pivot in that direction.

AS FOR THE WEDDING RING, that happened last fall. He was clipping his fingernails when he noticed it missing. He'd just returned from a two-week-long business trip at the time, going from meeting to meeting, city after city. He'd lost some weight during the springtime Covid lockdown, one of those mixed blessings. Through exercise and diet he'd managed to keep it off. The ring could have slipped off his finger anywhere.

He checked every corner of his apartment. The next day, he enlisted his cleaning lady to sweep again several times. He turned his office upside down, then downside up. He asked the building security to help him download footage of his entering and leaving the building, examined them frame by frame, and established the ring was still on his hand at least three days before the trip. He asked his assistant to call every single hotel, office, airport and airline, train and bus terminal in the cities he'd stayed in, every restaurant where he'd had a meal, and so on. No luck.

He was going to hide this from Fei for as long as possible in the hopes the ring would magically turn up somewhere. Failing that, he would order another one soon and pray Fei wouldn't notice the difference up close. One night, during their video call, he was drinking a beer in front of the camera and forgot to hide his hand. "Wait," Fei said. "Let me see your hand."

He'd had to come clean. Told Fei how sorry and upset he felt—it was the deepest loss he'd ever experienced for any inanimate object; the sadness chilled him to the core like nothing else had before. He'd hoped for some words of comfort from her, a virtual hug, a tear shed in sympathy, or at least a rueful expression. But instead she just stared at him mutely from across the Pacific. At some point, she said very casually, "So, I've been thinking we should get a divorce."

"Get a what?" Deckard was positive he heard her wrong. Was there some furniture piece that sounded like "divorce"?

"A divorce."

"Oh, that's just mean. You shouldn't joke about things like that. The ring wasn't even my fault, and I'm still hoping it'll turn up," he said.

"I'm serious."

She couldn't be. *Unless something's gone wrong with her head?* It was unheard of. How could anyone dissolve fifteen years of marriage over such a small thing? "I said I was sorry. If it doesn't turn up, you can help me make another one when I'm back in the Bay Area. Maybe we can both upgrade..."

"It's not about that." Fei cut him off.

"Then what is it about?"

Fei would not—*could not?*—respond, so he posed questions and supplied answers in his head—was what was to him an unfortunate accident, to her more proof he didn't care enough? No, that was ridiculous. Why else would he work so hard if it weren't for their family? Did she think he'd taken the ring off on purpose to pick up women in bars? After all these years together, she ought to know him better and have more trust in him. Was this still about his staying at the hotels? He couldn't believe she tried to track him. He told her the completely innocent truth—he went there to sleep because it was quieter and easier to sleep there than at home.

The real reason he kept to himself—he couldn't quite bring himself to face it: he was feeling oddly and completely exhausted and craved sleep. During the week, he self-medicated with alcohol, which disrupted his sleep so he could wake up in the morning. Shots of espresso would get him through the day. On the weekend, he just wanted to be in bed all day and never wake up. He'd been here before, when Fei and Jessica lived in the States. He knew he would eventually come out of it, if he slept enough, but he also knew this was abnormal and didn't want them to see him like this up close. He blamed it on work-related stress and thought Fei understood. Yet things hadn't felt quite the same since. Something fundamental had eroded from their relationship. He sometimes caught her watching him with a cold, appraising look like she was doing now.

"The ring was a small thing; stop fixating on that," she said finally. "Just a coincidence, bad timing, but perhaps there was something kismet if you insisted on looking at it that way."

"Kismet?"

"The last straw."

Deckard grimaced. He knew about the complaints Fei had privately registered with others: being a married single parent, having to meet Deckard's expectations for Jessica and for herself, always having to make accommodations for his schedule and put up with his forgetfulness, his workout regimes, his diets, his moods, his political activism. But she never said those things to his face, which he appreciated. And she did everything willingly, didn't she? That was the deal, right? This life they chose to build together wasn't an easy one, but one that allowed him—and their entire family—to achieve greater things. He wasn't the first person to run a company in China whose wife and child stayed overseas. It was a better life for Fei and

Jessica. There were communities of families like that; had Fei taken the initiative to join one from the very beginning, she could have learned from others about how to face the challenges instead of struggling alone. He thought they were partners in this, but apparently she was owed something, and the bill was now due.

"I know it's hard. I know you feel ignored," he said with utmost sincerity, his tone being the one he used when trying to persuade a valued employee not to quit. "But we decided to do this together; we're almost there." Hadn't they talked about this—once Jessica was in boarding school, Fei would come back to Shanghai so the two of them could be together. A new beginning; a fresh start; possibly another baby while she still could?

Fei's face tilted away from the camera. He saw the flaring of her nostrils—was she snorting? Then a thought struck him. "Is there someone else?"

She hesitated for a second, then denied it. That second was all he needed. The goddamn modern mobile phone—he could neither hang it up with a bang nor hurl it across the room without incurring significant inconvenience. He asked, calmly, so he thought, "Who is he? How long has this been going on?"

Fei poked her tongue against the part below her bottom lip, as she sometimes did while trying to maintain a look of forbearance. "I told you, there isn't anyone else. It's just something I've been thinking about for a while. I should've talked with you face-to-face about this; guess it just kind of slipped out. Any chance you can come here so we can talk things through?"

"Right now? You've got to be kidding. I'm in the middle of a fundraising round! I can't just take off to go to California—if I tested Covid positive on the way back I could be locked up for a month. You want to do this, you come here."

"We'll have to wait until winter break, then. It would be good for both of us to have a little more time to think."

Think about what? But he agreed to buy some more time. Fei was a child. He was the adult in the relationship and the one driving the decisions; he should always remember that. This way, he wouldn't get so angry with her errors in judgment. He would give her the time she needed to come to that realization. She would feel different in a couple of months, when she got tired of this idea, this man—if there is indeed one. Then she would want things to be back the way they were, and he would forgive her. For now, he had more important things to focus on, such as keeping his business afloat.

He couldn't sleep that night. When he turned off the lights and crawled into bed, images of his wife with another man assailed him in the dark. He jumped up and turned the lights back on. He lay stewing, eyes fixed on the ceiling, mind smoldering in slow circles: anger at her infidelity, her denial of it, and her picking this time to drop this on him turned to anxiety of what was to come, which turned to doubt of whether he'd chosen the right path for him and his family, which turned back to anger again.

There must be a way out of this. There had to be. When the morning came, he was wide awake but had his usual three shots of espresso. His person vibrated the rest of the day, and he was short with his direct reports over minor issues. He could sense the tiptoeing around him.

In the evening, he sat alone at home, eating dinner left for him by the cook. Fei planned a clean Paleo menu each week, ordered the groceries, and instructed the housekeeper on cooking. Will she continue to do so, or will he have to order takeout from now on? It would be around 4 a.m. California time now. He wondered what Fei was doing—was the space next to her in bed, the place that rightfully belonged to him, empty? She'd better not be bringing any guy home to his house. That singular notion rekindled his anger. Circular thoughts returned. How could she do this now, when he was barely keeping his head above water as is? Was this inevitable? Did they make a mistake somewhere? Could he have done anything differently? No, not when they thought this would work. She was to blame entirely. At midnight, he was abuzz with furious energy, pacing in front of the floor-to-ceiling windows in the living room and staring out at the taillights of cars on the streets below, suppressing the urge to shatter the glass with a kick and jump out. This was ridiculous. He had to get some sleep. He had wall-to-wall meetings the next day. He found a bottle of cognac, had two full glasses, and blacked out.

The next morning, he got up, had shots of espressos and went to work. What followed were more weeknights when he couldn't sleep and weekends when he did nothing but. He worked hard at work and the gym, doing everything he could to keep from slipping into that hollowness he sometimes experienced, the dark hollowness that threatened to swallow him up. The proverbial wolves were baying at the door, the compounding of all the other losses he'd experienced before, harbingers of more losses yet to come.

Then he met Lili.

35

Alice opens the bathroom door to catch the sight of Lili draped across the tiny sofa, long legs dangling over the armrest. She's looking at her phone while munching on a pastry, paying no attention to the crumbs falling on and around her.

"Help yourself to Rou Song Xiao Bei," Lili waves a hand at a pink box on the table. "Who were you talking to?"

"A friend," Alice says, picking up a quivering Pork Floss Baby and taking a tentative bite—it's a cake filled with mayonnaise sauce and rolled in soy sauce and sugar-infused pork cooked down to crunchy fibers, flecked with bits of seaweed. The disparate ingredients explode in the mouth and hit half a dozen tastes and textures at once. She's unsure if she loves it or hates it, so she puts it down and files it away as one of the strangest things she has ever had.

"It's weird to talk to people in the bathroom," Lili says, licking her hand like a cat with her paw.

Weirder to be talking with the wife while the mistress hangs about, Alice thinks. She takes the chair opposite Lili. "I may know where Deckard is."

Lili pops her eyes at her and waits.

"He's somewhere in Sichuan."

"That's great!" Lili starts to tap on her phone. "Let's leave first thing in the morning. I'll book us tickets. Which city?"

"It's out in the boonies. We'll have to get to Chengdu first, then figure out how to get there."

"Alright. There's a 9:25 a.m. flight…"

"No. Let's take the train."

"But it's much faster to fly."

Alice sighs. "I've got aerophobia. Flying is difficult for me. So, I'd like to take advantage of the train system here as much as possible. Really, you don't have to come along."

"But I want to."

"Deckard might not want that. He was pretty explicit about not wanting people to go look for him. I'm going against his wishes, but I don't care if he gets mad at me."

"I don't, either."

"I hate to sound dramatic, but I have the feeling someone is out to get him. This could be dangerous." Just thinking about it leaves Alice with a sinking sensation, like turning into a dark alley and finding oneself in a bad part of town. Except there are no real bad parts of towns here anymore, are there?

"All the more reason for me to go—you might need my help; he does too."

"Why would he?"

"There's a project we've been working on."

Funny that *she's never mentioned this before.* "What project?"

Lili leans back. "I'm not sure he wants others to know about it."

"He doesn't want a lot of things, does he? If you want to come with me, you need to tell me everything you know."

Lili reaches for another cake, takes a big bite, and chews for a long time. Then she takes a big gulp from a tall cup of boba tea, sucking up half of the tapioca balls from the bottom of the cup, leaving Alice to marvel at the metabolism of youth. Fortified by all that sugar, Lili looks up at the ceiling and says, "Deckard has a secure USB key with some important documents on it. He's forgotten the password, so he asked me to help him figure out the password."

Alice squints at her. "But he's a whiz at this sort of thing. What, are you more of a hacker than he is?"

"No! It's one of those secure USB keys that's password protected; you only get ten tries. If you fail on the tenth try the device self-destructs. He hasn't had much luck cracking the password. He's only got a few tries left, so he has to be careful not to waste them. He thought I might be able to help him jog his memory—the password has something to do with Wu Ying."

"How would you do that?"

"This is a little embarrassing, so promise you won't laugh," Lili says, giving Alice a sheepish look. "You know the Neuromersion headsets? He would program it in memory recovery mode and put it on. I would pose for him and he would look at me through the goggles, while electrodes on the headset sent out electric pulses to stimulate his brain for memory recovery."

A barking laugh escapes Alice, who immediately clamps her hands over her mouth. The situation and imagery are laughable, even though she knows the technology isn't entirely crackpot—scientific studies have shown that transcranial magnetic stimulation can indeed improve memory. But to retrieve a specific password he has forgotten? By watching Lili, who looks like Wu Ying? That sounds like science fiction. She can't help wondering if it was just a ruse to get Lili posing for him—with or without clothes on? Does it matter? They're two adults in a relationship. Albeit one of them is very young.

"He had a photo of her in one of those old-fashioned button-down white shirts. So he got one made for me and asked me to wear it during our 'password recovery sessions.'" Lili continues primly as if having read Alice's gutter mind. "I even had to cut my bangs in a dumb way to look more like her. But we weren't successful. He wasted some tries then sort of gave up on the whole thing. But I think I figured out a way to get back on track—I've done something big for him."

"What did you do?"

"Don't want to get into it now. I'd rather he be the first to find out."

"O-kay. What kind of documents were on the USB?"

"No idea," Lili says nonchalantly. She takes another gulp of the boba tea and masticates on the pearls like a cow chewing cud.

Alice doesn't buy it. How can Lili possibly not be curious? "C'mon, if you want to come with me, you've got to trust me," she says.

"I do trust you. So you should trust me when I say I don't know—because he wouldn't tell me," Lili says through her sticky teeth. Her annoyance seems genuine: things on a need-to-know basis are out of the purview of the young girlfriend; she only needs to sit and be a Wu Ying model. Alice wonders if the documents have something to do with the bitcoins. But if Lili has no knowledge of it as she claims, Alice doesn't want to be the one to tip her off.

"There's something I've been wondering," Lili says. "This Wu Ying character, she moved after the second year of high school, right?"

Alice nods.

"Before that, you all tried to go to Beijing. The truck broke down, so you never got there. I get the sense that something else happened to Deckard on that trip, but he doesn't want to get into it. You were there; what happened?"

Alice exhales. "Something did. But what it was, I'm not exactly sure, either. This is what I remember."

36

June, 1989

Cat and Aining stared at the gleaming black phone on the metal desk the way a bomb squad examined a bomb. At least there was only one curling tail of a wire coming out of it, so there was no question as to which wire they would have to cut, Aining thought drolly. She wanted to share the joke with Cat, but the fretful look on Cat's face stopped her. This was not the right time for that.

For them to reach this phone was no small feat. They had walked for hours to get here, gotten lost a couple of times and found their way by asking various strangers for directions. They came from Laijiachun, the village of the Lais. This was Caojiachun, the village of the Caos, a clearly more prosperous place. There were several newer buildings along a short street, including a flat government building with a telecommunications office that housed this telephone. For three yuan, they could call anywhere in the country for ten minutes, explained the clerk who led them into the room. They paid and gave the clerk Cat's mom's work number for her to patch the call through.

Aining sighed. "Are we really going to do this? There's no turning back."

"We have no choice," Cat said.

Aining had to agree. Because they had little clue as to what to do. So now they had to, baby-like, turn to the only adult who would do whatever she could to help them. In doing so, they would acknowledge how young, inexperienced, and foolish they were. Kids who made messes of things and had to be bailed out.

The phone rang, startling them both. Cat picked up and spoke into it. "Hello. May I please speak with Dr. Huang Qingcheng?"

The person on the other side was loud. "Is this Maomao?"

"Yes, yes, it's me," Cat answered to her baby name with a catch in her voice. "Is that Auntie Zhao? How are you? Is my mom there? Could I please speak with her? Thank you."

It was one of those things about Cat that Aining had always been impressed with, the ease with which she talked on the phone. Even now, Cat spoke politely with an even tone rather than shouting like so many adults were wont to do, a dead giveaway that they seldom used the phone. Cat had plenty of practice. When her mom first gave Cat her work number, Cat would call during recess, using the phone at the little store next to the school. For five cents a pop, she would report to her mother various trivialities: that she had worn her new leather shoes and forgotten to bring gym shoes for PE class; that she wanted to have luffa soup for dinner, so she would pick up some tender luffas at the market after school; that she would go to a photography exhibit at the Veterans' Club so would be home late, and would not pick up the luffas after all. Eventually the calls tapered off because they were depleting her allowance fast and because her mom had asked her to stop bothering her at work. Aining's own mother had a phone, a direct line at her apartment in Alabama, although Aining had never called it. Calls to the U.S. had to be made from the Central Telephone Office downtown and cost a fortune. They exchanged letters instead, somewhat formally and focused on important matters such as exam grades and changes in weather. Her mother never knew what she wore to school or wanted for dinner.

After a short silence, Dr. Huang came on the line. "My treasure! It's good to hear your voice! I've missed you so much."

"Mama," Cat said, choking up as she shook her head vigorously.

"Is everything alright?" Dr. Huang sounded alarmed.

At that, Cat started to bawl.

Aining batted away the desire to cry herself—now was not the time. She gently took the phone from Cat and spoke into it. "Auntie Huang, it's me, Aining."

"Where are you calling from? What's happening? Why is Maomao crying?"

"We're outside Jinan. We've run into some trouble here. The truck broke down."

"Oh, what rotten luck... Where's Qian? I'm sure he'll take care of it... I've spoken with his coworker who was a former patient of mine. Said he's got a good head on his shoulders. Is he there? Can I talk with him?" So Dr. Huang was not a fool. She'd done her due diligence before entrusting her precious daughter to a total stranger.

"No, Qian's gone to Jinan to get replacement parts. The thing is, Shen Weiguo has disappeared."

"What do you mean, disappeared?"

"We haven't seen him. Can't find him anywhere. We went to look for him all day yesterday; last evening we went to the woods. But we had to come back because Guihua was having stomach pains—she's pregnant. Then this morning..."

"Wait. Slow down. Who's Guihua? Go back to the beginning and tell me everything. Don't skip over any details."

Aining leaned back. Where was the beginning? She decided to start at the point where the truck broke down. How they got to the village. How Old Lai and his niece Guihua took them in. The next morning, Qian went to Jinan on a borrowed bike. Weiguo wasn't there to see him off. When later on he wasn't there to partake of breakfast, the girls wondered out loud if he'd gotten up. No, Junhu said, he didn't think Weiguo slept in the house at all last night.

Then where was he?

Nobody knew. There wasn't anything else to do anyway, so they set off looking for him.

At first, it was just a diversion, a rather aimless search between a hike and a meander. They checked in trees specifically. They went up to the little hilltop behind the village, which offered a good view. They scanned carefully at the fields below, hoping to catch sight of Weiguo lolling about. Instead they only saw a few farmers in wide-brimmed hats working in the fields. They came down the hill and went to ask the farmers if they'd seen a teenage city boy. No one had. By mid-afternoon, when there was still no sight of him, they were getting properly worried.

It was Wu Ying's idea to go back to the village and knock on doors. Those who answered gave them curious looks and shook their heads. They went back to Old Lai's house, hoping to find Weiguo mocking them with a smirk on his face. Alas, no such luck.

After that they spiraled out from the village, going in bigger and bigger circles to make sure they didn't miss anything. It was about five o'clock when they reached the woods. There was still plenty of daylight left. Looking at the dense thicket of growth, however, one could easily imagine getting lost in there. So they returned to Old Lai's house once more, telling their hosts that they were looking for Weiguo and asking for help.

If Old Lai was displeased by the trouble his guests stirred up he didn't show it. The night before, Qian had pushed a fistful of cash into Old Lai's hands to cover food and lodging. The kids were Old Lai's charges now. It was, however, impossible for Old Lai to join them on the search because of his leg problems. Guihua, who was back to help with dinner prep, said that she knew the trail through the woods well and could take them.

They ate quickly, then set off. The sun was setting and mosquitoes were out in force. Guihua had the foresight to give them fans made of woven leaves when they left the house, so they fanned at the bugs while calling his name in unison every thirty paces or so. By the time they reached the woods, dusk was falling around them. Soon they had to turn on an oil lamp. When they called out, the only responses were frogs croaking, crickets trilling, and moths sizzling as their powdery wings hit the lamp.

They went for miles along a creek. Guihua stopped to drink from the creek a few times, which the city kids refused to imitate for fear of parasites despite Guihua assuring them it was alright because it was "clean, living water." She pointed out fireflies winking in the distance, a sight that would be worth pausing and admiring had the circumstances been different.

They walked on. And on. Their energy was sagging. They called out Weiguo's name less and less frequently.

Then—this part Aining omitted in telling Cat's mom because she thought it was irrelevant—as mosquitoes buzzed around them, Junhu took Aining's hand by surprise. She'd not held hands with a boy since preschool. Did Junhu see Weiguo and Wu Ying holding hands the day before and somehow thought it was worth imitating? Was hand-holding catching? Did she want this? Was she supposed to feel happy? Aining had no definitive answers. She liked Junhu alright, but just not in that way. After a while, she felt an urge to withdraw, though she wasn't sure if it was the proper thing to do—was a hand freely recallable like a kung fu novel on loan? Or was it more like fifty cents, once given out, should be considered a gift and never be asked back? She couldn't decide. Then Junhu said something about how dark it was; only then did she understand that he was afraid. And she was, too. With that understanding, they continued to clutch each other's slightly moist hands, out of need for security, like babies clutching soft blankets.

At some point, Guihua called for a break. They should have realized that something was amiss: Guihua had been very quiet, not her bubbly self. "Ah," she said with considerable distress as she sat down on a rock.

"What's wrong?" Aining asked, lifting the oil lamp close to Guihua's face. Even in this light she could tell Guihua's coloring was wrong, dark red like pork liver. Rivulets of sweat were running down her hair along her nape. The front of her shirt was damp.

"My tummy hurts... It's the baby, I think."

But how could it be? People always said "nine months of pregnancy." Guihua had told them she was about six months along, her bump visible but not huge. Could the baby come this early? The friends looked beseechingly at Cat, the doctor's daughter. Would she know what to do if Guihua had to give birth right here in the woods? Even if she did, they would need stuff. Yet they had nothing. Wouldn't even be able to boil water, which seemed essential in all the birth scenes in movies. And there was also the other "water" that needed to "break"—something inside the woman's body, Aining dimly recalled from the same movies. When she asked Guihua about this, Guihua shook her head weakly. Was that good? Did that mean the baby wasn't going to come out? Nobody had any idea, including the expectant mother herself. One thing, for sure, they needed to get back. Quickly.

They looped one of Guihua's arms around Junhu's neck and the other one around Wu Ying, who was the tallest among the girls. Aining took the lamp and walked in front of them. Guihua moaned softly for a while. The pain lessened sometimes, and she would go quiet, but then it would start again, and she would be back to moaning. After some time, Aining and Cat relieved Wu Ying and Junhu. They did not last nearly as long, for Guihua was a solid girl.

When they finally got back to the village, the pain had miraculously dissipated for good. Should they take her to a hospital? they asked Guihua's mother-in-law. There was no need, the older woman replied. It was just a false labor—as long as there was no bleeding and the baby was still kicking, she was all good. They left Guihua's house with the sincere hope that the mother-in-law's claim that country women were much hardier than city women was true.

Exhausted, they went to sleep. When the morning came and there was still no sign of Weiguo, Cat and Aining made a decision and asked Old Lai where they could get to a phone. And here they were.

"How did Weiguo seem when you last saw him?" Dr. Huang asked.

"He was acting a little bit funny," Aining said. Maybe more than a little bit. He was more wired and agitated than she had ever seen him, or anyone, really.

Cat, who had stopped crying by now, stuck her face over the mouthpiece. "At first we thought he was just mad about not being able to go to Beijing. Then he started to act really weird. Said a bunch of nonsense about us being abduction targets and something about how he could channel Chairman Mao—he's lucky we're no longer in the Cultural Revolution—could have been a deadly offense!"

"Did he—did you all—have enough to eat and drink that day?"

The girls looked at each other. Aining licked her own chapped lips. She suddenly realized how thirsty she was, so much that her head hurt. It had been hours since they last had anything to eat or drink. "We didn't eat much all day. Guihua made us noodles for dinner, but Weiguo hardly ate anything. I don't think he drank much water either."

"So he might have been dehydrated. And possibly experiencing confusion from low blood sugar. It could be dangerous—you need to find him as soon as possible. Have you talked with the local police?"

"No."

Dr. Huang paused for a second, then barked out orders like she was treating an emergency patient. "Go find a policeman. Make him help you look for Weiguo. If anyone finds him, get him to drink sugar water mixed with salt first, then soft food like porridge. Take him to a clinic for some IV fluids if possible. I'll go talk with Weiguo's parents. Aining, you are neighbors, right? Give me their address. We'll come as soon as we can. What's the name of the village and how do we get to it?"

Dr. Huang and Auntie Liu arrived at the village around nine o'clock at night, their hair wild and eyes bloodshot. At the sight of them, Aining took note of the real difference between adults and children—adults had resources. Without train service, Dr. Huang found a former patient who worked for the airline and was able to get them to

Jinan on a circuitous flight via Xi'an. They hired a motortrike to get here.

By then Weiguo had been found. The lone policeman in Caojiachun rounded up a bunch of locals to carry out the search. They eventually found Weiguo by a pond behind a pig pen, which the earlier search party had somehow missed. He was naked, filthy, covered in scratches and red swellings of mosquito bites—apparently, he had jumped into the pond in an attempt to escape the swarm. Luckily the water was only waist deep and he was able to crawl out. He was raving, combative, but thankfully weak. He tried to run when they came for him but tripped and fell over. They carried him out, then put him on a flatbed cart, on which he lay shaking like a leaf in the wind. They debated whether to tie him to the cart so he wouldn't run away and decided he was too weak to do so anyway. There he remained, under the eaves of Old Lai's house, covered in a blanket, muttering to himself while the friends ministered sugar and salt water and kept watch.

Auntie Liu burst into tears when she saw him. But she dried her eyes immediately and went about feeding him porridge and putting ointment on his bites.

"He's lost balance in his qi," Old Lai said. "We all have negative qi and positive qi inside; when one overwhelms the other, the imbalance messes up the whole body. The yin and yang become disrupted, the circulation of qi and blood stall, the organs and meridians become misaligned—"

"He's just dehydrated," Dr. Huang cut him off. As a Western medicine doctor, she had little regard for this kind of mumbo jumbo. "We're going to take him to the hospital and get some fluids into him. He'll bounce right back."

"Thank you for taking care of him and all the other kids," Auntie Liu said, handing an envelope with cash in it to Old Lai. "But please, there is no need to mention this to anyone."

"That's right, this qi business makes everyone sound crazy. And that goes for all of you, too," Dr. Huang said, looking sternly into the eyes of the children one by one. "You all got sick with food poisoning;

Weiguo is sicker than everyone else and has to go to the hospital. Anything more, you'd get yourself into big trouble."

The moms took Weiguo to a hospital in Jinan that night. The rest of the kids remained at Old Lai's. The next morning, the moms sent two motortrikes for them. They met up at Jinan Hospital, where Weiguo had been given IV fluids and sedatives. He was asleep when they arrived. There was no problem with getting train tickets going south, so besides Weiguo and his mom, the rest of them returned to Nanjing Saturday evening, stinking and exhausted and hungry, their parents none the wiser.

Monday, June 5, was an ordinary day at school. The other kids in their class scratched at flea bites, stabbed the agricultural studies dodgers with envious looks, and goaded them with questions. The dodgers' responses were muted and concerted: It took nearly a week to get over the severe food poisoning, so agricultural studies might have been preferable. Weiguo was so sick that he had to be hospitalized. He would hopefully return the following week.

That evening, Aining and her dad were having dinner in front of the TV as usual. Aining had put too much salt in the tomato and egg dish. Ba didn't complain, but she could tell he was reluctant to eat it. As they trudged through the disappointing meal in silence, something unexpected happened: the seven o'clock news came on. Anchors Du Xian and Xue Fei were both wearing black as if attending a funeral. The color contrasted starkly with their pale, strained faces. Instead of the usual cheerful introduction, they took turns reading out the headlines in flat tones, their eyes downcast as if someone off-screen was holding a cudgel over them.

Then the program cut to a screen with no videos, just the words, "The martial law troops suppressed the counterrevolutionary riot and entered Tian'anmen Square." Du Xian read descriptions of how the troops were attacked and the litany of ghastly acts committed against them: rioters hit the soldiers and bystanders with bricks and sticks, several soldiers were beaten to death, one of the bodies was hung on railings, a military truck was set on fire and a dozen soldiers suffered burns; numerous tanks, trucks, armored cars, and buses were destroyed.

Aining was stunned. Was this what they had missed? Riots? Tanks? Fires? Beatings? Killing of soldiers?! She desperately wished she could run out and find Weiguo to make sense of all this. What had happened? How could the students, who were demonstrating peacefully the whole time, suddenly turn into rioters? How could life go back to the way it was? Only Weiguo was still on soft food in the hospital in Jinan. Chances were he was completely oblivious to all this.

"That doesn't sound so good," Ba said evenly, the way he usually did in response to terrorist attacks or industrial accidents or police suppression of striking workers that were common occurrences in the foreign news segment. He picked up a piece of egg, chewed as he gave Aining a rueful smile. "No point wasting food," he said.

THE NEXT DAY, Teacher Mike didn't show up for the English conversation class. Teacher Huang took over and turned it into a regular English class. She told them that Teacher Mike had a family emergency and had to return to America. No one ever saw him again.

37

The upshot of the long journey to Sichuan is the time Alice and Lili have together. When scrolling on the phone or staring out gets boring, they fall into conversation, chatting amiably as trees and houses fly past the train windows.

Lili is from Shengzhou, a place Alice has never heard of. China is full of such places, small cities with populations greater than that of San Francisco but barely register on the map.

Her father is an electrician and her mother had worked as a packager at a state-owned window factory until she had Lili. The one-child policy was still strictly enforced back then. To have her, her parents had to pay a hefty fine and her mother lost her job, a fact some of her family members, such as her brother and aunt, still like to remind her from time to time. It hadn't struck her until she talked with her coworkers about it just how unfair and mean such reminders were. All in all, though, her family was a loving one, and her life wasn't too bad aside from the fact her mom wasn't in very good health, so Lili had learned to look after her from a young age. Yes, she went into nursing because her family thought it would help her mom. Her brother, fourteen years her senior, went away for college when she was little, so for much of her life she'd lived as an only child.

She was short and skinny all the way through sixth grade. Then she grew thirty centimeters in two years and got boobs. Such a disquieting time it was, how she resented the way her body was changing, yet her relatives all exclaimed at how she'd blossomed. Boys started to vie for her attention. She received flowers and candy and other small presents each week and unending invitations to movies and karaoke—small-town boys are like that, her sister-in-law said contemptuously when Lili told her about all this during a visit. They would never do that in bigger cities, everyone being under so much pressure to study for school entrance exams and advance in life. The exception being Lili's brother, of course. That was how he got to where he was today, a rising star in government, already a vice director in his early thirties.

"Enough about me," Lili says, and turns to ask many probing questions concerning Alice herself, her husband and her children, which Alice answers thoughtfully. And what about her aerophobia? How did she get it?

Alice is surprised. Most people who learned about her affliction would politely assume it was a condition she was born with, like a genetic defect. Few have ever asked her about it the way Lili did, as if she'd caught it, like Covid, from the aerosolized droplets of someone sneezing at a party. She lets out a long breath, and when all the air is expelled from her lungs, she says quietly, "Alright, if you must know. This is something I haven't told many people."

38

August, 1989

"We are starting to board," a woman's voice announced over the loudspeaker. There was no need to mention the flight number or the destination, as there was only one plane sitting on the tarmac at the international terminal of Hongqiao Airport. People got up from their seats and moved toward the gate.

Aining stood up, too. Her dad put a hand on her shoulder. "We've got a few more minutes."

"Shouldn't we get in line?" Aining asked. Something years of scarcity had drilled into the population: When there was a line, one should stand in it as soon as possible so as not to miss out.

Ba glanced at her, then shifted his gaze to the ground. "I want to talk with you."

About what? she thought impatiently. Ba was never much of a talker. Besides, they would be on the plane for thirteen hours; they could do nothing but talk.

Ba took something out of his pocket and pressed it into her hand. She looked down at his boarding pass with the luggage ticket stapled to it, his passport, and an envelope with Mother's name written on it, then looked up in confusion. Something wasn't right about his chin. It was quivering. Then she saw his eyes, red and brimming with tears. One fat drop rolled down his cheek and he wiped it away with his palm.

"Ba, what's wrong?" she asked, scared. The only time she'd seen him cry before was at her grandmother's funeral.

"When you get to Atlanta, give the letter to your ma. And pick up my suitcases. I've packed them with your things."

"Why can't you do it? What happened to your stuff?"

He blinked, his voice barely audible. "I won't be going."

"What are you talking about? You want me to go by myself to America?" Aining asked furiously, a little too loud. A couple of people turned to watch them. This made no sense.

"We've practiced this. Your English is better than mine. You know how to ask for help. Ma has a friend with a car. They will pick you up at the Atlanta airport. You just need to be sure to make the transfer in Los Angeles…"

"No, why?" Why was Ba doing this after all that trouble of getting their passports and visas? Ma had found a job for Ba at a lab at her university, no easy feat in itself. When it came to getting the passports, his work apparently gave him some grief and he had to go around for weeks, begging up and down for letters, signatures, and stamps. And they'd had to travel to the consulate in Shanghai twice to get their visas—the first time in April they'd had the bad luck of drawing the cold blond immigration officer who was notorious for always denying people for "immigration tendency." The second time, in July, the kindly bearded man who stamped their papers actually smiled at Aining—he was about the same age as Ba; perhaps Aining reminded him of his own children. How elated she and Ba were, how sweet the soft serve ice cream they got to celebrate tasted. And there were the plane tickets, so expensive, costing nearly two months of Ma's stipend. All that effort. Why? She felt like crying and screaming at the same time, although neither would do her any good besides attracting more curious stares.

Ba took out a handkerchief and wiped his eyes. Then he blew his nose into it. "I wasn't planning on this," he said, sniffling. "I really thought I could go through with this. But then I realized I just can't..."

She was quick to catch his lie. "Then why did you pack your suitcases with my things? And the letter?"

"I don't mean today." He swallowed. "Confucius has a saying, 'When the parent is alive, the son does not travel afar.' You will understand when you are older..." He took her hand—his was hot to the touch, hers icy.

She shook herself free. Now! She wanted to scream. She needed to understand it now! What's this nonsense about Confucius? Nainai had already passed but Yeye was healthy and doing just fine; he could take care of himself for a year, the amount of leave she and Ba had gotten from her high school and his university, respectively. They would get really good at English in that time. Then Ma was going to finish her PhD and all three of them would come back together. Everything would return to the way they were, except they would have seen America and would speak excellent English. That was the deal. Why would he back out of it now? It didn't matter; she needed to persuade him with reason. She bit down on her lip and focused on the pain. A few seconds went by. When the blood that rushed to the top of her head receded, she said, "A year will go by fast. You said so yourself. We can do anything for a year, especially if it's just learning English and living in America." She tried to sound reasonable and convincing, but the wrenching look on her father's face made her feel like she was patching a breached dam with mud.

He hugged her and kissed her hair. She couldn't remember the last time he did this—probably not since she was still light enough to be carried. Her forehead was dampened by his tears. He whispered, "Do not tell anyone this before you get there: your mother is not coming back. She'll explain everything to you later. If anyone gives you a hard time about me not being on the flight, just tell them I got sick."

She tried to absorb this. From the corner of her eye, she could see a vein on his neck pulsing, pulsing. Could Ma just do that, not come back? The university would let her? America would?

"What about me?" she asked. "Do I stay with Ma or come back in a year?" She immediately caught the fallacy of her question—if Ma wasn't coming back, why would she, unless she, too, turned back now? But returning home with Ba seemed impossible. Not after this. She would get on that plane to get away from all this deceit.

"You should stay. You will have lots of opportunities. Be good. Study hard, get into a good university, listen to your ma. Write. I love you."

She should have been astonished—he had never said that to her directly, not in so many words. His generation showed acts of love, never told it in words. She pushed him away and hissed, "I don't believe you. If you loved me, if you cared about me at all, you'd come with me." With that, she grabbed her carry-on bag that was stuffed to the gills with winter clothes and walked toward the gate without a backward glance.

WHEN ASKED about the empty seat next to her and her lack of a guardian, she told the flight attendant that her father had just been diagnosed with late-stage cancer and must remain in China as she went to America to fetch her mother. She couldn't explain how she came up with the lie, yet she fervently wished it were true. They must have believed her, for she sobbed quietly the whole flight. They brought her hot towels and extra snacks. She asked for water, which she badly needed to replace what she had lost in tears.

There was trouble at the port of entry. She had to break out her English-Chinese dictionary and finally understood that the issue was with her H-4 visa, which was dependent on her father's H-1B visa. She showed the officer her father's passport and visa and stuck to her story: this was a medical emergency; they found out about the diagnosis right before the flight but couldn't get hold of her mother on the phone. She held her breath as the immigration officer took her to a small office and dialed her mother's number. No one picked up—her mother was probably in Atlanta to meet her. The officer spoke with his superior. She returned their questioning gaze stoically with peach-swollen eyes. *I want my mother*, she kept repeating. Finally they relented and let her get on her transfer flight.

In Atlanta, Ma tore open the envelope and read the letter at the arrival gate, leaving Aining to awkwardly engage in small talk with the young couple who drove the car. Ma's face turned scarlet when she was done. Aining waited for Ma to either break down or blow up—she was unsure which direction Ma tended to lean toward, as she really didn't know Ma that well, having spent only a couple of years living together, during which, besides working full time, Ma spent a lot of time studying English and taking the GRE and applying to graduate schools. Neither, as it turned out. Ma seethed quietly and held Aining's arm in such a tight grip that the message was unmistakable: This was somehow Aining's fault.

Back at her apartment, Ma sat Aining down in front of the television and inserted a tape into the VCR. What came on were dim, jerky images of apocalypse: crowds streaming down a lamp-lit boulevard with popping sounds like firecrackers in the background; dark sky filled with smoke, buses on fire, people cheering; trucks driving by, accompanied by booming gunshots. They were just like the one driven by Qian but sans the cover and full of soldiers. The narrating voice was that of a British woman. Aining understood the gist of what was said: gunfire, the center of Beijing, Tian'anmen Square, gunfire from "lorries," which must have meant trucks. She asked Ma to pause the video. "Is this..."

Ma nodded. "BBC News on the Tian'anmen Massacre. The reason why I will not go back, and you shouldn't, either." She resumed the video.

The disheveled reporter appeared on camera, the background lit with hellfire. She told the audience that the troop had been firing into the crowd but people weren't turning back. She, too, could have been shot. Aining thought of the British woman, then of herself.

Chaotic scenes of people ferrying the injured on bicycle rickshaws. Of ambulances. Of people shouting "Animals!" at the soldiers. Of students singing the Internationale.

The reporter was back on camera, her sooty face contorted from stress and emotion. "After hours of shooting and facing a line of troops, the crowd is still here. They are shouting, 'Stop the killing,' and 'Down with the government.'" An ambulance with sirens on went by. "The young man in front of me fell dead," the reporter said, and the camera cut to a collapsed body on the ground—a Dead Person! On TV! Shot by soldiers! Aining's stomach, barely recovered from the roiling of travel, flipped again. The chicken and rice she'd just eaten rose sourly to her throat, threatening to erupt.

The camera cut to a scene at a hospital. People were running, including a shirtless man holding a woman whose head was completely wrapped in a cloth, her shirtfront soaked in blood. More hospital scenes of people rushing the injured in on makeshift stretchers. One man was carried in on a park bench. A woman was lying prone with a gaping wound to her side. The camera returned to the burning inferno on the street. The reporter said something about the fear and anger of the people on the street. "Tell the world, they said to us," the reporter said at the conclusion of the segment.

"If Ba could see this..." Aining said, hugging her knee.

"He doesn't want to know. He told me that when we talked on the phone."

Was that why he was in such a foul mood that day after he went downtown? Aining had thought perhaps he had gotten wind of the failed Beijing trip from one of the moms, and nervously waited for the rebuke, but he never said a word about it to her. Just fumed and banged the pots and pans extra loud while he fixed supper. He must have gone to the Central Telephone Office to call Ma to figure out the logistics of their travels and had explosive news lobbed at him like hand grenades.

"Is there someone else?" Ma asked suddenly.

"What do you mean?"

"Like, another woman."

Aining was completely taken aback. The idea seemed wild and

absurd. But, was there? She raked her brain and thought about that friendly auntie who always said hello to them at the station where grains were sold, or that soft-spoken graduate student whom she saw at Ba's office a couple of times, even her own math teacher, who mentioned once after the parent-teacher conference that Ba was rather young-looking? What about his coworkers? Their neighbors? Could any of them be the "other woman"?

"I don't think so," she said finally. "But why wouldn't he want to know what actually happened?"

"Because he's a fool. All we can do is forget about him and live the best we can on our own," said her unrelenting mother.

And that was what they did.

39

At the high-speed rail station in Chengdu, the driver at the head of the taxi line frowns when Alice gives her the destination.

"Why would you want to go there? There's nothing there. Why not stay in Chengdu? Lots to do here—great food; you can go see the two-thousand-year-old dam at Dujiangyan and baby pandas at the panda research base," says the rotund woman with spiky bleached hair. She has already pegged Alice and Lili as tourists.

Alice catches her breath. Such good questions. What could Deckard possibly be doing in such a place? And what are they doing here, with nothing but two numbers to go on? Inertia, perhaps—once she started, she just wants to keep going until the leads run out. She feels woefully inadequate for what is to come. Didn't Ben Franklin say failing to prepare is preparing to fail? She has the company of Lili, and between them four water bottles, two rain parkas, a box of biscuits and some peanuts. These count for something, don't they? And a trip without a guidebook is always more exhilarating. To step into the unknown is to be alert, to navigate with unprecedented focus and excellent peripheral vision. It must be how a bloodhound feels when following the scent trail.

The driver clears her throat, still waiting for a change of destination. Alice says simply, "We'll pay."

"No!" The woman shakes her head like a bristling hedgehog. "It's too far. Like, eight or nine hours. And all those dirt roads would destroy my car," she says, gripping the steering wheel protectively in case Alice tries to wrestle it away from her.

The car of the next driver in the line reeks of cigarette smoke, so Lili slams the door on him, sending the man into a fit of rage as he cusses at them in Sichuanese. The third driver is also disinterested as his shift ends in an hour. People in the line behind them are getting agitated. When Alice explains their predicament to the old security guard in a yellow vest, he leers and says in a huff, "You two, by taxi tonight? On those mountain roads? You'll end up dead in a ditch."

Remembering the dozing taxi driver she encountered in Shanghai, Alice sees the folly in her original plan. They return to the ticket counter to figure out a more sensible strategy that is easy to execute: the evening train to Puxiong, a basic inn by the train station for an overnight stay, then, at seven in the morning, a boxy cucumber green local train heading toward the heart of the Daliang Mountains.

UNLIKE ALL THE high speeds Alice has taken so far, the green train is uncrowded. Once they choose their seats, Lili immediately opens the window to release the stale air of bodily odors and other unsavory scents. That's one advantage these old trains have—windows that open. Passengers for such trains are not hothouse flowers but wild willows, cacti in the sun. Wind in the hair is most welcome.

At Hongfeng, four young women get on and take the seats behind Alice. One of them is in a traditional Yi outfit, with a square hat and black embroidered jacket with asymmetric front plackets. They chat in an incomprehensible, sing-song language.

Alice tries to learn a bit about the area on her phone. This place has been the territory of the Yi people historically. It's always been poor: the hilly landscape, poor soil, and ever-changing weather conditions make it difficult to farm. Given the conditions, one crop that did grow and brought in profits was opium. In the late eighties, the region became a part of the illegal drug trafficking route from the Golden Triangle region. Heroine brought spikes of drug abuse, crimes, and the spread of AIDS. The government has cracked down on illegal drugs and poured money into poverty reduction in recent years. Things have gotten better, but problems are hard to eradicate and the region remains one of the poorest in China. The Hans like to claim that the Yis are impoverished because they're lazy and resistant to change. Of course, compared with the work ethic and adaptability of the Han Chinese, the rest of the world are slackers and reactionaries.

According to the Chinese Internet, in the 1950s, the poor and wretched local Yi people welcomed the new Communist government wholeheartedly. The takeover was touted by the Communist Party as liberation rather than annexation: The caste system and slavery that still existed in the traditional Yi society were abolished; the government brought schools and transportation to the villages. All this sounds too pat, too much like the kind of propaganda Alice was used to hearing growing up. Knowing what the government had done to the Tibetans and Mongolians back then, she wonders if there is more to the story.

A bit more digging with the help of VPN and Google, a more bloody counter-narrative emerges: In 1955, the government confiscated private property and set up class divisions. The locals didn't like that, and some clans put up resistance. The government sent troops to put down the rebellions. More conflicts erupted, and more troops were sent in. According to official records, between 1955 and 1957, there were over four thousand conflicts of various sizes. Once, a hundred thousand locals took part in a fight. The government ordered nearly a hundred and thirty thousand troops to the region, killing over fifty thousand locals. The facts of the armed suppressions were corroborated by the Chinese Internet, albeit characterized as the government putting down rebellious slave owners and turning the Yi from a backward slavery society into a modern socialist one.

With the destruction of familial clans and the lack of a dynamic leader like the Dalai Lama to turn the world's attention onto them, the Yi society became atomized and impoverished—a familiar page from the Communists' playbook, and indeed the playbook of powerful races against the weak ones the world over.

Alice's research is interrupted by the conductor, who has come around to collect money for the tickets—no online ticket orders necessary on this train. "This is one of the last slow local trains in the country," she tells them as she collects thirty-two yuan for two tickets, less than five dollars. Stopping every ten to fifteen minutes to gobble up passengers like a hungry caterpillar, the train is a lifeline that connects these villages to the outside. Train 5633 has been running for over fifty years now, fares are kept low since it's the commuter train for the locals. Alice notes that the seats look brand new. "We just got an upgrade a couple of months ago. Go check out the themed specialty cars when you get a chance," the conductor urges.

So she and Lili walk down the corridor together, swaying like drunkards. The health car is empty save for the first aid mannequin torso propped up on a metal table. A glass front cabinet is stocked with Band-Aids and such. They check out the wares in the market car, which has a seatless area in the front that allows vendors to lay out sacks of produce: fresh toona leaves tied in neat bundles, a fishy-smelling vegetable with white stems and sparse mint-like leaves, turnips, mushrooms, pale looking strawberries. Lili buys a bag of small cherries for ten yuan, which are so tart that she ends up feeding them to some ducks and chickens kept in the large item car. The poultry are stuffed in bamboo carriers, arranged to face out like baskets of flowers. The owners, a couple of wizen-faced farm women, laugh as the birds fight over the fruit tossed on the floor.

When they get to the student car, the train has already stopped and a group of kids in school uniforms are just getting on. Alice wants to get a picture of them studying on the train to show her children—look how studious these kids are in such difficult conditions! But instead of sitting at the built-in desk along the windows to study as they are supposed to, one boy grabs books from a shelf at the back of the car to build a wall around the perimeters of a desk, then starts a kind of air hockey game with his buddies using folded squares of paper.

Lili takes selfies and videos through all this. A worker passing with a broom stops her. "Don't do that. And don't post anything online," the man warns.

Lili puts away her phone without arguing.

"Why?" Alice asks, perplexed.

The worker gives her a meaningful look without answering. Alice has seen that look before, the one Chinese people like to use that says, *You know*. Only she doesn't.

"Why?" Alice insists.

The worker shakes his head at her denseness. "Up above don't like it," he says, sweeping a potato chip on the floor into the dustpan. "Just don't do it."

Who is "up above"? The gods? Alice turns to Lili. "What's that all about?"

"He probably doesn't want me to take pictures of things that are not good."

"Like what?"

"Who knows." Lili shrugs. "Maybe there are still drug deals going down on the train." She takes out her phone again to take a picture of several men smoking in the pocket between cars. The conductor's warning, having neither logic nor consequence, only needs to be complied with in his presence.

~

"THE GIRL in the Yi outfit is getting married." Lili elbows Alice as they get back to their seats.

"You can understand them?" Alice says in surprise.

"They're speaking a mix of Sichuanese and local dialect. I had a neighbor from Sichuan growing up, so I understand some."

Lili turns back and says something to the young women in Sichuanese. They reply in accented Mandarin, eyeing Alice to let her know it's for her benefit. They are lovely girls with smooth, sun-kissed skin and ivory-colored teeth. They and Lili make fast friends. Soon the five young women are giggling and talking over each other like a nest of baby birds.

The one sitting by the bride-to-be is her sister, the other two are cousins. The three younger girls are still in high school. The bride has graduated and is marrying a carpenter. They are on their way to visit a few tailors to check out the workmanship of the bridal outfits. After the wedding, the bride and groom plan to move to Guizhou for work. They don't want to have kids for a few years but will get cats. The other girls aren't sure about finishing high school—the college entrance exam is hard and there's less guarantee of a good job after graduation these days; it seems easier to find work in Chengdu or Guizhou. Lili puffs out her cheeks at this. "Just don't go into nursing."

They talk about the wedding plans and soon Alice and Lili find themselves invited. "It'll be nice-nice," says one cousin, laughing. "But you can't post it on social media—we don't want you to get into trouble!" Someone in the neighboring village, she explains, had a wedding recently. The whole village was invited, including some visitors. One of them posted videos of the wedding on Douyin, which somehow upset some local officials. He had to delete the video eventually.

"But why?" Alice asks, mystified.

The girls titter. Again, it's that look again—*you know*. This time, Lili presses for an answer, too.

"It was very low budget," the cousin says.

"So? What's wrong with a low-budget wedding?" Alice asks. Her own wedding was low budget and considered unbecoming by her mother: since no one offered to help pay for the wedding, they had a city hall ceremony followed by a lunch at a dim sum restaurant.

"The guests were sitting on the dirty floor, eating sour cabbage and tofu soup. It looked terrible," the sister says.

Alice finds the censorship offensive, but also reckons that's why she likes to use Weibo as opposed to other social media. Because the Chinese social media companies endeavor to present a censored, positive online world. There is a cost, however, to the content creators as well as consumers, to be stuck in Disneyland forever.

The bride adds, "Xi Dada was supposed to be coming for a visit soon. Our region used to have the label of poverty. Now that label has been removed, the video made the officials look bad. So the police found the man who took the video and took him to 'drink tea.'" She uses the euphemism for police interrogation.

"What happened to him?"

"He had to sign a letter of pledge, to only spread positive energy online in the future."

Lili rolls her eyes at the story, but Alice understands how a Xi Jinping visit might prompt any local officials to act sycophantically. In her own city of San Francisco, the government had scrubbed the downtown streets clean of graffiti and homeless people in anticipation of APEC. "San Francisco cleans up for Xi, why not for thee?" The newspaper headline inquired. But least the San Franciscan officials weren't asking vloggers to take down videos. There's the China the world is used to seeing, the one with humming factories and gleaming high rises, cities connected by freeways and subways and high-speed railroads, zipping toward economic progress, Chinese socialist-capitalist style. Underneath that glossy veneer, however, there are vast networks where dirt accumulates and things run according to their own rules. *Deckard may have slipped between these two Chinas, and I may be slipping down with him*, Alice thinks.

The conversation moves on to the groom. The bride blushes as the younger girls wonder out loud if they, too, could have the good fortune of finding someone who doesn't smoke or drink, is 170 centimeters tall, makes over five thousand yuan a month, whose family can afford the bridal price and is without a lot of siblings to take care of.

Lili listens with a wry expression on her face. She has told Alice her take on marriage. Lili has witnessed firsthand what happens to those who live in small towns and get married early. They live the kind of lives you can see all the way from here to the grave—marriage, kids, take care of the kids, work an easy job or be a stay-at-home mom if the husband makes enough money, then someday take care of the grandkids. And mahjong. She isn't going to let that happen to herself. Her plan has always been to get out of Shengzhou and live in Shanghai like her brother. To that end, she has had to make many compromises along the way.

"What would be marriage material for you?" Alice asks Lili offhandedly.

Lili answers without thinking, "Someone with ambition."

"That's ambition itself," Alice says, impressed. She'd never thought of that herself. Henry has the ambition of a two-toed sloth, but that's part of his charm. And Alice doesn't have great ambitions herself. Just a good job, a nice house, kids in decent schools, the kind of life Lili would find boring. But Deckard is another matter. Always trying, always striving for change, in himself, in others, in the world. It heartens Alice to know the young woman is drawn to Deckard not just for his money and sophistication but for something more innate. But would Deckard want to get married again so soon after ending things with Fei? If marriage is what Lili is after, she'll probably end up disappointed—but what is a little disappointment, when the path of youth to maturity is paved with it?

Lili gets up to go to the bathroom. When she returns, she whispers to Alice, "Don't look, but there's a guy in the back, two rows from the door, in a black T-shirt. Does he seem out of place to you?"

Alice doesn't know how to tell without looking, so she gets up and heads toward the bathroom herself. The man in question is in his mid-twenties. Medium build, crew cut, a light blue mask covering his face, attention fixed on his phone. Nothing about him would have stood out had they been on a train from Shanghai. Here, however, the majority of passengers are villagers with swarthy complexions. In comparison, the man looks like he sits in an office most of the day. Maybe a civil servant paying a visit to a village? As she passes him, she intentionally bumps his elbow, then mumbles an apology. The man doesn't even look up. How can anyone be so engrossed in a game on his phone?

"Yes," Alice tells Lili when she returns. "Why do you care?"

"I think it might be the same guy who followed me and Deckard before. His hair looks different—it was longer before. But I'm pretty sure it's him," Lili says.

"That's some super recognition power," Alice says without conviction. Sure, Lili is very observant, but can anyone really recognize another person they'd only seen once at a distance and wearing a mask? It's understandable that Lili might be jumpy because of what happened. But what if she's right? What could he possibly want? Should they confront him or, as more in line with Alice's natural inclination, run away?

Lili's face is taut. "Let's get off at the next station," she says. "We'll go to another car and get off right before the door closes so he can't come after us." With that, she takes her carry-on down from the overhead rack and makes a show of searching for something inside. When she doesn't find whatever she's looking for, she takes Alice's backpack down and riffles through that, too.

Alice helps move the luggage into the aisle. As she straightens, she catches the man looking up at them. He drops his gaze when their eyes meet. *That does it*. Alice's pulse quickens. She has never been followed by anyone before. Logically, that doesn't bode well and she's worried about it. Yet there's something a little childishly thrilling in this, too, like she's a character in *Emil and the Detectives*. "He's onto us," she whispers to Lili.

The train pulls into the station. When the doors open, bleating sounds flood in. Out on the platform, dozens of goats are milling about, and a goat herder is prodding them with a long skinny bamboo pole. It would be a wonderful scene to watch had there not been some goon tailing them.

Lili turns around to have another exchange with the Yi women. They tell her the goats are about to get on the train—the last car is reserved for livestock.

"Want to go watch?" Lili asks.

"More than anything else in the world." Alice stands up and hoists her backpack on her shoulder.

"Just take your phone. Leave the bag. Keep a watch for us, would you?" Lili says loudly to the young women behind them. "We'll be right back."

Before Alice can ask what the plan is, Lili says to her sotto voce, "Don't worry. You got your passport on you? I'll take care of the bags."

Alice pads the inside pocket of her jacket and nods. Lili steers Alice toward the back door, giggling softly all the way. The man is still fixated on his game, actively not paying attention.

The goats are more interested in getting under the train than onto it. The goat herder smacks the animals on the butt with the stick and makes clicking noises at them. It's turning into an all-hands-on-deck kind of situation, with the conductor herself jumping off the train to help with goat wrangling. Seeing Lili taking a video, she yells, "Don't just stand there and watch! Do something to help!"

Alice doesn't know what she can do besides standing there and watching, bewildered, as the goat herder grabs the goat by the armpits—or whatever you call that spot on a goat—while the conductor carries its hind legs. Together they shove the goat on the train. That's when the two women find their uses—they can block the entrance to keep the goats that have already gotten on the train from jumping off. Most of the goats are docile; a tug on the horn or a pat on the butt is usually enough to get the animal moving out of the way. For any truculent individual, Lili puts her face really close to the goat and hisses to scare it off. "Careful, they bite!" the conductor cries amid all the pandemonium.

A few more passengers are clustering around the door at the end of the car to watch the spectacle. Alice catches a glimpse of the man in the black T-shirt. Crap, he's looking at them, and she feels like a deer caught in his headlight eyes. *Are they supposed to get off here? What if he comes after them?* Lili gives Alice a nod—she, too, has seen the man. *Follow me*, Lili mouths.

All the goats have finally gotten on, so has their herder. The conductor blows the whistle and jumps onto the train. The train starts to move, and the onlookers are turning back, including the stalker.

As the conductor reaches for the button by the door, Lili rushes up to her. "No, don't shut the door yet," she says, pulling on Alice's arm. "Get off, now."

She's got to be kidding—the train is already in motion and gathering speed. And what about their bags?

"Don't worry about your stuff. We'll get them. Go, now." With that, she shoves the conductor aside and jumps off the train and sticks the landing. She spins around, jumps and waves her arms like mad, her figure shrinking as the train picks up speed.

"Wait, what?" the conductor gestures wildly.

Alice braces herself against the door. How they would get their bags is the least of her concerns right now; she has to stay with Lili. But how? The train continues to speed up and the platform has ended. She has stopped breathing as her heart jumps up to her throat and her brain screams, "No!" She's on the verge of panic when the image of her kids leaping from the dining chair comes to her. Something from that image takes hold of her legs and feet. "Geronimo!" she shouts as she goes airborne. Her life—and the weeds and gravel underfoot—flash in front of her eyes. She miscalculates the velocity of her landing and stumbles into a rolling fall. A sharp pain shoots up her right ankle. When she takes stock of her body parts, however, miraculously nothing appears to be broken. In her peripheral vision, something flies out of a window up ahead and hits the ground with a thud, followed by another thud. The train is chugging faster and faster and soon disappears into the distance.

Lili runs over. "You did it! I knew you could!"

Alice shakes her head, her breath ragged. "I don't know how—I can't believe it—we jumped out of a moving train!"

"The slowest one in all of China, but still," Lili laughs.

True, it ain't the *Orient Express* and she ain't no Tom Cruise, but she'll tell her kids, you won't believe what Mama did, and I did it because of you. She gasps, the spasming muscles in her face shudder into a maniacal laugh as she tries to relive the moment of the jump.

When the adrenaline rush recedes, they inspect their belongings. Lili's suitcase has suffered a broken wheel, while Alice's backpack has narrowly missed a pile of goat droppings. Alice unzips her bag to get out the laptop. It turns on without trouble. She thanks Goddess for the extra padding in the laptop compartment of her bag and silently promises a five-star review later.

"Who threw out the bags?"

"The bride-to-be behind us. I gave her a little something," Lili says.

"I hadn't seen that," Alice says in awe. Once again, she has underestimated this clever girl—she herself can never think on her feet like that or completely trust a stranger to help—except she has trusted Lili and things have turned out alright so far. She asks, "Do you think the guy was following you in order to track down Deckard?"

Lili nods. "That seems pretty obvious. I wonder what he wants from him exactly. Kind of wish we had asked him."

"Guess we missed the train on that one," Alice says.

40

They follow the street next to the train station to the center of the town, such as it is. No eating establishment appears to be open at this hour. Wind rustles the tree tops, sending shivers down Alice's back. An old memory creeps up—she and her teenage friends walking down a desolate road after their truck had broken down. Old Lai and his pregnant niece Guihua—where are they now? Is Old Lai still alive? What happened to the village, plowed under to build the new freeway or developed into a rest stop? And the baby, if it lived, would be in his or her mid-thirties now. Tempus fugit, as they say.

They find a convenience store that still has lights on. An old lady in a canary-yellow bathrobe, like a character conjured out of a fairy tale, answers the door and invites them in. With efficiency and attentiveness that would surely astonish the most experienced concierge at any five-star hotel, the proprietress at this whistle-stop convenience store solves the women's needs for food (instant ramen and tinned fish), lodging (a semi-clean room in the back of her house), and a guide to take them to the GPS location the next day (her grandson Zuomu), all in the time it takes to heat up water to pour into their paper noodle bowls.

When summoned, the fifteen-year-old Zuomu is initially reluctant to get up early on a Saturday but becomes more interested at the prospect of two hundred yuan and the sight of Lili.

So it is they set off for the misty mountains at daybreak. As she and Lili bounce on the back of a little electric cargo trike on dirt roads, Alice keeps her anxieties about the lack of helmets and battery range to herself. They arrive a little past noon at the foot of the mountain, the top of which is likely the GPS location. Zuomu locks up the trike, and they commence the ascent on foot.

Zuomu turns out to be quite a chatterbox, which helps to distract from the rather tiring hike. They learn he is a typical left-behind kid, his parents being factory workers in Dongguan, so he is raised by his grandparents.

"Me too," Alice says, "except I lived in the city and my parents worked in the countryside."

"Really? I'll bet you didn't have to go to school on the train line," Zuomu says. He tells them about how his school is under constant threat of being shut down due to the lack of teachers, which, Alice observes, appears to be a problem rural China (too poor, too remote) and the San Francisco Bay Area (too rich, too expensive) have in common. When he learns Alice is from the U.S., he guesses that America is three times the size of Japan, then laughs at himself because he knows he's probably wrong. What he lacks in geographical knowledge, he makes up for in curiosity. He peppers the women with questions regarding the places they're from—Are there lots of guns and drugs in America? Are kids worried when they go to school? Does Shanghai have the tallest building in the world? Is it really as expensive to live there as people say? etc. To which Lili tries to answer for both of them and gives half-true answers aimed at messing with the kid (yes; yes, they are worried sick; no, just the tallest in China; yes, unbelievably, some people have to sell their kidneys to pay rent) and Alice doesn't bother to correct her.

Then he asks what's at the GPS location. Alice deflects gently and says they will see.

The trail is poorly maintained after the first few miles. They aren't too worried about being lost, however, as there is cell phone reception—this is a country where there are 5G towers on Mount Everest, after all. Perhaps that is the problem: In the modern world where one can no longer get lost, a deliberate act of disappearance is all the more strange. Alice's mind is back once again to the time when she and her high school friends had roamed the countryside looking for Deckard. Here she goes again. At least he had been found only marginally scathed last time, and his mishap may have prevented a much greater disaster from befalling them all. As an adult, she has finally come to grips with Deckard's situation back then—not mere dehydration, but possibly a psychotic episode. The fact he hasn't had any problems since, at least none Alice is aware of, gives her little comfort. People hide things, and there's much about him she doesn't know. What if he's holed up somewhere in the mountains, having another mental breakdown? Only their mothers won't be coming to their rescue this time. She, now a mother herself, has to be doing the rescuing. Will they be as lucky? What other calamities lurk around the corner?

At some point they come to a picturesque hanging bridge. Had it been easier to get to, city folks would have turned it into a popular photo spot for social media. They train their sights on the far side, take cautious steps on the planks, scream and laugh when the bridge sways, and somehow manage to cross it without falling into the thundering, muddy river.

The GPS location is indeed at the top of the mountain. They stand at the highest point, scanning the ground, trees, and rock outcroppings all around them for any signs of life. Not even a squirrel is in sight.

Lili and Alice look at each other. It's one of the possible outcomes, indeed the more likely one. What did they expect, a GPS location in the middle of nowhere? Heaving a sigh of disappointment, Alice slumps to the ground.

"What are you doing?" Alice asks when Lili begins walking about with her eyes downcast.

"You said the tracker was inside his shoe. So I'm looking for footprints. He wears Hokas for hiking."

At least one of us isn't so easily defeated, Alice thinks. She gets up and makes motions of scanning the ground as she walks in circles. She remembers Leo's handbook on tracking and regrets not having read it. She ought to take a greater interest in the interests of her children. Suddenly, she catches the sight of a shoe print that says REI on it, her heart skips a beat—*what, do they have a store here?*—only to realize it's her own.

They scan fruitlessly until Zuomu bounds toward them. Panting, he points at a boulder standing on the edge of the hilltop. "Over there."

Behind the boulder is a trail snaking its way down toward the valley on the other side of the mountain, where green fields are flanked by rows of beige houses with red roofs. A place to spend the night, with hot food and a bed! What an unexpected treat. The idyllic setting reminds Alice of the story of the Peach Blossom Valley, where a tribe of people hid from war and lived in peace and harmony for centuries, separate from the rest of the world.

"There's no way we'll reach it by nightfall," Lili says with a pout. She must be exhausted, this girl who claims she doesn't like to exercise for fear of getting overly muscular legs.

Alice doesn't see the harm in trying. Sleeping in the middle of the mountain isn't much different from sleeping up here. "Come, the journey of a thousand miles starts with a single footstep," Alice says. What a terrific language her mother tongue is, with a hackneyed proverb for every situation.

As luck would have it, they don't have to go all the way to the valley. About halfway down, they come across a hamlet they hadn't seen from the top. From this vantage point, things open up in front of them: a ribbon of river carves out a canyon between the mountains; peak after peak ripple away into the foamy white clouds. In the distance, a patch of dark mist is casting a local thunderstorm. Not a bad place to live, if one can handle the isolation.

Stepping into the village is like stepping back in time. Not just pre-industrial, but pre-historical: a few lean-tos are built into the side of the mountain, with mud walls and thatched roofs. Chickens dart in and out of bushes. A particularly curious hen follows them and clucks along the dirt path. Somewhere, a horse whinnies.

Zuomu calls out. Several urchins tumble out of the lean-tos, followed by a few adults. An older woman is wearing a black hair turban but everyone is dressed in T-shirts and regular pants. Like the farmers Alice had seen on the train, these men's and women's faces are deeply tanned, their clear eyes curious. A girl with missing front teeth approaches them, but when Lili bends down to talk to her, she runs off, tittering like a little chickadee.

Zuomu talks with the grownups in the local dialect. He turns around to report that someone is going to find the chief.

Alice imagines someone imposing like Sitting Bull, but the man who comes to greet them is diminutive, with mercurial eyes and two slashes of wrinkles across his cheeks where dimples once had been. He seems pleased to see Zuomu, and the two fall into an animated conversation, completely ignoring Alice and Lili.

A dinner invitation is issued. Alice's first instinct is to refuse—to eat these poor people's food, to take calories away from their mouths! It's unthinkable. Except her stomach begs to differ. It longs for something warm and salty—some kind of soup, with a little protein, some vegetables, and crusty bread. She accepts the invite and asks Zuomu to offer a cash gift in return, which is gladly accepted.

A woman comes running with a knife—Alice blanches, then realizes she's after a chicken, the spotted, curious one Alice had seen before. The woman grabs it by its wings, bends its neck backward, plucks some feathers off, and slits its throat with practiced ease. A boy runs up with a metal bowl to catch the squirting blood.

"The chief insists on a special treat," Zuomu says. When Alice expresses dismay at having the villager kill one of their few precious animals, he assures her despite being guests from far away, they're not getting the treatment reserved for the most honored guests, for whom the villagers would kill a pig or even a cow.

"Why not?" Lili asks.

"It is... traditional," Zuomu says diplomatically.

"Is it because we are women?" Lili snorts.

Zuomu says nothing, just sucks in his lips. He seems to know instinctively how not to provoke Lili's ire. His bossy grandmother has raised him right.

"A chicken is great," Alice says. She's already looking forward to whatever chicken dish the Yi cuisine might produce. She can't wait to tell her family about this unexpected close encounter with an indigenous people unspoiled by tourism.

They are shown to the chief's house, which is minimally furnished with a couple of stools and a fire ring. She vaguely recalls something she'd read about the Yi people—that they worship fire. Or is it water? No, definitely not water. They had only seen a single running spout for spring water the whole time.

Several kids come in to fill the fire ring with dry leaves and branches they dragged in. The chief lights a match and holds it to some dry leaves, which instantly catches and fills the room with smoke. Coughing, Alice and Lili excuse themselves to go outside.

The mustachioed Bagan, the oldest of the chief's sons, follows them, then takes them on a tour of the hamlet. A haphazard orchard on the hillside—walnut, peach, mulberry, Sichuan peppers, all of which are untrimmed and some bearing sparse fruit in various stages of ripeness. A flowering cactus more than a person tall is next to an open air pen with pigs and goats, which is next to a lean-to. Up higher inside the lean-to, a girl's face is peering down at them through a tiny window cut into the wall. Alice is reminded of the Chinese character 家 (jia, family, house), which depicts a roof with a pig living under it. Lili doesn't hide her disgust for the arrangement, especially its odors.

At dinner, the chief tells them, through Zuomu, that the government had built a housing compound at the foot of this mountain and offered units at a steep discount to all the hill villagers around here. Nice, brand-new apartments. Most of the villagers took up the offer and moved. But he turned them down for his entire family.

"Why?" Alice asks. She feels a bit uneasy, partly due to the probing nature of the question and partly due to the awkward seating arrangement: the chief, Zuomu, and the chief's three sons are sitting in one circle with stools, while Lili, Alice, and the chief's daughter and daughters-in-law are sitting in another circle on the ground to the side. Cushions don't seem to be a thing here. Alice has to twist her body to talk with the men.

The chief's answer surprises her—because they had already moved once.

The village used to be further down, close to the river. A few years ago, the government wanted to build a hydroelectric power station. They had to move or be flooded. So they abandoned the village they'd been living in for generations and came to this spot. Although not as good as their old home, it is a decent location sheltered from the wind and has a natural spring. They were able to plant some trees and cultivate a bit of land. If they moved to the housing compound, they would have to travel a long distance here to take care of their animals and the land.

While Zuomu is translating this, the chief's voice turns higher pitched, his face flushing with agitation. The interjections from his children fan the emotions higher. In the end, the men are all clenching their jaws and the women are glowering.

"Why do they seem so upset?" Lili asks.

"It was a difficult time for them," Zuomu says. "The chief didn't trust the government not to change their minds and make them move again. It was hard for them to argue with the government; the officials said he was unfit to be the chief, and the villagers who moved turned against him and his whole family. But in the end, they let them be."

"Good for you!" Alice says. The chief understands her endorsement, and his expression softens a bit.

Lili gives Alice a look, telegraphing her view on this: *Really? Whatever for? To live in this squalor?*

For their principles, Alice telegraphs back. To defend their way of life, such as it is. After generations of suppression, here is a family who have stood up to the government and won. Alice cannot fathom how difficult that must be, the pressure they faced, the courage required. Perhaps the chief descends from a generally cooperative clan. Perhaps the government had no designs on this little scrap of land; otherwise the whole family might have been chased off the mountain and forced to live in cookie-cutter housing. But might they be better off for that? Better sanitation; easier access to medical care and schools; a more prosperous, more urban, albeit less free life. Surely they have considered the trade-offs and chosen one over the other. Like the villagers in Peach Blossom Valley, the family decided to band together and stay away from civilization, even though the younger generation must have had some education as they all seem to speak some Mandarin. Their children are growing up and will need to go to school soon. For how much longer can they continue to hold out, to resist the siren songs of the modern world outside?

She wants to ask them all this and whether their clan was impacted by the military suppressions of the 1950s, but the family are completely absorbed in the meal. So she picks up a creamy roasted potato and bites into it. She has turned down the chicken because, in spite of the wonderful aroma, the bird is ash-covered and gritty looking, and also because the women's circle has received only one thigh and a wing, offered on a metal plate to the guests. Lili, however, has no compunctions and digs in. She peels off the skin and lifts strips of meat into her mouth. "You should try this; it's actually pretty good," she says happily, licking her fingers.

Through Zuomu, the chief asks Alice whether she is married.

"Yes, with three children."

"Is the young lady one of her children?"

"Do I look that old?" Alice guffaws. "No. She's a friend."

"What an asshole, he totally doesn't care whether I'm married or not," Lili whispers to Alice.

"Maybe because you are young and still have plenty of time," Alice says.

"No, I think he's out of sons."

The chief asks what they are doing out here without their families.

To get away from them, Alice almost says. When she thinks of her family lately, their absence only leads to a feeling of lightness—she'd had no idea how much burden she'd been under. "We're on a work trip," she says. "We're looking for a colleague who has probably been in this area. Lili, can you show him a recent photo?"

Lili takes out a wet wipe from her pocket and carefully cleans her hands first. She finds a photo on her phone, of her and Deckard sitting at a cafe table with greenery all around, smiling at the camera. Actually, only Lili is smiling. Deckard looks like he was reluctant for the camera but arranged to turn his mouth upward.

The chief reaches for the phone. Lili pulls back and takes out another wet wipe and wipes his hands for him. Only then does she hand over the phone. The chief examines the photo with his rheumy eyes for a bit, then shakes his head. Lili takes back the phone to show it to the rest. They look and chat among themselves. Finally, a woman, the chicken killer, says in accented Mandarin, "We don't recognize him. But does his work have something to do with the hydroelectric dam downstream? They have a compound for the workers there."

Something pings inside Alice's head. One of the major benefits of hydroelectric dams, besides clean power generation, is flood control. Can this have something to do with the nonprofit Deckard is involved in? It's as though she'd downed an energy drink and her fatigue is gone. How can they get there as soon as possible?

"That place used to be a good spot to go dancing. There's a natural stone platform." says one woman, probably a daughter as her face has the characteristic curvature of the family, made more concave by her sour expression. "But we can't go anymore. It's been fenced off."

"They're always doing stuff like this," the youngest brother says, his baby face in a scowl.

They continue to talk in Yi mixed with Mandarin, and the conversation soon gets heated. It doesn't take a genius to figure out they're pretty incensed about the situation, the continuous taking of what they consider theirs, in a country where all land is owned by the government, therefore, by everyone and no one.

"We should head up there tonight—to dance under the full moon, like we used to," Bagan says.

"But you said it's fenced off."

Bagan grins. "Have you heard of a bolt cutter?"

41

Torches are brought out for the outing. Made of dried reeds and dipped in some kind of oil, these are the real deal, the same type used in the Torch Festival. With a line of flames lighting up the night, there is indeed something festive about the whole affair.

Alice, Lili, and Zuomu follow behind the villagers, walking single file on the narrow, winding path. They speak very little, but there's plenty to listen to: the rhythmic banging of a drum by one of the brothers up ahead, the melodious cooing of songs by a couple of the ladies, and during stretches of silence in between the performances, the distant roar of the river, the chirping of crickets, the occasional hissing crackle followed by a falling spark, prickling the air like bubbles popping the surface of water.

All this, plus the monotonous steps, the amber glow of the fire, and the sweet, grassy scent of the smoke, are so mesmerizing that they send Alice into a kind of fugue state. She momentarily loses track of time, space, and what she's doing, which, when she thinks about it, amounts to going on a lark with a gang who plan to enter a power station by force. What if the station operators called the police on them? And what if Deckard weren't even there? Then it will be an adventure nevertheless. If they want to deport her and ban her from entering this country ever again, so be it. She didn't know she had the capacity for such defiance, such madness inside. A week ago she was ensconced in a comfortable house in Mountain View, living within the tight confines of being an upstanding American citizen and the ethics rules of the California State Bar. Now she's marching down the hill in the middle of nowhere in China with a veritable mob, ready to do some breaking-and-entering—albeit with no intention to commit any real crime. The torchlight is indulgent, cloaking her in both recklessness and invincibility. These red flowers are the talisman that promise to keep at bay whatever predator, evil spirit, or bad luck lurking in the dark.

They walk like this for almost two hours, stopping only occasionally to swap in new torches or, in Lili's case, put a Band-Aid over a blister. Once, in a clearing, something shadowy gets very close to their heads—an owl has swooped down then up soundlessly toward the moon.

The posse stops under a big crooked tree at a bend. The gate is up ahead. Bagan asks everyone to put out their torches so they won't be spotted by the cameras. Lili mumbles something about infrareds but no one seems to be paying attention. A brother runs up the road to check things out and returns to report that the gate, as expected, is indeed locked. They turn off the path, walk in parallel with the fence. When they have walked about three hundred paces, Bagan tells them to stop. This time they get close to the fence. Using the flashlight on Alice's phone, they appraise the barbed wires on top of the chain-link fence and decide they will not attempt to scale it. Bagan hands the cutter to Zuomu, who, without hesitation, runs up to the fence and gets to work.

Zuomu grunts once as he squeezes the arms of the bolt cutter together. The fence shudders. The first wire is severed. Only then does the gravity of the situation hit Alice—here's a kid, not yet graduated from high school, being asked to take part in a criminal venture. If for some reason they get caught, what this might do to his future is unthinkable. She takes the cutter from Zuomu and hands it back to

Bagan. "Let him do it since it's his idea. And it might be best for you not to go in at all. Just wait for us back by the big crooked tree."

Bagan cuts dozens of wires, making a hole big enough to fit through. They wriggle through like fish from a broken fishnet, except going in the wrong direction. Once inside, the villagers head west toward the dance rock, while Alice and Lili are drawn, like moths, to the lights coming from a building standing on a hill. They want to check it out first in case someone inside knows Deckard's whereabouts.

As the women get closer, Alice takes off, dashing at what she imagines is her top speed. Running up the hill is inefficient even for the supercharged athlete, and in her depleted state, she wouldn't get there much slower had she walked. Yet even a few seconds of delay seems too long. She has the premonition that she will be able to push open a door and find Deckard—open-mouthed, hands hovering above the keyboard of his laptop, eyes as big as lanterns—she will take a picture of the look on his face before saying to him, "Gotcha."

Just as she puts her hand on the handle of the front door, however, she hears a steely voice saying, "Stop right there."

42

Alice wheels around, squinting at a white beam of light. Behind the flashlight, the silhouette of a man gets bigger as he gets closer. He must be over six feet tall—his shoulders appear to be almost twice as wide as Alice's—impressive physique for an Asian dude. Her people are getting bigger and stronger physically.

Alice takes a deep breath. Not that she hasn't prepared a response. In fact, this exact scenario played out numerous times in her mind on the way here. Stay calm and be congenial. Tell the truth. Ask polite questions. Only now it's happening, it's as if her brain has been swapped out with that of the proverbial deer. She has achieved a perfect understanding of the animal: of course the mouth runs dry, because the lungs are on fire; of course the chest constricts, how else could the body contain the exploding heart? Of course the knees buckle as the body readies itself for leaping away. "Um," she says, her effort to swallow thwarted by the thick, dry lump in her throat.

The man jiggles the flashlight up and down at her. He asks impatiently, "What are you doing?"

Lili has caught up and comes to Alice's aide. "We're looking for someone," she says. "Shen..."

The man cuts her off. "How did you get in here?"

Before Lili answers, voices drift up from below. Laughter and shouts—it's the villagers. With no dogs or guards going after them at the moment, they're getting bold. Someone claps and whoops, the rest of them join in, sending the hillside abuzz with ululations. The man swears.

"They aren't with us. We don't know them," Alice says.

The man talks into a walkie-talkie. "Get the team out to Building 1. We have intruders. Bring weapons."

"Hey!" Lili says, raising her arms in the air. "We aren't intruders. We don't mean any harm. We're just looking for somebody who's gone missing."

"Don't move. You're under arrest," the man says. The flashlight dips down for a second as he searches for something.

"You can't do that! You are not the police!" Alice yells as she watches in horror as the man tries to grab Lili's arm. The man, dressed in a polo shirt and khakis, is probably just a security guard. Can private security make a citizen's arrest for a misdemeanor here? What does Chinese law on false imprisonment involve? She has no idea.

Lili twists herself free and darts toward the side of the building, screaming, "Run, hurry, run!" Alice takes off the other way. The man swears again and shouts into the walkie-talkie, calling for backup.

ON THE OTHER side of the building, Alice sees a shadow moving toward her. She meets Lili midway, both of them doubled over and panting. The big man hasn't followed, but it would only be a matter of time before he and his "team" would show up.

"Did you see another entrance?" Lili asks. "We should at least take a look inside."

That sounds like a harebrained idea to Alice, but she can't resist it —they've come this far. If they had to run away from crazed security guards, they should at least take a look. And why would anybody try to arrest them for real? If it comes to that, she'll play the sweet dumb old American tourist lady who got mixed up with unruly locals. She'll offer to pay for the fence repairs plus something extra for their troubles and they will let them go, won't they? Chinese people are easygoing that way, not at all the sticklers of law and order the way Americans are. Flexibility with rules is their hallmark.

There's no other entrance in the back. The only windows they can see are at the second-story level. "Let's go back to the front. Hopefully the villagers will have distracted the guards," Lili says.

They sneak along the back side of the building, stopping at the corner to peer out. Alice's heart pounds, as if ready to jump out of her chest and run into hiding.

"It seems safe; let's go to the front of the building," Lili says.

They turn the corner and stop again at the next corner. They hear shouts but can't see anything. The guard appears to have been drawn away. Alice and Lili run up to the gate—locked, of course. Alice pulls a credit card out of her wallet and tries to push in the latch with it—what's the second breaking-and-entering in a day, anyway—but the lock doesn't budge.

"C'mon," she mutters, wishing they had brought the bolt cutter. A terrible thought comes to her. "I hope Zuomu got away," she says.

Instead of replying, Lili puts a finger on her lips and turns her head.

They listen to the shouts coming from below the hill. Much of it is in Yi, mixed with what sounds like angry cursing in Mandarin and Sichuanese. Someone is yelling in Mandarin, "Put your hands up!"

Alice and Lili run behind a tree on the edge of the hill to look down—two of the men, trapped in a semicircle by about half a dozen guards, are waving torches to stop the guards' advance like hunters keeping back a pack of wolves. Then four or five people come out of nowhere and jump on the guards, tackling them to the ground. As the rest of the guards turn to help their mates, the first two men seize the opportunity to charge at the guards with the torches. One man's back catches on fire. He rolls on the ground screaming as he tries to put out the flame.

A crackle rips through the air, leaving a resonating echo that fades into the surroundings. A gunshot. The melee scene below freezes for a second as if a movie director had ordered "cut!" A villager shouts something, and all jump up to run down the path. The guards give chase. One is captured but fights his/her way to freedom and disappears with the rest of them into the dark.

Lili says, "Can you beli—"

She's cut off mid-sentence as she pitches forward—something has struck her hard. Her arms flail in the air then one of her hands grabs Alice's left arm. As Alice struggles to keep balance, there's a hard shove on her own shoulders, and she falls down with a face plant next to Lili. She lifts her head. In the second miracle fall in two days, despite the blooming pain on her chin, nothing on her face seems broken. She tries to get up but something is pressing down on her back—the knee of a heavy person. Her arms are yanked back. Something bites into her wrists, then her ankles. Something goes over her head. Something else around her neck tightens and stops just short of choking her.

"Lili!" Alice tries to shout but her voice is faint even to her own ears. "Lili, are you okay?"

"Let me go! Let..." Lili's voice becomes muffled, and Alice soon comes to understand why: The drawstring of her hood loosens, and her captor's hands reach in, pinch her jaws open, and stuff a wad of something into her mouth. *Holy crap, I'm bound with zip ties and gagged with socks!* The stale, mildewy taste makes her want to retch. *Please,* she begs the higher being, *don't let me throw up now. I don't want to choke to death on my own vomit.*

43

Alice is picked up and slung over someone's shoulder like a side of pork. She instinctively thrashes, trying to get down.

"Don't move. Or I'll throw you down the hill," the man says with the exaggerated menace of a schoolyard bully. Not wanting to test him, Alice goes limp. *I must preserve my life and limb,* she tells herself. *Oh God. It's come to that? Preservation of life and limb? I'll do whatever it takes.* What had she been thinking? How stupid it was to dismiss the possibility that something like this could happen, even in China. It only dawns on her now that since she's never been in any physical altercation before, she has acted as if no one could touch her. She, like the young protesters in Shanghai, didn't believe that truly terrible things would happen to her because she has never experienced them firsthand. Surely there are people who grew up in war zones or crime-ridden areas who don't tread the earth the same way. Those who are more leery, used to looking over their shoulders, wouldn't get into a situation like this. She's been privileged, and that privilege has expired. Blood, along with regret, rushes to her downward-pointing head.

Once the man starts walking, the way his arms hold her legs and his shoulder jams into her stomach has an almost gentle quality to it, like an adult carrying a tired child. Perhaps he has a child, too. Or a quadriplegic parent he has to carry in and out of a wheelchair. If only she didn't have those disgusting socks in her mouth, she would try to find out.

An old memory surfaces at this odd moment: When she was maybe five or six, her father took her to Xuanwu Lake Park. There was a series of display cases containing miniature dioramas of people at work—hospitals, schools, farms, etc. Those were the days before Legos, so everything was handmade using clay or cardboard and propped up with wooden sticks. One of the diorama was a scene of a chemical factory, where several model workers were standing next to a vat of chemicals and stirring in the vat with long poles. One of the model workers' head had broken off, left with only the torso and legs.

"Look," her father joked, "that poor guy has lost his head, and his coworkers are fishing for it in the vat." Only it wasn't so funny to her —the thought of a severed head seized her with an intense horror. At the same time, she was assailed by a wave of exhaustion and immediately closed her eyes to shut out the diorama. She pretended she was tired. Ba picked her up and carried her much like this man is doing now. Then, as now, her body was fatigued by fear. Whatever happened to the fight-or-flight response? Perhaps it's the other evolutionary trick of survival, to play dead until the danger passes. Perhaps it's the lack of oxygen in this stupid hood. All she wants to do is close her eyes and let the steps lull her to sleep.

THE MAN IS CARRYING Alice up some stairs. For a thug he doesn't smell too bad—no stale cologne or strong body odor or even cigarette smell, just the clean scents of soap and laundry detergent. He breathes hard, not because she's heavy but because he's out of shape, Alice prefers to think. She hears muffled noises—*must be Lili*—carried by someone else. She makes similar noises back. At least they're in this together.

A door beeps open. The man enters and switches on the lights—

Alice sees red, the color of the hood. She can't see anything through the dense weave. His shoes squeak on the floor. Perhaps they're walking down a hallway. Another door beeps.

"Here we are," the man says, almost cheerfully, and lowers Alice to the ground on her feet.

Alice wobbles a little, disoriented, but manages to keep standing. Lili is no longer with her. She remains surprisingly calm when the man puts a hand on her shoulder—he is going through her backpack. Taking the backpack off would require undoing her zip tie, which he is not about to do.

Alice grunts—*please, check the inside pocket of my jacket! Look at my passport! My driver's license! My business card! You have abducted an American! You are creating a diplomatic incident! The U.S. consulate will come after your ass once my family reports me missing! There will be a woman hunt! They will send a SEAL team to extract me!* She only hears the crunching sound of a plastic shopping bag—might be the one holding the snacks. The man is filling it with her stuff.

Well, just wait until you find out who I am.

But the thought further unsettles her. Anti-American sentiment has been rising in China in recent years. What if these people hate Americans, and especially Chinese Americans, because they see immigration as an act of betrayal? And what if the U.S. government doesn't care enough? How long did it take for those hikers who were abducted by Afghans to get freed? Years? And they weren't even rescued by Americans, were they? Will she see her children again before they become adults, or ever? And what about Henry? How will he keep the mortgage paid and the children fed? Will he have to declare her legally dead to make a claim on her life insurance policy? Is kidnapping covered?

The man eases the pack back onto Alice's shoulders. Then, he lifts her arms one by one and sweeps under her armpits; his hands lightly glide down her pants like he's trying to smooth wrinkles out. He doesn't touch her chest or her crotch.

Hey, Alice wants to say, *I've had a rougher pat down at the airport. What happened to the sexual assault I was promised? Am I too old for you?*

And a part of her is relieved: *Please be as gentle with Lili. Please, please don't hurt her.*

He reaches into her jacket pockets, then pants pockets and relieves her of all her documents, her phone, some change and receipts. He harrumphs once as he riffles through the items, probably when he sees her passport, but says nothing. The door slams. He is gone.

ALICE SHAKES her head violently to lose the bag over her head, only it doesn't budge. She tries to wriggle her hands, but they're bound as tightly as can be. In fact, she realizes she's losing sensation in them. A new terror grips her—if circulation is cut off long enough, she could lose her hands and feet. She pictures the stumps at the end of her limbs and remembers a prosthesis client the firm has—prosthetic technology is getting really good these days. Perhaps they'll give her a discount. Perhaps she will start a GoFundMe campaign, or write a popular memoir like that rock climber who cut off his arm in order to free himself from being trapped under a rock. She already has the perfect title: *Power Struggle, How I Survived My Kidnapping at a Chinese Hydroelectric Plant*—predicated on her actually surviving this, of course. Her situation seems worse than the rock climber's in many ways, not the least because she has neither a free hand nor a pocket knife.

And there's the stuffing in her mouth. Her jaw is getting sore from the pressure. She strains to open her mouth wider as she pushes the mass out with her tongue. Bit by bit, it loosens, and finally, success.

Breathing freer, she hops in the direction of the door and immediately bangs into the wall. She catches her breath, keeping her body flat against the surface as she shuffles along, more carefully this time. Within a few feet, her fingers brush a light switch, then a door handle. She grips the lever, a futile exercise. It's locked from the other side. She keeps going, turning whenever she hits a barrier and continues to hop along the perimeter. She finds no windows or furniture.

A different approach. She tries hopping across the room, venturing further before doubling back. She pants, feeling like a trapped fly. But she pushes on. After about five minutes of zipping back and forth, running into walls, she's certain of one thing: the room contains only herself and an empty plastic trash can. She's shut inside a plain box.

She needs to conserve energy. Who knows for how much longer she would have to stay inside this prison. Her stomach is empty, but it's not food that she's concerned with. Humans always die of thirst before they do of hunger. She also needs to pee. There's no hope of her doing this without wetting herself, so she'll just have to hold out for as long as possible. Perhaps her captors will have the heart to let her use the toilet? Would they free her hands, then? Will they watch, to get some kind of kinky thrill out of watching a peri-menopausal woman relieving herself? Or will they just leave her here to die? But if they wanted to do that, they could just as well have left her outside? What do they want with her?

And who are these people? Definitely not the police, given the number of them present at night, the lack of police uniform, and the fact they gagged her with socks and used zip ties instead of handcuffs. Yet they obviously had some training in anticipation of intruders. Private security guards and maybe workers living on site who felt the need to defend themselves. Do they really need to resort to such extremes? Why not give her a chance to explain?

She hops over to the light switch again and flips the switch on and off. Three short blinks, three long blinks, then three short blinks. SOS. She's glad to have practiced that with her children on camping trips. Perhaps the room has a transom window above her. Transom, a letter away from ransom. Perhaps someone will notice the signal, someone who is in the vicinity and understands what it means. And gives a damn.

When no one answers her distress call after she repeats this a hundred times, she puts her head against the wall and slowly shifts the fabric in between. She lifts the bottom of the bag all the way up against her chin, then drops her head against the other shoulder, rotating the bag until she can feel the cord lock between her cheek and the top of her shoulder. She twists, angling her head to catch the lock between her teeth. She whips her head several times as she bites down, loosening the string bit by bit until, finally, a triangle of light opens up under her nose. She gives the bag a hard shake like a wet dog shaking off water, and she's free.

She gulps down air, her eyes blinking and seeing green in everything. She looks down. The hood is a reusable shopping bag with a cartoon cat and the words "Xinchong Natural Pet Food" printed on it. Goddamn amateurs. She looks around. The room is vacant and windowless. She stands leaning against the wall, her eyes on the door that obstinately stays shut.

Minutes pass as she counts her breaths. As long as she's breathing, she's alright.

She hears something—on the other side of the door, someone has dropped something on the ground with a thud. She darts behind the door. She even considers putting the bag back on. But what's the point of that? Instead, she turns off the light.

The lock beeps. Someone enters and turns the light back on.

"There you are," the man says when he sees her, mildly surprised. "You got your hood off. Alright. I'm going to untie you in a minute."

Alice breathes out.

The man's stubby face lifts for half a second in an almost-smile, then turns downward again. "Please sit." He points at the plastic folding chair he's brought in.

Alice is torn—why should she do anything her captor tells her? But a chair is a welcome change from standing. And he said please. She takes the seat. "I need to go to the bathroom," she says.

He nods. "I will take you after we talk." His small, rodent-like eyes focus on her from their meaty sockets, his face congealed in an expression of concern. "You shouldn't be here," he says.

"I don't want to be here, either. I'm being held against my will—you guys bound and gagged me," Alice says, holding tight onto the edge of the chair. Now the possibility of going to the bathroom has become real, she can't think about anything else.

"Because you broke in," the man says.

"Then call the police!" Alice is suddenly very irritated. "Who are you to arrest me? And with those methods—it's kidnapping and false imprisonment." She squirms and grimaces. It's hard to maintain dignity when you're being denied toilet access. But this is China. The concept of cruel and unusual punishment is nothing.

"What are you doing here?" the man asks with the deliberate ease of someone who can empty his bladder whenever he wants to.

"I'm here looking for someone. Shen Weiguo, the CEO of Danyang. Sometimes he goes by Deckard. Do you know him?"

The man studies her without reply.

Alice exhales. If he doesn't deny it, does it mean Deckard is here? She sees the first ray of hope in a long time. "I've got important business to discuss with him. And I really need to go to the bathroom. Please, take me now."

"You should've thought of that before you broke into a secured area," the man says, stroking the stubbles on his throat.

"Secured area? Why does a power station need to be secured? Never mind—I don't care. So you don't want people to trespass. I get it. I'll leave."

"It's not that simple."

"What do you want from me?"

Before the man answers, there's a knock on the door. The man frowns as he pulls the door open. Who can be standing in the doorway but Lili, her hair wild and her eyes wilder, her hands behind her back.

"Aya, how did you get out? I was going to come to you next. You can't be here," he says, reaching his hands to grab Lili.

Lili swings something from behind her and smacks the man across the head with it. Hard. The man curses, reaching for his ear. She brings it down again from overhead, this time with a wet cracking noise.

"Ow, you broke my nose!" The man doubles over, covering his face with his arms.

Lili is about to swing the rock in the sock again, but Alice screams, "Enough, don't kill him!" Lili pauses for a split second and the man reaches to wrestle the sock away from her. Alice falls to the floor and swings her tied-together legs at the man's groin—more a push than a kick, but he wobbles. Lili takes advantage of his imbalance and gives him another good smack on the head. The man collapses to the ground and stops moving. Alice watches the man's bloody face in horror.

"He's alright; he's breathing," Lili says as she feels the man's neck. She rips the card key off his belt. "He'll wake up any minute. Let's run!"

"I can't. Still tied up."

Lili sighs. She checks the man's body and finds a box cutter in his pocket. At least he wasn't lying when he said he was going to untie Alice.

"How did you get out? How did you find me?" Alice asks when they reach the woods behind the building. To their relief, no one has come out to chase after them so far.

Lili smiles, her white teeth catching the moonlight. "Watch," she says. She bends down with her arms behind her, her fingers interlaced. She moves her arms toward her head until it reaches an angle that looks rather painful. Yet she presses on, moving more slowly until her arms are nearly in the same plane as her torso. She bends her elbows and gives out a soft little cry as she shakes her shoulders. Now her arms are in front of her, her hands still impossibly clasped together.

"I don't understand—what did you just do?"

Lili sighs and does the trick all over again. This time, Alice doesn't blink. She's certain Lili hasn't opened up her fingers then re-closed them.

"So you are..." Alice searches for the word for double-jointed in Chinese and can only come up with "soft-boned." "But how did you break the zip ties?"

"I saw a video once—you just go like this." Lili raises her hands overhead and rams them down on her hip bone. "Hurts your wrists a little bit but the zip tie just breaks. Then I broke a window—I used the bag they put over my head to wrap around my fist—and used the glass to cut the foot tie. I jumped out and ran around the building, found an open door, ran back in, then started knocking on all the doors until I found you."

"I don't know who you should work for, the circus or Mossad," Alice says in disbelief.

"You weren't so bad yourself; he might've gotten to me if you hadn't kicked him in the nuts."

"Self-defense class from Freshman year. First time I had to use it in more than thirty years!" Alice high-fives Lili, then ducks behind some shrub to relieve herself. Hot urine comes out not in a gush but at a trickle, as if her overworked bladder is weeping over the joy of the sweet, sweet relief.

"Don't tell me you didn't pee the whole time," Lili says over the hedge.

"Well, I've had no access. Did you find a bathroom?"

"No. But it was the first thing I did when I freed myself. Right on the floor!" Lili laughs savagely.

They follow a trail downhill toward the river, their path illuminated by the moon. A low hum fills the air, a sound distinct from the rushing water sound of the river. As they advance, the noise gets louder. Soon the path turns, and what stands in front of them is a two-story rectangular building. It's the sort of thing built as cheaply as possible, its blocky, unadorned shape as if constructed out of Legos by a four-year-old. It is also the source of the low hum. When they get next to the building, the noise nearly reaches a level of discomfort. Not quite a jet engine, but much louder than city traffic, punctuated with occasional high-pitched noises like long spikes poking into one's ears.

They peer through the security bars over one of the windows. Inside is a cavernous space. Blue and green LEDs, like a tide of bioluminescent algae with an occasional blinker of red or orange, dimly illuminate banks of computers on which the lights are installed. As their eyes adjust, they see rack after rack of computers stacked from floor to ceiling, connected by snaking cables. And odd looking machines these are, with one side made entirely of fans and vents. These are powerful servers designed to handle computationally intensive operations that constantly generate a lot of heat. Are they what she thinks they are? She tsks.

"What?" Lili looks at her askance.

"Just as I suspected, this is a data center. That's probably why Deckard came here—he didn't lie; this really is a client project."

"But this is in the middle of nowhere. Why would any client want to..." Lili stops herself, then raises her eyebrows as she puts it all together. "Oh. It's the hydroelectric power plant—makes sense to put the data center next to a cheap source of energy."

"Exactly right. Let's check out the place quickly, then get out of here," Alice says. The noise from all these computer servers' cooling fans is driving her crazy, not to mention the possibility of another goon squad waiting to get them.

They slither along the wall until they reach the front door—locked, of course. They go around the building and find a set of stairs. They go up as quickly and stealthily as they know how.

The door on the second floor is also locked. They take the stairs to the roof. On the flat deck space sits a dark, blocky shape—a shipping container. A picture of a horse on roller skates is painted on the wall, with neon paint that glows under the moonlight.

This must be another one of Qian's works—what was it he did for Deckard? An anechoic chamber. Why would it end up here?

Before Alice asks if they should knock, Lili has already pulled the door open and disappeared into it. Alice hears a soft *ahh*, though no tumbling sound.

"Are you okay?" Alice asks.

Lili's answer is barely audible but sounds like a yes.

Alice takes a tentative step into the dark. The ground underfoot is all wrong—not solid flooring but some kind of netting. Her toes slip through holes as she crouches down. It's eerily quiet in here, a welcome reprieve from the noise outside. The air has a strange pressure and her ears pop. She stands up again, searching for a light switch by the entrance and finding it.

The blinding light illuminates a disorienting room. Alice fumbles at the slide beneath the switch to adjust the dimmer. Lili is lying on the net, shielding her eyes. The walls and ceiling are completely covered with protruding blades the size of large clipboards, arranged in different orientations, as is the floor underneath the netting they're standing on. There's no one else in here. In the center of the room are several computers and a helmet-like device. Alice has seen pictures of it before but this is the first time she has seen a Neuromersion set up in person. Next to the setup is a small mattress pad topped with a pillow and a folded blanket. So this is Deckard's R&D lab?

"It feels so weird in here," Lili says, her voice tinny. "Like you are underwater but can still breathe."

"Because it's an anechoic chamber," Alice says.

"A what?"

"It's a chamber built to completely absorb sounds that hit the walls—anechoic, no echo. Qian told me he built one for Deckard, for Neuromersion testing. I just don't get why it would end up here."

"That's great. So he's here." Lili crawls toward the mattress, yawning the entire way. She shuts her eyes and says, "Let's wait until he gets back."

Alice shakes Lili. "You can't go to sleep now. We don't know what he's doing here; for all we know, he may be a prisoner just like we were. And the goons are probably searching for us. We need to hide."

"Mmm," Lili says. "Just a few minutes. A catnap."

If Lili is anything like Alice's own children, once sleep hits, she would sooner be carried out than roused. Alice sighs and ends up finishing with a yawn. Exhaustion rushes over, threatening to dunk her under. It's so tempting to just lie down. But the goons are coming. And the quiet inside the chamber is starting to be deafening: her ears ring; her heartbeats resemble a chugging train engine; and her breathing sounds like howling wind.

Alice steps outside and walks unsteadily down the stairs. At ground level, she finds a bush that offers cover and through its bottom, a view of the path. If anyone comes this way, she'll have a couple of minutes to run in, hopefully wake up Lili, and run toward the river. *Is this a good idea?* She isn't sure, but her mind, churning slowly and limply, has trouble coming up with an alternative. The moon is higher now, casting a silvery wash. She sits down, feeling her bottom sinking into the soft duff. So, this is what it feels like to be deboned.

44

Something is next to Alice, watching her. She tries to wave it away, but it hovers over her. A very bright owl that carries its own sun. She opens her eyes.

A pair of dark eyes are staring down at her. The mouth seems to be frowning, though she quickly realizes it's doing the opposite, as the face is upside down. She sits up to face the man, who is half kneeling as if ready to propose.

"What do you want?" she asks.

"The better question is, what do *you* want? Fancy seeing you here, Alice. How did you get in?"

"Deckard? You look totally different!" She stares at him. He is unprecedentedly shaggy, sporting a beard and untamed hair. Also much thinner than she remembers, his facial features having slackened with an asymmetry, as though a molar has gone missing on one side. Martyr is the word that comes to mind, replete with feverish, bloodshot eyes.

He answers by passing his finger through his hair, a gesture Alice copies, combing for sticks. Lili is nowhere to be seen. Young people and their need for sleep.

"What are you doing here?" they ask again simultaneously. A little chuckle, then both fall silent.

It seems too soon to bring up the invoices, so she says, "We came looking for you."

"So you've found me."

"What are you doing here? Everyone's worried about you," she says, omitting that Danyang is falling apart like an iceberg in July. Again, too soon, and how can he not know?

"Work," he says, standing up.

"Kaipeng said there are no clients in this part of the country."

"Ah, Kaipeng. She doesn't know everything about our clients. This is a special one that requires a lot of individual attention."

Lili chooses that moment to appear. She gives them a little wave. A smile breaks out on Deckard's face, but halfway through, it freezes.

Not quite the kind of lovers' reunion Alice is expecting, but then again, the Chinese aren't into PDA. Should she leave and give them the privacy to... do what, exactly? Hug? Kiss? Have sex? Whatever they want. She doesn't need to be the third wheel. As she searches for a way to excuse herself, Deckard is watching Lili's face intently, a muscle under his eye twitching with concentration.

"How are you?" Deckard's voice is quiet.

"Well, Danyang is falling apart. I got laid off. Then I met Alice, and we came looking for you. Some guys tried to tie us up. I broke out, and we escaped. Now here we are. I slept in that shipping container last night, now my back hurts," Lili says with a pout. Then she catches the expression on Deckard's face. "Why, you don't want us here? Have we disrupted your work?"

No, this is all wrong. Alice has the urge to stage direct the young woman: *Our presence isn't an intrusion to be tolerated. We aren't going to apologize for being here. Be righteous, be outraged; he needs to know what hell we've gone through to find him here, what distress he's caused, in so many, by running away. And no, we haven't disrupted his work; he has disrupted ours.*

"What happened to..." Deckard touches his nose.

Lili lifts her chin to show off her profile. "What do you think? It's better, isn't it? Much more like Wu Ying?"

"Mmm."

Alice narrows her eyes at Lili. *What exactly is going on?*

"I had a nose job," Lili tells her.

Alice is floored. Is this the "big thing" Lili had done for Deckard? Why would she do such a thing, to have a nose job so she can look more like Wu Ying? It's weird and degrading. "Why haven't you mentioned this before?"

"Because it hasn't come up. Besides, you would just disapprove—like you clearly do now. Why give me that look? A nose job is no big deal; lots of people get it. I never liked my nose before; it was too flat. The surgeon says Wu Ying had a great nose, an excellent model to base mine on."

Alice has to remind herself that this is modern China. Cosmetic surgery is as common as any other beauty treatment. People here have a much more liberal take on it than her circle of middle-class American friends. "The surgeon had met Wu Ying?" she asks dumbly.

"No, silly, I showed him her photos—the ones Deckard kept," Lili says.

"But you told me you broke your arm from the accident, and you were going home so your parents could take care of you," Deckard says.

"I told everyone that. How else would I get the time off to recover? Besides, I wanted it to be a surprise for you. But when I went back to the office, you were gone. Then they laid me off—can you believe it? You wouldn't do that if you were there, right? Anyway, can we talk about this later? I'm starving. Where can we get some breakfast?"

The "cafeteria" is just a trailer with a kitchenette inside. Deckard fetches hard-boiled eggs and soy milk in plastic cups from the refrigerator. There is no cook on staff, Deckard informs them as he heats up the soy milk in the microwave.

Lili smacks an egg on the table and rolls it around to break up the shell. She peels it, breaks it in halves, and frowns at the greenish yolk inside.

"No cook, but plenty of security guards?" Alice asks pointedly.

"There aren't any security guards," Deckard says.

"Who are those people who tied us up last night, then?"

"All regular employees. Although they've had security training," he says, pushing up his glasses, which immediately fall back into the same place. "Sorry about the misunderstanding last night. They have orders to arrest any 302s—any suspicious persons. We are too far away to get assistance from the police quickly."

"A data center militia? How is it necessary?"

"The client has had trouble with people coming to steal equipment before, so they've got to take precautions."

"There was a boy with us. What happened to him?"

"He must've gone off with the gang that was chased off by our men."

"Have you got any raw eggs? I can fix something up some for us," Lili pipes up. This conversation seems to bore her. She doesn't seem to care about why Deckard is here. That he is alive and well seems good enough for her. Even his ambivalence at her new nose doesn't seem to bother her. How pure and simple her love, how sanguine she is about the situation—Alice in her twenties would never have tolerated a self-absorbed boyfriend like Deckard. But then, she was well educated, had a good job, and her family wasn't pressuring her to move back to her hometown to get married. Before she starts to judge, she needs to remember that Lili hasn't had the same advantages.

Deckard nods at the fridge. Lili goes over and opens it. "The peppers are wrinkled," she calls out, then walks over to the sink to wash the vegetables. Deckard takes a napkin to wipe the eggshells off the table.

Soon the kitchen is filled with the aroma of fried garlic. The range fan is deafening. Alice stares at them—this tableau of domesticity, this bizarre normality. *This ain't Sunday brunch at your house*, she wants to say to Deckard. She has hard questions that demand answers. She pulls her chair closer to his.

"So the equipment your client has is very valuable," she says.

"Yeah."

"Except they aren't Danyang servers, are they?" It would be better if he just owns up to it—although, does anyone own up to anything anymore these days?

"No, they aren't. They are custom," he says, and his right leg starts to shake like the needle on a running sewing machine.

Alice puts her hand on his knee to stop the shaking. A kind of heat pours from his person, along with a faint odor, although Alice can't be sure that isn't coming from her own body.

"Deckard, are things alright?" she asks.

He returns a high-wattage smile. "Yes, of course."

"I talked with Fei before I came."

"Ah, Fei. Is that how you found me? I thought I'd found all the trackers she planted on me."

"Apparently not." Alice scrunches up her face. "Do you want to talk about the divorce?"

"Not really," he says as he brushes off some invisible speck of dust from his pant leg. A moment passes, and he asks, "How is she?"

Oh, she's great, probably riding with her Hells Angel and drinking at a biker bar as we speak. But what's the point of goading him with this information? "She seemed alright. We didn't exactly hang out," Alice says.

"You never liked her."

Alice bristles. "That's not true. And why does that matter? I respect her."

"As do I. Always will."

"And you show that respect by going out with someone five years older than your daughter."

Deckard looks at her askance. "We were already separated when I met Lili. And you aren't going to moralize me, are you?"

"No—yes, maybe. I know it's none of my business, but the girl is young, things are confusing enough for her as it is. If you aren't serious about her, don't lead her on. Just leave her alone."

"I know. I know. Of course I wouldn't do anything to hurt her." He shifts a little in his seat. "But you know what, that's how a person grows—through relationships, successful ones or failures, they are all valid experiences. She can do a lot worse than going out with me. And honestly, you don't have to worry about her. She's tougher than you think."

"Tough enough to get cosmetic surgery for you."

"That's something, isn't it?" He sounds awed.

"It's not nothing. Must be nice to be you," she says.

They drink soy milk in silence. Alice is about to bring up the invoices and ask about the USB key when the fan suddenly stops. Lili walks toward them, holding a plate topped with a mound of veggie scrambled eggs.

"Let me know what you think. Learned to make this last spring—we call it the lockdown scramble," she says brightly.

AFTER BREAKFAST, Deckard takes them on a walk along a path that loops around the compound. In front of the server farm, they run into a man whose head is wrapped in a bandage, a la Humpty Dumpty—it's the guy whose nose was broken by Lili last night. Alice considers turning the other way, but it's too late.

"Good morning, Shen Zong and guests," the man says nasally.

"Good morning, Lao Mo. So you've met my friends: Alice from America, and Lili, also known as Rambo from Shanghai."

Lili's face is blank, probably hasn't caught the eighties American action hero reference. She says, "We could've told you that had you not bound and gagged us." She apparently knows how to stand her ground; it just depends on who it is. Around Deckard, she's a puddle.

The man does a fist-palm solute like a character in a kung fu movie. "Apologies; we were just doing our job. I'm Mo Jiajiu. They call me Lao Mo (Old Mo)." He grins. "Bu da bu xiang shi."

That phrase, "from an exchange of blows a friendship grows," has always struck Alice as one of the odder expressions in her native tongue. The Chinese like to proclaim they're the most peace-loving people, except phrases like this tend to debunk that notion. Perhaps sentiments like this—the acceptance of former rivals as friends—are at the core of pacifism? They shake hands, everyone feeling magnanimous.

Deckard has to go to a meeting, so Lao Mo volunteers to show Alice and Lili around because, thanks to Lili, he's got the day off.

The three of them walk in silence for a while. Then Lili taps at her own nose and asks, "Does that hurt?"

"Just a bit."

"You'll want to have it set properly, preferably by a cosmetic surgeon. Shouldn't take that long to heal," Lili says. She of all people would know.

"Lucky for me there's a visiting doctor here at the moment—mostly he's been working with Shen Zong. He put this poultice on me and the swelling went down right away. I don't feel much pain."

"I could use a doctor for some acupuncture," Lili says. "Slept on an uncomfortable mattress last night. My back is killing me."

"Why is Shen Zong working with a doctor? Is he sick?" Alice is alarmed.

"Well, I wouldn't put it like that," Lao Mo says. "Not like he's caught something. But everyone can see he's got weak nerves. He's working like a fiend, only it's on irrelevant things, when there's real work he should focus on."

"Real work? What's that?"

"Getting the data center up and running, of course. The management wants it operational before the rainy season starts, but we might not make it, mostly because Shen Zong isn't paying attention to his stuff. There's just a little bit left but he just can't get his part finished, no matter how much we cajole him. Maybe he wants it that way—as long as this isn't finished, he doesn't have to go back to Shanghai, so he can keep working on that wacky brain helmet thing. The thing is, we'll all lose our bonuses if we miss the deadline." Lao Mo looks Alice in the eye to let her know the serious nature of this. "We were hoping Dr. Chang would do what he could to help with Shen Zong's nerves and make him focus, but from what I hear, the doctor is now being pulled into working on that helmet thing, too." He shakes his head.

~

He takes them to the biggest building, the turbine hall, where they peer down from a height at a series of turbines in the ground that look like giant blue plugs.

"A hydroelectric power plant is the most efficient and environmentally friendly way to supply electricity to a data center," he tells them, as if reciting from some brochure.

"Or a bitcoin mine," Lili says.

Lao Mo stands still, then turns very slowly to face Lili, as if ready to throttle her. Alice is flabbergasted. That had been her guess as well—she had read a design patent case recently where the dispute was centered around the unique look of the fans on the state-of-the-art brand of crypto mining servers. They looked just like the ones she saw last night. Without further proof, she hadn't been ready to share with Lili her suspicion that somehow Deckard is involved in a bitcoin mining operation. But how does Lili know? Is she able to read Alice's mind?

"Shen Zong told us," Lili says, her hands in her back pocket. "Don't worry, we are very good friends of his. We can be trusted to keep a secret."

Lao Mo exhales. "Good."

But when did Deckard say anything to them about it? Alice is pretty sure she had seen Deckard before Lili. She frowns, and Lili catches Alice's eye—now she understands that Lili is bluffing. There is one problem: Crypto mining has been illegal in this country since 2021 and now carries criminal penalties. What is Deckard doing getting mixed up in this? What else is he hiding? It occurs to her that she, too, ought to push Lao Mo a little. It's a gamble, but she has very few dots, so she's going to connect them the best she can and see how much more she can squeeze out of Lao Mo before she confronts Deckard.

"This client of Shen Zong's—Tong Zheyu—he's some kind of financier, isn't he?" Alice asks.

"A rich guy is what I hear."

"What's he doing with a bitcoin mine?"

Lao Mo grins, displaying his crooked yellow teeth underneath the bandages. "What do you think? Is it for the children? Or the poor? Oh, is it for the environment? Is he doing it out of the goodness of his heart?"

Alice frowns.

Lao Mo cackles. "None of the above, of course! He just wants to make money! Rich people can never have enough money. And a bitcoin mine makes a lot of money."

"But it's ill-gotten gains."

"How's it ill-gotten? He's not stealing from anyone."

"It's illegal. He might go to jail if he gets caught," Alice says.

"Yeah, what if someone reports to the police?" Lili chimes in.

"The police," Lao Mo scoffs. "They're all in Tong's pocket. So are all the local officials in the district. They all like getting paid in crypto; so much better than hiding a suitcase full of cash at home. How do you suppose he got to lease the power plant before it even got finished?"

So, support local economy. Bribe with farm-to-pocket bitcoins. Jokes aside, they are playing with fire here. Even if the local government is totally corrupt, what about the central government? Is this what attracted the attention of the State Security Bureau people? Was the stalker sent by the government? Alice has a bad feeling about this. A puckeriness coats her tongue; she hates that she can always taste aggravation, which tastes nasty.

Lao Mo's walkie-talkie crackles. An urgent voice says over static: "We've got a potential 302 at the north entrance. Subject is male, ran back on the road after he was spotted. Da Fa took off after him. Team 2, come quick for backup."

"Weren't we the 302s?" Alice asks.

"Someone else must be trying to breach the compound. Is Shen Zong expecting more guests?"

"I doubt it."

Lao Mo ushers them to the door. Seconds later, he has locked the door behind them and is running down the corridor, the guided tour over.

"Don't just gag the person you catch," Lili shouts at his back. "Give them a chance to explain; might spare you another blow to the nose."

When Lao Mo is out of view, Lili asks Alice, "Do you think the stalker has found us?"

"That's what I was wondering. I hope he gets caught; then we'll at least know for whom he's working," Alice says, turning to face Lili. "When did Deckard tell you he's running a bitcoin mine?"

"He didn't. In the conference room they locked me in, there was a whiteboard. Somebody must've had a meeting there, then forgot to erase the drawings. They were all layout diagrams for the data center. Some boxes were labeled as bitcoin servers. So I just guessed."

Alice puts her hands over her temples. "I can't believe it! I would never have had the presence of mind to study that before freeing myself! And you tricked Lao Mo!"

"You were pretty tricky yourself, getting him to confirm that Tong is behind all this."

"Yeah, we are so clever. But this isn't good. Tong must be holding something serious over Deckard. I don't like what's going on at all—he can get into big trouble over this."

"What can we do to help?"

Bewildered, Alice comes up short for an answer. Aside from the invoices, she came here because she was worried she might once again find a raving, broken-down Deckard. She's relieved to see he seems alright, if a little stressed out—what normal person wouldn't, to be a law-abiding executive one day then a part of a criminal syndicate next?

"We should get him out of here," she says, then adds lamely, "although, if he had a choice, he probably would have left already."

"Well, I've come here to help him figure out the password for the USB key, so I'm not leaving until I've done that. If it's as important as he says, maybe it will help."

"Maybe," Alice says. She thinks, *You have no idea*. A warmth is creeping up her cheeks. She should be the strategist here, the one who analyzes the situation and comes up with a solution. Instead, Lili is the one who has kept focus on the crux of the problem. Without knowing the actual content on the USB key, she has intuited an answer—the money should help, at least with Danyang's fiscal situation. Only it's a series of ifs—if there really are as many bitcoins on the USB key as Fei claimed; if they can actually figure out the password; if Danyang is Deckard's main problem, rather than something else that can't be solved by money.

45

Alice finds Deckard alone in a lab on the second floor of the data center building. The lab bench he is working in front of is crammed full of equipment: oscilloscope, signal generator, power supplies, multimeters. Cables and wires crisscross like rhizomes. Ordinarily she would have asked him what the setup is for, but she has more important things on her mind at the moment.

"We need to talk," she says.

He takes off his glasses and looks up at her.

"Look, I know you're setting up a bitcoin mine for Tong."

Deckard studies her, perhaps still trying to think of some subterfuge. He pats his pockets. When he finds a coin, he hands it to her. "You are hereby hired as my personal lawyer. Here's one yuan for your retainer."

Alice bats his hand away. "I can't do that. I already represent Danyang. And our communication won't be privileged if you are doing this with the intention of committing or covering up a crime. Also, I know next to nothing about Chinese law, so you'll need to talk with someone who does if you are in hot water here. But I'm your oldest pal. You can unburden your secrets with me. I want details. Whys and wherefores."

He coughs a little but owns up to everything. After China's crypto ban in 2021, lots of mines moved out to Kazakhstan for its cheap electricity. Things went well for about a year. Then there got to be so many crypto mines that they drove up electricity prices in the country. The locals protested. There were vandalisms and thefts, and the government threatened to cut power on the mines in the winter, which would have caused the machines to freeze in the subzero winter and become damaged. The owner of a mining operation decided to fold and live large off the earnings. Tong, whose nose is specially tuned for bargains, somehow got wind of this and bought their equipment at a steep discount.

Meanwhile, the crackdown back in China had tapered off. Timing was good; Tong had connections—ones he made through Deckard's charity—that allowed him to lease this power plant before it was even completed. He had two problems: there was a drought through the winter, and he didn't have the technical know-how to set up a mine, let alone disguise its traffic. Finally, the rainy season was starting, and the power plant was going online. When Deckard came to him for a loan, he saw the solution to his remaining problem. Tong proposed a Faustian bargain: in exchange for the loan, Deckard would set up the bitcoin mine, and handle things personally both for security reasons and so he had "skin in the game."

"In other words, *implicated*. But why would Tong do this? Surely there are legal ways to make money? Why risk jail time?"

"Legal means aren't always as profitable these days. Or as thrilling," Deckard says. "Tong didn't get to be where he is today by coloring inside the lines."

"Once a coal boss, always a coal boss—even though he was actually trained as a lawyer."

"He has his own views on what a just legal system should be like, which is not this." Deckard draws a circle in the air.

Alice can hardly contain herself. "So he's got grudges against the whole Chinese legal system, and this is his way of thumbing his nose at stupid laws? Hadn't he come close to going to jail before? Didn't he learn anything? How about this simple rule: Anyone who lives here, in this country, should obey its laws. If you don't like it, maybe you should move somewhere else. Tong can afford to do that. Not that it would be any better—you've lived in the States; you know what that's like—plenty of stupid laws. But wherever you go, you don't get to pick and choose which ones apply to you and which ones don't."

"Two answers to that. First, this country needs people willing to stay and fight for changes from within. Tong and I choose to stay here and make changes happen. Second, we have no effective ways to challenge stupid laws here, so the best we can do is take the matter into our own hands. And that means small steps. Minor acts of civil disobedience. Whatever an individual can do." His eyes gleam, and he has that fevered look whenever he is overtaken by his fight-for-not-flight-from-the-country patriotism.

Alice has to cut him off before he's swept away by his own oceanic feelings. "Look, I wouldn't call illegal mining a minor act of civil disobedience. And trying to fight the government is like throwing eggs at a rock—at a mountain. Your little criminal acts make no difference at all. And we aren't having some intellectual debate over port and cigar. You guys have actually broken the law, and there are real consequences. Tong might get caught. You might, too. And if somehow they found Lili and me here, how would we prove our innocence?"

"You should leave."

"I would. But Lili wants to stay and help you."

His expression softens. "Look, we're not getting caught if you don't blabber about it. The power station is completely off-grid. No one can detect anything by monitoring electricity usage. All the data is encrypted. There's tight physical security, and Tong's careful with the people he chooses to run things."

"Really? Haven't two ordinary women just breached this tight physical security last night and figured out what's going on here? And what if it weren't Lili and me but someone else with a vendetta?" Like the stalker dude, Alice suddenly remembers with a shudder. "Did they ever catch the 302 guy? Somebody was following us on our way here. Possibly the same stalker who stalked you and Lili at the restaurant in Shanghai a few months ago."

Deckard shakes his head. "No. For the record, nobody ever stalked us. Lili is always paranoid about stalkers—as pretty young women are sometimes. I see she's gotten to you, too."

Alice is speechless. She was quite certain the man on the train was stalking them, but looking back, what real evidence was there besides Lili's saying so? Did they jump off the train for no good reason? Who is gaslighting her, Lili or Deckard?

"We've had intruders here from time to time," Deckard continues. "So far none as clever as you gals. But really, don't worry about it. In the worst case, Tong has people in government."

"I see. What's the point of having money if you can't buy influence? Only that adds to the list of offenses; I'm pretty sure bribery carries worse penalties than mining a few bitcoins. Look, you have"—she almost says, a family—"a child. You don't want to go to prison over this."

"Let's just drop this, alright? I'm not here because I have a choice."

"Alright. Tell me about the USB key, the one you and Lili were working on the password of. Does it really have tens of millions of dollars' worth of bitcoins on it?"

He blinks. "How did you know about this?" he asks quietly.

"Fei told me. Is it true?"

He looks at her, his expression complicated. "Who told her?"

"Somebody anonymously texted her with the info. Is it true?"

He sighs, rubs his eyes, and puts his glasses back on. "But you aren't going to tell her that. This is my confidential information, and I'm interviewing you to be my lawyer. Have you said anything to Lili?"

"No. It wasn't my place. But don't you think you should?"

"I do plan to tell her, when the time is right. Just don't want to freak her out or put any undue pressure on her."

"Yeah, hard to know what other surgical procedure she might have undertaken if she had undue pressure. But this is your big chance—why did you give up on working with her to recover the password?"

"I didn't. It was her—she got in her head that we weren't succeeding because she didn't look sufficiently like Wu Ying. But it never was her. The problem was with Neuromersion. It wasn't sophisticated enough to reach deep into the mind to fetch the password. Then she had that 'accident'—now I understand what she was trying to do. It had always been a long shot anyway, thinking that her presence would somehow shake the password loose from some hidden crevices inside my brain. But it's not going to happen. Her having a new nose isn't going to change things. There may be another way."

"Like what?"

"I've been trying to work on a hardware solution using side-channel attacks," he says. "I'll show you." He goes on to explain what SCAs are. The technique involves operating a chip in conditions it's not designed for. He has tried different things to the USB's processor chip: varying the supply voltages and clock frequencies, applying a magnetic field, shining ultraviolet light, in the hopes of tricking the chip into spitting out the unencrypted password on startup. It's a high-wire act, since he is unable to find another USB key like the one Hikaru gave him, there is no reference he can study or experiment on. He has to take extra caution not to damage the device. It's like fording a river in the dark. One slip, it could be all over.

As he speaks, he draws diagrams on a whiteboard and uses markers and an eraser as props to illustrate the interactions of the components. He keeps pushing up his glasses and letting them fall back down. He literally rolls up his sleeves. He seems glad for an audience who's interested in following along the technical nuances of what he's doing. As usual, Alice finds his explanations clear, concise, and engaging. This is the kind of thing he'd rather do, solving technical problems, not setting up illegal crypto mines for crime bosses.

"So did it work?" Alice asked innocently, already knowing the answer.

"No. Twice now I thought I had the answer, but it turned out to be two wasted tries," he says, slumping back into the chair.

"That's discouraging."

"Discouraging? Because it failed?" Deckard's bloodshot eyes

widen, the dark pupils sucking in light. "No, it just means I have to attack from another angle. Think bigger, out of the box—destroy the box."

"What are you talking about?"

"The key to all cryptocurrency—the actual cryptographic algorithm itself, ECDSA."

Alice has to think hard about what that acronym stands for. Elliptical Curve Digital Signature Algorithm, if she recalls correctly, is used to generate Bitcoin keys and signatures. It's the basis of Bitcoin security. "What do you want to do with it?"

"I'm going to crack it."

Alice hears a snorting sound and realizes it's her own laugh. "Sure, crack the encryption algorithm, then you would have broken all of cryptocurrency—and the Internet. And why not get some other problems wrapped up while you're at, like, completing the unified field theory? End global warming? Achieve artificial general intelligence and world peace?"

Deckard is unruffled by her dismissiveness and coolly reminds her he was a part of the team that identified the weakness in the Data Encryption Standard back in the late nineties.

"But that was different—your graduate lab just built some special hardware that did the computation super fast. Mining hardware is already extremely optimized. You can't improve much unless you've got a quantum computer." Alice catches her breath. "You haven't got a quantum computer here, have you?"

"No. And anyone trying to speed up current hardware and brute force the solution is on the wrong track." His tone suggests that he finds this approach truly regrettable. "All those attempts in finding vulnerabilities—looking for back doors, implementation errors, parameter injection attacks—are all just tinkering at the edges. There is a better way."

"I imagine if there is a better way, cryptographers would have found it by now."

"Listen to yourself—if that were the case, no progress would ever be made. People haven't tried everything. There are an unlimited number of transforms. You've got to look beyond your own dimensions."

Alice feels the conversation slipping away and reaches for the nearest thing floating her way that she has some understanding of. "Transforms? Like Fourier?"

"Sort of. Fourier gets you from time domain to frequency domain; what I'm looking for also takes you from domain A to domain B, only we don't necessarily know what A and B are. Standard transforms aren't going to solve computationally intractable problems like the elliptical curve discrete logarithm problem. We've got to transcend our smallness, our three-dimensionality."

"How?"

"Multi-dimensional transforms, over manifolds, both Euclidian and non-Euclidian. There are so many of them to try. Looking for them is like hunting for comets, the faintest patterns of light. You realize how vast the universe is, how infinite the possibilities…"

One of the possibilities is that he has gone completely off the rail. "Alright, how are you testing out the possibilities and when will you be done?" She asks, swallowing back *Before Danyang runs out of cash? Before we all die? Before the universe shrinks back down to a black hole?*

"I don't know," Deckard says with an unexpected vehemence. "But it will happen, I guarantee it—when it does, it will change everything. *Everything!*"

Alice feels tiny pricks of cold on her face—Deckard's spittle has traveled far. She watches in horror as her friend plunges his hands into his hair and grabs fistfuls, as if trying to lift himself up. This is crazy, and all this mumbo jumbo is just that, empty, crazy talk; he doesn't actually have anything. He's not anywhere close to solving ECDSA, or getting the bitcoins off the USB key, or even completing Tong's little illicit operation so he can get the loan. Too many irons in a fire that's burning out fast. Deckard has gone mental. Danyang is over. So is her own partnership track.

There's a knock on the door, as if the person has been listening and waiting for a break in the conversation. She jumps up and opens it.

It's a portly Black man. Standing behind him is Lili.

46

"When I got up this morning, I noticed a southerly wind. And surely enough, it brought Miss Lili into my humble on-site office," the man says in nearly perfect Mandarin with just a trace of Sichuanese accent. He turns toward Alice. "You look very surprised," he says.

"Ah, sorry, I wasn't expecting..."

"I know!" Lili says. "A Black doctor who speaks Chinese like a native! And an excellent acupuncturist to boot."

"Black person doctor, not Black doctor, which would sound like I'm practicing medicine without a license," the man says with a diastematic grin.

After a round of introductions, Lili says, "Earlier, when Dr. Chang was putting needles in me, I noticed this interesting design painted on his medical bag, so I asked him if it was supposed to be an African mask."

"You might call it a kind of family crest—my grandfather used to paint his face like that. Grandpa was a Nganga, a healer. He painted his face when he performed iboga ceremonies—that's a traditional West African spiritual practice, a journey," Dr. Chang recalls with fondness. "Grandpa was resigned to the fact that, like my dad, I too wouldn't follow his footsteps to become a shaman, but he didn't want the knowledge to be lost. He tried to teach me. It was just one of those things I am so glad to have learned when I was young, now that Grandpa is gone forever. It's a true gift." He closes his eyes and palms as if in prayer.

"Do you still practice?" Alice asks.

"Yes. I still do a journey by myself at least once a year, usually when I feel uncentered."

"Interesting," Deckard says. "I didn't know that."

"Well, it hasn't come up," Chang says.

Alice gives Lili a look. *What's this about?* Lili blinks back. *Patience.* "Tell them what that's like, the ceremony," she says.

"It takes a full day. Before the ceremony, the followers fast. Then the Nganga gives them iboga, a bitter-tasting plant with special properties. Once the followers ingest iboga, the Nganga begins to chant, dance, play the mungongo harp and the ngoma drum, and generally guide the journey. After a couple of hours, the iboga will set in, and the visions will come, like a vivid dream but full of insights."

"What kind of insights?" Deckard asks.

"Depends. Sometimes the messages are very clear, other times more subtle. Sometimes they come in the form of helpful spirits. Some people are aware of their surroundings during visions, some are not and rather feel like they are dreaming. Personally, I've experienced lots of different things: understanding of death and nature and the circle of things; knowledge about how to heal traumas; connection to my ancestors and my past lives; connection with others and the world; finding what's lost; accepting the loss…"

"Did you hear him?" Lili cries. "Finding what's lost! He can help find what's lost!" She raises her arms at Deckard. "He might be able to help you get unstuck."

Alice eyes Deckard, who stands expressionlessly. Does Lili actually believe this man and his plant medicine has that kind of power? The young woman is past the age of believing magical wish-granting genies, though not by much. Yet something Dr. Chang said struck a chord with Alice, too—healing traumas. If only iboga could do that for her.

"Well," the doctor says, "the ceremony is not about finding lost things or forgotten memories per se. The Nganga guides the follower on a journey, where the follower has visions. It isn't about knowledge or soothsaying—the visions can't help you figure out the winning lottery number or which stock to buy. They are about gaining insight. Reaching parts of the subconscious, if you prefer to think of it that way. Things you have forgotten may turn up."

So iboga sounds like some kind of psychedelic, like ayahuasca or magic mushrooms. Alice had read *How to Change Your Mind* by Michael Pollan, and knows about the mind-expanding properties of these medicines. But Chinese drug laws are very strict. The doctor, practically a Chinese person, ought to know this. Perhaps that's why he has come out to the middle of nowhere, where chances of getting caught while trying to "center himself" is practically zero.

"Where do you get the iboga?" Alice asks.

"I've got a license for importing herbal medicines from Africa. I use their native names. Customs has never raised any fuss."

"It just might be what you need," Lili says to Deckard, her eyes sparkling. "To pair with Neuromersion, give you the boost needed to recover the password."

"It just sounds so." Alice frowns as she searches for the word and is only able to come up with "woo-woo" in English.

"You are right," the doctor says. "Consider this: most indigenous cultures have something like this. The word 'Shaman' originates from the Tungus tribe in Siberia—doesn't mean they were the first people to practice it, but they had the brand, the word for it that caught on. The neighboring Mongolians have similar customs, as do Native Americans and Aboriginal Australians."

"But not the Chinese," Alice says.

"Not true. The Manchus of Qing Dynasty practiced Shamanism. And the traditional Chinese 巫术 (wu shu, witchcraft) matches the Shamanic practices almost exactly."

"I mean, the Chinese don't use psychoactive drugs."

"Probably untrue, also. Look around, lots of woods here, little brown mushrooms everywhere. You don't see the practice today doesn't mean it never existed. Let me show you something else. How can I access the Internet here?"

Deckard shows him the secure terminal. Dr. Chang types in something and brings up a photo from the Shanghai Museum website of an ancient bronze goblet with fluid outlines, standing elegantly on three legs and covered with decorative writing. 亚矣侯 (Ya Yi Hou), the text said, ceremonial vessel from the Shang Dynasty, 1300–1100 BC.

"Look at this," he says, enlarging the photo and pointing at a couple of protrusions on the lip of the vessel.

"I'll be damned," Deckard mutters. They are staring at two little Psilocybe mushrooms: long stems, tiny caps, green patina and all.

"Never knew anything about this. Do you think they—the governments, the mainstream Confucian culture—suppressed these traditions?" Alice asks. There is some irony in asking this Cameroonian all the stuff about Chinese culture, but the man is clearly knowledgeable. She's reminded of the Confucian way—in a party of three, there must be someone who's my teacher.

"Possibly, but there is another theory," the doctor says. "Most of these psychotropics have side effects—nausea, GI distress, bad taste. Iboga is no exception. By the way, some purging might occur. Anyway, your people are agrarian and developed alcohol fermentation early on. It's easier and tastier to achieve an altered mental state by drinking alcohol, even if it may not unlock your subconscious quite the same way. That, and later the Buddhist emphasis on meditation, which aims to achieve such states from within—what do you think enlightenment means? Meditation is a trainable, more predictable process with no side effects, if more difficult to master. But you people always prefer things you have to work at. Perhaps those were the reasons why the practice of ingesting magic mushrooms fell out of favor."

Alice is tickled by his use of "your people." She has always thought of her people as hard-eyed realists, not worshipers of magic mushrooms or sojourners to other worlds. But if the erudite doctor is right, those ancestors are as much her people as Confucius and Mao Zedong.

"Is it safe?" she asks.

"Generally, yes. The Nganga keeps watch to make sure one doesn't journey too far. I've had to do it by myself but there's never been any problems."

"Is it addictive?"

"No. In fact, iboga has been used to treat addiction."

"I'd like to try it in conjunction with Neuromersion—it could be the missing piece, what I need to open up more and reach deeper into the subconscious," Deckard says with a kind of clenched decisiveness—or perhaps desperation—of a man with little to lose.

The doctor nods. He turns to ask Alice and Lili, "Do you want to try, too?"

"Of course—it's as safe a setting for this sort of thing as it gets, isn't it?" Lili says eagerly.

"Yes, it is. The biggest risk is you might learn something about yourself you didn't want to."

Do I want this? Alice asks herself. Until recently, she had never so much as been drunk. Yet ever since reading the Michael Pollan book, she has been curious. She does want to try. Curiosity and desire for healing are just front matters, backed by Dr. Chang's cautiously confident guarantee of safety. And there is something deeper, more illogical and difficult to explain: Ever since she landed in this country, she has been sensing a kind of rupture, as if a new self is bursting out, whose main purpose is to surprise herself.

IN THE DARKENED ANECHOIC CHAMBER, the three of them lie on the net floor. Deckard has on the Neuromersion helmet. Alice and Lili are on each side of him, wearing eye covers. Dr. Chang sits in a corner, drumming on an upturned bucket. The sound is muffled rather than sonorous, but the point is in the beat. He calls out to the spirits around them.

So here goes nothing.

47

Alice finds herself in a field. It's dark at first. The drum beats are like strobe lights at a disco, illuminating her surroundings. There's grass under her feet; a water tower looms to her left. So it is the field in front of her childhood apartment. Not quite the wonderland she was expecting. Then she feels the soft fabric of her dress, the one with purple and pink flowers and princess sleeves, a favorite from her tween days that she outgrew too quickly. She looks around for signs of spirits but finds none. What's happening? Will this be a failed journey?

The drumming continues. She holds on to it like a lifeline. She needs to keep going. Approaching the water tower, she spots a mallard sitting in a nest of grass. The mallard sees her, too, and stands up courteously. A clutch of eggs peek out from underneath its butt. A mallard hatching ducklings? Is this a patriarchal conspiracy?

She goes up to the duck—not walking, but weightless gliding across and closing the distance—and asks it if it's there for her.

Through its beady eyes, the mallard beams back the message "yes."

Well, good. Yet she can't get her question out. She's having a momentary lapse of memory. She tries to focus—it's about something she can't figure out. There have been lots of those lately, but this one has puzzled her for a long time. What is it? "I'm sorry, I've forgotten my question," she says.

The duck sits back down on the eggs, indicating to her that he has all the time in the world. Then she remembers she can ask questions for others. In fact, it is often easier to do so, according to Dr. Chang.

Of those, she has many. She picks the most pressing one, what she's here for. "How about this: Could you tell me the password to Deckard's USB key?"

The mallard actually smiles. Not an outward smile but a telepathic one, not unkindly. "If I told you, would you believe me?"

True. On the one hand, there are bitcoins worth tens of millions of dollars at stake. On the other, an imaginary duck. How can she resolve the absurdities of the situation? How can she answer honestly without sounding rude? Is it okay to be rude to an imaginary duck?

"No, it's not okay, except I won't consider this one rude. Honesty can seem rude, but dishonesty actually is. I can tell the difference. Yes, it takes a little while getting used to these mind-to-mind conversations."

Well, suppose I believe you, then what?

"Then nothing. I don't possess that knowledge."

Of course. It's like asking about the winning lottery number—she needs to remember that the duck might be her subconscious. If she doesn't possess that knowledge, how can it?

"But Deckard does," the duck reminds her.

She raises her head to meet those shiny beady eyes, which blink twice. Do ducks blink? Well, this one does.

Sure, Deckard possesses the knowledge, but it's lodged somewhere in the crevice of his synapses. He can't retrieve it, so it's useless.

"He needs this." The duck shows her something on the ground.

A piece of some kind of transparent bone. Cartilage?

"Courage."

You are funny. What does courage have to do with it?

"Everything."

He has plenty of courage—he isn't even afraid of breaking the law.

"Courage to embrace failures."

As do all of us.

"You catch on quick."

It isn't about me.

"It's about all of us."

Oh, I know how to handle this kind of vagueness, Alice thinks. *I do this for a living, squeezing concrete details out of inventors who like to wave their hands and gloss over the details. Please clarify. Explain more fully what you mean by that.*

The duck is mellow about it. "Why don't we just sit here for a bit."

So she takes a seat next to the brooding duck. A comforting warmth comes over her. She hugs it, and it rests its blue-green neck in the crook of her arm. They have a very nice moment listening to the drums.

After who knows how long, the duck nudges her with the feathers on its wing. "There he is," it says.

A man is standing with his back facing her. Someone she wants to see. She runs in front of him.

"Ba," she says, surprised. He's younger than she is, barely into his forties. That would make sense, if the body she inhabits now is that of a teenager. "Are you here to help me?"

Her dad looks at her. His smile is shy, though he was not known as a shy man. He nods.

It's all coming back to her now, the thing that puzzles her. "What made you decide to stay in China? Why wouldn't you join Mom in the U.S.? No, don't just repeat what was in the letter; I remember what you wrote. But there is more to this you didn't tell us."

His smile fades. His brows come together, and three short vertical lines are squeezed between them. "Because I was dyslexic. I could never quite figure out whatever I read in English. The letters and words were just jumbled together. I had to use a ruler and run my thumb across the words to spell things out one letter at a time, and even then they didn't make much sense. As soon as I figured out one word I'd forget what the word came before it meant. It's like my brain turned into goop as soon as I started to read English."

"But how could that be? You were a college professor."

"The strange thing is that I could read Chinese just fine. And numbers weren't a problem, either. Perhaps because different parts of the brain are used in processing character-based language and math. It was a strange brain deficiency—I just couldn't do English. So, there was never a chance in hell I could come to the U.S. and go to grad school and get a job like your mom wanted me to. I would be illiterate, completely dependent on your mother. I didn't want that. Nor would she."

All the blame, the resentment, the self-pity flood back and smash into a single point and collapse. "I'm so sorry," she says.

Her father is silent.

Wish you had told me, Alice almost says. But what good would it do for her to know this? Would it have changed anything?

"Probably not," her father says. She forgets he can hear her thoughts. "It was my own shameful secret. I took it to the grave. I'm sorry you've had to bear the weight of that all these years. Let it go now. Be free."

The duck soars in the sky. Her heart does, too.

48

"How did it go?" Peter looks up from his reading glasses.

"Well enough," Alice says, taking a seat in the visitor's chair across his desk. "They were almost in a crisis situation but the CEO pulled a rabbit out of the hat and got some funding last minute."

"Excellent!" Peter smiles brightly, his near-white lashes batting along. "See how useful an in-person visit is?"

As if that had anything to do with anything, Alice thought. And if only the real story were that neatly wrapped up in a bow. The truth was that Deckard never was able to recover the password. The iboga journey did help with his focus, however, and he was thus able to complete the last bit of work he owed Tong, which was really the best outcome they could practically hope for. He would get the loan and promised to pay the invoices. What the future holds for Danyang is still anybody's guess. If the economy doesn't turn around soon, they'd be back in the same place in six months.

At Alice's muted response, Peter adds, "I'll mention your efforts at the partnership meeting. It won't go unnoticed."

"About that," Alice says. "Thank you, but it's not necessary."

"Huh?"

"I'd like to go away for a while."

Peter puts his pen down. He takes off his glasses. "A sabbatical? Well, it's not the firm's official policy, but considering how long you've been here, we ought to give it some serious consideration. Maybe a month or two? I know the past couple of years have been exhausting for folks with young children..."

Alice shakes her head. "I need more time than that."

"It might be tough to find people to cover your clients for much longer..."

"You'll have to. Because I'm leaving."

Peter's blue eyes are glassy. "What do you mean, leaving?"

"As in, I quit."

"Surely you are joking..."

"No, I'm not. It's been wonderful working here. I appreciate everything you've done for me." Alice stands up and extends a hand. Peter sits, unmoving, so she takes his hand in hers and gives it two vigorous shakes. "Bye now."

At home, Henry is apoplectic. "It's one thing to turn down the partnership. But to quit completely! Without a new job lined up, in this economy? What were you thinking?"

Alice just sits there.

"What's your explanation? What are we going to do now?"

"You can cash out my 401k. That'll pay for tuition and mortgage for a while. Do talk with Gary first about taxes. I'll sign the paperwork electronically."

"Then what?"

"You'll figure it out."

"You can't do this. It's completely irresponsible. Have you gone nuts?" He grabs her arm. "Go back, grovel, say you made a mistake. Get your job back!"

Alice goes completely limp. Henry lets go of her and watches open-mouthed as Alice stands up, takes out a duffel back from the closet, and starts to pack.

She walks down the hall to her children's rooms, planting kisses on each of them and silently says her goodbyes. Tears roll down her cheeks, leaving hot tracks. She starts to walk away before they hit the floor. She can't waver now.

She packs the car with her clothes, some camping gear, and canned food from their pantry, which has always been well-stocked since the pandemic. She withdraws ten thousand dollars from the bank and drives north.

It's still shoulder season, so she has little trouble finding spots at campgrounds. She sleeps in the van most nights. When the mood strikes, she moves the narrow air mattress outside and watches the Milky Way. She alternates between takeout and cooking on the camp stove. She stays for two or three days in a place, does some hikes, then moves on. It takes her nearly two weeks to reach Vancouver, where a spell of unusual solar storms brings out gorgeous northern lights like a fantastic dream.

In Surrey, she eats an exceptional tomato she bought at a farm stand. When she returns for more she notices a wanted sign. She applies for the job, ignoring the curious looks of the other farmhands and answering vaguely to the pointed inquiries of the boss. She gets a work permit and starts to work as a tomato picker, earning C$17.50 per hour. It's exhausting work but her skin has never been more hydrated—the hot house is humid like a steam room. She constantly has the feeling that moss is growing out of her nape.

In time she befriends Jimena and Ana Paula. She moves into their tiny place on the farm, mostly just to take showers, use the toilet, and cook food. They go to the laundromat together. She still sleeps in the van. She talks with them via Google Translate and learns enough Spanish to get through a meal. The days are stretching longer and longer. Jimena, who is Guatemalan and wants to become a hairdresser someday, would cut their hair. Some evenings, Alice would drive her roommates to Mud Bay Park to watch birds. The scenery reminds her of the Baylands, where she used to go biking with her family.

She gets a new telephone number. She doesn't call her family. Now and then, she snaps a photo of something she sees—a monarch caterpillar, a tomato that's half green and half red like Sleeping Beauty's apple, a bright orange-colored mushroom growing on a log—and sends them a postcard using an app. *Love you, miss you*, she always writes. She hopes they know she means it.

The tomato farm shuts down in late fall for the year. She considers staying, but in the end decides to travel across the country with her roommates to Leamington, Ontario, where there are farms operating year-round. Looking at the map, she realizes that it's about the same latitude as the northern border of California. How could she not know that before?

She drops off her roommates and heads south. She has the vague notion that she wants to be somewhere warmer for the winter. Perhaps she'd go back to Alabama, which she hasn't visited since high school graduation. In Memphis, her van breaks down in the Walmart parking lot on Elvis Presley Blvd. So she gets a store clerk job there, and finds out about the fringe benefit of being able to park the van in the parking lot at night and sleeping there. She brushes aside the attention from a security guard offering his home to her and instead gets a trial membership at a gym nearby for showers. When she's driven to the brink of insanity by the Christmas jingles at the store, her van is finally fixed, so she quits and takes a job as a delivery driver for Amazon. There are several law firms on her delivery route; one of them does intellectual property law. She calls them and dials the phone directory at random. When someone answers, she hangs up—what is she thinking? She's not licensed to practice in Tennessee.

She stays in Memphis for four years. She gets an apartment and takes in a stray cat she names Marshmallow. Gradually, the memories of her family get hazy. The postcards become infrequent, and eventually the photo-to-postcard app company goes out of business, and she doesn't sign up with another one. She keeps her gym membership and works out there daily. She's mostly healthy, save for a molar problem that first required a root canal, then extraction and a dental implant.

One day, while she's walking, a disorderly bicyclist on the sidewalk runs into her and knocks her into traffic.

When she wakes up, she asks the young attending doctor about her injuries. His widow's peak reminds her of Casey. "Fractures in the upper right arm, collarbone, hipbone," he says as he looks through her charts on the computer terminal next to her bed.

"How come I can't feel my arms and legs?"

A pause.

He tells her the good news first, then the bad: Her legs and feet aren't broken. But there are injuries to the spinal cord.

"What does it mean?"

"It's too early to say. Each case is unique. Your recovery will depend on many factors, including the extent of the injury, how well you respond to treatment, and your overall health—you seem pretty healthy, which is good. We have a team of specialists who will be working closely with you throughout your recovery. Our goal is to help you regain as much function as possible and to support you in adapting to the changes in your life."

"What kind of changes? Why do I need to adapt to them?" Then she realizes he is talking about the life of a quadriplegic.

A woman named Clarissa comes to see her. She is the caseworker. Does Alice have any family she should contact?

"No," she answers, closing her eyes. The bicyclist was long gone. She will have to deal with all the insurance stuff later. Maybe she'll have to declare bankruptcy? If she told them who she really is, she could get Henry into trouble—they're still legally married, as far as she knows. Her debts would become his. A more thoughtful, decent person would have taken care of that. But she had long given up on being such a person. *These are my comeuppances.* She wishes she had stayed in Canada with their socialized medicine.

When food comes, she refuses it. That throws things into a loop. Several doctors come together for a consult, one of them a psychiatrist. They look at her with earnest eyes and discuss the pros and cons of force-feeding. She returns their concern and empathy with logical persuasion: I have nothing to live for. I am not the sort who would want to become a Paralympian. It is morally wrong to keep me alive against my will. You'd want the same for yourself. They ask her if she needs a chaplain or the equivalent in her religion. Or you can just give me a big hit of morphine, and that would save all of us a whole lot of trouble, she tells them. You can't keep me here forever.

Days pass like this, when they are locked in a contest of will. Finally, one of them mentions MAiD, Medical Assistance in Dying. There are only a handful of states where it's legal, and Tennessee isn't one of them. Even if she moves to one of the legal states, there will be hoops to jump through. She will need a lawyer.

She perks up. *I am a lawyer—was. I am all about jumping through hoops, though at this point only metaphorical ones. Just help me get a computer with dictation setup.*

They all smile at her. Alright. So transparent is their optimism: this could turn into something positive. Figuring out how to die might make her want to stay alive. Perhaps even turn into a new career opportunity for her, to help others die with dignity.

If only.

Sunlight comes through the windows. All she can see is snow. She's drugged up and feels no pain. She sees the faces of all her friends: Deckard, Cat, Wu Ying, Junhu, Lili, Dr. Chang. How did they get here? Then they leave, and Ba hovers nearby.

A tender sadness swamps her like a flash flood. She starts to weep. "So I know what it is like now, to die alone," she says.

He doesn't answer.

She asks, "Do you have regrets? I do."

He doesn't answer, just holds out a plate of food toward her. Succulent grilled chicken glistening in glaze, plain rice, a simple cucumber salad. The smell is beyond delicious; it's magical. He motions—whatever you do, eat something first.

She reaches for it.

49

"She's coming back." Lili's voice sounds like it's from an expanding space.

Alice struggles to open her eyes. Her eyelids experience a tearing sensation as the glued-shut eyelashes are pulled apart. She rubs the crud off with the back of her hands—so she has no trouble moving them. Her attempt to sit up fails—her body is still heavy, as if encased in scuba gear; the world around her is gently swaying like a ship. The walls are yellow-tinted. The sky outside the windows is dark. There are little rainbows around the edge of the lights on the ceiling.

"What happened?" she asks.

"You were gone a very long time."

There's a clock on the wall. The short hand is pointing down, the long hand is pointing down in the other direction. She has trouble figuring out what that means. So she asks, "How long?"

"For about thirty-four hours, which is an unusually long time. We were getting worried you might have gotten lost on your return journey," Dr. Chang says, bending down to take her pulse. His smile is familiar. Kind, concerned, relieved, just like the doctors she had conjured up. "But you are good. Welcome back."

They help her sit up. Only then does she notice the room is redolent with the scent of grilled meat basted in soy sauce and sugar. When Lili hands her a plate, however, her stomach signals resistance, and she asks for water instead. Everything she sees, smells, and hears is vivid. This isn't a dream. This is real life, solid as the little bumps her tongue feels on the inside of her lower lip.

She looks around. "Where's Deckard?"

"In the lab. He had real insight—an epiphany about how to rig the SCA," Lili says as she hands Alice a bottle of water.

Well, that's a start. "Did he mention anything about the ECDSA?"

"No."

That's a relief, Alice thinks. *At least the Internet is still intact.*

"What are you doing now?"

"Waiting. And cooking and eating. Speaking of which, I'm going to drop off a bowl for him at the lab."

When Lili returns with a set of dirty dinnerware, Alice tells her and Dr. Chang about her encounter with the duck, her dad, and her years as a vagrant. She wept unabashedly at points because she knows Lili and Dr. Chang would be sympathetic. Lili had a short, uneventful journey. She tells her she met Koko, Lloyd's mom, who tells her to "be fancy."

"I know who that is," Alice says. "I've seen Ninjago too many times."

"Take it easy," Dr. Chang says. "Go to sleep if you are tired."

He hardly needs to remind her of that. She's hesitant, however, harboring an irrational fear that she might get lost in her dreams again.

Deckard comes to them in the afternoon the next day, wild-haired, pucker-faced, and rank-smelling.

They look at him expectantly. "So?"

He exhales. "I've got it. Thought I was given a more complicated clue but turns out it's extremely straightforward and simple."

"That's great!" Lili cries. "But why does your face look like a bitter melon?"

"Because I had it all along. It was deckardshen, the original password."

"I don't believe this," Alice says. "Surely you have thought of that before?"

"I have, but I was so certain I changed it, I didn't want to waste any attempt on it. I thought, you know, there was just no way. But the latest SCA confirmed it."

Jaws drop collectively. Then Alice laughs, and everyone besides Deckard joins in. The absent-mindedness is so Deckard. But that's life—full of blind spots and surprises.

"Well, have you tried it?" Lili asks.

"No."

"What are you waiting for?"

He exhales again, turning the corner of his mouth downward to make the melon more bitter. "It's the last try. What if it's still wrong?"

Then at least you know, Alice is tempted to say. She also wants to say something about courage, but such banality, unless she is personally willing to type in the password on Deckard's behalf, might as well come from a duck.

"I'll do it," Lili says. "As long as you don't blame me if it fails."

THEY GATHER OUTSIDE THE LAB, the grim suspense feels like an execution. *If you're smart, girl, you'll do it as quickly as possible to minimize the pain.* Alice wishes she could send the message to Lili telepathically. Perhaps Lili has heard her. A minute later, they hear a squeal coming from inside.

THEY CROWD BEHIND DECKARD, who is back in the driver's seat in front of the computer. A few mouse clicks and he opens up a text file consisting of two lines. He pauses.

"What are we looking at?" Dr. Chang asks.

"The address and the private key of some bitcoins a friend gave me a long time ago," Deckard says.

Seeing these unassuming alphanumeric strings, Alice is buffeted by an uneasy mix of anticlimax, anticipation, and wonder. The strings themselves haven't changed for over a dozen years and can remain the same for dozens more. From the moment these jumbles of numbers and letters were created, the arrow of time shot forward: a part of humanity, aided by computers, continues to ascribe values to them—nothing, millions, anywhere in between. Some of those humans have gotten richer, some lost fortunes. Some are dead. Some are in jail. None got younger.

Deckard raises his hands over the keyboard, then puts them back down.

"Do you want us to leave?" Alice asks, sensing the loss of nerves. She would want to be left alone if it were her. Then again, she wouldn't have forgotten the password in the first place.

Deckard looks at her and shakes his head twice. With a deep inhale, he brings up the browser and navigates to blockchain.com/explorer, copies and pastes the shorter string into the search box, then hits the little magnifying glass button next to it.

Lili is the first to react. She shakes Deckard's shoulders, then puts her arms around his neck and hugs him from behind. "Congratulations! This is awesome!"

"This isn't for real, is it?" Dr. Chang asks, putting his face close to the screen, squinting.

Deckard stands up. He turns to shake the doctor's hand, then pulls him into a bear hug. "As real as gold and silver, my brother. You made this possible, Dr. Chang, and you, sweetheart." He reaches for Lili with the other arm and plants a kiss on her cheek, then beams at Alice. "And you, Alice, for bringing us together. Let's go celebrate."

He unplugs the USB key and puts it in a zippered breast pocket. Alice is tempted to ask him if he should put the bitcoins somewhere more secure. But where? FTX? Genesis? Binance? Some other platform that's possibly co-mingling customer funds and might go bankrupt tomorrow? Until he figures out how to exchange the funds, a hardware wallet next to his chest seems as good a place as any.

They are almost out of the door when he turns back toward the desk. "I just want to look at it again," he says, giggling.

On the screen, in a light peach-colored box, under "Bitcoin Balance," are the unmistakable numbers: 2000.00000000 $56,686,400. With a deep satisfied sigh, he closes the browser.

THEY'RE DRINKING white wine mixed with sparkling water—the closest thing to champagne they can find in the kitchen—when Lao Mo barges in, panting.

"Shen Zong, we got the guy—the 302. He claims to know Ms. Duan Lili. Can you come with me?"

IT IS the man on the train. Zip-tied but not gagged, he is slumped sideways on a chair in the small room, fuming.

"You need to go home," he says when he sees Lili.

"Who the hell are you?" Lili asks.

"Zeng Dongxuan, if that's his real name," Lao Mo says, removing a wallet from his pocket to show them the man's ID.

"What do you want?"

The man tilts his head. "For you to go home."

"Did my brother send you?" Lili crosses her arms and scowls.

The man hesitates but nods.

Deckard steps closer. "Miss Duan is an adult. She can decide what she wants to do. If you promise to just go back and deliver that message to her brother, I'll untie you and let you go."

The man shifts, looking like he's about to agree.

"No," Lili says, then gestures for them to go outside. Shutting the door behind, she tells them, "It's not that simple. My brother works for the government. Ministry of State Security."

Deckard gives her a severely annoyed look. "You never mentioned that before."

"You never asked."

It seems pretty obvious that something like this may be of concern. But Lili, skilled at picking up the minute details around her, seems to have missed that clue. Another blind spot.

"There were some supposedly State Security guys who visited Deckard's mom's house. Do you think he could be one of them?"

"Possibly."

"Maybe we can just offer him something—a little bitcoin—to keep quiet," Dr. Chang suggests. The good doctor has lived in this country too long.

Lili shakes her head. "You don't know the type that work for the Ministry, do you? They consider themselves incorruptible. They've been brainwashed to really buy into the 'serving the country with two empty sleeves' crap. Besides, penalties are stiff if they get caught. Even their family members would be barred from schools and government jobs."

"There's no reason Zeng would know about the mine," Alice says. "Perhaps just tell him he shouldn't have broken into a private data center. Give him a warning this time and send him off."

Deckard bites on his lower lip, thinking. After a while, he says, "Dr. Chang, do you still have some of that iboga left?"

"Yes, what do you want?"

"Give the guy a dose. He would be a perfect candidate for our experiment—we've shown that iboga and Neuromersion can open up our minds to other possibilities; let's see if we can change his beliefs."

Lili's face is flushed. "And we should record his trip. If he doesn't keep his mouth shut, we'll send it to his boss's boss."

"Blackmailing?" Alice asks in disbelief. "That sounds like a dumb idea. He'll just say he was set up."

"It would be good insurance," Deckard says. "He's running a side job for Lili's brother. This can't be sanctioned; he probably got something for it. It'll be pretty complicated for him to explain all this to the disciplinary committee, let alone prove it. Point is, it would be in his own interest to keep quiet."

The doctor scratches his chin. "I can try." He grins, showing his gapped teeth. "You know, the clinic could use a remodel. Won't take much, five or six hundred thousand yuan will make a huge difference for the patients..."

"Of course. Consider it done."

LILI and the doctor administer the iboga: Lili pinches Zeng's nose to force open his mouth; the doctor pours the brew from a teacup down Zeng's throat.

Deckard and Alice watch from the side. Once again a weary disbelief washes over Alice. *Why am I here? How is this all happening?* She pinches herself just to confirm she isn't dreaming. She's complicit in all this now. She hasn't become as corrupt as Tong or even Deckard. Yet, little pieces are taken somewhere to make her law firm and herself whole, and she isn't going to be choosy about where the pieces come from, whether they're clean. She just wants this over with.

Twenty minutes later, Zeng starts to heave like he's dragging a heavy sack uphill. He moans and thrashes as if in pain.

"It's alright, we all had to go through with it," Deckard says as he unties Zeng and starts to record with his phone. The moaning gets louder, beads of sweat form on Zeng's head and soon form rivulets. Alice is starting to sweat, too. The room is so damn hot. Zeng clutches his chest. Dr. Chang gestures for Deckard to turn off the recording and crouches down to take the man's pulse. The doctor frowns. "He's having arrhythmia, and his pulse is weak," he says. He takes out a blood pressure cuff from his medical bag and straps it to Zeng's upper arm. "His blood pressure is too low." A minute later, he tries again. "BP is dropping." He turns Zeng over and pinches his mouth open, then hollers at Lili to get him a tongue suppressor. Lili stuck her fingers in Zeng's throat directly to induce vomit. Zeng gags and coughs but nothing comes out.

"We need to get him down to the clinic, now," Dr. Chang says.

"What?" Deckard is bewildered.

"You heard me. He's having an allergic reaction. He needs to get his stomach pumped right away, plus medication for his heart. I've got everything at the clinic. Get your ATVs here. We're taking him down the mountain."

What happens next is a blur: Deckard and Lili both run out. They come back on two two-seater ATVs. They lift Zeng off the floor and strap him into one. Dr. Chang hops into the driver's seat and takes off. Deckard and Alice get into the second ATV. It occurs to Alice it might be good to have Lili the ex-nurse along but she's gone inside for something and there's no time to wait.

They bump along the dirt road, following Dr. Chang. Alice hopes the jostling would make Zeng throw up on his own but that hasn't happened by the time they arrive at the clinic. Zeng is carried inside. Alice and Deckard are clumsy nurse assistants as Dr. Chang injects Zeng with medication, intubates, and suctions Zeng's stomach like pumping up a football. He then hooks Zeng up to an IV drip. Once that's done, the doctor rustles up a patient monitor from a corner and straps Zeng's arm into it. He's planted in front of the monitor like a captain steering a ship through a storm. There he stands, for several hours, until Zeng's blood pressure eventually returns to an acceptable range.

"Is the allergy common?" Alice does her best not to sound accusatory.

"It's exceedingly rare. I know it can happen in older people, but it's unheard of in someone so young. He might have some pre-existing heart condition," Dr. Chang says, wiping his face with his upper arm as he plops down on a stool.

∼

THEY SPEND the night keeping vigil as Zeng slumbers. Around 5 a.m., he stirs. When he wakes up, he is frightened. Alice gives him warm water and tries to soothe him.

"Excuse me, you over there," he says, squinting at Dr. Chang. "You look completely Black to me. Has something happened to my eyes?"

"Your eyes are fine. I am Black."

"A Black doctor?"

"A Black person doctor," Chang says. "I came originally from Africa, Cameroon to be exact. Do you remember who you are? Where are you from?"

Zeng turns his face at the ceiling, breathing hard. "I'm Zeng Dongxuan, originally from Wuzhen but I live in Shanghai now. What's this place?"

"You're in a clinic in Hongzhen, Sichuan."

"What am I doing in Sichuan?"

Dr. Chang exchanges looks with Deckard and Alice. "I'm not sure. Don't you remember?"

Zeng closes his eyes, struggling to recall. "There was some kind of store, maybe. I can't remember why I was there, though."

"What's the last thing you can recall with reasonable certainty?"

Zeng stares at the ceiling vacantly for a while. Finally, he says, "Going out with a couple of buddies to a hotpot place to celebrate me starting my new job."

"When was that?"

"When the quarantine ended, mid-December."

"Did any of you get Covid?"

"I don't know."

"Ministry of Security. A public servant," Deckard says. "You ought to be more discreet."

"What do you mean?"

"You were at the train station. Thrashing on the floor, spouting anti-government nonsense. Several people got videos of you; I told them not to share it but don't know if they would listen. You were on something, weren't you? You would have ODed had we not found you and taken you here. Dr. Chang saved your life."

Zeng looks ashen. He turns his head a little bit toward Chang. Tears suddenly burst out of his eyes. "I don't know. I'm no druggie. But I saw things. Not good things. It was a nightmare I couldn't wake up from. I felt very close to death. Thank you, doctor. I am so grateful to be alive."

∼

WHEN ALICE and Deckard decide to return to the power station, it's nearly three o'clock in the afternoon. Dr. Chang wants Zeng to stay another night at the clinic for observation, but Zeng feels well enough to go home and refuses. Reluctantly, the doctor agrees. The last train leaves in thirty minutes but they can still make it if they hurry. Dr. Chang takes Zeng in the doctor's car, while Alice and Deckard leave on their ATV.

"Do you think he's pretending?" Alice asks as she and Deckard bump along the road on their ATV.

"Zeng?"

"Yes. Don't you think it's awfully convenient for him to lose four months of memory? What if he was just pretending?"

"Did he seem like he was?"

"No. But he could be a really good actor. And what if he regains his memory as time goes on?"

"We'll deal with it then. But it's in his interest to keep quiet about this."

Suddenly, the ATV stops, sending Alice lurching forward. "Ow, what's that for?"

"I don't have my jacket."

"So?" It's just like him to leave his clothing behind. Then the significance dawns on her—the USB key is in the breast pocket of the jacket. "Oh, shit. I don't remember seeing it on you when we left for the clinic. You must've left it in the lab in that kerfuffle."

Deckard doesn't answer. Instead, he slams on the accelerator.

∼

IT'S EERILY quiet in the lab. Of course no one would be here. Heat is still on full blast. On the back of the chair is the navy blue jacket.

"Thank goodness," Deckard mutters as he races toward the jacket. He grabs it from the chair back, sticks his hand into the breast pocket, and turns to stone.

The two of them turn the jacket inside out. They run around the entire compound. The USB key is gone, so is Lili. They find Lao Mo watching TV in his room. He has no idea where Lili went. Nobody else does.

50

"So did Deckard call the police?" Henry asks from behind the wheel. He picked Alice up half an hour ago, and it has taken her nearly the entire drive to fill him in on her trip—with a few omissions about her other journey under the spell of iboga.

"Yes."

"But the police didn't find her?"

"No. The CCTV showed her leaving the compound right after we did. They did a sweep of the surrounding areas but found nothing. So they reported up to the provincial police. When the provincial police heard about what was on the USB key, they said it would be treated as a missing property case only for the value of the device, not the bitcoins. They gave Deckard a form to fill out and put the estimated value of the item at 10000 yuan, the max they would give to an electronic storage device."

"That's ridiculous! What about the FBI? They've cracked crypto theft cases before."

"They'll only investigate crimes on foreign soil under special circumstances, by invitation from foreign governments. Besides, Deckard is a Chinese national; the FBI couldn't care less."

"There are services, right? Bounty hunters who would track down lost crypto?"

"Trouble is, Deckard didn't make any backups—he didn't even have the address information for the bitcoins; the browser on the computer he used to check the bitcoins was set not to keep track of anything. They wouldn't know where to start."

"So that's it?"

"Easy come, easy go." Alice takes a sip from her water bottle.

"Who tipped Fei off?"

"The best we could come up with was that Deckard had let something slip when he was drunk with Lili—which he did from time to time. Perhaps Lili somehow let her brother know, and her brother tipped off Fei in order to figure out where Deckard was."

"If there is indeed a brother."

"Exactly. She could just as easily have pulled the con by herself. We tried to find out if there's someone with the last names of Duan or Zeng working for the Shanghai branch of the State Security Ministry, but haven't had any luck so far."

"Pretty slick con. None of you saw it coming?"

"With twenty-twenty hindsight." Alice purses her lips.

And where is Lili at this moment? On a private yacht? A luxury villa? How wrong Alice was about her. She thought they were friends—she laughs at that naive notion now. Actually, she never thought they were equals. She kept thinking she had something to teach the young woman, but ended up being the one schooled.

"What are you going to tell your boss?"

"The truth. Deckard fell apart. He threatened to jump off the dam; Lao Mo and a couple of guys had to subdue him and take him to a hospital in Chengdu. He was on suicide watch but finally stabilized. I called Fei. She arranged for appointments with some psychiatric specialists at Stanford, then flew out to bring him back to the USA."

"So she decided to patch things up with him—a good woman. Family is all a man's got in this kind of situation."

"I don't know about patching up. All I know is she thinks it's wrong to abandon him now—for Jessica's sake. She's doing her best."

"As did you."

"Yes, even though it wasn't enough. But I have stopped blaming myself for bringing Lili to him. I still don't quite believe Lili had planned all this—it feels like a crime of opportunity."

"But she must have planned it from the start, the only surprise being how easy it was to get the key in the end."

"Again, hindsight," Alice says, fixing her eyes on the dark road ahead. "And there's a bit of good news, too. Kaipeng and I spoke when Deckard was in Chengdu. She told me a couple of AI clients the company had been courting came through, giving them enough revenue to live and fight another day. We've worked out a payment plan for them to pay the invoices over the next twelve months. Fingers crossed they'll deliver on that."

"Phew! So you did it! You're back on track," Henry says with a great exhale as he pulls into the driveway.

The children are fast asleep. Alice steps into the twin's room. The curtain is half closed. Moonlight coats the ends of their bunk beds, just like in her dream journey. Her eyes get misty as the urge to sob rises within her, but she kisses their foreheads instead.

BACK IN THE LIVING ROOM, she checks her phone and asks Henry, "Are you free this Saturday morning?"

"Of course. What do you want to do?"

"Take the kids to the post office."

"What for?"

"To get their passports."

Henry stares at her, his mouth open.

"I thought we could take a trip overseas this summer. I need to work on the flying thing some more. So Europe? Australia?" She puts her hand on his shoulder. "Or China?"

ACKNOWLEDGMENTS

Starting the book was easy but finishing it was a four-year long marathon. My gratitude goes to those who helped me through this seemingly impossible process:

My family for continued support;
Susan Y. for your valuable advice;
Solveig P. and Kevin F. for beta reading;
Lee V. P. and Bobby C. L. for teaching me about Bitcoin;
Rhonda A., Amy S., Vlada T., and Faye W., for always being there and sharing ideas;
Elizabeth Gaffney for developmental editing;
Vicki M., Jonathan S., and Thomas P., for reading my early draft;
Kathy Waghorn for copy editing;
Don Huff for cover design;
Michael C. for book club guide;
My teachers: Elizabeth Gaffney, Rachel Herron, Valerie Mathews, Lisa Cron, Paul Bradley Carr, Seth Harwood, and Chris Baty, for teaching and coaching.

I learned things and drew inspiration from the following books and websites:

The Promise of Bitcoin by Bobby C. Lee
The Tiananmen Papers Compiled by Zhang Liang, Edited by Andrew J. Nathan and Perry Link
Mastering Bitcoin by Andreas M. Antonopoulos

Burn Rate by Andy Dunn
The 35th of May; or, Conrad's Ride to the South Seas by Erich Kästner
Emil and the Detectives by Erich Kästner
https://www.youtube.com/watch?v=icBD5PiyoyI
https://www.aboluowang.com/2017/0228/889285.html
https://www.lexology.com/library/detail.aspx?g=345139ba-c8fd-400f-9f4b-5c1e4265b6a2
https://www.youtube.com/watch?v=kMKvxJ-Js3A
https://www.haodf.com/neirong/wenzhang/6475094270.html
https://www.darkreading.com/risk/https-security-encryption-flaws-found
https://zhuanlan.zhihu.com/p/612144815
https://www.jfdaily.com/wx/detail.do?id=235651
https://www.bloomberg.com/features/2023-china-ev-graveyards
https://www.sc.gov.cn/10462/10464/10465/10595/2023/2/13/a775ae72302d41eaa313f244013acd9b.shtml
https://www.youtube.com/watch?v=CubPBhOyJ_0

The lyrics of *Sailing the Seas Depends on the Helmsman* were written by Li Yuwen in 1964. The lyrics are in the public domain because the first copyright law in People's Republic of China was enacted in 1991.

WHAT DID YOU THINK?

I am so grateful you chose to spend your time with these characters. If you enjoyed the book, I would truly appreciate a one-sentence review to help others discover the story. Ebook readers can use this Amazon link; others can scan the QR code below:

To get a **bonus scene** of how Lily met Deckard and other special offers, please sign up for my newsletter. Ebook readers can use this link; others can scan the QR code below:

Many thanks for your support,
Diana Hongcha

ABOUT THE AUTHOR

Like the protagonist in her book, Diana Hongcha grew up in China and emigrated to the United States more than 30 years ago—but that's where the similarity ends. Diana travels to China frequently for family and work, and stays closely connected to her home country. These trips continue to shape how she sees the country.

Diana has worked as both an attorney and a part-time middle school teacher. She dreams of one day splitting her time between Chengdu, China and Bozeman, Montana, while wrangling a busy family life. For now, international living remains more of a fantasy than a plan. Find out more at www.dianahongcha.com.

BOOK CLUB GUIDE

Discussion Questions

Part 1: Characters & Relationships

1 Alice's Journey: How does Alice change from the beginning of the novel to the end? What does her willingness to confront her fear of flying symbolize about her personal growth?

2 Female Partnership: Discuss the relationship between Alice and Lili. How do their generational differences both challenge and strengthen their partnership? What does each woman learn from the other?

3 Deckard's Character: What drives Deckard to make the choices he makes? Do you sympathize with him, or do you see him as reckless? How does his brilliance both help and hurt him?

4 Marriage and Sacrifice: Compare the marriages in the novel—Alice and Henry vs. Deckard and Fei. What different forms does sacrifice take in each relationship? What ultimately breaks Deckard and Fei's marriage?

5 Motherhood: How does the novel portray different experiences of motherhood through Alice, Fei, and the mother figures in the flashbacks? What pressures do mothers face across cultures?

Part 2: Themes & Social Commentary

6 Two Chinas: The novel contrasts 1970s-80s China with modern China. What has changed, and what has remained the same? Did anything about modern China surprise you?

7 Censorship & Freedom: Discuss how censorship affects the characters' lives—from Cat's suspended Weibo account to Deckard's WeChat ban to the broader surveillance state. How does living under such constraints shape behavior and relationships?

8 Identity & Belonging: Alice describes feeling like neither fully American nor fully Chinese. Have you or someone you know experienced similar feelings about cultural identity? How does returning to China after 30 years affect Alice's sense of self?

9 Technology's Double Edge: The novel features various technologies—from data centers to Bitcoin mining to Deckard's Neuromersion brain device. How does technology serve both liberating and oppressive purposes in the story?

10 Economic Anxiety: Financial pressure drives much of the plot. How do economic concerns affect characters' decisions across different social classes? What does the novel suggest about the American dream vs. the Chinese dream?

Part 3: Structure & Craft

11 Flashback Structure: The novel alternates between Alice's present-day search and memories from the past. How do the flashbacks enhance your understanding of the present-day story? Which historical period interested you most?

12 The 1989 Journey: The flashbacks to the teenage trip toward Beijing during the student protests form a parallel to Alice's current journey. What connections do you see between these two quests?

13 Suspense & Mystery: Did the mystery of Deckard's disappearance keep you engaged? Were you surprised by what Alice discovers? At what point did you suspect what was really happening?

14 Setting as Character: From Silicon Valley to Shanghai to remote Sichuan villages, the novel spans diverse locations. How do these settings shape the story? Which setting was most vividly rendered?

Part 4: Broader Implications

15 Female Empowerment: The novel centers on women—Alice, Lili, Cat, Fei—navigating male-dominated worlds. How do these women support or undermine each other? What strategies do they use to survive and thrive?

16 Cultural Revolution Legacy: How do the traumas of the Cultural Revolution continue to affect the characters decades later? What does the novel suggest about intergenerational trauma and memory?

17 Business Ethics: Alice navigates gray areas in her quest—from illegal Bitcoin operations to dealing with loan sharks. When, if ever, do the ends justify the means? Where would you draw ethical lines?

18 The Title: "If You Don't Go, You Don't Know" is a recurring phrase in the novel. What does it mean in different contexts? How does it apply to Alice's journey, both literal and metaphorical?

19 Friendship Over Time: Alice and Deckard have known each other since early childhood. How realistic is their enduring friendship despite decades of distance? What keeps them connected?

20 Contemporary China: What did you learn about contemporary China that you didn't know before? Did the novel challenge or confirm any preconceptions you had?

For Further Reflection

21 Ending Thoughts: Without spoiling for others, what did you think of the novel's resolution? Did it satisfy you? What questions do you still have?

22 Personal Connection: Did any character or situation resonate with your own experiences? Which scenes stayed with you after finishing the book?

23 Author's Perspective: This is Diana Hongcha's first novel. She is described as "a part-time middle school teacher with dreams of splitting her time between Chengdu, China and Bozeman, Montana." How might her own transnational perspective shape the novel?

24 Genre: The book blends mystery, literary fiction, and cultural exploration. Which genre elements did you find most compelling? Did the genre blend work for you?

25 Recommendations: Who would you recommend this book to? What other books does it remind you of?

Activities for Your Book Club

Food: Serve Chinese dishes mentioned in the novel, such as High Mountain Oolong tea, lemon chicken, mini wontons, tofu-and-pigeon-egg soup, or crayfish.

Map It: Create a map tracking Alice's journey from California to Shanghai to Nanjing to Sichuan.

Research Topics:
- The 1989 Tiananmen Square protests
- The Cultural Revolution and its aftermath
- China's one-child policy
- Bitcoin mining and cryptocurrency in China
- The Chinese tech industry and government regulation
- Chinese censorship and the "Great Firewall"

Character Debate: Divide into teams and debate Deckard's choices—were they justified?

Key Themes

Identity and Belonging - Alice's struggle with her Chinese-American identity, feeling neither fully American nor fully Chinese after thirty years away.

Past vs. Present China - Stark contrasts between 1970s-80s China (Cultural Revolution aftermath, poverty, political turmoil) and modern China (technological advancement, censorship, economic complexity).

Friendship and Loyalty - The enduring bond between Alice and Deckard despite decades, distance, and divergent life paths.

Female Solidarity - The unlikely partnership between Alice and Lili across generational and cultural divides.

Technology and Memory - Deckard's Neuromersion technology explores themes of memory, trauma, and the desire to enhance or alter the past.

Censorship and Freedom - The constraints of living under an authoritarian system, social media censorship, and self-censorship.

Economic Precarity - Financial pressures on characters across social classes, from Alice's partnership concerns to working-class struggles in China.

Motherhood and Family - Alice's guilt about balancing career and family, generational trauma.

Risk and Courage - Alice confronting her fear of flying; characters taking physical, financial, and political risks.

Corruption and Moral Ambiguity - The gray areas of doing business in China, illegal activities, and compromised ethics.

Made in the USA
Coppell, TX
11 February 2026

71759980R00215